"Delectable stuff.
Sharp prose that's punched up
by lines worthy of Bogart or Mitchum."
—*THE WASHINGTON POST*

"A delicious synthesis of menace and glamour,
historical fact and rich imagination."
—*THE SEATTLE TIMES*

"Kanon's prose is eminently noir, all cigarette
smoke and magnesium flashbulbs."
—*ENTERTAINMENT WEEKLY*

"Comes within a whisker of being flawless."
—*KIRKUS REVIEWS*

"Kanon's atmospheric, character-driven latest comes within a whisker of being flawless. . . . Time and place are so vividly evoked, and the writing is so strong."

—*Kirkus Reviews*

"Kanon perfectly balances action and introspection, while smoothly integrating such real-life figures into the plot."

—*Publishers Weekly*

"Kanon manipulates his plot and setting expertly, evoking both a James Ellroy–like postwar noir atmosphere and, at the same time, capturing the surface glamour of Hollywood's fading golden age. . . . The novel re-creates a time and a place with pinpoint accuracy and reminds us once again that the wounds of war take time to heal."

—*Booklist*

"With his usual mastery of historical milieus and the subtleties of complex characters, Kanon immerses the reader in the glamour of Hollywood just before it comes under investigation."

—*Library Journal*

"Spectacular in every way . . . wonderfully imagined, wonderfully written, an urgent personal mystery set against the sweep of glamorous and sinister history. Joseph Kanon owns this corner of the literary landscape and it's a joy to see him reassert his title with such emphatic authority."

—Lee Child

"The perfect combination of intrigue and accurate history brought to life."

—Alan Furst

"Sensational! No one writes period fiction with the same style and suspense—not to mention substance—as Joseph Kanon. A terrific read."

—Scott Turow

This title is also available from
Simon & Schuster Audio and as an ebook.

STARDUST

ALSO BY JOSEPH KANON

Alibi

The Good German

The Prodigal Spy

Los Alamos

STARDUST

A NOVEL

JOSEPH KANON

WASHINGTON SQUARE PRESS
New York   London   Toronto   Sydney

WASHINGTON SQUARE PRESS
A Division of Simon & Schuster, Inc.
1230 Avenue of the Americas
New York, NY 10020

First Washington Square Press trade paperback edition July 2010

WASHINGTON SQUARE PRESS and colophon are registered trademarks of Simon & Schuster, Inc.

For information about special discounts for bulk purchases, please contact Simon & Schuster Special Sales at 1-866-506-1949 or business@simonandschuster.com.

The Simon & Schuster Speakers Bureau can bring authors to your live event. For more information or to book an event contact the Simon & Schuster Speakers Bureau at 1-866-248-3049 or visit our website at www.simonspeakers.com.

Designed by Davina Mock-Maniscalco

Manufactured in the United States of America

10 9 8 7 6 5 4 3 2 1

The Library of Congress has cataloged the hardcover edition as follows:

Kanon, Joseph.
    Stardust : a novel / Joseph Kanon. — 1st Atria Books hardcover ed.
        p. cm.
    1. Family secrets—Fiction. 2. Hollywood (Los Angeles, Calif.)—Fiction. 3. Cold War—Fiction. 4. Domestic fiction.
    I. Title.

PS3561.A476S73 2009
813'.54—dc22   2009011719

ISBN 978-1-4391-5614-8
ISBN 978-1-4391-5632-2 (pbk)
ISBN 978-1-4391-6481-5 (ebook)

Again, for Robin

A MAN RIDES INTO TOWN

As it happened, Sol Lasner was also on the train. Ben spied him first on the red carpet at Grand Central posing for photographers, like one of his stars. Shorter than Ben remembered, his barrel chest wobbling on thin legs, storklike, but with the same tailored look, natty. He gave a quick, obligatory smile to the flashbulbs, then herded a group of men in suits onto the train, back to business. At Croton, where they switched over to the steam engine, most of the suits got off for the ride back to the city, but two stayed on through dinner, so Ben didn't have a chance to talk to him until they were past Albany, when the landscape had already turned dark and there was nothing to observe from the observation car but blurs of street lamps and platform lights streaking past.

He'd been sitting near the rounded back of the car, smoking and staring out at nothing, when Lasner came in, holding a cigar. He nodded to Ben, not recognizing him, and for a moment Ben was tempted to let it wait, talk later on the Army's time. The next few days were supposed to be his, little shrouds of time to wrap himself up in, prepare for the funeral, stare out windows, get used to it.

The long-distance call to Danny's wife has taken hours to put through, her voice scratchy with bad connections, or grief. What kind of accident? "A fall. It's in the papers as an accident. You know, anyone can fall. So they put it in that way." But it wasn't? Ben had asked, disconcerted, feeling his way, listening to the precious seconds tick by. "Look," she'd said finally, "you should know. You're his only family," but then went quiet again. You mean he tried to take his life? "Take his life?" she'd said, confusing him until he realized that it was a translation problem, an idiom she hadn't picked up. Hans Ostermann's daughter. Tried to kill himself, he said. "Yes," she said reluctantly, then drew a breath, moving past it. "But they didn't want to say. You know what it's like here. Everything for the good name. Nothing bad ever happens. It's better if it's an accident, in the papers. So I said it, too." There was a snort of air, like a shrug over the phone. "But his brother— you have a right."

Rambling on, making no sense to him now, or maybe he had just stopped listening, his head dizzy with it. Not a crash, a virus, some act of fate, but something willed, a scream of unhappiness. "I'm sorry for this news," she'd said before he could ask more. "Is it possible for you to come now? He's in a coma. So still alive. I don't know how long. They don't expect—so if you could come." And then the reserved time was running out, and instead of questions there were logistics and plans. But what answers could anyone have? Something that only made sense to Danny, the most private act there was.

To his surprise, there had been no problem having the Army move up the trip. The problem was getting there, with the trains the way they were. Then something last minute opened up on the Chief, if he was willing to sleep sitting up on the Century to meet it, so he'd packed a duffel, sent the wire, and now found himself riding with Sol Lasner. Who could wait—the Army's assignment—while he took his personal leave, brooding. Days to think about it, all the way to California. Meanwhile, Lasner was lighting the cigar, looking out the window and then at his watch, checking some invisible schedule.

"Any idea where we are?"

"Just past Schenectady."

Lasner drew on the cigar, looking out again. "Upstate," he said. "Goldwyn's from here. Gloversville. They made gloves. That's what he was, a glove man. Well, why not?"

Just talking to himself, not really expecting a reply, but suddenly Ben took the opening anyway. The meeting had fallen into his lap, personal leave or not.

"Mr. Lasner?"

Lasner turned, peering at him.

"Sorry. You probably don't remember. We met last month overseas, on the Army trip. Ben Collier." He held out his hand. "I was one of the liaison officers. Translator."

Lasner took his hand, looking closely, still trying to place him. "The guy with the rooms, right? The one got Eddie Mannix the Ritz in Paris."

Ben smiled. "And Zanuck. And Balaban. Colonel Mitchell arranged it. He figured they'd want the Ritz. Kind of people used to it."

"I got news for you," Lasner said, pointing with the cigar. "You think Harry Cohn's used to the Ritz? Some hot-sheet place down on Flower—that's what he's used to." He shook his head. "I still don't know what that trip was. A stunt. Army puts a bunch of us in uniform, takes us around. What did they get out of it?"

What did they? Harry Cohn played poker in his suite, ignoring Paris. Everywhere the jockeying for the best hotel rooms, the special transports. Ben remembered the winding road up to Berchtesgaden, lined with jeeps, a new tourist attraction, GIs hunting for souvenirs while the executives stood at Hitler's vast picture window, little tyrants finally humbled. A ride on Hitler's yacht. Hamburg, where people had melted into the pavement during the firebombing. The camps, even worse. A few survivors still there, too emaciated and stunned to be moved. In town, packs of children, foraging. How much had they seen from their requisitioned rooms?

"It was Ike's idea. Thinks people should see it. What happened. So the State Department sends groups over. That was the studio tour. There was another for the newsreel editors. See what it's like."

"At the Ritz."

"And Dachau."

For a moment there was no sound but the click of wheels beneath them.

"I was there," Ben said quietly. Watching Lasner stagger against a building, his face in his hands, sobbing. "I know it made an impression on you."

Lasner rounded his cigar in the stand-up tray, smoothing off the ash. "We're making a picture about it."

"Who's making?"

"I'm in the Signal Corps. We shot film there. What the newsreels didn't."

"You personally?"

"No, I collect the film. See it's put together for briefings, whether we can do something more. Information length, maybe features. If not, V shorts. Depending on the footage. What you do, in a way. Produce."

Lasner waved his hand. "And now you're out of a job."

"Not yet. *The Battle of San Pietro* got a lot of play. And the Tokyo film did okay on general release, so the exhibitors are still interested. And there's Ike's film coming."

"Who's releasing?" Lasner said quickly.

"Columbia."

Lasner grunted.

"You know how it works. War Activities Committee—Freeman, at Paramount—assigns the pictures on a rotating basis. All the majors. It was Columbia's turn."

"The majors. What am I? They still think Continental's a Poverty Row shop? Next year, we'll outgross RKO, but me they give the training films. You know what it costs me? We get four to five thousand a reel. But we throw in the production, the overhead, the *salaries* for chrissake. Add it up, it's more like seven thousand a reel and we just eat the difference." He tapped the cigar again, calmer. "Not that I mind. You know, for the war. But you don't hear Freeman calling me with a feature, either."

"He will be."

Lasner glanced up at him. "What's this, a pitch?"

Ben leaned forward. "We're sitting on a ton of footage. They're setting up trials. This is what they're all about. People need to see this. We want to work with a studio to put it together."

Lasner shook his head. "Let Columbia do it. You think people want to see this? Nobody wants to see this."

"They should."

"Should. You know, Freeman asks, it doesn't mean we have to do it. These war films—it's all strictly voluntary. And now, *after* the war? Nobody's going to make this picture."

"I thought you'd want to."

Lasner looked at him for a long minute, then sighed.

"Let me tell you something. Nobody needs a picture about killing Jews. What else have they been doing? Since forever."

"Not like this," Ben said quietly, so that Lasner busied himself putting the cigar out, avoiding him.

"Wonderful," he said finally. "Cohn gets Eisenhower and I get— I'll think about it. Let Freeman call. We'll see." A dodge.

"I'll be at the Signal Corps base in Culver City. A local call."

"Fort Roach." He caught Ben's look. "Hal Roach's old studio. The Army took it over. They've got some of my people down there. Drafted. My best cutter. Splicing film on VD. How does your prick look with crabs. Talk about a waste of a good technician." He glanced up. "You want to make the picture there? Fort Roach?"

"No, I want to make it at Continental. With you."

"Because we were such good pals in Germany. Looking at things."

"Freeman said you were the first call to make. You were there for the Relief Fund. You hired refugees in 'forty. You—"

"So back to the well."

"He said the others think they're Republicans."

Lasner snorted. "Since when did Frank get funny? If I heard two cracks from him my whole life it's a lot." He shook his head, then snorted again. "Mayer keeps a picture of Hoover in his office. Hoover. And now with the horses. A Jew with horses. So he's fooling everybody." He paused. "Don't push me on this. We'll talk. In an office. We make a picture if it makes sense to make a picture. Not just someone tells me it's good for the Jews. Anyway, what kind of name is Collier?"

Ben smiled. "From Kohler. My father. It means the same thing."

"So why change it? Who changes names? Actors."

"My mother. After the divorce, we went to England. She wanted us to have English names. My father stayed in Germany."

"Stayed?"

"He was a *Mischling*. Half."

"And that saved him?"

"He thought it would."

Lasner looked away. "I'm sorry. So it's personal with you? That's no good, you know, in pictures. You get things mixed up."

"Not personal that way. I just want to get this done and get out of the Army. Same as everybody."

Lasner picked up the cigar again and lit it, settling in.

"Why'd you pick the Signal Corps?"

"They picked me. My father was in the business. Maybe they thought it got passed down, like flat feet. Anyway, I got listed with an MOS for the Signal Corps."

"What's MOS?"

"Military Occupational Specialty. Civilian skill the military can use. Which I didn't have, but the Army doesn't have to make sense. They probably wanted guys with German but everybody did, so they grabbed me with an MOS. And once you're assigned—"

"Well, at least it kept you out of combat."

"Until last winter. Then they needed German speakers with the field units."

"So you saw some action?" The standard welcome-back question.

"Some. The camera crews got the worst of it. They had to work the front lines. We lost a lot of them."

Sometimes just yards away. Ed Singer, so glued to his lens that he never saw the shell that ripped his arm off, just turned and looked down, amazed to see blood gushing out. Ben scooting over. To do what? Dam the blood with a wad of shirt? A stump, spraying blood as it moved, even the camera covered with it. Ed looking at him, frantic, knowing, until his eyes got calmer as shock set in, then closed, no longer there to watch his life run out.

"I was lucky," Ben said. "The closest I came was in a plane. When nothing was supposed to happen. You see *Target Berlin?* Some of the night footage in that. They told us the AAs had been wiped out, but they forgot to tell the Germans. Our gunner was hit. We get back, the plane is full of holes."

He stopped, embarrassed, then took out a cigarette.

"Sorry. What am I doing now, telling war stories?" He inhaled, then blew smoke up toward the round observation roof, in this light oddly like the glass bubble of the Lancaster. "The thing was, I used to live there. Berlin. So it was the enemy, but also someplace you knew. It's a funny feeling, bombing someplace you know. You think what it must be like on the ground."

Lasner stared at him for a minute, saying nothing. "And then— what? You're showing Zanuck around Europe. In uniform. He had it made, you know that? A tailor." Almost a wink, a joke between them. "And for that they needed—what's it again?—an MOS. Because your father was in pictures. Where, Germany?"

"Uh huh," Ben said casually, sorry now that he had brought it up. "He came here for a while. Years ago. I was born here, in fact. California. But he went back."

"Collier," Lasner said, thumbing a mental file.

"Kohler then. Otto Kohler. He was a director." The old hesitancy, as if the name, once his own, would somehow brand him.

"Otto? My god, why didn't you say so? Wait a minute. I thought his kid was already over here—at Republic or some place. We were going to do something with him once, but then it didn't work out. I forget why." He stopped, confused. "Same name, though, as Otto. Kohler."

"My brother," Ben said, about to say more, and then the moment was gone. Why not tell him? But why would Lasner care? Something still private, and somehow not real. "He changed it back. Kids pick sides in a divorce. He was closer to my father." Moving away from it. "You knew him? Otto?"

"Of course I knew him. He *worked* for me. You didn't know that?" He glanced at Ben, a slight suspicion. "We made *Two Husbands*. You must have seen that."

Ben spread his hands. "I was only—"

"That picture was a classic. He didn't keep a print? Never mind. I'll run it for you. You should see it. The talent that man had." Lasner was off now, waving his cigar to draw Ben along with him. "He was the one that got away. The Ufa directors who came over. The great ones." He raised three fingers. "Murnau—well, he got away, too, that car crash. Lang we've still got. And Otto. His trouble? Expensive. Sets. He thought we were making *Intolerance*." He looked again at Ben. "Why didn't you tell me before? Now I know who you are," he said, leaning back and opening his jacket, visibly relaxing.

Ben smiled to himself. An industry, but still a family business.

"He was ahead of his time with those sets, you know," Lasner was saying. "But they were all like that, the Ufa people. Even the ones who came later. You know why? No Westerns. They never learned to shoot outside. It was all controlled light with them. Of course, they had the facilities. In those days, what they had in Berlin—I'm still knocking my brains out in Gower Gulch trying to borrow arc lamps, and over there they're making cities. Otto," he said, shaking his head. "I can see the resemblance now, around the eyes. I knew your mother, too. A looker. So what happened? They split, you said."

"Another woman, I guess. That's what I heard. My mother never talked about it."

"Well, he was like that. He always had an eye. So that's why he stayed there? Some skirt?"

"I don't know. He probably thought he'd get through it—that's what people thought then. He was making pictures with Monika Hoppe. Goebbels liked her. Maybe he thought that would protect him, they'd look the other way. Anyway, they didn't. He was arrested in 'thirty-eight. They sent a notice to my mother. This was when they still thought they had to explain it."

"So," Lasner said, looking away. "Some story."

With everything Ben remembered left out. The good days in the big house on Lützowplatz. The parties, sometimes with just a piano, but sometimes with a whole band, the air full of perfume and smoke, Ben looking down through the banister. Faces even a child recognized. Hertzberg, the comedian with the surprised round eyes; Jannings, jowly and grave even with a glass in his hand. And afterward, sometimes, the quarrels—were there women even then?

Sunday mornings, the room still smelling of stale ashtrays, his father got them ready for their walk. Scarves in winter. Umbrellas if it rained. But the walk without fail, because that's what you did on Sundays in Berlin. Down Budapesterstrasse to the zoo, afterward a cake at Kranzler's, his father desperate by now for a drink. Later, when they were too old for the zoo, they would head straight for the cafés, where his father met friends and Danny tried to sneak cigarettes. Then, a few years after that, they were on a train for Bremen, an American woman with her two boys, their father back on the platform at Lehrter Bahnhof.

They were meant to go home, but stayed in London. Did his mother think Otto would follow, that it was somehow important to be near him, at least on a map? When it didn't matter anymore, after the official letter, she lacked the will to leave, and they stayed longer. By the time Ben finally did get back to America, to the Army training camp, he was grown up. The accent they teased him about now was English so he lost that one, too. And then, full circle, the Army wanted the old language of his boyhood. They polished off the rust, and it came back, as fluent as memory, bringing everything else with it, even the smell of the cakes, until finally the war took him to Berlin and he saw that it was gone for good—Kranzler's, the zoo, all of it just rubble and dust, as insubstantial now as his father, all ghosts.

"Then what?" Lasner said, an old hand at story conferences. "She remarried? A woman like that—"

"No, she died. During the war." He caught Lasner's expectant look and shook his head. "She got sick." No drama, a daily wearing away, medicines to keep the retching down, then a final exhaustion.

"So now it's just the brother?" Lasner said, suddenly sentimental. "Let me tell you something. Stay close. What else have we got? Family. You trust blood. Don't be like—" He took a puff on the cigar, moving farther away, drifting into anecdote again. "Look at Harry Warner. Jack makes him crazy. Screaming. Shouting. Sometimes, they're in the same room, you don't even want to watch. Don't be like that."

"But they're still—"

Lasner shrugged. "Who else would work with Jack? He is crazy. You know, I said to him once, you hate him so much, come work with me, partners, your name first, I don't care. At the time, this is worth a fortune to him. You know what he said? 'You want that bastard to run my studio?' His studio. So they're stuck with each other, till one of them keels over. You put that kind of pressure here," he said, touching his heart, "and sooner or later they wheel you out on a stretcher. Well." He stood up, glancing at his watch again, then out the window. "What I hate, this time of night, is you never know where you are." He put his hand on Ben's shoulder, an uncle. "Remember what I said. Don't be like Jack. Stay close."

And what was there to say to that? Danny had gone to California in '40, using Otto's name to get a Second Unit job at Metro. Just to see what it was like. And then the war had closed the door behind him, eight thousand miles away, so that all they'd had for years were sheets of blue tissue V-mail. Danny playing parent. Keep safe, out of combat. Their mother's health. War news. But still Danny's voice, the same wink in it. Stories he knew Ben would like, could pass on to his friends. Meeting Lana Turner. Going to hear the King Cole Trio. You have to come out here. The whole make-believe world real when Danny wrote about it, the same kid sneaking cigarettes, talking late at night from his bed across the room. About what? Anything. Ben wrapped up in the sound of it.

He got up, feeling Lasner's hand still on his shoulder. "Don't forget to call Freeman."

"I don't forget anything," Lasner said, peering at him. "I'll tell you one thing I don't forget. Your father cost me a bundle. So maybe I'd better watch out—you're an expensive family."

"No sets this time," Ben said.

Lasner nodded, finally dropping his hand. "We'll talk. Where are you staying in Chicago?"

"I'm just changing trains."

"The Chief? That's seven fifteen. That gives you what? Nine hours to kill." Everything measured and counted. "What're you going to do for nine hours?"

"See Chicago, I guess."

Lasner waved his hand. "You've seen it. You need a place to rest up, I'm at the Ambassador East. They get me a suite. Plenty of room." He started to move toward the end of the car. "Otto's kid. You live long enough—" He turned. "He was shot?"

"That's what the letter said."

"But who knows with the Nazis." The unspoken question, a quick bullet or days of pain, clubs and wires, and screams. Years ago now.

"Anyway, he's dead," Ben said. "So it doesn't matter."

Lasner nodded. "No. It's just my age, you think about the how." He was silent for a minute, then looked up. "You got a budget on this thing?"

Ben held up his hand, checking items off his fingers. "Hard costs. The footage we've got. Prints, I can req the raw stock from the War Production Board. You do the prints. And the sound—an engineer for the track, some bridge scoring, somebody to do the narration. American. Fonda, maybe?"

Lasner shook his head. "Use contract. Frank Cabot?"

"Fine. All I need is a cutting room and a couple of hands. We can do it either place, but yours would be better—Army studio, someone's always taking your equipment. You provide the space, I can get the hands from Fort Roach. The stock would be an Army expense," Ben said, looking at him directly. "We'll make it for you. If you put it out."

"Nobody makes pictures for me," Lasner said, looking back, the rhythm of negotiation. "At my studio." He held Ben's eyes for another second, then smiled. "You know, if your father had been like you, he'd still be—" He looked away, at a loss. "I mean—"

Ben said nothing, waiting.

Lasner held up a finger. "Don't take advantage. People don't forget that." He lowered the hand, a dismissal, and walked away, followed by his moving reflection on the glass roof. "We'll talk in the morning," he said, the words in a slipstream over his shoulder.

But when the train pulled into LaSalle Street it was the scene from Grand Central all over again—Lasner surrounded by hats, tips given out, telegrams handed over, the group moving down the platform in a huddle. Ben followed behind, not wanting to interrupt, then lost him outside in the line of waiting taxis. Dearborn Street, where the Chief would pull out, was only a few blocks away, but what would he do there? He turned east instead, past the murky bars and shadowy streets under the El, light poking through the girders in latticework patches. Off the train, things seemed to pass in a plodding slow motion. Nothing whizzed by the window. He had all day.

He crossed Michigan to the lakefront, hoping for a breeze, but the lake was flat, a sheet of hot tin. In the park, dogs panted under bushes. He thought of Warner being wheeled out on a stretcher in Lasner's imagination. But anyone could have an attack, even someone as young as Danny. Except he hadn't. What had his life been like? Maybe the same pressure cooker the Warners steamed in. Not the easy California you saw in magazines, men in open-necked shirts. Did he look like that? His wife would have pictures. Hans Ostermann's daughter, the only thing Ben knew about her. She'd be at the hospital now, waiting things out.

He got up from the park bench, restless. How could he not know Danny's life? Ben had followed him everywhere, just wanting to be part of things. Wild, just like your father, his mother had said, meaning impulsive. But he wasn't. A letter every week, staying in touch, still taking care of him. And now gone, without even a note. Maybe he hadn't really meant to do it, not at the very end. A fall. How did she know for sure it hadn't been like that? He stopped in the street, caught not just by the heat and the night of half sleep, but a deeper weariness, tired of thinking about it, going round in circles.

On State Street he saw an AIR COOLED banner running along a marquee and went inside. The picture was a Betty Grable on second run, something with snow. Caesar Romero danced. Charlotte Greenwood did her split high kick, right over her head. Betty was put out over some romantic mix-up with John Payne, all of it so airy that it melted away as you saw it, like touching beer foam. The newsreel brought him back with a jolt. Europe in grainy black and white, where he'd been just two weeks ago. People going through PX garbage cans. Then war criminals passing sentences on themselves before the courts could—cyanide capsules for the privileged, amateur nooses for the others. Not a botched accident, a Hollywood indulgence. Meaning it. In the camps, they threw themselves on electric fences. You never asked why, not over there. He stood up, desperate to move again.

Outside there was everything he'd been too preoccupied to notice before. Taxis. Buildings with glass. Stores. No debris in the street. Doormen walking dogs. The bar at The Drake, with silver dishes of nuts. A country so rich it didn't even know its own luck. Where anyone could be happy.

At the station, busy with redcaps pushing luggage carts, he saw flashbulbs near the Chief. Not Lasner this time, real stars. Paulette Goddard. Carole Landis. Two girls he didn't recognize. All of them smiling, holding up a bond drive poster as they perched on the compartment car steps. Other passengers stopped to watch. You'll never guess who was on the train.

They left at seven fifteen exactly, sliding out so smoothly that it wasn't until they began clicking over the points in the yard that Ben looked up to see they were moving. Past sidetracked box cars, then clotheslines and coal sheds and scrap metal yards, the backside of the city, until finally the open country of the prairie. Another day before they saw mountains. Los Angeles Monday morning, half a continent in under forty hours. He opened his bag to change. People dressed up for dinner on the Chief. A wash, a drink in the club car. He looked out again at the late summer's light on the unbroken fields, a pale gold. Farther away from the newsreel with every mile. And then, not paying attention, he nicked his finger on his razor and watched, dismayed, as blood welled out of the cut. Had there been blood? She hadn't said. A pool spreading under his head? Where had he fallen? But there must have been blood. There always was.

THEY WERE three deep at the bar in the club car, talking over each other, a party roar of indistinct voices and ice tinkling against glass. Just a few uniforms, officers with their own money. One of the starlets he'd seen on the platform, lipstick refreshed, was taking a light from a man she'd obviously just met, all eyes and what-are-my-odds. The way every trip should begin, Ben thought, the air bubbling like the tonic in his drink.

"So what happened to you?"

Ben turned to the finger poking at his shoulder.

"I thought you were coming up. Talk some more."

Lasner had changed suits but seemed to have kept the same cigar, now just a stub between his fingers. He was with a young man whose eyes darted around the car, a quick sweep, before they settled on Ben. He stuck out his hand.

"Lou Katz. Morris Agency."

"Lou works with Abe Lastfogel," Lasner explained.

"I'm his number two," Katz said, evidently a point. "You're with Continental?"

"The Army," Lasner said. "He's making pictures for the Army."

"Oh," Katz said, his eyes beginning to move away.

"You know who this is?" Lasner said. "Otto Kohler's kid."

"Really," Katz said uneasily, not sure he could admit the name meant nothing.

"The director," Lasner said. "Silents."

"Right, silents," Katz said, relieved. "Let me get us some drinks. You're fine?" He nodded at Ben's hand and without waiting for an answer headed into the bar crowd.

"Watch this," Lasner said. "You want a drink right away, always travel with the Morris office."

"Sorry about today. I thought you'd be busy."

"So come now." He glanced at his watch. "We've got the eight seating. It'll be a help to me. You have dinner with Katz, you always feel a hand in your pocket. Look at this, what did I tell you?"

Katz was slipping through the crowd, drinks in hand.

"Looks like a full train," he said. "You see Julie Sherman over there?" He nodded toward the starlet from the bond drive. "You know Fox isn't picking up her option."

"Lou, don't peddle," Lasner said. "Anyway, what would I do with her?"

"Nobody ever lost money showing tits. Your health," he said, raising his glass.

"Then what happened at Fox?"

"Too much like Tierney. Who needs two? She should be somewhere they work with the talent. You know she can sing? Test her. See what she can do. You can't run a studio on loan-outs."

"How many times, Lou? Contract talent's okay for the programmers. That's your base," he said, demonstrating with his hands. "Up here you don't want to carry around that kind of expense. You get top-heavy. For A pictures, buy what you need. How many A's do I make? Sell her to Metro, they can afford it."

Katz shook his head. "You got it backwards. *You* should do the loan-outs. Look at Selznick—he's *living* on his contract list. Every time he loans out Bergman, he's making what? A couple of hundred?"

"There's a name for that."

"Producer."

"Producer. What's he doing now, some *farkakte* Western with that girl played the saint? One picture. You know how many pictures Continental's releasing this year?"

"That's my point. You're not a small studio anymore. People should be coming to you for the talent."

Lasner held up his hand. "You got something going with her, is that what?"

"Just ten percent."

"Do you believe this guy?" Lasner said to Ben. "She's gone down on half the Fox lot and with him it's still business."

"You've got her wrong. She can sing."

"You remind me of Gus Adler. The way he was with Rosemary. All he could talk about. Test her, test her."

"And you did. And signed her," Katz said smiling, sending a ball over the net.

Lasner shrugged. "All right. Set it up with Bunny. Then we'll see." Katz started to speak, but Lasner stopped him with a hand on his shoulder. "Now take a step back. You push too hard, you knock people over. Learn from Abe. You know what he decided? Act like a gentleman, people always take your calls. There are ways to do things."

"Jesus, Sol. I was just trying to say thank you."

There was a stirring in the car, a shift in the air, as if someone were holding a door open. Paulette Goddard was walking toward them, people pretending not to notice as they let her pass. The bond drive dress was gone, traded up for a dark silk top that glittered with sequins, almost as bright as the diamond earrings setting off her face. It wasn't just being beautiful, Ben thought, amused—she seemed to have brought her own lighting with her, a spot following her through the car.

"Sol, I had no idea you were on the train," she said, kissing him, the air denser now with perfume.

"You look like a million," he said fondly.

"I should," she said, holding up her wrist to show off a strand of diamonds. "You like?"

"If I don't have to pay for it. What is it, from Charlie?"

"Are you kidding? He still has the first dollar. Well, from him in a way. The settlement." She laughed, an infectious giggle. "Imagine his face."

"So everything's friendly?" Lasner said, a concerned relative.

"Darling, it was ages ago. You know Charlie. He's wonderful. He's just impossible to live with."

"You two go way back," Lasner said.

"Not that far, Sol," she said, laughing again, then turned to Katz. "Hi, Lou. How's Abe?"

"Busy," he said, almost blushing, grateful to be recognized. Ben smiled to himself. No one was immune to stardust, not even those who lived on it. "Can I get you a drink?"

"Can't. Date with the Major. To celebrate the end of the drive. Sol, would you believe it, we set a record? And it was just me and Carole and a few other girls."

"Julie Sherman," Katz said, getting the name in.

"Yes, Julie." She had turned her head to him and now took in Ben, her smile as bright as the bracelet. "I'm sorry—"

"Ben Kohler," Lasner said, the way he now remembered it. "Otto Kohler's boy." Ben could tell from the fixed smile that the name meant as little to her as it had to Katz. "He makes pictures for the Army."

"Really?" A glance to the other wrist, another flash of diamonds. "God, look at the time. I'll call Fay." Evidently Mrs. Lasner. "We don't start shooting for another week." She looked up at him, suddenly serious. "Milland. What do you think?"

"You'll make him look good," Lasner said, then leaned over and kissed her forehead.

"Liar," she said, smiling. "Love to Fay. If you want to buy a bond I'm in car twenty-two. At least I think it's twenty-two. Just go to the end and holler. Lovely to meet you," she said to Ben, grazing his hand with the tops of her fingers. And then, to Katz, "Give my best to Abe," and she was off, turning heads again.

"That's a nice girl," Lasner said.

Ben looked at him, surprised at the word.

"Paramount signed her to seven years. Seven years, Sol," Katz said.

"So let Freeman buy the bracelets."

"I'm just saying—"

"Besides, she's a friend. Who hires friends?"

"Everybody."

"I don't mean relatives. She and Fay started out together, for chrissake."

"Another round?" Katz said, letting it drop. A porter had started the first dinner chimes. "One for the road," he said, beating the rush to the bar.

"Your wife was an actress?" Ben said, curious.

"Actress. They were Goldwyn Girls. On the Cantor picture. *The Kid From Spain*, whatever it was called. That's how we met. The wrap party. I'm meeting with Sam, and he says, 'I've got to go put in an appearance.' So we met. Thirteen years now. Thanks," he said, taking a new drink from Katz. "But Paulette, that was something different. She wanted it—pictures. After Goldwyn she was with Hal Roach. Then Chaplin found her. Or maybe she found him. Anyway, Charlie's a great teacher. And she learned. But fresh—that you can't teach. You look at *Modern Times*, that's just the way she was."

"Before the bracelets."

Lasner glanced up. "There's nothing wrong with bracelets. Depends how you get them." He made a face, as if he were stifling a belch. The porter came through again with the chimes.

"I don't know about you, but this drink is going right through me," Katz said. "I gotta take a leak. Sol, I'll see you in the dining car." He took Ben's hand. "Nice talking to you."

Ben watched him head for the restroom, then heard a gasp and turned. Lasner was looking at the floor, bent over. "You okay?"

Another gasp. Ben took Lasner's arm. Not just the drink. He felt a clenched spasm. Lasner reached behind with his other hand, grabbing onto the window curtains for support. Geometric flowers. Around them the cocktail buzz went on, not noticing. Lasner looked up, his face contorted, white, sweat forming on his forehead.

"Help me," he whispered. "Don't let him see."

Ben grabbed Lasner's elbow, propping him up and hiding him from the rest of the car. "Do you need a bathroom?"

Lasner shook his head. "Heart. Get me out of here." His mouth tight, a grimace.

"Don't move. I'll get a chair."

But Lasner was already stepping forward, leaning on Ben. "Next car," he said hoarsely. "Before he sees."

They started toward the other end, away from the crowd moving into the dining car, away from the restrooms, each step heavy as lead, his whole weight falling on Ben. Only the bartender seemed aware of them, a blank expression taking in another one-too-many. At the end of the car, another gasp and shudder as Ben fumbled with the door handle.

"I'll get a doctor."

Lasner sank into a porter's jump seat, his face tight with strain. "No, make some excuse," he said, short of breath, waving toward the dining car. "Make some excuse. With Katz. Before he comes looking. Then come back."

Ben opened the top of the window, a rush of air.

"Lean back," he said. He started to undo Lasner's tie. But did it matter? It occurred to Ben for the first time, a moment of panic, that Lasner might really be in trouble. The chimes went again. In the next car over, people were sitting down to dinner.

"I have pills," Lasner said, as if that answered anything. "Come back. After." He looked over at Ben, eyes large. "Please."

The word, so completely unexpected, had the force of an order. Ben nodded.

"Just try to breathe normally. Don't force it, okay?" Which came from where? An old first aid manual? How to tie a tourniquet.

He waited until Lasner had taken a breath—steady, not a rattle—then hurried back into the club car. And what excuse could he make? An agent expecting dinner. Ben looked into the dining car. Not there yet. No one he recognized, in fact. The Major must be hosting the bond drive table in the other dining car. Maybe a private party. Behind him, he heard the bathroom door close with a whoosh.

"There you are. Sol asked me to wait. Look, he's sorry but he has to beg off dinner. Miss Goddard came back for him. You know Sol, he can't say no to her." This all in a rush, as if he were short of breath. "He said he'll make it up to you. It's just—"

"What? Just *now*?"

Ben shrugged. "I think she didn't want to be alone with the Major. Sol couldn't say no."

"No," Katz said, evidently used to excuses.

"He said he'd make it up to you."

He left Katz standing in the dining car, wondering how, and raced back through the club car, pushing past the crowd at the bar. Lasner hadn't moved, leaning against the window, holding on to the rail underneath, still white.

"All right, now let's get you a doctor."

"Next one," Lasner said, pointing down the corridor toward a drawing room car, presumably his own. He leaned again on Ben. "No porters. They tip them."

"Who?" Ben said as they started to move. Was Lasner becoming confused? Did that happen?

"Polly. All of them. They tip the porters."

Meaning Paulette? Ben glanced at him, then let it go. "The pills are in your room?"

Lasner nodded, clutching the handrail as they moved down the car. "What did you tell him?"

"That Miss Goddard sent for you."

"He buy it?"

"I think so. You shouldn't even be moving."

"So they can lay me out in the club car? We're almost there."

It was a two-chair drawing room, top of the line, the settee already extended and made up, crisp white sheets folded over at the head. Ben lay him down, taking off his tie, his shoes, then suddenly went shy, not ready to draw the pants off the bird-like legs.

"Dopp kit," Lasner said, pointing to the bathroom.

Ben rummaged through the leather case and pulled out a brown pill bottle. Hillcrest Pharmacy. As needed. He splashed some water in a glass. "These?"

Lasner took two, then lay back, half closing his eyes, as if he expected instant results. Ben stood for a minute, helpless, then put the water down next to Lasner and went to the door.

"I'll find a doctor."

"I don't need—"

"I'll be right back," Ben said, ignoring him.

"No porters," Lasner said, raising his voice so Ben could hear it after he closed the door.

But, in fact, how could he find a doctor without one? Another story, a sick wife, the porter too polite to contradict.

By the time he got the doctor back to the compartment the pills seemed to have had some effect. Lasner's breathing was deeper, pushing some color back into his face. The doctor glanced with a quick nod at the pill bottle and took out a stethoscope at the same time. "There still some pain?" He reached into the shirt, placing the metal disc on Lasner's chest.

"Not as much."

"This happen before? Must have, if you have these." He nodded again at the pills. "And you kept walking around? Don't you know better than that?"

"I'm here."

"You're lucky." He leaned over, listening more carefully.

"With doctors," Lasner said. "It's like lawyers? It's all private?"

"You should be in a hospital. To be on the safe side. I can ask them to stop the train," he said, glancing out at the open prairie, "or wait until we get to Kansas City. We can wire ahead, have things ready."

Lasner shook his head. "Carry me out? In front of the Morris office? No."

"What's he talking about?" the doctor said to Ben.

"Nothing," Ben said, not bothering. "Is he really in danger?"

"He could be."

"Listen to me," Lasner said, his voice steady. "I know what this is. It gets better, or it doesn't. You ride it out. What are they going to do in a hospital? Put me in bed. I'm in bed."

"Well, I can't take the responsibility then," the doctor said, sounding so exactly like George Brent that for an instant, thrown, Ben almost laughed.

"Kohler will keep an eye on me," Lasner said.

The doctor sighed. "Anyway, you're *not* in bed. Here, give me a hand, will you?"

"What do I do?" Ben said to the doctor as they undressed the head of Continental Pictures. The stork legs, just as imagined. Boxer shorts. The suit hung up neatly. Wispy gray hair laid back against the propped pillows.

"Nothing. He's right about that. You ride it out. Just keep him quiet. I'll check in again in the morning." He wagged his finger at Lasner. "Stay in bed. Or they will carry you out in Kansas City." He turned back to Ben. "I'll leave these," he said, handing him a small envelope with pills. "In case he can't sleep. If it gets bad again, you know where to find me." He picked up a cigar from the standing ashtray. "Wonderful," he said to Lasner, "just what you need." Another Brent line, shaking his head as he left.

"Fascist," Lasner said when the door closed. "They're all fascists."

Ben looked at him for a second, then dropped into one of the chairs, drained, holding on to the armrests to calm his hands.

"What's the matter, I give you a scare?" Lasner said, a faint smile now on his face.

"It's not funny. You should do what he says. Get off in Kansas City."

"He's just covering his ass. If I'm going to peg out, I'll do it at Cedars. Here's what we do. Kansas City, that's two twenty-two." Ben looked over at him, impressed again. On schedule. "We get five minutes there, not enough to call and get through. Anyway, that hour she's asleep. So send an overnight. Are you getting this? There's some paper over there. Tell Fay to meet the train in Pasadena. Not downtown. Pasadena's eight thirty-five. She always forgets. And tell her to bring Rosen. Then another wire to Jenkins at the studio, tell him *not* to meet the train. Tell him Fay's meeting me. Otherwise, he'll start calling people."

"Anything else?" Ben said, playing secretary. "You're not supposed to be talking, you know."

"I'm not supposed to be breathing, either," he said, but his voice was softer, winding down. "Don't forget the wires, okay? The address is in my wallet."

"I'd better go. Let you get some rest."

"No, sit. Sit. Stick around," Lasner said, trying to sound casual.

Ben turned off the overhead, leaving just a small side lamp and the faint light from the sky outside. The land below was already dark, anonymous.

"At least till Kansas City. Make sure they don't take me off. Okay?" he said, asking something else.

"Okay," Ben said, taking a chair and turning it so that he was facing both Lasner and the window. A clean horizon line, flat, the dark beginning to take over the sky, too. He lit a cigarette, watching the red tip glow in the window reflection.

"You want something to eat? We can have something brought."

"No, I'm fine. Go to sleep."

"Who could sleep now. You just wonder if you'll wake up." But he half closed his eyes.

Ben said nothing, listening to the wheels.

"Talk to me," Lasner said after a while, still there.

"What did you mean about the porters? Who tips them?"

"The columns. Hedda. Polly Marks. All of them." Polly, not Paulette.

"What for?"

"Items. Who's in whose compartment. Who got tossed out of the bar. Who's on the train. You know, N.Y. to L.A. Everybody meets the Chief."

"Like the boats in New York," Ben said, looking at the land outside, now as black as the night sea. Soon they would cross the Mississippi, something out of books. "And you don't want them to know. What does it matter? I mean, what if Katz sees you? Any of them?"

Lasner said nothing for a minute, then grunted. "You're not in pictures. You don't know the first thing about it. Not the first goddam thing."

Ben sat back in the chair, waiting for more, but Lasner was quiet, drifting. When he spoke again even his voice had changed, pitched to a different role.

"You know how I got started?"

"How?" Ben said, the expected response.

"Fourteenth Street. On the east side, near Third."

Ben looked over, surprised to start with an address. But Lasner was smiling to himself, his voice stronger, buoyed up by memory, as if the past, already known, could steady his irregular heart.

"By Luchow's, where the cheap beer gardens were. Next to one of them there's a dry goods store. Like a shoe box, you know, just a long counter, some drawers for notions. Lousy space for retail, long, but at night they clear the counter and put a projector in. There's a sheet at the end of the room. For this the space is perfect. So, a nickel. On benches. The first time, I'll never forget it. I didn't even have English yet. Just off the boat, and I'm sitting there laughing like everybody else. An American. This *thing*—I thought, here is something so wonderful, everybody will want it. A nickel. You couldn't move in the place. I wonder sometimes what if I hadn't gone in, on Fourteenth Street. But you know what? I would have gone in somewhere else."

"And after that you wanted to make pictures?"

"Make? No. Show. You rent the stores at night—who was using them at night?—and you rent some chairs, you got a film from the exchange, and you were in business. Get a little ahead, you take over the store in the day, too. People came. Of course I'm not the only one seeing this. Then it's theaters and it's serious money. Banks. Fox, that prick, is squeezing right and left. Zukor. How do you compete with this? You don't. I thought, I don't want to be in the real estate business. They can gobble up everybody and then what? They still need something to show. So I sold the theaters and came out here to make pictures."

Already "out here," Ben noticed, still two thousand miles away.

"The right place," Ben said.

"Well, not then. That all came later. There was nothing here then. Oranges. Goyim with asthma. Nothing. But every kind of country, sun every day. It was all outside then. You put up walls and hung cheesecloth over it. To cut the glare. Right out in the open. We used a ranch out in the Valley for Westerns. For years, the same ranch."

"That's how you started? With Westerns?"

"Everybody started with Westerns. What's to know? A man rides into town. That's it. Just go from there."

Ben smiled. "But what happens?"

"What happens. Guns. Chase. Gets the girl. It's a picture."

He stopped, distracted for a moment, then picked up the thread again, enjoying himself, and Ben sat back, letting the words circle around him. The Lasner style, growls and purrs and easy intimacy under the sharp eye.

"The first place we had was on Gower. In the gulch, right across from where Cohn was. With all the fly-by-nights. They go out of business, we'd pick them up. Just kept moving down the street. Those days, it was hand-to-mouth. Sometimes not even." He looked up at the ceiling, absentmindedly smoothing the blanket. "You know what you miss? That age? You never think about being sick. Dead, maybe, the idea of it, but not sick. Your body's just something you carry around with you. Then one day you're lying here with a bomb in your chest, waiting for it to go off. Just when things are going—since the war, everything's doing business. Then something you never figured. I'm on two kinds of pills. And you know what Rosen says? Slow down. In pictures. You show weakness for five minutes and—"

He let the words hang in the room. Ben got up and went over to the wash basin.

"Well, it wouldn't be a weakness to get some rest. Here, take this." He handed him a pill from the small envelope.

Lasner held it in front of his mouth, a bargaining chip. "But you'll stick around."

Ben nodded, watching him lift the water glass. "Don't worry. I'll stay till you're asleep."

"And after that?" Childlike, pressing.

Ben took the glass away. "After that you'll be asleep. If anything happens, ring for the porter. I don't care who's tipping him. You don't want to take any more chances with that." He pointed to Lasner's chest.

Lasner grunted. "People try to see me all day long and here you are, and all you can say is go to sleep."

"Mr. Lasner—"

"Sol. For chrissake, you took my pants off."

Ben sat down. There was nothing to do but wait for the pill to kick in.

"All day long," Lasner said. "No wonder I get episodes. You think it's a picnic, running a studio?"

"Maybe you should think about retiring."

"Hah. Then who would call me?" Said so simply that for a second Ben thought he was joking.

"But if you're sick—"

"What do you think, it's something you can just walk away? I built the studio. All of it." He sat back against his pillow. "Nobody sees the work. They think it just happens. But it's work. Look at Paulette." He raised a finger. "You're wrong about her. I saw it in your face. You thought she was a Peggy Joyce."

"Who?"

"Gold digger. She had a career for about two minutes. You never heard of Peggy Joyce? She was in a *song* for chrissake."

Ben shrugged his shoulders. "Before my time."

"I forget you're a kid. She married—well, who remembers? Her they remembered. Or did," he said with an exasperated look at Ben. "Paulette never married for that. You know how old she was, she started to work? Fourteen. She's fourteen and making a living."

"On the stage?"

Lasner nodded. "Chorus. Then Ziegfeld. Next thing, she's out here. Pretty. But that wasn't it. Pretty you can get anywhere. She was raring to go. Fun. That's what Charlie spotted in her. Not just pretty. You know where they met? Joe Schenck's boat. So, another girl for Charlie. But no. He works with her. And the way he works, every little thing perfect. And she does it. Even now, you see the picture, she's terrific. Casual, like she's not working. But she's working since she was fourteen. And now she's a star." He lowered his voice, suddenly pragmatic. "But not to carry a picture. Not yet. And they want to put her in a hoop skirt—where's the sense in that? The way she wears clothes? What do you see in a period picture? Shoulders."

"What's wrong with shoulders?"

"What's wrong with you? I'm trying to tell you something here. You have to know what you're doing. You make a bad picture, that's one thing. You make a few—" He spread his fingers, letting the thought slip through them, like luck itself running out.

Ben stared at the hand, curious. Every gambler's fear, that it might all go away. Danny's world.

"Nothing's the way you think out here," Lasner said, his voice weaker, drifting again.

Ben looked over at him, not sure what he was talking about now, some earlier thought, and saw that the eyes had finally closed, his chest moving slowly, night breathing. Resting comfortably, nurses would say. After his scare. Five minutes of weakness. Their secret. He could go now, leaving only the dim night-light. But he stayed, listening to the wheels, keeping watch, sure somehow that Lasner felt his presence, felt safer. What happened in a deeper sleep? Did you hear anything in a coma, voices, faint rustling sounds around you? Would Danny even know he was there, had come all this way to see him? Maybe Lasner didn't know, either, breathing steadily now. But when Ben woke, hours later, and finally left, he tiptoed to the door and opened it quietly, without a click.

LASNER WAS still in bed in the morning, now propped up against pillows in a patterned silk bathrobe.

"Where've you been? The doctor was here an hour ago."

"And?"

"I'm great."

"He tell you to stay in bed?"

Lasner waved his hand in dismissal, but made no move to get up. "You want some breakfast?"

"I already had. What do you keep, banker's hours? Let's talk about the picture. There's nothing to see till New Mexico anyway."

Ben looked out the window—endless yellow fields, silos and telegraph poles, a hot, bright day.

Lasner held up a finger. "It's not because I owe you. I don't want you to get that idea."

Ben nodded and sat down. "Sure you're up to this?"

"How much footage have you got?"

"Lots. And some captured Nazi film—they actually filmed it. We can also get stock from Artkino, the Russian agency."

"You want to use Russian film?"

"They were the first ones in. The quality's okay—I've seen it."

"Never mind the quality. It's Russian. You use it, that prick Tenney will be all over you."

"Who?"

"Jack Tenney. You've been away for a while. He used to write songs. *Mexicali Rose,* one hit. Now he's a politician, with a bug up his ass about Reds. He's got a committee up in Sacramento. Making lists. You don't want him making trouble for you."

"Over some footage?"

"If the Russians shot it, he'll say it's a lie. Which leaves you where? Saying it's not. People wondering. Don't go near it. You got plenty of Army film, right? Why buy trouble?"

The knock came before he could answer, a light rap, then a tentative opening.

"Sol? You there?"

"Paulette. Come in, sweetheart. You're up early."

She took in Ben with a quick smile to cover her surprise, then frowned at Lasner. "What are you doing in bed? You all right?" she said, crossing the room. She was wearing cream-colored slacks and a dark jersey top with a single strand of pearls, day wear.

"Something I ate," Lasner said.

"When? At the dinner you ate with me except you didn't?"

"You saw Katz."

"Don't worry, I covered. Next time I'm the excuse, let me in on it, will you? I had to have a *drink* with him. So he could tell me his troubles."

"What troubles does he have?" Lasner said.

Goddard laughed. "What's going on?" She turned to Ben, who had already caught Lasner's signal.

"Doctor says it's probably just flu."

"You had a doctor?" She sat down on the edge of the bed, looking at him closely. "You want me to call Fay?"

"It's done, it's done. Ben took care of it in Kansas City. She's meeting me in Pasadena. Don't make such a big deal."

She put her hand on his forehead, the bright red tips touching his hair. "Tough guy," she said, then looked at Ben, raising her eyebrows. "No fever. Some flu."

"It's a bug is all," Lasner said. "Now let me get dressed. How about I take you to lunch?"

She smoothed back his hair. "We'll have it in. I'll bring some cards, what do you say?"

"What's my end?"

"You stay in bed. And don't cheat." She tapped a finger on his nose, then stood up, not waiting for an answer. "Help me find his porter, will you?" she said to Ben, blowing Lasner a kiss.

In the corridor her face was serious.

"What did the doctor really say?" When Ben hesitated, she brushed past it. "I know, you can't— He thinks nobody knows. Fay would kill me if anything happened and I was right *here*." She looked up at him. "What's the connection again?"

"We're going to make a picture together. For the Army."

She shook her head. "You'll have to explain that to me sometime. Right now, he's taken a shine to you, so help me keep him in bed."

"How?"

"He can't resist a game. They're all like that."

Ben thought of Cohn in his Paris suite, throwing chips on the pile.

"Get a deck from the club car. I'll order lunch. I know what he likes."

She was right about the cards. Lasner only picked at his chicken sandwich but brightened when the trays were cleared and she brought out the cards and score pad, kicking off her espadrilles and sitting cross-legged on the bed, Indian style, to make a circle.

Outside there was nothing but fields, and Ben lost track of where they must be, cut off even from the rest of the train in their private party. A million miles from Europe, playing cards with a movie star.

The first shadows made him look up. They were finally leaving the steady glare of the flat landscape for the real West, mountains and stretches of old conifers, dirt the color of bright rust. Lasner checked his watch.

"We hit Albuquerque in ten minutes. Four thirty-five."

"My god, the hairdresser," Paulette said, getting up. "Why don't you get some beauty sleep. I'll check in later. I do *not* want to see you in the dining car. Use room service—you can afford it."

"Now I'm an invalid," Lasner said, a mock pout.

She picked up the cards. "No more of these, either. Come on, Ben, let's take a hike. You rest."

"You *deserve* Milland," Lasner said, then turned to Ben. "See if they got papers on the platform. Anything. Even local."

Ben nodded, already one of the suits on the red carpet, a Lasner man.

The Los Angeles paper was yesterday's but he bought it anyway. While he was waiting for change, he noticed a bundle of old papers, tied up to be sent back. His eye stopped. Not even a big headline, just a story near the bottom, easy to miss. He slipped the paper out from under the twine.

DIRECTOR IN FREAK FALL

Daniel Kohler, director and head writer of the Partners in Crime series, was rushed to Hollywood Presbyterian Hospital after an accidental fall at the Cherokee Arms Hotel in Hollywood. Kohler, who was alone at the time of the accident, had a long history of dizzy spells, according to his wife. Kohler used the hotel room as a writing office. Neighbors in the building summoned police after hearing sounds of the fall in the adjacent alley. Kohler, son of the late silent film director Otto Kohler, had been a Second Unit director at Metro before originating the detective series at Republic Pictures. Herbert Yates, President of Republic, said the studio intended to continue production while Kohler recovers. *Partners in Crime* features Larry Burke and Bruce Hudson.

Ben looked up at the metal sides of the Chief, shining like coins. Not even about him, really. An industry item. Was anyone fooled? Not the reporter, his skepticism poking out between the lines. Why rent a hotel room to write? Didn't he have an office on the lot? Not really about him at all.

He got back on the train just as it was leaving, his mood seesawing back down to where it had been when the first telegram had arrived, a quiet panic. But Lasner was too busy dressing to see it, his attention focused on the mirror.

"Don't start," he said, nodding down to the clothes. "Two nights and they notice. Get the paper?"

"Take the pills with you. Just in case," Ben said, putting the paper on the bed. "You know *Partners in Crime*? The series?"

"Over at Republic? If Herb had any brains, he'd fold it. I heard the last one did so-so. Oh," he said, stopping, embarrassed. "That's your—?"

"I mean, what's it like?"

"*Boston Blackie,* except two brothers. One chases girls, gets into trouble, you know. The other one solves the crime. The good one's Bruce Hudson."

No, it's me, Ben thought, suddenly light-headed. The way they'd been as boys.

"You never saw it?"

Ben shook his head. "They never sent it overseas." He tucked the other paper under his arm and turned to leave. "Don't forget the pills."

Lasner looked at Ben in the mirror. "I don't forget things." A kind of thank-you.

Back in his roomette, relieved to be alone, Ben opened the paper again. A piece with everything between the lines. Except why. Because a B series was failing?

Outside, they were heading up through cactus and sage into the wild high desert. At this time of day even the rocks glowed, golden with trapped heat, the shadows around them streaked with violet and terra cotta, as if the Chief had planned it all for dramatic effect, a show before dinner. He imagined Lasner on that other train forty years ago, the dry goods store behind him. No air-cooled compartment then, just hot gritty air and something new at the end. Maybe that's what all of them had wanted, not just sunlight for film, a new place. What Danny wanted, too, and didn't find.

Ben looked down at the paper, disturbed. Everything about it was wrong, not just between the lines, but in the lines themselves. He thought of the high railing along the Embankment, Danny perched on it like on a balance beam, arms outstretched and fearless, a boy who had never been dizzy in his life.

BEN SAW Lasner once more before they arrived, this time by accident. He'd been up since dawn, watching the last of the desert slip by, the brick sand turning white in the Mojave. They passed Barstow, houses without shade, then over the ridge to San Bernardino and the miles of orange groves, planted straight to the San Gabriels, at this hour still smelling of the night perfume the guidebooks promised. Ben had lowered the window, leaning out in the morning air. In Europe there had been no oranges at all, not for years. Here the land was bursting with them, an almost supernatural abundance. Royal palms began to appear in front yards, rows of peeling eucalyptus along the tracks.

On the rest of the train, he knew, suitcases were being snapped shut, lipstick dabbed on for the last half hour to Union Station, but the morning held him at the window, head stuck out like a child's. It was still there as they pulled into Pasadena, sliding by tubs of bright flowers, so Lasner saw him when he stepped onto the platform. He came over to the window, his face troubled, oddly hesitant.

"That was your brother that fell? You didn't say anything? All this time."

Ben looked for a response, feeling caught, but said, "How did you hear?"

"Katz said it was in the trades."

Ben imagined the news spreading through presses, across wires, all the way to tables on the Chief, Katz bending forward to gossip, a montage of rumor. But at least Danny hadn't been ignored, forgotten. News for five minutes.

"It wasn't your trouble," he said finally. "I figured you had enough of your own."

"A shame," Lasner said, shaking his head. "I never heard he was a drinker. They must have had some party. Him and the skirt. It's a hell of a thing. He gonna be all right?"

So now he drank, the rumor swelling, branching. A drunken party, something Lasner could understand. Where did the woman come from? His own invention, an inside tip from Katz? But before Ben could say anything else, Paulette Goddard got off the train with a group of porters and a cartload of suitcases. Her hair was brushed out, shiny, every inch of her in place.

"She doesn't trust me to find my own car," he said as she came up, putting her hand on his arm.

"I'm just cadging a lift," she said.

The lift, or at least its colored driver, was moving toward them on the platform, behind a blonde in a wide-shouldered dress and spectator pumps, still trim but thickening a little now.

"Paulette," she said with a quick hug, then turned to Lasner and put her arms around his neck and held him, not caring who saw. "Dr. Rosen's in the car," she said, nodding toward a black Chrysler waiting at the curb.

"I feel fine."

"Big shot," she said fondly. "Just get in the car. Stanley's sniffing around somewhere. Florabel Muir's old leg man—he's working for Polly now. You want to talk to him or to Rosen?"

"That's the choice?"

"Oh god," Paulette said, "not Stanley. He's been after me since Charlie. Fay—"

"I know, I know. Henry, get her to the car, will you?" She turned to Lasner. "You send a telegram from Kansas City and now you don't even want to see him?"

"He sent it," Lasner said, pointing at Ben.

Fay looked up, puzzled, then went back to Lasner. "I was worried sick."

"I just hired him. We met in Germany."

This seemed to make even less sense, but she smiled up blankly, polite, the boss's wife.

Lasner held his eye for a minute, what Ben took as a last silent exchange about the train, then moved on.

"Call Bunny Jenkins at the studio," he said to Ben. "He'll fix everything for you. And order the stock now—they say tomorrow, it's always next month. Check the list at Roach, see if they've still got a cutter, Hal Jasper."

"The VD guy?"

Lasner smiled. "Yeah. Tell him I bet they were his crabs."

"Sol, I mean it, no more business. I'll walk right out of here. I've been worried *sick*. This is the second time—"

"Tell the world."

She bit her lip, then sighed and fixed him with an or-else stare. "This isn't a house call. I had to get him out of bed to come here. Now are you coming or what?"

He shrugged, beginning to move off, then paused and looked back to Ben. "If you need a few days, that's okay. You know, to visit at the hospital."

AT FIRST, scanning the crowd, all he saw were the dark glasses and thick blond hair, pinned up in a pile on her head. Then she came toward him, a smooth stride, and he recognized the woman in her photograph, the same long face as her father, the high forehead. What it hadn't shown was the skin, a tawny cream that held the sun in it. She was in a white short-sleeved blouse, slacks, and canvas shoes, as if she'd just stepped off a tennis court.

"Liesl?" he said, peering at her.

"Yes," she said, extending her hand. Then, "Excuse me," taking off her sunglasses, "so rude. Sometimes I forget. So we meet."

"How is he?"

"The same."

"What do the doctors say?"

"He's not responding. It's a long time now. We're just waiting. You understand, there's no recovery. I don't want you to expect—"

Her eyes, uncovered now, darted sharply, flecked with light. She seemed to be wearing no makeup at all, lips bare, not even a hint of Paulette Goddard's glossy red, just the flush of anger or worry that made her movements jerky—handshake to questioning glance, all quick, angular. Only the voice was smooth, held a second too long in her throat, still with a trace of accent. When she said, "This is all?" nodding to his bag, he heard the rhythm of German, not quite forgotten yet.

"That's it. I'm sorry to get you down here so early."

"No, I was glad to get a break," she said, colloquial, fully American now. "It's been—" She let the phrase finish itself.

"You're sure it's all right? To stay? If it's not convenient—"

"No, no," she said, dismissing this. "We were expecting you." Another awkward pause. "Of course later, not so soon. He was excited you were coming."

"He was?" Ben said, unexpectedly pleased. "Then—"

He stopped before "why," catching himself. Danny wouldn't have thought about him, about anyone. They didn't. Something that happened only to you.

"Yes," she was saying. "So many years."

"Liesl? Is that you?"

A tiny woman, teetering in high heels, was hurrying toward them from the barrier. She was wearing a suit with a matching hat, the veil thrown back, as if she didn't want to miss anything. Behind her, trying to keep up, was a man holding a camera.

"Polly," Liesl said, taking a step backward.

"My dear, I can't tell you—"

"Thank you," said Liesl, anticipating her. "This is Daniel's brother, Ben."

"You must be *shell*-shocked," Polly said, ignoring him. "I know Herb Yates is. I talked to him."

She spoke in a rush that was a kind of suppressed giggle and the rest of her moved with it, head turning to keep the passengers in sight, so alert that her body actually seemed to be vibrating. The effect, Ben noticed, was to make Liesl recede, wary as prey.

"Did you see the column, dear? The item about Dan? I didn't mention the bottle. I thought, Herb has enough on his plate without—and, you know, it just gives the industry a black eye. I was never one for that."

"No," Liesl said, noncommittal.

"And how is that other man?" Polly said, almost winking, some sort of joke between them. "Such a shame about *Central Station*. Sometimes, a book like that, you wonder if it's *too* rich. But he must have been disappointed."

"Oh, I think he was grateful for the money," Liesl said, evading.

"What is he working on now?" She stopped swiveling to look straight at Liesl, a reporter with an invisible pad.

"You know he never says."

"But you're his translator, dear."

"Only at the end. When he's finished."

But Polly, not really interested, was looking around again. "Oh, there's Carole Landis."

Ben followed her look to the end of the platform where Landis, Julie Sherman, and the other girls were getting off the train. They were all back in their bond-drive dresses, as next-door as the Andrews Sisters.

"You're meeting her?" Liesl said, eager to be off.

Polly shook her head. "Paulette Goddard's on the train."

"No, she got off in Pasadena," Ben said.

Polly whirled around, surprised, glaring at him.

"We met on the train," he said, explaining himself.

"The studio said Union Station. Stanley's in Pasadena. He doesn't do interviews. Now the best I can do for her is an item. Is that what she wants?" Still fuming at Ben, somehow holding him responsible.

"I don't think she knew."

"Maybe she thinks she doesn't need it anymore, a good word here and there. I'd be more careful. Given where she's been."

For a second Ben thought she meant the chorus days, less innocent than Sol imagined, but Polly had gone elsewhere, almost spitting now with irritation.

"You know, you lie down with a Red, a little pink always comes off. If I'd been married to Mr. Chaplin I'd be a *little* more careful before I threw away a friendly interview." She looked over her shoulder to see Landis getting nearer. "Well, I guess it's Carole's lucky day. Won't she be pleased."

"We'd better let you get on with it," Liesl said, beginning to move away.

"Believe me, dear, she'll wait. Nice running into you." She patted Liesl's arm. "You'll be all right. You tell that other man I'd like to have a chat sometime. As a friend. You know, he's been signing things and you have to be careful what you sign. Carole!"

She stuck out her arm, waving, and without saying good-bye hurried over to the surprised Landis, the photographer trailing behind. Liesl stared at her for a minute, face flushed.

"My god. 'You have to be careful what you sign,'" she said, her voice bitter.

"Who was that?"

"Polly Marks." She caught Ben's blank look. "She writes for the newspapers. One hundred and twenty-three of them."

"Exactly one hundred and twenty-three?"

She smiled a little, a slight softening. "My father told me. He's always exact."

"Who's the other man? Him?"

She nodded. "You know my father is Hans Ostermann. So Thomas Mann is also here. And she imagines they have a rivalry—well, maybe it's true a little—and so he's the Other Mann. The names, you see. Warners bought one of his books, so now he exists for her. Otherwise—" She turned her head, annoyed with herself. "I'm sorry. She does that to me. I'm sorry for such a greeting. So, welcome to paradise," she said with an indifferent wave toward the station.

She started through the barrier, leaving Ben to follow on his own, moving sideways with the bag through the crowd to keep up. The main hall, streamlined Spanish colonial, was noisy with leave-taking, voices rising over the loudspeaker announcements, so Ben had to speak up.

"What did she mean about the bottle?"

"They found one in the room," she said, slowing a little but not stopping. "They think—you know, for courage. I don't know who told her. One of her little mice. Maybe the maid. She pays them. Or the night clerk."

Or porters on trains, Ben thought. They were passing through a waiting hall with deep chairs and mission-style chandeliers.

"I don't understand about the hotel."

"It's an apartment hotel. People live there. But there's a switchboard and a maid to change the sheets. A service, considering. You rent by the month."

"And he used it as an office?"

"What do you think?" she said, looking at him.

They reached the high arched entrance, where Ben had to stop, blinded by the sudden glare. She had moved aside to put on her sunglasses and now was rummaging through her bag for cigarettes.

"I suppose it takes the guesswork out of getting a room. They asked me if I was going to use up the month. Since it was already paid for. They want to move someone else in. Collect twice." She lit a cigarette, her hand shaking a little, then looked away, embarrassed. "I'm sorry to involve you in this. Such a welcome. But you'll hear it anyway. So it was like that."

He looked over at her, not sure what to say. A marriage he knew nothing about.

"I didn't mean to pry," he said finally. "You didn't know?"

She shook her head. "Isn't that the point? *Cinq à sept*. Like the French. Just get home in time for dinner." She drew on the cigarette, her expression lost behind the glasses. "Or maybe he didn't want to come home. So that's that." She lifted her head. "I wonder what she felt when she saw it in the papers. Maybe she left him. Maybe it was that. Well," she said, the word like a thud, so final that for a moment neither of them spoke. Then she stepped away from the wall. "So come. With any luck we'll have the house to ourselves. These last few days— Why do people bring food? Salka brought noodle pudding. Noodle pudding in this climate." She turned to him, still hidden behind the glasses. "Please. Don't listen to me. All this—business, it's not your problem. It's good you're here." She dropped the cigarette, grinding it out, and started for the parking lot, lined with spindly palms, then stopped again, staring at the rows of cars, gleaming with reflected sun. "You know what's the worst? I didn't know he was unhappy. Isn't that terrible, not to know that about someone? Maybe the woman was part of all that, I don't know. So maybe it's my fault, too."

"No. It's nobody's fault."

"I didn't even notice," she said, not hearing him. "I don't know what I'm supposed to feel. One day, one thing, the next—" She put a hand up to her forehead, covering her glasses. "I'm sorry. I must sound like a crazy woman. Talking like this. You're here five minutes—"

"It's all right. I don't know how to feel, either."

She turned, dropping her hand. "Yes. I forget. It's not just me, is it?"

He followed her to a convertible with the canvas roof down, shining with chrome, the metal handle already hot to the touch. She opened the door, then stood still for a second, looking at him.

"What?"

"Just then, with the bag, you were like him. Not the looks. You don't look alike. But the gesture."

He got in, flustered, and watched her start the car.

"I know it's hard, but—tell me what happened. I want to know. The papers. I mean, dizzy spells."

"That was their idea. I said, why not a stroke? Anybody can have a stroke. Even young. But they said a doctor could tell, if he looked. A fall, it doesn't matter."

"Who said?"

"The studio. They're superstitious. Bad things. Maybe they *stick*. They're not supposed to happen." She glanced up at the bright sky. "Just sunshine."

"But how? Through a window?" he said, still trying to picture it.

"There was a balcony. Just enough to step on. You know the kind?"

"A Juliet," he said automatically.

"Yes? Like the play? So if you got dizzy, you could fall."

"If you got dizzy."

She looked at him, then up at the rearview mirror, backing out, physically moving away.

"Look," she said, nodding toward the station doors as Polly came out with Carole Landis, arms linked. She waved and moved the car forward in the line to the exit. "Did you really meet Paulette Goddard on the train?" Not wanting to talk about it. "What was she like?"

"Nice," he said, forced to go along.

"Maybe you are."

"No, she was."

"She won't be after Polly's through with her."

"What was that about? With Chaplin?"

"Polly hates Chaplin. So he must be a Communist. Everyone she hates is a Communist. She hated Daniel, too, when he was in the union. She thinks they're all Communists in the union."

"Then why is she doing him a favor? Covering."

"It's for Yates. Daniel was important to him. *Partners* made money. So he was giving him a big picture to do. You know at Metro you have to wait years for that. That's why he left there. You know what he's like. Everything today. A skating picture, but still. A good budget."

Not failing, on his way up.

"Skating. Like Sonja Henie?"

"Vera Hruba Ralston," she said, drawing out the name. "You know her? Yates is in love with her. So it was a good job for Daniel. They paid him while they fixed the script."

"Hruba?"

"'She skated out of Czechoslovakia and into the hearts of America.'"

Ben did a double take, then smiled. "Really?"

She nodded. "On the posters," she said, lighting another cigarette at the stop sign.

"Who's Mr. Ralston?"

"She got it off a cereal box."

"You're making it up."

"You don't have to, not here." She looked up at the sky again. "The fog's burning off early. Sometimes it takes all morning. Shall we go to the hospital first?"

She pulled out of the lot, looking straight ahead. Smoke curled up from the cigarette between her fingers on the steering wheel, then flew back in the breeze as they sped up, mixing with loose wisps of hair. What California was supposed to be like—a girl in a convertible. But not the way he expected.

Across the street, they drove past a sleepy plaza of tile roofs and Mexican rug stalls, a village for tourists. Behind it, just a block away, the American city began: office buildings, coffee shops, anywhere. Harold Lloyd had dangled from a clock here and the Kops had chased each other through Pershing Square and dodged streetcars (red, it turned out), but all that had happened in some city of the mind. The real streets, used so often as somewhere else, looked like nowhere in particular.

They drove out on Wilshire, the buildings getting lower, drive-ins and car lots with strings of plastic pennants.

"The first time, you think how can it be like this," she said, noticing his expression. "The *signs*. And then you get used to it. Even my father. He likes it now."

"Well, the climate—"

"Not so much that. He's hardly ever outside. For him it's a haven," she said, her voice so throaty that it came out "heaven." "All those years, moving. One place. Another place. Then here, finally safe, and other Germans are here, so it's good. The sun, I don't think it matters for him. He lives in his study. In his books."

"What was *Central Station*? I never—"

"*Anhalter* before. They changed it. So it wouldn't sound German. You know it?"

"*Anhalter Bahnhof*. Of course."

"Tell him. He'll be pleased."

She made a right on Vermont, pointing them now toward the hills.

"Do we pass Continental on the way?" Ben said.

"We can, if you like."

"But if it's out of our way—"

"It doesn't matter. He's not conscious, you know. We just sit there. Maybe it's better for him. There's so much damage, the brain—if he were awake, what would that be like for him? Sometimes I think it would be better if—and then I think, how can you think that?" She bit her lower lip. "But he did. I don't know why. But that's what he wanted. Not this."

He looked away, across the miles of bungalows.

"Did he leave a note?" he said finally.

"No."

The crucial prop, the writing of it sometimes a scene in itself, looking up from the paper into a mirror, eyes moist. In the movies. In real
life you just did it.

"Just his 'effects.' I had to sign. You know that word? I didn't know
it. Effects." She looked at him. "They would have said. If they'd found
anything." She turned on Melrose. "That's Paramount down there,
where the water tower is."

After a few blocks he could see the roofs of the sound stages,
humped like airplane hangars. She slowed near a gate of swirling
wrought iron so that he could get a glimpse behind—a tidy factory yard
with people in shirt sleeves gliding past, the tall water tower rising above
everything, just like its mountaintop logo, ringed with stars. In front of
the gate, a thin line of pickets walked back and forth carrying signs.

"There's a strike?" Ben said. A prewar image.

"Daniel said it was jurisdictional," she said, careful with the word.
"One union against the other." She looked away, no longer interested.
"He always wanted to work here. More than any of them. Maybe if—
well. That's RKO, at the end."

They turned onto Gower under the model of a radio tower on a
globe.

"Continental's up there," she said, pointing. "Across from Columbia."

This gate was modern, no more than a break in the walls with
streamlined trim. Beyond it, unseen, Lasner's empire, built from nickels,
a private world made invisible by sentries and passes. Outside, the street
was empty—no pickets, just a small cluster of people near the gate.

"Who's that?" Ben said.

"They wait here, to see who drives through."

"For autographs?"

"No, just to see them. For a minute."

Hans Ostermann was waiting for them in Danny's room, reading in
the corner next to the window. The shades were half-drawn so that even
the light seemed hushed, a hospital quiet broken only by the nurses
outside and the clank of a meal cart being wheeled down the hall.

Ostermann stood when they came in, taking Ben's hand. He was wearing a suit and tie, as natural to him as his perfect posture and formal nod. Ben wondered, a darting moment, if he wrote dressed this way, erect at his desk in a white collar, keeping German alive.

Ben approached the bed, his stomach tightening with shock. Not just sick. Danny's face was beaten in, bruised, one eye swollen shut, jagged laceration marks crossing the rest. What happens when you hit. Ben stared at him for a minute, trying to see something familiar, but all he could see was the fall itself, the smash at the end. Why this way? Danny primping at the mirror for a date, deliberately doing this to himself. Why not sleeping pills, an easier Hollywood exit? Why would he want to look this way?

Ben stepped closer, taking in the IV drip, the monitor, all the hospital tools to keep him alive, bring him back. But you only had to look at the broken face to see the truth. The teases, the grins, were gone. They were just waiting for the rest of him to go. Ben took his hand, half expecting some response, but nothing moved.

"Danny," he said, keeping his voice low, waking someone who's just dozed off. He turned to the others. "Can he hear anything?"

"No," Liesl said.

"We don't know that," Ostermann said. "There's no way of knowing. Talk if you like."

"Nonsense," Liesl said, moving over to a vase of flowers.

"No, the doctor said, head injuries—we don't know. What really happens." He looked over at Ben, his voice reassuring. "The first two days were the critical ones. So perhaps—"

"But he's no better," Liesl said, bluntly pragmatic, facing it. "Why do people send flowers when he can't see them."

The room, Ben noticed now, was full of them, covering side tables and window sills.

"It's a sign of concern," Ostermann said. "A gesture."

"For you," Liesl said. "They send them for you."

"You're tired," Ostermann said, as close, Ben saw, as he would come to a reprimand.

Liesl was reading one of the cards attached to a vase. "From Alma," she said. "So she's forgiven you."

"For now," Ostermann said, a weak smile.

Ben looked at the bruised face. When you're unconscious, where does the mind go? Functioning somewhere beyond pain, or simply floating in white? Now that he was here, what was there to do? The usual business of a hospital visit seemed beside the point—fetching nurses, chatting idly to keep up spirits, plumping pillows.

Instead they waited, Ostermann returning to his book, Ben sitting at the bedside gazing at Danny's damaged face, Liesl pacing, making lists of the flower cards for thank-you notes, glancing over at the bed as if she were still deciding how to feel, wearing herself out with it.

By lunch, in the cafeteria, she was visibly exhausted.

"Go home and rest," Ostermann said. "You were here all night."

"How can I leave? What if I'm not here if— What would people say?"

"That the family was here. Get Ben settled in. I'll stay."

"How can I sleep?" she said, putting things on her tray, standing up.

Ostermann looked at her fondly. "Then have a swim." He turned to Ben as she left the table. "It's no good, being here day and night. Look at her, all nerves. Take her home. He'll be here later, you know."

"What if he isn't?"

"I know how you feel. When Anna was dying, in Paris, I never left. Nuns. I didn't want to leave her with nuns. Leave her alone. But it was for me, not her. When she died, I was there and it didn't matter. She was alone. I didn't know it until then. We die alone." He looked up. "I'll call if there's a change."

THEY DROVE up into the hills, the narrow road twisting upward in a series of blind curves past tall bushes and steep, hidden driveways. With each turn the houses seemed to get bigger, villas and a few white boxes that once must have been daring and modernist, softened now by middle-aged gardens. The trees were bigger, too, mature oaks and tall needle pines, as if the cooler air above the flats made it easier for them to grow. The new cars parked along the side of the road were buffed and shiny, like children after a bath.

"Here we are."

The house, just visible through the driveway shrubs, was Mediterranean, fronted with a row of French windows. They pulled up next to a Dodge coupe.

"Oh, good, Iris is here. I asked her to come in an extra day." A maid with a car. In Germany, bicycles were traded for food.

The house inside was light and open, filled with books and contemporary furniture, a piano covered with framed photographs in the corner. Iris, a wiry, pale woman in a dress, not a uniform, was in the dining room polishing silver.

"I put the messages by the phone. You better call the caterer again. I told him no ham but he wants to talk to you."

Ben looked at Liesl, surprised.

"I thought I'd better start arranging things," she said, flushing, "just in case. So we won't have to at the last minute. Iris, this is Mr. Kohler's brother, Benjamin."

"Reuben. Anyway, Ben," he said, distracted, noticing her feet in pink bedroom slippers.

Iris nodded. "I'm sorry about Mr. Kohler," she said, formal but genuine, then cocked her head to one side, appraising him. "You don't look alike."

"No, he took after my father."

Liesl started toward the hall. "You're down this way. You'll have your own bath, so it's private."

Through an open door on their left he could see a big desk and more shelves. Danny's real workroom, not rented by the month. A club chair in the corner and, next to it, a day bed made up as a couch.

"I'm here. Daniel's dressing room opens from the hall, too, so you won't be bothering me. If you use it. That door." She pointed, still moving.

"You better call the caterer," Iris shouted from the dining room.

"All right. I don't see what's so difficult. I said poached salmon."

"Well, he heard ham."

She opened a door at the end of the hall. "You're in here. I'd better phone or she'll nag me about it. If you'd like a swim, just use those stairs—the pool's out back. I won't be long."

A swim. Something he hadn't had in four years. He gestured toward his bag. "I didn't bring—" Who had bathing suits?

"Use one of Daniel's. He's got a drawer full of them. Just root around and pick what you like."

He threw his bag on the bed and went over to the window. The pool was below, blue and rippling, catching the light in quick flashes. It had been set off from the rest of the hill by a private wall of trees, with the far end left open, so that the land seemed suspended in air before falling away to the distant grid of streets. Around the edge were large pots of geraniums, a few lemon trees, and a row of trimmed oleanders, high enough to flower but not block the view. Ben stared at the pool, unsettled, as if a wrong note of music had been hit, jarring the whole piece. He'd thought of Danny as somehow desperate, not lying on a chaise in the sun, picking fruit off trees. How did they fit? An acre of paradise and a room at the Cherokee Arms.

He went to the dressing room, curious. More money. Rows of sport jackets on hangers, shoes laid out. A drawer full of bathing suits: tropical flowers, chevron stripes, finally a pair of navy blue trunks that could be anybody's. He looked through the other drawers quietly, feeling like a burglar. Socks rolled up, a stack of handkerchiefs, pressed and folded. But Danny's drawer at home had been neat, too. Under the handkerchiefs there were old passports, kept for some reason, filled with the stamps of their childhood, crossing into Germany, crossing out of Germany, Dover and Calais, Berlin-Tempelhof, the last with an eagle on a swastika, just before the pages ran out. He looked at the photo. In his next passport he'd be grown up, but here he was still young, the hair brushed to one side.

Where would the other pictures be? His study, probably. He crossed the hall, carrying the trunks, and surprised Iris, who was putting papers away in drawers.

"I'm just cleaning up in here. You get people in and out, you know they're going to come snooping. They go looking for the bathroom and next thing they're at the desk, just happening to read what's on it. I've seen it. Something I can help you with?"

"No, I'm just snooping myself," Ben said. "Trying to find some pictures. You know, we haven't seen each other in a while."

She went over to the shelves where a few small frames rested against the books.

"This is pretty recent," she said, handing him one.

Ben looked down. A group on the beach, Danny with his lopsided grin, making a face at the camera. The whole row smiling, enjoying the day. Liesl wore a two-piece suit with polka dots, like Chili Williams, her hair blowing behind her.

"You planning to stay long?"

Ben raised his head.

"I only ask because of the food. So I can plan."

"I don't want to make things worse for her," Ben said, a question.

Iris shook her head. "Far as that's concerned, she could use the company. You know what it's like in an empty house. She's already taking it hard. It's the suddenness of it. And the way—" She stopped and went back to the desk. "Don't mind me."

Ben put the picture back, then glanced down at the day bed. "He spend a lot of time in here?"

"What kind of question is that?"

"I just meant—"

"I know what you meant. I suppose you've been hearing things? People like to talk. When it's none of their business. I'll tell you, I never saw it. But people have different ways. You take Mr. Baker—that's my ex. That man was a hound. I threw him out. I said, 'I know you can't help it, you got to chase anything runs in front of you, but I don't want any part of it.' Now Mr. Kohler, I never saw that. Two years I've been working here. Since they got the house. So you live and learn." She closed the drawer and looked up at him. "He seemed the same to me. Like always. Well." She moved to the door. "You want to help, people have to eat. She hasn't touched a thing in days. Melon. What's melon? Water is all. Get her to eat something."

When she'd gone, Ben looked at the other pictures, more wrong notes, as jarring as the pool. Danny and Liesl on a picnic blanket. With another couple around a nightclub table covered with glasses. Hans Ostermann, unintentionally comic in his somber European suit, surrounded by Danny and a few other young men in tennis whites. A croquet game. A pool party. Danny smiling in all of them. A happy life. But everybody smiled for the camera.

He went over to the desk, intending to start on the drawers, but Liesl came in, carrying flowers. "Oh good, you found one," she said, nodding to the bathing suit. "I'll be right down. As soon as I deal with these. I have to put them where she'll see them. She'll ask otherwise. Now what?" she said, as the phone rang. "Why does everybody want to talk?" But she picked it up anyway, not waiting for Iris, and immediately switched into German. She had the rich, fluid German he remembered from before the war, before all the coarse shouting, and her voice sounded relaxed, at home in it.

"Salka wants to drop off a cake," she said wryly, hanging up. "But she wants to know if Alma's here. They're not speaking to each other."

"Alma who sent the flowers to Danny?"

Liesl nodded. "Mahler. Well, Werfel now, but if you leave out the Mahler she puts it back in."

"And Salka?"

"Viertel. Berthold's wife. Well, when he's around. Everyone goes to her on Sundays—like a real salon. So of course it makes Alma crazy. Two queen bees in one hive. I suppose they'll have to see each other, if there's a funeral. For five minutes anyway. They'll all come. It's like a village. They'll come to see who doesn't come. So, you'll be all right?"

she said, gesturing again to the trunks, then glanced at the desk. "Were you looking for something?" She met his eyes, her face suddenly soft. "He didn't leave a note. You can look, but he didn't."

The drawer was a mess of papers: letters, odd pages of scripts with margin notes, bank statements with canceled checks, more private than clothes. An envelope with a doctor's return address. He pulled out the letter. An annual physical, boxes checked in columns, blood pressure, heart rate—everything had been fine in January, perfect in fact, except for the lazy eye that had got him a 4-F. He put the form down, suddenly embarrassed. What exactly was he looking for? An explanation? An apology? He looked at Danny's handwriting again—swooping caps and then tight, closed letters. Which meant what? Would he even have given it a thought a few days ago? This was like looking at tea leaves or chicken entrails. He shoved the paper back and closed the drawer.

Downstairs, sliding glass doors led out to the pool. There was a wet bar, some bright patio furniture, and a galley kitchen with a serving window that opened to the terrace. Ben imagined parties with platters of food, umbrella tables by day, the million lights by night. To the side was a closed door. The garage? No, a screening room with red plush seats and musty velvet drapes, so dated it must have come with the house. He turned up the lights. Except for the sound speakers, it was the kind of room Lasner might have used to run *Two Husbands*. Maybe even for Chaplin, a lifetime before Paulette. Did Danny still use it?

The projection room, at any rate, was functional, the equipment newer than some he'd used in the Signal Corps. A few cans of film lay next to the projector, waiting to be put back on the metal shelf lined with hexagonal storage boxes. Ben went over to look, expecting a row of Republic serials, but they were Ufa films, titles on the boxes inked in German. *Drei Mädchen, Ein Tag in Berlin, Sag Mir Adieu*—all the silly comedies and shopgirl dramas their father had made out in Babelsberg, a kind of shrine to Otto Kohler. All here, even the ones from the thirties, when Otto still thought he'd be safe. Ben ran his fingers across the boxes. Films he hadn't seen, then never asked to see later, all faithfully collected. The father's son. Even *Two Husbands,* probably moldering away now in its canister.

He moved from the shelf, his eye caught by a wall of framed photographs. Another Kohler homage. Otto on the set with Marika Rökk. A group picture with Jannings, Lorre, and Conrad Veidt. Dietrich showing him her leg, a gag shot. A formal premiere, probably at the Zoo Palast, in gowns and white ties with—yes, Goebbels at the end of the row. Otto on a crane. Otto blocking a scene. A wall of Otto. And finally, at the end, a picture of the family, all four of them in Lützowplatz, his mother smiling broadly, her hand on Ben's shoulder. Danny making a face.

He took the picture from the wall and stared at it, suddenly moved. His life, too. How old had he been? Eight? He remembered the day it had been taken, Frau Weber telling Danny to stand still and then not finding the shutter button so he'd laughed at her again, making another face, the whole afternoon still so real that Ben felt he could touch it, right through the glass frame. His face flushed, a warm surge of recognition. Not someone else.

"There you are. I saw the light. I've been looking—" Liesl stopped, seeing his face. "What?"

"Why would he do it," Ben said flatly.

She had put a terrycloth wrap over her bathing suit and now pulled at one of the lapels, a nervous drawing away.

"I've been acting for days as if he's someone I don't know." He held out the picture. "But I do know him. It's not something he would do."

"Don't," she said softly. "It makes it worse. I know. I did it, too."

"But it doesn't make sense."

"You want it to make sense?"

"It does to them, somehow. He wasn't sick—I saw his physical. He wasn't depressed, either. Iris said he was the same as always."

"Oh, Iris."

"You did, too. You said you didn't know he was unhappy. But why should he be?" He waved his arm to take in the house, Danny's life.

"We don't know what was in his mind. We don't."

She turned and headed out toward the pool. He glanced down at the picture again, then followed.

"But to do this—"

"What, then? Do you think his girlfriend pushed him out? Like some cartoon?"

"Somebody could have."

Liesl shook her head. "No one else was there. The police talked to the night clerk. No one went up. No one. The door was locked."

"There has to be a reason."

"So what could it be? Maybe his marriage. Is that what you think? The others do. You can hear it in their voices. How could he do such a terrible thing? And then they look at *me*."

"I didn't mean—"

"Ouf," she said, cutting him off, then tossing the robe on the chair. "Enough."

"Liesl—"

But she turned away, stepping over to the edge of the pool, and dove in, a perfect arc, slicing into the water, then streaming under the surface, out of hearing. When she came up she swam the rest of the length in fast, efficient strokes, a quick, sideways turn for air. Someone who swam every day. He watched her as she turned for the second lap, hair flowing, the long, golden legs scissoring effortlessly, at home in it. The kind of girl everyone noticed, pretending not to, but imagining the smooth body without the suit, beads of water running off the tan skin, all anyone could want. But not enough for Danny. The father's son in every way. That same careless urge for the next thing, not expecting any damage, until families were broken up and what should have been held close had been let down.

He turned his head away, flustered. Not just some girl in a pool. There were cigarettes on a side table, and he lit one, looking away toward the hazy city. Behind him he could hear the regular splashes of her strokes, then a pause and a noisy gathering of water as she lifted herself up the pool stairs. She came over to where he was standing, toweling her hair.

"Marta says I should wear a cap. The chlorine burns the hair. My hairdresser," she said, the change of subject a kind of apology, moving on. She glanced at him, waiting, then lit one of the cigarettes, joining him. "Would you like to know about me and Daniel?"

"It's none of my—"

"Yes. Otherwise you'll wonder. That's how it is now." She looked at him. "We need to be friends. To get through this. Sit," she said, indicating the next chaise. She sat back on hers, lifting her face to the sun. "He got me out. That's why he married me. My father, there was a visa for him. You know, for the culture. They could get artists out on special visas, especially if they were known here. But not me. I wasn't an artist. I wasn't anything. You know, after we left Germany we were officially stateless. Not even resident permits, always temporary papers. So, no visa. But of course my father wouldn't leave me, and it was dangerous for him. So Daniel married me, made me an American. But I think he was fond of me, too." She turned to him, her eyes direct. "It wasn't a *mariage blanc*. Don't think that," she said, then looked away again.

"This was where?" he said after a minute. "Germany?"

"No. Germany? We would have been dead. My father was one of the first to leave. His name was already on a list, because of the articles. And, you know, my mother was Jewish so it was for her, too. First Vienna, to keep the language. Then Paris—she died there. I think her heart gave out from the worry. Then, after the Nazis came, we went south, like everyone. You don't know this? That's where I met Daniel. In Marseilles. He was helping people get out. You wouldn't think such a place—it was like here, the good weather—but it was a death trap. Who could trust Vichy? So Daniel helped people get to Spain. Sometimes over the mountains, on foot. He walked them out. They never forgot it." She paused, taking in some smoke. "Neither did I. He was my hero," she said, staring at her burning cigarette. She looked up, self-conscious, her wistful tone now shaded with irony, almost bitter. "So it wasn't for love. But we made a life. He never asked to leave, afterwards, when it was safe for me. We were—comfortable together." She sat up, rubbing out the cigarette.

"And the others? You seemed surprised."

She made a half smile. "Maybe I'm like Germany. I didn't want to know. So I didn't. And now everyone will know—" She stopped. "But how can I be angry? He didn't owe me that." She covered her eyes with her hand, a pretend sunshade. For a moment neither of them said anything, the air so quiet he could hear the drain flaps in the pool. "You know before, when I said I didn't know he was unhappy? I should have known, because I see it now."

"Everybody says that after. They should have seen—"

"No, it's true. Not unhappy—troubled. Maybe this woman. I don't know." She looked at him. "I still don't want to know, do you understand that?"

He walked toward the pool, thinking.

"How long? I mean, when did you notice?"

She got up, gathering her robe, the movement like a reluctant sigh. "Not long. The summer, the end of the summer. So now you can find the girl and ask her, what happened this summer, all right? Then maybe you'll be satisfied." She belted the robe. "But it wasn't us. We were all right. We were just the way we were."

THE HOSPITAL seemed busier at night—trays being collected, nurses changing shifts. Danny was alone in the room, oblivious.

"He wouldn't just leave," Liesl said, looking for her father, then spied him at the end of the corridor in the smoking lounge with another man, not as tall, looking around hesitantly, like someone trying to make small talk. "My uncle Dieter," she said. "Look how they stand. See how stiff?"

"His brother?"

"My mother's. The truth is they don't like each other. When my mother was alive, it was different. Now he only comes when you have to, for appearances. My father's birthday, things like that."

"Or like this."

"Yes," she said, looking down. "But not only for that. He liked Daniel. Everybody did." Already in the past.

"He lives here, too?"

"Pasadena. Come, before they quarrel."

But when they joined the men, the mood seemed polite, not at all contentious, Danny's situation overriding whatever irritation there might have been. Introductions were made, doctors' visits discussed— and then they were all back on watch, drifting between Danny's room and the hall, fidgeting, looking for something to do. Only Ben stayed fixed, holding Danny's hand again, convinced against all sense that Danny could feel it, use it to climb back. When the two men got up to go to dinner Liesl went out with them to the hall, a family huddle, leaving Ben alone. Talk to me, he thought, tell me why before you go. At least that. The battered face had lost its power to upset him, used to it now, but the waiting itself had become oppressive, making him logy, his mind dense with still air. When the first sound came, he wasn't sure he'd actually heard anything, just his own wish, but the second was real. He lifted his head sharply, as if someone had snapped fingers in his face.

"Ben." Still faint, a little croaky, but there. He grasped Danny's hand, waiting for his eyes to flutter open.

"Yes. I'm here."

"Ben," the voice said again, the tone slightly puzzled, working things out.

"Danny, my god."

The eyes open now but blinking against the light.

"You're in the hospital. Do you remember anything?"

The blinking stopped, his eyes steadier, wetting his lips, focusing.

"Danny."

Then his eyes closed, a kind of resignation.

"Danny, let me get the others. They're just outside. Everyone— Liesl, her father, Dieter. We didn't know if you'd make it—"

He got up, ready to bolt across the room, but Danny made a hiss, an attention-getter, his mouth so dry it was difficult now to speak. Ben leaned close to his face.

"Don't leave me," he whispered, his voice raspy, urgent.

Ben lifted his head, disconcerted. Did Danny know it was him? All these years, and now suddenly clinging. Maybe what happened at the end, any life raft.

"Don't," he said again.

"No, I won't. It's going to be all right now." Elated by the unexpectedness of it. "I'll just get Liesl," Ben said, excited, racing across the room and flinging open the door. "He's awake!"

They all looked at him, stunned. Liesl got to the bed first.

"Daniel?" she said, then, when there was no response, turned to Ben. "You're sure?"

"Of course I'm sure."

"Daniel? But he looks the same."

"He was awake. I'll get the doctor," Ben said, still excited, heading for the door.

"I'll go," Ostermann said.

But Ben was already on his way, racing down the hall to the nursing station, everything around him a blur. The nurse, alone on duty, looked up in alarm, Ben's hands now pounding on the desk, an emergency signal. Dr. Walters was on another floor. She picked up the phone to call the station upstairs.

"Never mind," Ben said, not waiting for the elevator, leaping up the stairs, his eyes looking for the recognizable white coat. Down the hall, jotting notes on a clipboard.

"He woke up," Ben said, a little breathless.

Dr. Walters, startled, put the clipboard down without a word and followed him to the stairs. Ben could hear their feet clumping, an echo effect between floors. Ostermann and Dieter were at the nursing station now, then Liesl, everyone running, the corridor filling with people, the same blur as they raced back. Dr. Walters dodged past an aide, not stopping till he pushed the door and ran across the empty room to the bed, taking up Danny's hand.

"You said if he came to—" Ben started, watching the doctor lower his head to Danny's face, then take his wrist. "What's the matter?"

The doctor took out a stethoscope and bent lower again, a repeat check.

"I'm sorry," he said. "He's gone."

Ben looked at Danny, winded, his own body suddenly cool. Could you tell just by looking? The body still, mouth slightly open, no movement at all.

"But he can't. He was just here," Ben said.

The doctor looked at him. "Maybe he was saying good-bye. A last effort. Nurse."

She hurried over, turning off the monitor, and drew up the sheet. The doctor glanced at his watch, already mentally filling out a certificate.

"It may be for the best," he said calmly, an attempt to comfort. "This kind of injury. A full recovery isn't possible. It's unusual, to last this long. If we do a complete examination, maybe we'll know more next time. Mrs. Kohler, I'll need you to sign some forms."

Liesl didn't answer, staring at the bed, dazed.

"We can wait till tomorrow, if you like."

"You mean an autopsy," Ben said, imagining the knives.

"It can wait," the doctor said.

Liesl turned from the bed. "No, I'll come," she said, her voice a monotone. "He wanted to be cremated." Danny in a box.

"That's not a hospital—"

"No, I just meant, it won't matter, the examination." She touched Ben's arm. "That's right, isn't it? You don't object?"

Ben shook his head. "He knew me. He was conscious."

And then he wasn't. When? What everyone always said, it happened so fast, a part of a second.

"Mrs. Kohler," the doctor said again and then he was leading her out, Ostermann following, everybody, even the duty nurse, until Ben was alone in the room.

In a minute orderlies would come and wheel the bed away. Ben went over and pulled back the sheet, a last look, shaken. On the train, he'd thought of Danny as already dead, but that was an idea. This was worse, a flash of contact, then gone, actually cold now to the touch. Another body. When he was a child, death was something remote, an event for old people. Then, in the war, it happened to everybody. But you only got used to it when they were already dead. Dying itself was new each time, something you could feel. Ed bleeding away. Now Danny. Don't leave me, he'd said. But he was the one who'd left, just the way he always did, when it suited him, leaving Ben behind.

He was still standing by the bed when he heard the door open. He turned, expecting the orderlies, but it was Liesl. She glanced toward the white sheet, then away.

"Do you want more time?" she said.

"You're finished?"

"A few papers only." She walked over to the bed, staring at the body for a minute, eyes soft. "So it's over." She looked up. "What should we do with the flowers?" she said, her voice shaky, snatching the phrase out of the air, something to say. "What happens to them?"

"I never thought about it. Maybe they give them to other people."

"It's true? He was awake?"

Ben nodded.

She looked down, then folded her arms across her chest, as if she had caught a chill. "We should go. All the arrangements. There'll be so much to do. For the widow." Another glance to the bed, her voice catching again. "So now this. I've never been a widow before."

THE PHONE started ringing early and continued for most of the morning, through the deliveries and the extra help and Iris directing the table setups, the whole house in motion. The mechanics of mourning had taken over. No one sat and brooded, or even mentioned Danny.

"You're about the same size," Liesl said, handing him some of Danny's suits. "They should fit."

He smiled to himself. Still wearing his hand-me-downs.

"You'll need something," she said, misinterpreting his look. "But if you feel funny—"

He shook his head, cutting her off. "It's fine."

"I thought you might like his watch."

Ben took it, his finger grazing the crystal. Not Danny's, their father's. Another piece of the Otto shrine. When did Danny get it? On one of those last trips to Germany, probably, a sentimental gift to the loyal son who stayed close.

"Thank you," he said, touched. "There must be something I can do. Except be in the way."

"No, really—" She stopped. "That place. Where he was," she said, hesitant. "Somebody has to go there. If he left things. I don't know, nobody said. But I could send Iris."

He shook his head again. "I'll go."

"Take his car. You'll need one out here anyway. Two now. And so hard to get. But now you—"

"You have the key?"

"The key?" she said, a new idea. "I don't know, maybe here." She went over to the desk and pulled out a ring with several keys. "They were in his pants. So it must be one of these. So many keys," she said, looking at them, other parts of his life.

He missed a turn and had to backtrack west on Hollywood Boulevard, past the Pantages, a name out of radio broadcasts, then right on Cherokee. The Cherokee Arms was a five-story pastel building with an alley along the side connected to a parking space behind, not grand, but not seedy, either. A place you used on the way up or the way down, but not at either end. Ben parked across the street and looked at it for a minute, fingering Danny's keys. If the fall could kill him, he must have been on the top floor. He got out and walked across. An apartment building with a lawn in front, quiet in the bright light, no shadows. He passed through the alley. There were a few cars parked in back, garbage cans. He looked up to the top balcony. The railing wasn't high, if you staggered against it. The back door was locked. But it would be, wouldn't it? A convenience for residents on their way in from the parking lot. No need to go through the front, where the desk clerk would see you go up. If you had a key.

The third one worked. From here you could either go directly up the back stairs or down a hall on the right that led past mailboxes and what looked like an elevator door. From this angle Ben couldn't see the front desk switchboard where the clerk must be. He went up the stairs, walking quietly, expecting to be stopped. Instead he found the landings empty, the building still except for the sound of the elevator going down. On the top floor he went to what he assumed was Danny's door, using a key that resembled the one that had worked downstairs.

The room, a studio, was neat—bed made, no dishes in the sink, a hotel room just after maid service. Nothing in the bathroom; nothing in the closet, either. He started opening cupboards. Glasses and dishes that came with the place. On the counter there was an ice bucket and a bottle of brandy, opened. Nothing on the desk but a message pad and pen. No personal presence at all. Ben went over to the French windows and opened them, looking at the balcony, trying to imagine it. He stepped out, placing his leg against the railing. If he'd been wobbly— possible. But so was the other, the leap off. He went back in. What was the point? He took one last look around, then opened the door to leave.

"Moving in?"

The man was leaning against the opposite wall, clearly waiting for him to come out. Young, without a hat.

"You the desk clerk?"

The man—the kid—shook his head and flipped open a press pass.

"I saw you go in. I was out back. So I figured maybe they'd been giving me the brush. About the room. I mean, you have a key. Mind if I look around?"

"What for?"

"They didn't tell you? Scene of the crime," he said, starting in. "Last guy had the room went out the window. Mind?" All the way in now. "What are they charging, you don't mind my asking."

"I don't know. I'm not moving in."

"No? Where'd you get the key?" he asked, but almost offhandedly, moving over to the counter, looking at everything.

"I'm his brother—the guy before."

The kid stopped. "Sorry. I didn't mean—"

"What do you want to see? There's nothing here."

"Honest maids," the kid said, picking up the brandy bottle. "Usually the liquor's the first to go." He went into the bathroom, checking the medicine chest, behind the door. "You come here to pick up his stuff?" He went over to the balcony, retracing Ben's steps, even putting his leg against the railing.

"There's nothing to pick up."

"I noticed. Funny, isn't it? Somebody must have been here already."

"What do you mean?"

"What do you think he used the room for? We said writing office, but what the hell, be nice to the wife. What *would* he use it for? You ever meet a woman yet who didn't take over half the bathroom? Cream here, powder there. Douche bag on the door. And what's here? Nothing. She must have cleaned it out. I don't know when, though. I've been watching the building."

"What for?"

The kid looked at him. "To see who else had a key."

"You think someone was with him?"

"Not then. She'd have been spotted. Every window's got a head sticking out. You know, taking an interest. Cops had to use a passkey to get in. There's no one in there with him. It had to be later."

"Unless she'd already moved out. Maybe that's why he—"

"I get it. You think he jumped. The breakup, huh?"

"You don't?" Ben said, interested.

"At first. We get the police call, nobody else is interested, but my position, you need the inches, even the blotter stuff. The cops are already here and the night clerk's going 'oh-my-god, he must have fallen'—you know, don't make the place look bad—and the cops are going along with it but I can see they're looking at it as a jump. You know, taking pictures and everything. And it's Hollywood, where you get this. Not Hancock Park or someplace—people have been known to jump here. But I'm thinking, it's a funny kind of jump."

"Why?"

"You know anything about jumpers? I covered a few. They like it a little higher. To make sure. Maybe for the show of it. Why not just go to the Roosevelt and jump off the roof? Four, five stories? You *can*—I mean, he did, he's dead. But you could also just wake up in a cast somewhere. That's one thing. Then the angle of the fall. All the jumpers I've seen, they don't back out. Face forward. So I figure the LAPD are looking for a little excitement, pick up a slow night. I wouldn't let this get to you. You believe what you want, but my guess? He was plastered and tripped." He nodded toward the brandy bottle on the counter.

"Then why are you watching the building? If that's all it was?"

"Look, why have a separate place anyway? Under a different name. They got him as Collins downstairs. All right, he's seeing somebody on the side. Not a one-night stand, a longer-term thing. Still, why not a hotel? Unless they don't want to be seen in public, take that chance. Maybe she'd be *recognized*. So who is she? I'm wondering about this and then something funny happens. I know the cops wrote it up as a jump, I was here, but when I'm doing the story the next morning they got it as an accident. How come the change? That's when I get interested, because that kind of change, the only people in this town get favors like that are the studios. So I figure there's a story."

"Why would a studio do that for Danny?"

"Him? They wouldn't. Anyway, he was a goner. They look to the living. And now what do we find?" He looked around at the clean apartment. "Nobody was ever here. But she must have been. And she must have been more than a fuck."

Ben looked at him, sorting it out. "You don't know any of this," he said finally.

"You'd rather have him as a jumper?"

Ben said nothing.

"Maybe we could help each other out."

"How?"

"You're family. Go through his stuff. If he's seeing somebody, he has to call her. There must be a number somewhere."

"So you can find her and put her in the paper," Ben said, thinking of Liesl reading it.

"If she's in pictures, it's a story. Don't you want to know?"

"Seen enough?" Ben said, ducking it, starting to leave.

"I'll do the legwork. That's what I do," the kid said, a half grin on his face, playing reporter, the kind he'd seen in the movies. "I just need a number." He took a business card from his jacket pocket and handed it to Ben. "Day or night."

Ben looked at it. Tim Kelly, a name you'd forget without a card.

"What if she isn't in pictures?" he said. "Just a secretary or something?"

"A secretary—and he gets a place like this?" Kelly said, breezy, still in character. "Then I'd like to fuck her myself."

BEN STOOD beside Liesl and Hans Ostermann at the funeral, the immediate family. Around and behind them, all in black, the émigré community sweltered in old high collars, hats with veils, mourning clothes that belonged in the drizzle and cloudy skies of Middle Europe. Thomas Mann had come, a courtesy to Liesl's father, and Ben recognized a few others—Lion Feuchtwanger, slicked-back hair and eager eyes behind rimless glasses; Brecht, rumpled and smelling of cheap cigars. They were standing in front of the plain marble wall where Danny's box of ashes would be placed. The rest of the cemetery was more elaborate, carved headstones and obelisks and flamboyant tombs from the 1920s. Valentino was somewhere over to the left. Beyond the cypresses and the high wall, Ben could see the water tower of the Paramount back lot, as close as Danny would ever get now.

There were Americans, too—people from the studio, glancing at their watches, expected back—and while they all waited, Ben wondered what made it so easy to tell them apart. Not just the clothes or the haircuts, maybe something in the way they held themselves, an attitude. Or maybe, like Tim Kelly, everyone here slipped naturally into a part, hitting marks under the giant arc lamp. Wasn't he? The grieving brother. Liesl, the stoic widow, dry-eyed behind her dark glasses, leaning on Ostermann, all formal Weimar dignity, as publicly correct as the other Mann. Ben saw that Polly Marks had come, keeping close to a man in a double-breasted suit whom Ben assumed was Herb Yates. Who were all the others? Ben looked at the faces, bored or genuinely sad, and realized again that he knew nothing about Danny's life.

He was still scanning the crowd when he caught someone doing the same thing—a man in a gray suit standing near the edge, looking at faces methodically, as if he were counting. When he met Ben's eyes he didn't even pretend to be embarrassed, just looked, then moved on. Ben stayed on him, watching him fix on Ostermann, then on the others, each in turn. What part was he playing? Not from the studio, certainly not an émigré. Holding a hat in his hand, like a policeman.

He heard a crunch of tires and turned to see a black Packard pulling up. The others had had to park near the gates. A driver hopped out to open the doors. First a little man Ben didn't know, then Alma Mahler, making her entrance. She was dressed for a Viennese funeral the emperor himself might have attended, long black silk with a sizable hat, and without hesitation made her way to the front of the crowd. Ben watched her approach, fascinated. Everybody's mistress, now broadened and grown outward, a kind of pouter pigeon effect, but still turning heads. She put her hand on Liesl's arm as she took her place near the family, then nodded to Ben, her eyes interested, someone new.

Her arrival seemed to give permission to start: a man went to the wall and turned to face them, opening his hands. Ben had been told there would be a rabbi, but his dark suit was like all the others and the service was so secular, no religion specified, that Ben wondered if the cemetery had rules about who could be buried there. *Judenrein.* He looked at the flowers, bouquets, and wreaths with long name ribbons in the German style, then at the open square where they would put the box. After which everyone could move on. He felt Liesl next to him, holding herself erect, getting through it. What would Kelly find, a tabloid love triangle, with pictures of the Cherokee nest? Bury him. Why not a tipsy fall? What difference did it make?

"Heinrich Kaltenbach will say a few words."

The little man who'd come with Alma opened a piece of paper, then closed it, visibly upset, his round face drawn.

"Only a few, not a speech," he said, his accent thick, uncomfortable. "I speak also for Alma and Franz, for many of us here. There is for us a great debt. We owe this man our lives. He came with us. On foot. Only a little farther, he would say. To the border. You remember, Alma?" he said, looking at her, waiting for her nod, a little drama. "And you know what she's carrying, in the suitcase? The manuscript. Bruckner's Fourth. So not just lives, culture, he's saving culture. For this everybody owes him. Please, if you don't mind," he said, then switched into German, his speech picking up pace, fluent now.

The Americans stood respectfully, trying not to look blank, but for the Germans it was a release, something real after the generic service, with the heft of language. Ben looked at them. Just the sound could take them back—the lucky ones, the ones who'd left. But what choice had there been? If they had stayed, they'd be dead. Like Otto. Ashes, too.

His mind wandered, the sound of German fading into the background, overheard but not distinct, as if it were coming up the stairs from one of his father's parties. Danny would be down in the kitchen, sneaking drinks from the indulgent staff.

He froze. He looked at the marble wall, seeing Danny as a teenager, his head over a toilet bowl, retching, swearing he'd never touch brandy again. And never did. An almost allergic reaction, not his drink at all. But there was the bottle sitting on the counter at the Cherokee, suggestive. A prop. Which meant someone had put it there.

Ben felt a prickling on his neck. Someone else in the room. The door had been locked—the police had needed a passkey. But there could have been another, a duplicate to lock the door behind you. Without thinking, he turned, looking back at the crowd for the man in the gray suit. Near the edge, still watching, like someone on duty. But why come to the funeral if you'd already filed it as an accident? Case closed. Unless it wasn't. His mind darted to the stairs, the alley, trying to work out the logistics, as if somehow that would make it all plausible. But how could it be? Could someone really have killed him? Why? Why were people murdered? Jealousy. Revenge. Because they were in the way. In stories, not in real life. Then he thought of the film clips waiting to be assembled at Continental. Why. Millions and millions for no reason at all.

Kaltenbach finished, the sudden quiet like a touch to Ben's shoulder. His eyes went to the rabbi, placing the box in the square, then handing Liesl a flower to put with it. She stood still for a second, then took Ben's hand, drawing him with her to the wall. He was given another flower and then, as if it had been rehearsed, they put them in together, one on each side of the box. When she finished she gave Ben a weak smile, her eyes confused, still not sure how to feel. He looked at the box, suddenly overwhelmed, feeling a loneliness he'd resisted before. Danny was gone, for good. Not just gone, taken away. By what right? And it wasn't just Danny. A death spread out in shock waves, touching other people, changing them, taking pieces of them, too. Demanding some kind of justice. You owed the dead that much. How could he want it for millions and not this one?

ONLY A few Americans came back to the house afterward, so the lunch turned into a German gathering, the language floating warm and familiar around the buffet table like the wisps of steam from the chafing dishes. The caterer had come through with the salmon and what looked like a dozen other dishes, but people had brought things, too, brisket and cakes, an unexpected homey touch. All of it was being eaten, heaping plates and seconds. Liesl, who might have sat in a corner, receiving, instead was everywhere, seeing to people, playing hostess. Ben watched her, waiting for signs of strain, but he saw that the nervous activity, with its chin-high assurance, was also a kind of protective screen, like sunglasses. There were no whispered concerns, no side glances to see how she was holding up. She was right in front of them, busy, in control.

Instead, to his surprise, he found that he had become the center of attention, new ears for old complaints. The curfew during the war. The five-mile restriction for aliens. Gas coupons. All that over, thank god. And then, in lower tones, what was it really like now in Germany? You hear such stories. And the newsreels. You can't recognize things anymore. That madman. Ben heard half of it, distracted, back at the Cherokee, his head noisy with questions. A bottle that shouldn't be there. Someone else. An idea, once there, you couldn't leave behind, not for polite conversation. So he nodded, answering with only part of his mind, and they backed away, respecting what they took for grief, not wanting to trouble him further. But keeping an eye on him, intrigued.

"It's like any colony," Liesl said when they got a moment. "They like to be with each other, not the natives, but they get a little bored, too. So you're something to talk about. Here comes Heinrich. Be nice. I don't know how he lives." She leaned forward to kiss Kaltenbach's cheek. "Heinrich, thank you. It was lovely."

"From here," he said in German, tapping his chest, then turned to Ben, the rituals of introduction.

"I didn't know," Ben said, "about his time in France. Getting people out."

"Yes, many," Kaltenbach said, still in German. "Some by boat, but that was difficult. So, Spain."

"Over the Pyrenees?"

"Yes. The mountain crossings were easier than the trains. Not so strict. One guard, maybe two. Sometimes you could walk in. If you got up there. Imagine, Franz and Alma, at their age. Not hikers, you know, not young men like your brother. It's a very dramatic story."

"Excuse me," Liesl said. "There's Salka."

"Very dramatic. A film," Kaltenbach said. "I think so. Think of it, everybody waiting to get out. The noose tightening. You know what we called the house? Villa Espère Visa. But your brother *acted*. It would be a tribute to him. His story. I have a treatment of this, I'll show it to you. *Exit Visa*. See what you think. They could do it at Continental. That's where you are, yes? Your brother's story. It would be a gift to his memory."

Ben looked at him, feeling ambushed.

"I'm not really at Continental. Just putting something together there for the Army."

And how had he heard about Continental anyway? Ben marveled again at the speed of news here, Lasner in touch even on a train.

"But you'll read it. You'll see," Kaltenbach said. "An exciting film. And you know I can work with another writer. For the English. But who knows the story better? Who lived it?"

"Ben," Liesl said, coming up to them, a short, plump woman in tow, "you have to meet Salka. She's everyone's mother."

"Everyone's cook," the woman said, taking Ben's hand. "They come for the chocolate cake, not for me."

"No, your good heart," Kaltenbach said.

"Daniel liked it," she said, waving this off. "So maybe you'll like it, too. Come Sunday. Any Sunday you like."

"Thank you. I'll look forward."

"Even Garbo comes sometimes," Kaltenbach said.

"So Lasner, now he's letting people go to funerals? On his time?" she said, raising a finger. "Make sure he pays you for the day."

"He doesn't pay me for anything. I'm still in the Army."

"You're at Continental for free?" she said, amused.

"How did you know? About Continental. I mean, how does everybody hear these things?"

Salka looked at him, puzzled. "It's in Polly. You didn't know? You should keep up," she said, a gentle tease. "Of course," she said, catching herself, "on such a day. Who has time for papers." She nodded to the room. "It's too soon for this. A young man. But we don't pick our time, do we?"

"No." Somebody else had.

"I knew your father, too. Tell me something. I've always wondered. Why did he stay in Germany?"

The question mark of his life.

"I don't know. I suppose he thought he'd be safe."

"No one was safe," she said, a settled matter. "Even then."

"I don't think he thought about politics. Just movies."

"Otto? Children never know their parents. When he was young, he and Berthold could argue for hours. Hours. All the problems of the world. No, he knew." She shook her head. "To make those comedies. To stay for that."

He found the paper in the den, already opened to Polly's column.

Off the Chief: Ben Kohler, new at Continental, here early to attend funeral of brother Dan after last week's tragic accident. The surprise death suspended production on the upcoming Vera Ralston picture, which Dan was slotted to helm. Word on the lot: the picture's set to be a breakthrough for Republic's new star. Polly's prediction: a new director and Vera skates over this rough patch of ice to big box office.

The funeral just a plug for Herb Yates.

"Spell your name right?"

Ben looked up. A burly man in a suit a little too tight for him stuck out his hand.

"Howard Stein. I just wanted to pay my respects. I can't stay."

"Thank you," Ben said. "Actually, they got it wrong."

Stein noticed the column logo. "Polly? She can't even spell her own. Used to be Marx, like Groucho. But also like Karl. Somebody points this out to her—one of the Hitler Youth she pals around with—so the next day it's Marks, k-s."

"You're not a fan."

"That bitch?"

Ben smiled. "Not a fan."

"I'm with the CSU. You know her with the unions. Like another goon with a club." He looked up at Ben. "Sorry for the language. I don't think she's a joke."

"Is that how you knew Danny—the union?"

Stein nodded. "He was a good friend to us. When he first got here. You don't forget that."

"But not lately?" Ben said.

"No, not lately." He shrugged. "It happens. People fall away. It's a hard place to hold on to something. You want—" He looked around at the house. "You want a lot of things. So you make some trades. But he was a good man. I'm sorry about this. You just get in?" he said, his voice gruffer, moving away from anything soft.

"Few days. Those pickets I saw in front of Paramount—that was you?"

Stein nodded. "Studios want the union they already got, not us. Why not—they've been paying them off for years. After Willie Bioff got sent up, they tell everybody they're cleaning house, but nothing changes. That's four years now."

"Sent up for what?" Ben said, not really paying attention, a local dispute.

"Racketeering. So you've got the head of the union behind bars, it's time for a change, right? Your brother thought so—we all did. And look. Four years later and we're out there walking with signs and the studios are still paying off. Cheaper than paying the employees. In a year like this, when they're making so much money it's like sitting on a fucking oil well. I'm sorry. I didn't mean to get started. This isn't the place." He looked again at the newspaper. "And now we've got her making it worse. Now we're all Reds."

"There weren't any pickets at Continental."

"No, you start with the majors—the big five. Then everybody else comes in. Who's going to follow Lasner?" He looked at Ben. "Not that he's any different. Dump the cash on some hotel bed and get yourself a new contract. They like doing business that way. It's an outlaw town, they still have that mentality. You know, one day they're at a meeting, the studio heads, and I see them walking out of the commissary and I say to myself, Jesus fucking Christ, it's the boys from Chicago. Same look. Well. This isn't the place." He looked at Ben, hesitant. "I liked him," he said, shaking Ben's hand, then glanced around the room. "It's some place he's got here." He turned back to Ben. "I don't understand it."

He followed Stein back into the busy main room, half-hoping he could pass unnoticed out onto the terrace, but Liesl caught his eye, flagging him down. Somehow the funeral had made them a temporary couple, alert to each other's signals. She took his arm lightly, lowering her voice as she steered him toward Alma Mahler, eating pastry near the table.

"She thinks you're ignoring her," she whispered. Then to Alma, "Found."

But once they were past the introductions, the sympathies, there was little to say. She was a woman of such regal self-absorption that Ben suspected she had no conversation outside herself, so he fell back on the usual, how she liked California.

"For us it was very pleasant. Before Franz died. Now I never go out. But before—you know Stravinsky is here? Schoenberg? Like Europe, with sunshine." Her eyes twinkled a little, waiting for him to respond, evidently a phrase that had worked before. "Of course, we were fortunate. Franz's success." She let the rest of the thought hover there, leaving Ben to imagine the riches. "You know it was a promise he made. He said if we survived, he would write about Lourdes, and look. So Bernadette blessed us, too. Who would have imagined it then? Such a success."

"And the film."

She nodded, accepting tribute.

"Of course, not serious art, like Mahler. Gropius." Listing former lovers like credits. "But it's important here, to have a success. It's what they respect. And of course it's nice, too, to be comfortable. Look at poor Heinrich. In Germany such an important name. I remember passing a bookstore, a whole window, all Kaltenbach, no one else. And here? No one knows who he is."

"The books aren't translated?"

"No. Franz, Lion, Hans of course," she said, tipping her head toward Liesl. "But Heinrich, it's too European maybe. So it's hard for him. We all help a little. Not charity, we tell him, a loan until better times, but of course he's proud. Once in all the windows. Liesl said you were just in Germany?"

"Yes," Ben said, surprised at the veering off.

"It's bad there, everyone says. Heinrich wants to go back. 'I want to be a writer again,'" she said, quoting, but shaking her head. "Well, you know what it's like. I had a letter. My friend Beate. She says people are like zombies. Numb."

"They're hungry," Ben said.

"Yes, hungry," Alma said, not even glancing at her own plate. "But not reading. Not reading Heinrich."

"They will again. Someday. Let's hope so anyway."

She looked up quickly, as if she had been corrected.

"But not here, I think. He doesn't have the popular touch, Heinrich. Like your brother. He had the popular touch. Detectives," she said airily, sliding it in as easily as a pinprick. "Heinrich is an artist."

They were rescued by Kaltenbach, slightly hunched, like a courtier, who came to say their car had arrived.

"You'll excuse us? These cars, they don't like to wait. Such delicious food," he said to Liesl. "But you must be tired. All these people. You should rest."

"Yes," Alma said. "It must be terrible for you." She paused, another prick. "So unexpected."

She patted Liesl's arm, then nodded at Ben and handed him her plate, leading Kaltenbach across the room, tipping her head to people as she went. Just a hand on his elbow, enough to move him along. Ben stared at it. To push a man over you'd need a tighter grip. Had Danny screamed? He must have. At least a startled grunt. Only suicides made no noise, grim with purpose, not taken by surprise. Nobody had said. But it might be in the police report.

"Is something wrong?" Liesl said, peering at him.

"Sorry," he said, snapping back. "Is she always like that?"

"You don't like her?" Liesl said, a mock innocence, then laughed, the first time Ben had seen her really smile. She covered her mouth with her hand, a girl's gesture.

The police report. Tomorrow.

They went out on the terrace, picking up wine glasses off a passing tray.

"Daniel didn't like her, either."

"What did they see in her?" Stay on Alma. "Kokoschka. Mahler. She had half the men in Vienna."

"She used to be a great beauty they say."

"Who says?"

She laughed again. "She does, mostly."

He looked at her, caught by the laugh. It seemed to come from some private part of her, something you only saw in glimpses, like her ease in the water.

"I shouldn't," she said, putting the drink down. "They've only started coffee."

"It's going by itself now," he said. "You can sit one out."

She glanced up, working out the idiom, then took a sip of wine.

"Did you notice? They don't talk about him. Anything else. They're embarrassed."

"How are you doing?" he said, a private question.

"Well, Alma's gone, so that's one thing," she said, evading it. "Now there's only my father to worry about." She nodded toward the end of the pool where two men were smoking cigars. "He always quarrels with my uncle. Well, not always. Then it's like this, polite."

"Quarrels about what?"

"Germany. Dieter says my father blames the people. You know the article he wrote. The German character. And how can you blame the people? It was Hitler. So back and forth. They're all like that," she said, looking around. "Their house burned down and they argue about why it happened."

"But it's important. To know why it happened."

"You think so? I don't know. It doesn't change anything. It's gone. They all want to go back. But to the old days. *Heimat.*"

"Do you?"

"Me? I almost died there once. You don't get rescued twice, I think.

Who would marry me next time?" She tried to smile, then looked away, restive again. "Well. There's Salka waving so Mann must be leaving. He'll expect—oh god, not Polly."

She was looking toward the pool again, where Polly Marks had wedged herself between the brothers-in-law.

"Who's the guy in the gray suit? Do you know? I saw him at the funeral."

"He came with her—I suppose he works for her."

Ben smiled to himself. "I thought he was a cop."

"A police? Why police?" she said, her head jerking around.

"But he wasn't. Just a legman."

"Why would you think that?" she said.

He looked at her, but this wasn't the time, not with people around them, not with nothing more to offer than a feeling and the wrong bottle.

"I'll go play referee," he said, heading toward the pool.

The group at the end, like actors in a silent, were telling the story with their bodies—Ostermann leaning away from Polly, who was cornering him with attention, her back to his brother-in-law, the legman off to the side, smoking and watching them with the same quiet sweep he'd used at the funeral.

"Hello again," Ben said to Polly, interrupting them.

She turned in mid-sentence, caught slightly off guard, trying to place him.

"Ben," Ostermann said, cueing her.

But Polly had already found him in her mental file and only gave him a quick nod before she went back to Ostermann. "They sure sound like a front to me. You think it's all innocent—I'm for world peace, too, who isn't?—and the next thing you know they're using you. Your reputation." The same rushed voice, quivering.

"Do you think I'm so famous?" he said gently, making light conversation. "No."

"You're not just anybody, you know that. Your name speaks—"

"I tell him he has to be careful," Dieter said.

Polly didn't even turn, brushing this off with a blink. A relative from Pasadena.

"You listen to Polly," she said. "Warners doesn't buy just anybody. If you have *any* doubts, people asking to use your name, call me. I've been here a long time. Turning over rocks."

"That's very kind," Ostermann said flatly. "To take so much trouble."

"It's no trouble. I love this country."

"As we do," he said, a courtly half bow. "Who took us in?"

"Terrible about all this, isn't it?" she said, looking back at the house. "I don't know how Liesl does it. So strong." She shook her head. "Of course he was no angel, but I'm not one to speak ill of the dead."

"No."

She took his hand and patted it, oddly flirtatious. "Glad we could talk. We'll have lunch soon." She looked at Ben. "You never mentioned you were going to Continental," she said, a black mark, holding out, all that needed to be said.

Without being signaled, the man in the gray suit slipped away from the oleander and followed her.

"So it begins," Ostermann said slowly. "Enemies everywhere. I wondered what would happen when they won. Now look. Like Germany last time, when we lost. 'I love my country.' That's what they said in Berlin, remember?" This to Dieter, who looked at Ben.

"Hans is writing about that time, so it's all he thinks about." Then, to Ostermann, "Don't pack your bags yet. It's not the same."

"It starts the same. I remember it."

"When you've been here as long as I have—"

"When did you come?" Ben said.

"'Thirty-seven. With Trude. I wanted Hans to bring Anna, too. It was still possible then. Perhaps if they hadn't waited, things would have turned out differently."

Ostermann went stiff, annoyed, evidently a sore point between them, the sister who died.

"But we're all here now," Dieter said, making peace.

"You don't want to go back?" Ben said, testing Liesl's theory.

"Now? My work is here. All my colleagues. Hitler was a catastrophe for German science, but a gift to America."

"You're a scientist?" Ben said, surprised. Not in pictures, not even connected. Another California.

"No, no," he said, diffident. "A teacher. Mathematics."

"A teacher," Ostermann said playfully. "Very distinguished. In Germany, a doctor doctor."

"But not at Cal Tech," Dieter said pleasantly. "One doctor only."

"Thank you for being there," Ben said. "At the hospital."

Dieter nodded. "You know what he liked? The observatory. On Mount Wilson. Not the science of it. He was like Hans here—everything a mystery, even the simplest numbers. But he liked to see the stars. It's a good lens, you know, a hundred inches, the largest. Would you like to go sometime? It was hard during the war, but now we can take visitors again. You have to stay over. The road is too dangerous at night."

"You mean camp there?"

"No, we have places to stay. Dormitories for the staff. A few rooms for guests. It used to be very popular, with the other stars," he said, smiling. "Hubble liked to take them up. Fairbanks, Pickford, all of them. You can see the pictures. So if you like, I'll arrange it. A family excursion. But now—" He looked around, ready to go. "A sad occasion. It's a pity you did not get a chance—"

"No, only at the hospital. For a minute."

"He spoke?"

Ben shook his head, not wanting to go back.

"No last words. I'm sorry," Dieter said, taking Ben's hand. "So we'll make a trip. Hans," he said, now reaching for Ostermann's hand, "be well. You should listen to her, you know. That woman. No petitions. No letters in the paper. It draws attention to all of us."

Ostermann watched him leave, a politer version of Alma's exit, then sighed and busied himself relighting his cigar.

"More American than the Americans. Except for the accent. He thinks no one hears it." He nodded toward the city below, spread across the flat basin. "Look at that. You know, every building you see, it's the first. There was nothing on this land before. Imagine. In Europe we live on layers. Here it's only the first. So what will it become? It's interesting. But do any of us care? We don't really live here. I'm still in Berlin. My study even, it's like before. Writing *1919*. You like the title? Just the year. No one here will be interested, it's for me. What happened to us. Mann's writing Bible stories. Bible stories after all this. The conscience of his country."

"I thought that was you."

He smiled a little. "The bad conscience maybe. I'm sorry. Such gloomy talk. Your brother used to call it the exile mentality. Always half-empty. But it was different for him. He never had to worry about leaving. Being asked to leave. He was born here. Sometimes I think we got out with our skins but our lives—they're somewhere in-between. Still waiting for the knock."

"Not here."

"We're still watched." He caught Ben's skeptical look and nodded. "We're German, we have a sixth sense for this now. The phone I think sometimes, the mail I know."

"Really?"

"There's a group, more exiles, in Mexico—it was easier to get a visa there. So they write to me sometimes and I think the letters are being read. You know, opened and resealed. So, a test. I tell them to write in English and you know what? The letters arrive three days earlier—the censor doesn't have to translate. So I know."

"But why? Did they think you were a Nazi? You?"

Ostermann smiled weakly. "Anybody foreign. There's no logic to this. It's like Polly. You start turning over rocks, you have to find something, or why did you start? So you keep doing it. I'm used to it. In Germany it was the same—well, worse. But you have to be careful. You say things and it might go against you with Immigration. It's better since the war, but Brecht says they're still watching him. Even now." He shook his head. "Such a dangerous person. In Santa Monica." He moved away from the potted geraniums, taking a chair and leaning back in it, his eyes still on the view. "It's an irony, yes? What we came to escape. Like poor Connie Veidt, playing Nazis. They wanted to kill him there, and then here it was all he can do, be a Nazi. It was the voice. Like Liesl."

"Like Liesl?" Ben said, confused.

"The accent. You know she was an actress. Small theaters only, but good, I think. Of course the father says that. But Salka says she had talent. And then we left and she lost her voice."

"Couldn't Danny get her work?"

"Here? Even Lorre, an actor like that, couldn't play American." He smiled. "Mr. Moto. A Japanese. A girl with a German accent? Not so many parts for her. And you know, I think Daniel liked her at home. So she gave it up. Became the *Hausfrau*."

"And your translator."

"Yes," Ostermann said, looking up. "A help to me, too, I admit. And now? It's a worry. When someone dies this way, you think, I never knew him. You turn it over and over in your mind, trying to make sense of it."

"Yes," Ben said, an almost involuntary response.

"Everything becomes a lie. Your own life. I don't want that for her."

"But everything wasn't."

"No, not everything. But which?" He drew on the cigar. "How little we know about each other," he said, brooding. "Even when we think we know."

GOWER GULCH

AT THE POLICE station he was directed to a basement room that resembled a post office will-call window, with rows of files behind.

"Accident report? Kohler?"

"You're with the insurance?"

"His brother."

"Companies usually get it direct. Not through the family."

"But I could see it?"

"You could ask," the clerk said, then got tired of himself and went
to get the folder.

In fact, there was little Ben didn't already know. A more precise
time. No eyewitnesses to the fall itself. Neighbors alerted by the sounds
of garbage cans knocked over when the body hit, an unexpected detail.
No scream. At least none reported. Police response time. Alcohol in the
room (dizzy spells not even necessary here—already unsteady). Taken
to Hollywood Presbyterian with head injuries and multiple lacerations.
Several boxes with numbers and acronyms for internal use. Everything
consistent.

"I was told there were pictures."

"Told how?"

"They took pictures."

The clerk stared at him, annoyed, then checked the report again, glancing at one of the numbered boxes.

"Give me a minute," he said, going back to the file room, a martyr's walk.

He returned opening a manila envelope. "We don't usually show these to family."

"What do I need? A court order?"

The clerk passed them over. "Just a good stomach."

Danny in the hospital had been hard to look at, but still a patient, sanitized, wrapped in bandages, the lacerations stitched closed. Here his face was torn open and the gashes poured blood, his head lying in a pool of it. Ben flipped through the pictures—the body from several angles, limp, legs twisted, a shot of the balcony (for a trajectory?), the alley crowded with onlookers and ambulance workers. Crime scene photographs.

"Why weren't these in the file?"

"You're lucky they're here at all. Should've been tossed. No reason to keep them in an accident file."

"Can I have them?"

"Police property."

"Which you were going to toss."

"Still police property. What do you want them for?" Genuinely puzzled, looking at Ben more carefully now. A morbid souvenir.

"How about some paper then? I need to take some notes. For the insurance."

The clerk reached below and brought up some paper.

"Next time bring your own. That's taxpayer money."

"I'm a taxpayer."

"Don't start." He went over to his desk and lit a cigarette.

Ben held up one photo, then jotted down a note, waiting for the clerk to get bored and turn away. The one thing you learned in the Army: The answer was always no, unless you could get away with it. All bureaucracies were alike. The clerk, still smoking, looked up at the clock. Ben drew out the rest of the photos, negatives clipped to the last. He copied another note, then began feeding paper into the envelope. When the clerk answered the phone, he slid the pictures under his newspaper, added some more paper to the envelope and closed it, pushing it back along the counter.

"Thanks for your help," he said, turning away with the newspaper.

The cop waved back.

The day clerk at the Cherokee could have been the policeman's cousin, the same wary indifference.

"You here with the key?"

"I thought it was paid through the month."

"You're going to use it?" the man said, oddly squeamish.

"I might. I mean, it's paid for."

The clerk gave a your-choice shrug.

"Anybody else have keys?"

"They're not *supposed* to. Just the tenant. Otherwise we have to change the locks. Why?"

"Just wondering if you ever saw anybody else. Use the apartment."

"Anybody else who?"

"A lady, maybe."

"I'm on days. It's quiet days."

"You were on that night. I saw you in the police pictures."

The clerk looked up, a new scent in the air. Just the word police.

"That's right. I was filling in. What's this all about?"

"I'm his brother. I just want to know what happened."

"He fell—I guess. Whatever it was, it was a mess."

"And you didn't see anyone go up that night?"

"The police asked me this. I told them, I'll tell you—no one. I didn't even see *him*."

"He used the back door."

"I guess. All I know is, I didn't see anybody."

"So she could have done that, too. Without being seen."

"If she had a key. Which she's not supposed to have."

"She's not supposed to do a lot of things."

"That I don't know. I just run the board and collect the rent. We've never had any trouble here, you know. Never. I got a lot of people upset about this. Maybe moving out."

"Many stay long?"

"More and more. Used to be, people didn't want the extra service expense. But the war's been great for us. Hard to find anything, and we already had the phone lines. You couldn't *get* a phone during the war, so we did all right."

"He make any calls that night?"

"I'd remember that."

"You might."

"No."

"Sure?" Ben raised his eyes, the cliché promise of a tip.

The clerk frowned. "I'm not looking for anything here. I don't remember. I don't keep tabs. Half the people I don't even know. I'm on days, right? The only reason I knew him is I rented him the room."

"So you wouldn't necessarily have recognized everybody."

"Not unless they're here during the day. You're asking more questions than the police did. What's this about?"

"I'm trying to find out who else came here. He didn't take the room to be alone. The family need to know. There might be money in it for her."

Bait that bobbed back, not even a nibble.

"Then I hope you find her. Now how about I get back to work? Are you going to keep the room, or what? Hey, Al." This to the mailman coming in with his bag.

"Joel. How's life?"

"Overrated."

"Hah," the mailman said, opening the front panel of the boxes with the post office key and beginning to fill them. Catalogues from Bullock's, a girl in a sundress, ordinary life.

"Let me know if you want to extend," Joel said. "The lease. It's month to month. And he was leaving at the end, so I need to know."

"You mean he gave you notice?" Ben said, surprised. Because the affair was over?

Joel nodded. "End of the month." Involuntarily his eyes shifted toward the alley. "I guess he had other plans."

Ben went over to the elevator, then turned. "When he came in to rent—how did he know? There was an ad?"

"No, we just use the window," Joel said, jerking his thumb toward it. "Put out a sign. Somebody always sees it. Like I say, it's been busy since the war. What with the phone."

The apartment was exactly as he'd left it, tidy, with the empty stillness of unoccupied rooms. The brandy bottle was on the counter, untouched, not even moved for dusting. He opened the French window, looking down from the balcony just as he had before, but imagining it differently. You wouldn't need a lot of leverage with the low rail—even a woman could have done it. But wouldn't Danny have reacted, reached out, grabbed something? No marks on the rail.

He went out to the hall, looking down the back stairs, the door that led to the roof. Someone could have gone up there, waited it out, then slipped away after the excitement died down. But why would she have to? A transient building—not even the clerk knew all the tenants by sight. She'd be just another face in the crowd. Why bother with the roof? Walk down Cherokee to Hollywood Boulevard and hop a red car. Unless she'd been driving, parked around the corner. Then no one would see her at all.

Ben went back inside and sat in the quiet. The empty bathroom, the empty desk. Whatever prints there'd been would have been wiped away by the maid. The fact was there would never be any physical evidence. The how was unknowable. The only way in was the why.

Downstairs, he put the keys in his pocket, then took them out again—one for the room, one for the back. No mailbox key. But why would Danny get any mail? An apartment registered to another name. Just a place where they changed the sheets. Still, they must have given him one, if only to clean out the catalogues and restaurant flyers. He turned back to the clerk.

"I don't have a mail key," he said. "For 5C."

"You'd better find it. We'll have to charge. We can't keep making keys."

Ben looked at the mailman. "He get mail here? Collins? 5C?"

"Mister, you think I keep track? If it's U.S. Mail, we deliver it."

"But you might notice—if it piled up. Or if someone never got any."

"Never? I'd buy him a beer." He waved his hand toward the boxes. "Everybody gets mail."

"Did you check his desk?" the clerk said. "Sometimes people keep it there."

But it wasn't in his desk or in the desk at home, at least not in any of the shallow paperclip trays in the top drawer, where it logically should be. And not in any of the boxes on top. Ben began taking papers out of the drawer, not rummaging through as he had that first day, but systematically putting them in piles—canceled checks, bill receipts. He started with the address book, as if somehow a number would leap out at him, but none did. Who would put his girlfriend in a book? An odd scrap of paper that no one would see, even a matchbook cover, but not in a book.

The checks were more interesting, like shards of pottery you piece together to reveal a whole society: tree surgeons and pool tilers, landscapers and caterers, an account at Magnin's, a life so far removed from Ben's that it seemed to be otherworldly. Like the thick terry robes by the pool, the drawers of cashmere. He thought of Howard Stein, looking around. And this was only someone with a B series about detectives. Mayer was the highest paid man in America. Still, nobody had killed him because Liesl kept a running account at Magnin's. He flipped through the stubs. No checks to the Cherokee Arms, presumably a cash expense, discreet. The appointment book was even less revealing: no coded notes, *M 5:30*, just straightforward studio meetings and doctors and dentists.

No wallet, either. But he must have had one. Maybe in his dresser, with the tie clips and cuff links. He crossed the hall to the dressing room and opened the door that covered the built-in shelves, the inside panel a mirror to check your tie. He reached for the top drawer then stopped, standing motionless. The mirror, some optical trick, reflected the mirror on the partly opened bathroom door. A leg, resting on the rim of the tub, just one, her hands moving up it slowly, as if she were putting on nylons, moving together toward her thigh, then out of the mirror. The hands again, the same smooth drawing up, rubbing. Not nylons, some kind of cream, maybe suntan oil. He stood there, unable to move, his eyes fixed on the mirror. A perfect leg, arched. He imagined his hands moving along it instead of hers, slick with oil, an image that came like a pulse beat, fast, involuntary. Now the leg leaned farther in, more thigh showing, the hands moving. Close the door. Instead he held his breath, mesmerized, wanting the hands to go farther. He could feel himself fill with blood. Unexpected, just like that, without thought. He wanted to see more, where the leg met the body. But it dropped and the other one came up, the same hand motion, just for him, even more exciting because she was unaware.

What could he say if she saw him? Find the wallet and get out. But he stayed, still not breathing. The other thigh now, an almost unbearable second, her sex just beyond the edge of the mirror, and then it moved forward, not hair, a wedge of bathing suit, then more, her whole body bent over, moving into the mirror, her head turning, looking toward her door. He closed the cabinet, a snap reflex, and crossed back to the office, his body flushed, slightly shaky. Had she seen him? The mirrors had to reflect each other, didn't they? What would she have seen? Standing there, mouth half-open, looking where he shouldn't, eyes fixed, caught in a kind of trance.

He picked up the checkbook again, pretending he could read the stub notes, listening for footsteps.

"What are you doing?"

He looked up, startled, feeling caught. She was pinning her hair, on her way to the pool.

"I was just—going through his things. I should have asked."

Nervous, waiting for her to say something. But she seemed not to have seen him in the mirror.

"No, please. Somebody has to. I've been putting it off. I've been a coward a little bit. In case I found—you know, if it's somebody I know," she said, turning to go now, anxious, her movements as darting as they'd been that first day at Union Station.

A new idea. "Did he leave a will?"

"The lawyer has it. Everything comes to me, so that part's easy. Oh," she said, a hand-to-mouth gesture. "I never thought. Is there anything you would like? I'm sure he—"

Ben shook his head. "I don't need anything. Anyway, you're his wife."

She smiled a little, trying to be light. "It's lucky we're living now. Not like in the old days. Bible times. You would have to take care of me. The brother's wife. Like a sheep or a goat. I'd belong to you."

He looked up at her, thrown off balance, then passed it off by smiling back.

"I couldn't afford it." He motioned to the check stubs. "Magnin's alone."

"You think I'm extravagant. Really, it was Daniel. He liked going out. He liked me to dress. And now how much is left? I haven't thought." She stopped and came over to the desk for a cigarette, her hands nervous. "I haven't thought about anything, really. What I'm going to do. Since you won't take me," she said, smiling again, blowing out smoke. "I should sell the house. My father's already asking, come live with me, but it's enough the way it is. Milton's daughter. An apartment somewhere, I guess. But I'd miss the pool." All said quickly, as if she were filling time, avoiding something else.

"You don't have to stay here."

"I couldn't leave my father. Anyway, I like it here. Maybe I'm lazy. Everyone complains, so ugly, so boring, but I like it." She started to put on her bathing cap, then stopped. "I know why you're looking," she said suddenly, nodding to the desk. "You want to know who it was. The other one. But what does it matter now?"

He took a breath. "Because we need to know. I don't think he killed himself. I don't think he tripped."

She said nothing for a minute, staring back, her body almost weaving. "You're not serious," she said finally, her voice faint.

"There was someone else in the room."

"How can you know that?"

"It's the only way it makes sense."

"Sense," she said, still trying to collect herself. "To think that. Things like that don't happen, not in real life. Do you think he was a gangster?"

"That's not the only reason—"

"Why then? She was so jealous? He was leaving her? Maybe it was the wife. Maybe you think that. Isn't it always the wife?" she said, her voice rushed, flighty.

"Not always," he said calmly.

She took up the cap again, fidgeting. "It's not true. Think what it means."

"It means he didn't kill himself."

Her shoulders moved, an actual shiver. "It changes everything, to think this. Why would anyone kill him?"

"I don't know yet."

"And you think it's her? She's so strong? To push a man like Daniel? Ouf." She shook her head, dismissive.

"She's a lead. He got the apartment for her."

She nodded at the desk. "What do you expect to find?"

"A number, maybe."

"Clues, like his detectives," she said. "Ben."

"You think I'm imagining this."

"No," she said, her face softer. "I think you want it to be true. It's easier for you." She frowned. "But how could it be true?" she said, not really talking, thinking. "To make someone do that. Kill you. He wasn't like that." She looked back at him. "It's so hard for you to accept this? What he did?"

"He didn't."

"The police think so."

"The police made a mistake."

"But not you. Just like him. You get some idea and then you won't let go."

"It's not some idea."

"Because it's better this way. He didn't do it."

"Isn't it?"

She said nothing, at a loss, then turned to go. "There's more," she said, flicking her hand toward the piles on the desk. "Boxes from his office. In the screening room. The next installment of *Partners*. Maybe it'll give you an idea."

"You think I'm crazy."

"Not crazy. Something. I don't know what. Like him. So sure."

"You don't want to believe it."

"I want it to be over. It's something you learn, when you leave. You can't look back. Not if you want to keep going. He's gone," she said.

"And if I'm right? We just walk away?"

She held his gaze for a second, her eyes troubled, then turned again and started for the pool.

He looked at the piles on the desk. Check stubs and an address book. Receipts. The life you could trace. Not the one that rented a room. In cash. He reached for his wallet and took out Tim Kelly's card. Someone interested in the other one.

Kelly answered on the second ring.

"Heard you had a talk with Joel. The day guy at the Arms."

"Heard from who?"

"Himself. I told him to let me know if anyone came around wanting to have a chat. And there you were." The same breezy tilt to his voice, like a hat pushed back on his head.

"And he did this for free," Ben said, curious.

There was a snort on the other end.

"Since you bring it up, if we're going to help each other out, I could use a little contribution to the tip box. I can't put everything on the paper."

"He didn't know anything."

"Joel? Not much. But you have to go through him to get to the others. The maid, say. So it's worth something. Spread the wealth."

"How much?"

"I'm not keeping books. Buy me a drink some night and throw a twenty on the bar and I'm a happy guy."

"Okay," Ben said, sitting back, interested. "So what did the maid say?"

"Her favorite tenant. Hardly ever there. She doesn't even have to make the bed."

"So he doesn't sleep over. We knew that."

"Or do much of anything else. Not exactly a hot affair. Neat, though. No stains."

"Oh," Ben said. A peephole world he'd never imagined, not in detail. "What about the usual night clerk? Joel said he was just filling in."

"Check. Night guy knew him. Saw him a few times. Never saw the playmate."

"So she used the back."

"Or they arrived different times. Or she said she was going to some other room and didn't. There're all kinds of ways to do this." None of which so far had occurred to Ben.

"But if she didn't want to be seen—I thought that was the idea."

"That was the hope. A face they'd know. Which is still the way it looks to me."

"Why?"

"This careful? Their own place, back doors, nobody sees them together—you go to this kind of trouble for who? Some dentist's wife?"

"You still have any credit left with Joel?"

"It wouldn't take much. What?"

"Could you get a list of the tenants?"

"Why? You think she's living there? Where's the sense in that?"

"Nowhere. But maybe somebody she knows. Joel says he just sticks a sign in the window when a room comes up, but how many times would Danny be walking on Cherokee? So how did he know about the room?"

For a second there was silence on the other end.

"Okay. It's an idea. Somebody she knows. A helper, like."

"Juliet's nurse."

"What?"

"Nothing. Let's see who's there. I don't know what else to do. I can't find anything here."

"Forget there. You got better places to look. When do you start work?"

"What do you mean?"

"Well, while you're wasting time making Joel nervous I spent a little time downtown. Always pays. Boys keep their ears open and like a drink after work."

"And?"

"And it's just like I thought," he said, almost a grin over the wire. "He's a jumper, then he trips. And who gets the report changed? Didn't I say?"

"Studios. But why would Republic want to change it?"

"That's the beauty part. They didn't. The favor was for Continental."

He first had to report to his commanding officer in Culver City, but that took less than an hour. His reassignment had been waiting for days, and the film he'd shipped from the Signal Corps already sent over to Continental, along with Hal Jasper to cut it. Colonel Hill, in fact, seemed eager to hurry him out, too. Now that the war was over, Fort Roach had the feel of a camp waiting for orders to pull out, an uncertain mix of khaki uniforms and open-necked Hawaiian shirts. No one bothered to salute. He was at the Continental gate before noon.

This time there were pickets, a handful with signs walking slowly back and forth, more a polite show of force than a threat. No shouting or heckling. They let him pass through without a word.

"You go to Mr. Jenkins," the guard said, checking his clipboard. "Admin, room two hundred and one." He pointed to an office building with Florida jalousie windows that faced Gower. "Park over there in Visitors till they get you a slot."

As a boy he'd loved the surrealism of the Babelsberg lot, the street fronts and women in Marie Antoinette wigs, and sailing ships beached against a wall at the end of a street. Now what struck him was the blur of activity. Outside, in the dusty orange groves and parking lots, things moved at a desert pace. Here everyone seemed to be running late—grips pushing flats and carpenters and extras filing out of wardrobe, everyone hurrying while the sunny oasis over the wall stretched out for a nap.

The look was utilitarian—no country club flower beds or Moorish towers. Lasner hadn't even bothered with the Spanish touches the other studios couldn't resist, the arcades and fake adobe walls. Here buildings were whitewashed or painted a cheap industrial green. The only visible trees were the bottle brush palms up in the hills and a few live oaks behind one of the sound stages, probably the western set.

Inside things were sleeker—modern offices with metal trim and secretaries with bright nails and good clothes. He thought of the offices in Frankfurt, the piles of unsorted papers and drip pails and girls with hungry, pinched faces. This was the other side of the world, untouched, not even a shortage of nail polish. The war had only made it richer. Everyone in the hall smiled at him.

Room 200 was the corner, presumably Lasner's office, and Jenkins was next door. Ben was shown in and announced without even a preliminary buzz, clearly expected. Or had the guard called up from the gate?

Jenkins was slight, with a boyish unlined face, sharp eyes, and hair so thinned that he was nearly bald. He came out from behind the desk with the easy grace of a cat, as smooth as his camel hair sport jacket.

"I'm Bunny Jenkins. Mr. L asked me to get you settled. He's on the phone with New York," he said, implying a daily ordeal.

Ben looked at him more closely. "Brian Jenkins?" he said.

"*Yes*, that Brian Jenkins," he said wearily. "Which dates you. The kids on the lot haven't the faintest. Not exactly a comfort."

"But—"

"Well, we all change," he said, a put-on archness. "I'll bet you used to look younger, too."

Just the voice, still English, would have placed him. Faces wrinkle but voices never change. He was still the boy in *The Orphan,* then the reworking of *Oliver Twist* and the other fancy dress adventures that had followed. Ruffled shirts and wide liquid eyes, everybody's waif.

"Sorry, I didn't mean—"

"Never mind. It has been a while. They don't know Freddie, either. Funny, isn't it? They brought me over to keep Jackie in line and then they brought Freddie to keep me in line. I mean, really. Freddie. They could have saved a ton and just let the hair do it." He touched his head.

"Freddie Batholomew?"

"Mm," he said, glancing up, as if Ben hadn't been following. "With all his wavy curls. Still, I hear. And much good it did him. They don't know him, either," he said, nodding toward the window and the anonymous kids on the lot. "Well, let's get you started. I'm the tour guide. He wants me to show you Japan, which means the serious tour. I gather you're here to give us some class."

"He said that?"

"I've seen your budget. You might want to explain the project to me a little. I've already had Polly Marks on the horn. I said, 'Darling, if you don't know, how would I? He hasn't even arrived yet.' But she'll be back. Walk with me. Oh, and you're expected for dinner. Saturday. That must have been some chat the two of you had on the train. He never has line producers to the house—not this soon anyway."

"That's what I am, a line producer?"

"Well, you have your own budget and nobody seems to be in charge of you."

"Not you?"

"Me? Oh, I'm a glorified assistant. Technically, vice-president, Operations, which is a nice way of saying I do whatever he needs me to do.

You know, you grow up on a set, there's not much you don't learn. About the business, I mean."

"In other words, you run the place."

Bunny looked at him. "No. Mr. L runs the place. Every nook. You wouldn't want to make a mistake about that."

They were almost in the hall when the phone rang. Bunny stopped, glancing over at his secretary. She covered the receiver, mouthing a name at him.

"Hold on a sec. I have to take this." He went over to the phone. "Rosemary, I thought you were being fitted." He listened for a while, concentrating. "But, darling, she's the best. I asked for her. Have you looked at the sketches? Forget the mirror. We never see ourselves, not properly. I tell you what, I'll swing by in an hour, all right? But meanwhile all smiles, yes? You don't want her to— Yes, I know. But she used to work for Travis. She *sewed* for him." A pause. "Travis Banton. He dressed Marlene, Rosemary. Now go have a ciggie and calm down and I'll be over later. *All smiles.*"

After another minute of reassurance he hung up, facing Ben again.

"A little *crise de nerfs*," he said lightly. "Still, that's the business. I know, you're going to make a documentary. Show us how ghastly it all was," he said, affecting a shiver. "But that's not the business. You know what it is, pictures? Attractive people. That's all it's ever been. So you want to look your best." He put his hand to his head again, smiling slyly. "Keep your hair. Come on, I'll show you Japan."

They made it out of the building without another interruption, Bunny giving a running description as they went.

"That's Payroll and Accounting. You'd get your check there, but I gather you don't get a check." A point to be cleared up.

"The Army's still paying me." He looked at the closed door. "They'd have a list, wouldn't they? Every employee."

"If we're paying them. Why?"

"In case I was looking for someone."

"Check the phone directory," Bunny said simply. "There'll be one on your desk." He looked over at Ben, as if he were hearing the question again, then let it go. "We've got you in B building, next door. Mr. L wanted you in Admin, but there's no room at the inn so you're out in the stable. Be grateful in the end—nobody looking over your shoulder. I wish I were there sometimes. I'm afraid you'll have to share a secretary. I wasn't sure how much help you'd need."

"That's fine."

"Bunny," someone said, waving hello.

"How'd you get the name?" Ben said.

"You know, no one's ever asked. All these years. Not rabbits. Pets, I mean. My mother, when I was little. Because I got my lines right away. You know, 'quick as a.' Anyway, it stuck. Editing rooms over there. I understand you got Hal back for us. He's a great favorite of Mr. L's. An A-list project," he said, leaving it open, wanting to know how involved Lasner would be.

"How old were you when you started?"

"In the womb. I don't know, four or five. Before I could read. She'd say the lines, and I'd have to remember them. But then you grow up. Nobody makes it past that. Look at Temple. Who wants to see her necking?"

"How did you end up here?"

"Through Fay. Mrs. L," he explained.

"Yes, we met. At the train station."

"Did you?" he said, another opening, then went back to the thread. "A great lady—not exactly thick on the ground out here. And smart. But she started late, so she needed somebody to help. You know, which fork where. How to do this and that. So, me. Anyway, the more I did for her, the more I got to know Mr. L, and he figured there were things I could do for him, too. So it all just happened. Here we are."

He opened the door to a sound stage and flicked on the light. Ben had thought Japan would mean a *Madame Butterfly* set, tea house and garden, but this was Japan itself—a huge, three-dimensional model made of plaster, set up table height on a series of trestles that covered most of the floor.

"It's built to scale," Bunny said. "Every bay, river. Took months. Mr. L's very proud of it."

"But what—"

"You set the camera up there, on the crane, and you move it along what would be the flight plan. Pilot watches the film, he knows what he's going to see when he gets there. The exact topography." A craftsman's pride.

Ben walked over. Mountains, cities, before you released the bombs. Up close, just plaster and canvas, like a train village under a Christmas tree.

"This must have cost—"

Bunny nodded. "It was the time. We had special effects do it after hours, so you run up overtime. The Army just paid for the materials." He caught Ben's surprise. "Our contribution to the war effort. We didn't just hand out doughnuts at the Canteen."

"What are you going to do with it now?"

"Well, that's the question, isn't it? It's just sitting here taking up space, but Mr. L can't bring himself to get rid of it. The Army doesn't want it. They can do actual aerial photography now. Funny thing is, the film quality's not as good. They were better off with this."

They made a circle of the back lot past the prop department, a hangar full of furniture, and the New York set. Everyone nodded or acknowledged Bunny, as if he were taking roll call. Lasner caught up with them on Sound Stage 5, in front of a plywood Hellcat fighter, sliced in half. A few grips were adjusting lights, fixed on the painted flat sky, but everyone else had gone to lunch.

"Well, at last," Lasner said, putting his hand on Ben's shoulder. "Everything all right at home?"

"Yes. Thanks."

"Hell of a thing. Anyway, you're here. Bunny have you all set up? Anything you need, see him. It's like talking to me." He turned to Bunny. "What's this about Rosemary's dress?"

"Good news travels fast."

"I happened to be over there."

"What did you think?"

"What do I know? You're the one knows this stuff." He paused. "She never complains."

"She's nervous, that's all. It'll be fine." He looked at Lasner. "It's already paid for."

"Don't pinch. This is the picture we put her across. So what's that worth?"

"I'll look at the dress," Bunny said, case closed. Ben watched the play between them, a practiced volley. It's like talking to me.

Lasner nodded, then turned to the plane.

"Two more weeks on this. Think we can get it out before November?"

"We still have to score it."

"The longer we wait— Who the hell's going to want to see a war picture now? Would you?" he said to Ben. "I'm asking you. Seriously. These last two years, you show any goddam thing, you do business. Now we got all these guys coming back, kids over there seeing things, like you did. What do they want? Maybe they're sick of this," he said, gesturing to the plane. "War pictures."

"Not with Dick Marshall," Bunny said, indicating the pilot seat. "He's had three in a row."

"That's no guarantee. Maybe Hayworth, that's it. And that prick Cohn has her." He cocked his head toward the studio across Gower, then looked at Ben. "You got the message about Saturday? Just a few people. Bring somebody. Nice."

He left them at the door, heading back to his phones.

"It makes him crazy," Bunny said. "Cohn having Hayworth."

"Why?"

"They both started out down here. Same street. You don't expect to get a star like that, not here. Well, maybe Rosemary will do it for him. She's worked hard enough."

"I thought it was all magic."

"It helps if you help. Let's get you back."

"I met Cohn in Europe," Ben said as they walked.

"You get around," Bunny said, raising an eyebrow, having fun with it.

"I was an interpreter."

"Cohn into English?"

Ben smiled. "Almost. He's a little rough around the edges."

"And he speaks so warmly of you."

A policeman passed, touching his fingers to his hat. "Mr. Jenkins."

"Bert," Bunny said back.

"Not an actor?"

"Studio police. We have our own force."

"Under you. Operations," Ben said, thinking.

"It's a small force."

"And who deals with the outside police?"

"What do you mean?"

"You know, runs interference. If somebody gets in trouble."

"You think this is Metro? Benny Thau and his house detectives? There, no wonder. Just handling Mickey's a full-time job. The rest of us just toddle off to bed and say our prayers like good children. Why, do you need to get a ticket fixed? Already?"

Ben shook his head. "Thank somebody."

"For what?"

"Getting an accident report changed."

"Changed."

"To make it an accident. You know Danny Kohler was my brother."

Bunny looked at him carefully. "Mr. L mentioned it."

"Somebody at Continental got the report on him changed. Saved the family some embarrassment, so—"

"According to whom?"

"The police." Ben shrugged. "People talk."

"Through their hats. We don't have that kind of influence."

"Everybody says the studios have an in with the police."

"Look, before you run away with yourself, let me tell you how things work. Somebody drives when he's had a little too much to drink and naturally Publicity wants to keep that out of the papers. So we make a nice donation to the Benevolent Fund and people are nice back. When they can be. Strictly parking ticket stuff. The kind of thing you're talking about—nobody here can do that."

"Not even you? I thought you might—"

"Not even me. In fact, *not* me."

"I just wanted to thank—"

"And I'd hear about it. I hear most things on the lot. Somebody's telling you stories. Anyway, why would we? Your brother wasn't *at* Continental."

"Maybe he had a friend here," Ben said, looking directly at him.

Bunny returned the look, then sighed. "Do you know what our police do? They check the padlocks, make sure the lights are turned off, equipment's where it should be, not walking off the lot. They're guards. They're not on the phone with downtown fixing cases."

"Somebody was," Ben said.

Bunny stared at him, a standoff. "So you keep saying."

He turned away, leading them around a corner. "Here we are, B building. I gather you asked for Frank Cabot for the narration. I'll see what I can do, but I can't take him off a picture if it's shooting. I put a contract player list on your pile—in case he's not available. When do you want to record?"

"It's not written yet."

"You'll want to hop to, then. Not really something for the hols, is it? And Hal Jasper likes to take his time. It's worth it, but you can't hurry him. You're just in here."

Walking a little faster now, eager to get away, but then caught at the door.

"Bunny, Lou Katz. You remember Julie? Julie Sherman. She's making a test."

Julie nodded and smiled, her lips moist with gloss. She was in low-cut satin, held up by a single diagonal strap. Lou, hovering, glanced nervously at Ben, not recognizing him but not wanting to offend.

"Of course," Bunny said. "Nice to see you. Everything okay? They take care of you in Makeup?"

"Yes, everyone's been wonderful," she said, meaning it. A pleasant voice, modulated, not what Ben expected.

"You'll be, too, sweetheart," Katz said. "Bunny, we appreciate this. You're not going to be disappointed. They said you didn't want the song."

"Lou, musicals? Here?"

"I just thought, to get the full range. This is a real talent."

Julie blinked, her only sign of protest, but otherwise kept smiling, evidently used to being discussed.

"You were on the train," she said, acknowledging Ben. "With Mr. Lasner."

"Yes. And you were with Paulette. Selling bonds, right?"

She smiled, pleased to be remembered. Bunny glanced at them, taking this in, his attention diverted.

"Bunny, we'll catch up with you later," Katz said, checking his watch. "You're going to like this one. Maybe they can run it for you with the dailies."

"I'm looking forward to it," he said politely, their cue to leave, then turned to Ben. "Paulette? Is there anyone you haven't met yet?"

"Whoever called the police."

Bunny stared at him. "So you can send a thank-you note. Just to be polite. It means that much to you." He cocked his head toward the building behind them. "Third door down on the left. Nice to have you with us. We could use something different. Mr. L's right, you know. Nobody on God's earth is going to want to see Dick Marshall shooting down Zeros. Let me know if there's anything else you need."

He headed to the Admin building, glancing back once over his shoulder.

The office was adequate but basic—typewriter, couch, Venetian blinds—a place for passing through, not unlike the apartment at the Cherokee. Ben sat down at the desk, annoyed with himself for pressing Bunny. The studio string-puller, now wary, protecting his flank.

Things had been stacked on his desk in neat piles: budget, a provisional time-line schedule, technician availabilities, an inventory of film already sent over from Fort Roach, the contract player list, personnel forms. The Signal Corps had had all the sloppy confusion of the Army, arrangements so haphazard they made the work itself feel improvised. This was a precision machine, waiting for him to set it in motion. To make something important. About millions. And all he could fix on was a police favor, worrying it like a sore tooth. Unable to leave it alone.

He picked up the phone and got an outside line.

"Meet any movie stars yet?" Kelly said when he heard Ben's voice.

"Who made the call from Continental?"

"You tell me."

"He didn't give you a name? Whoever you talked to?"

"That would make it real. I get a tip. But that doesn't mean it ever happened. My lucky guess. And nobody asks how I got there. Anyway, who would it be? Somebody in Publicity. Whoever. Who do you think makes these calls?"

"It wouldn't be somebody further up the food chain?"

"Not likely. They like the cleaner air. We're down here with the messenger service. The point is, who'd they call *for*. Who do they protect? They protect themselves. They protect the talent. This case, I'd go with the talent. He's not renting an apartment for a business meeting. Just keep your ears open. Something like this happens, there's always talk. I like the makeup girls. They always know who's been out the night before. One look. Ask them out for a drink, you'll hear what's going on. Get in their pants, you'll hear everything. You don't even have to pay. Speaking of which, I could use a little contribution."

"Why?"

"I got the resident list you wanted from Joel. Past year, right? He got all huffy. Why did I want it? Damned if I knew. Why do I?"

"I told you. Danny wasn't driving around looking for FOR RENT signs. He knew the building. So, how? Maybe she used to live there."

"Or somebody knew somebody. Or somebody heard—how far do you want to stretch it?"

"He had to know about it somehow. If we're lucky, there's a match."

"Okay, I'll swing by and leave it for you at the gate. Maybe—you got me curious—maybe I'll run it by Polly's files. She never throws anything out. Every rumor since Fatty's Coke bottle."

"She lets you go through her files?"

"Are you kidding? But it so happens it takes her hours to drink her lunch, and the secretary's a friend of mine."

"You have friends all over."

"And I'm just the lowlife. Run a studio, you got the whole town in your pocket."

Except the police, according to Bunny. He sat for a minute looking at the desk, then pulled over the contract list. Work backward. Who would they protect? A woman. Worth making a call for. He checked the credits. At Fox or Metro there would have been a slew of names, but Lasner borrowed stars so the featured players here made a much shorter list. Speaking parts, not hat-check girls or window shoppers. Recognizable. Rosemary Miller. Ruth Harris. Someone who met Danny on the side. Already married? One of these few, easy to check against the Cherokee records. Assuming she'd used her real name. Danny hadn't. He thought of Lasner on the train: Who changes names? Actors. Or Danny, with something to hide.

He spent the rest of the day with Hal Jasper, a short, wiry man, still in uniform, with a permanent five o'clock shadow that suggested sprouting hair everywhere else. He was one of those technicians for whom film was tactile, a physical thing, not another form of theater. There was a reverence in the way he handled it, each splice a weighed decision. He'd already screened most of the footage, waiting for Ben, and now was full of ideas about it, eager to start.

"For the opening?" he said, framing his hands. "There wasn't enough in the Dachau reel, but if you add some of the other material—Belsen, I guess, right?—you can go in just the way a GI would. The fence, the gates, everything. First time you see it. Walk in, looking around. What the hell happened here? Let it sink in. The faces. You don't say a word. Just look. Put a big chalk mark on the floor."

"A crime story," Ben said.

"It's the way in. I mean, if you see it that way."

"A crime," Ben said, thinking. "Why we need trials."

"Trials. How the hell do you judge people like this, I don't know. Unless you string them all up. Then you're doing what they did."

Ben looked up at the intensity in his voice. Thinking of Germans in greatcoats with attack dogs, not the kids eating out of PX garbage cans, both things true.

"Signal Corps said there's more footage coming, but let me start with this."

Ben nodded, feeling like an assistant, the machinery of the studio already whirring around him.

There were technician reqs to fill out and discarded film to be sorted and sent back to Fort Roach, so it was late by the time the gate called to say there was a delivery for him. Kelly, almost forgotten. It was still light, but the lot was quiet now, only a few distant carpenter hammers banging on a set somewhere. In the Admin screening rooms, they'd be setting up the rushes for Lasner and the producers, but most of Continental had gone home. The east sides of the sound stages were in shadows.

"Anything?" Ben asked, taking the manila envelope.

"*Nada,*" Kelly said. "Only a Red. If he is. Polly's got them under every bed, so who knows?"

"A woman?" Ben said, interested.

"No. Guy. No connection. Probably some name she got from the Tenney Committee. They feed her stuff they can't use—can't prove. Then she runs it and they watch what happens. What pops out of the hole. Cozy."

"And nothing else?"

"Not at the old Cherokee. You know what, though? She's got Frank Cabot as a fruit. That'll come as a surprise to his ex-wives." He grinned. "Or maybe not."

"Where does she get this stuff anyway?"

"Little birds. Chirp, chirp. And once in a while she gets hold of something real and makes *him* sing. 'You wouldn't want me to—' And of course he doesn't. Can't. So he feeds her someone else."

"Nice."

Kelly shrugged. "Hooray for Hollywood. Don't work too late," he said, making a mock salute with one finger. "Let me know if you get a match."

But no one on the Cherokee list appeared in the Continental directory. Ben looked at the short list of contract players he'd set apart. Not even similar name changes, like Kohler becoming Collins. Who changed names? Actors. Didn't any live at the Cherokee, grateful for the phone lines? Somebody there had to be in pictures. He picked up the personnel form from his to-do pile and stopped. One box for Name, one for Birth Name. The office files would have everyone's real name, maybe the one used to rent apartments. He filled out his own form, an excuse to hold in his hand, then took the lists and walked over to the Admin building.

It was dark behind the translucent glass panel, but the door, luckily, was unlocked, part of the protected village behind the studio gate. Ben turned on the light. A wall of filing cabinets. He started with the most likely featured players, working quickly. Arlene Moore used her real name, but Ruth Harris had been Herschel; Rosemary Miller, Risa Meyer. Ben smiled to himself. Hollywood's own Aryanization program. But neither of them, nor any other birth name, was on the Cherokee list.

When he heard the voices outside in the hall he pushed the file back in the drawer, closing it gently so it wouldn't slam. A click, inaudible to whoever was coming down the stairs. How could he have explained it? A clumsy snoop after hours. He was almost at the door when it opened.

"Oh, it's you," Bunny said, Lasner behind him. "I saw the light."

"I was just dropping off my personnel form," Ben said, indicating the sheet on the desk.

"So diligent and good." Bunny looked quickly over the room, as if he expected to find someone else. "They should keep this locked." He went over to the far filing case, test-pulling it open, looking relieved when it didn't budge. "Well, the salaries are, so that's all right. We wouldn't want people dipping into that, would we? Makes for ill feeling up and down." He switched off the light, following Ben out into the hall.

"You're here late," Lasner said, pleased. "You meet Hal?"

"We've already started. He's just what I need. Thanks for—"

"What did I tell you? He's got an instinct. His father was a cutter, you know. With Sennett. It's in the blood. Like you. You on your way out? Come look at the rushes."

"Sol," Bunny said, his tone suggesting a breach of some unspoken protocol.

"If you're going to learn the business," Sol said.

Bunny looked at Ben, annoyed, then bowed to the inevitable.

"Mostly bridge shots tonight. Fair warning. No comments to the directors, understood? They're touchy about tourists."

But in fact, slumped down in their chairs, they seemed to expect a barrage of arrows, at least fired by Lasner.

"Eddie, what the hell's the light on the left? What is that, sun on the wing? Except he doesn't see it? Just us?"

"We can cover it, Sol," the director said, not bothering to turn around. "It'll be fine."

Sol and Bunny were perched in the last row of the small screening room, everyone else scattered at random, leaving them a buffer zone of space. Lasner talked throughout, a back-and-forth flow, but Bunny sat quietly, looking over fingertips raised to his mouth in a pyramid, a line manager, carefully checking for scratch marks.

On the screen, Dick Marshall was leaning forward in his pilot seat, eyes squinting, taking sights on an unseen fighter plane. Then a closeup, his face registering the hit. A cover shot, another. There was no sound of gunfire or people yelling or the popping of AA fire outside—all the things Ben remembered—just Dick Marshall's face, taking aim, taut with cold calculation.

After a few more cockpit shots they were in a western saloon, the camera turning away from the bar to take in the front door, the looming shadow behind it. The same shot, another angle. There seemed to be no order to the sequence, just what had come out of the lab first. Now a city street, someone getting out of a cab. The cab pulling away. A woman's back, squaring her shoulders as she walks into an apartment building. Ben wondered how many pictures were in production, who kept track of the output, not just dialogue scenes but these, bridge shots, filler, seconds of screen time, the whole day's work reduced to a few nuts and bolts, then welded to other pieces of film, like steel sections in the Kaiser yard, one ship a day rolling down the slipway. When the clip ended, Lasner started squirming, bored by the sudden lull.

"Where's Rosemary?"

"She's coming," Bunny said, his head still resting on his fingertips.

The screen crackled to life, the first clip with sound, the snap of the clapper with the take number. Rosemary was standing at a bar, smoking, her low-cut dress lined with beads, little darts of light. Dana Andrews, the star on loan, was questioning her, the kind of detective who didn't bother to take off his hat indoors.

"We can do this hard or easy," he said, the rich baritone turned tough.

"I don't know where he is," Rosemary said, disillusioned, not meeting his eye.

"You expect me to believe that?"

"I'm telling you, I don't know." She rubbed out the cigarette in an ashtray. "He left me."

"Then one of you got lucky."

A new clip, a fresh cigarette, this time facing him. "I'm telling you, I don't know." The ashtray. "He left me."

"Then one of you got luck." A second. "Lucky. One of you got fucking lucky." Laughing now, the crew laughing behind him, somebody yelling cut.

"Wonderful," Lasner said. "A thousand a week, he's laughing."

Another clip, this time without a flub, Rosemary turning away, a more sympathetic nuance, the camera close on her.

"Better," Bunny said. "How do you like the dress?"

"Another inch and her tits are in the shot."

"That's her character."

"No, what you want here is she should show them but she doesn't *want* to show them."

"Eddie?" Bunny said to the director, a few rows down.

"Keep watching," a voice said in the dark.

And there it was, in the next clip, Andrews looking down, a gesture with her arm, the camera more aware of her body than before, but her own feelings more ambivalent, just what Lasner seemed to have ordered up.

"That's it," he said. "Christ, Eddie, I don't have to tell you anything."

"You know where I got that? Andrews. He said, 'Let's try it. I look down her dress but don't tell her I'm going to, see how she reacts.' And he's right, the arm goes up, she doesn't even know she's doing it. But now we know her. Nice."

"Actors," Lasner said.

There was more of Rosemary, reaction shots, close-ups, all gleaming, like her beads, then a kiss with Andrews, which she first resisted, then gave in to. After that, a series without Andrews, simply raising her head, her hair swept up now, the way Liesl's had been at Union Station. Ben leaned forward. Not unlike Liesl—harder, her mouth thinner and her face lacquered tight in studio makeup, but the same kind of look, the same cheekbones. Men married the same woman, over and over. Or was that just an old wives' tale? But she'd be someone the studio would protect, worth safety shots and endless close-ups, a simple phone call. Then she looked to the side, a different profile, not Liesl. Grasping at straws. Still.

The woman who'd got out of the taxi was back, now full-face, Ruth Harris on the building's penthouse terrace, confronting a gangster Ben didn't recognize. The picture was clearly a B, shot for speed, not star making. No dewy close-ups. The scene seemed barely blocked out, the man uncertain of his marks. He had grabbed Ruth by the shoulders, a prelude to roughing her up, pushing her against the balcony. She fought back, trying to scratch his face, slipping out of his grasp. When he reached for her again, she pushed him hard and then, before Ben could react, it happened. The man staggered against the rail, off balance from her push, wheeled around, his weight now plunging forward, pulling the rest of him with it, too late to reach out, a scream, falling over the side. Close on Ruth's eyes, wide now with terror. Ben blinked. Could it have happened that way? A fight, a push, the unintended pitch over—then, appalled, running. Ben looked away from the screen. The way he wanted it, not the way it had been.

"This is a woman's picture?" Lasner said.

"The DA falls in love with her," Bunny said, deadpan. "Well, here's your little friend," he said to Ben as the next clip appeared.

Ben looked back at the screen, but the terrace scene kept playing itself in his mind. Couldn't it be possible? Not intentional, not someone coming up from behind. A woman, a love quarrel gone wrong. Two men struggling. Over what? It might even have gone the other way, Danny left standing with the appalled face. But it hadn't.

On the screen, Julie Sherman was getting up from a piano and walking over to an older man in what looked like some variation of *Intermezzo*. She had been talking earlier, but Ben hadn't been paying attention. Now her voice caught him, the same surprising modulation he'd noticed when they said hello. Nothing remarkable happened. She kissed the man, patting his arm, then walked across the room, turned, and said good-bye.

"Satin," Bunny said. "Lou would dress his mother like a hooker."

"Forget the dress," Lasner said. "Sam likes her. He thinks he can do something with her."

"She can't move her arms."

"So she can practice yanking his dick."

"Sol," Bunny said, then picked up the phone. "Any more dailies? Okay." He looked down toward the directors. "We're done here. Thanks. Rosemary looked great, Eddie." He watched them leave, then turned to Lasner. "Sol," he said, the rest unspoken.

"Sam's girl—she looks good," Lasner said stubbornly.

"She's last year, somebody you could get into the sack before you ship out."

"You're an expert on this."

"And now they're coming back. What do they want? A quickie with a waitress or somebody you can bring home?"

"They want to fuck Loretta Young?"

"Sol, I'm serious. We don't need her."

"Sam Pilcer's been with me a long time," Lasner said quietly, a little embarrassed. "He doesn't ask much."

"So let him slip her a fifty every time."

"We can always use a girl."

"Fox dropped her."

"Zanuck doesn't see it. It wouldn't be the first time. Lou doesn't see it, either—he keeps saying she can *sing*. We could get her for a hundred a week with steps, and he'd be grateful."

"Not as grateful as Sam," Bunny said.

Lasner turned to Ben. "What do you think? You're a guy off the boat. She look good to you?"

"Everybody looks good to me." He glanced at Bunny, an offering. "She has a nice voice."

"You want to sign her for her voice?"

"Try a shorter option," Ben said, the thought too sudden to be filtered. "You don't have to pick it up."

Bunny looked at him, surprised, then waited for Lasner's reaction.

"It never lasts long with Sam," Lasner said finally, staring at Ben. He turned to Bunny. "Tell Lou you like her voice," he said, amused now.

"Start her with a voice-over," Bunny said, thinking. "If we had any." He looked at Ben. "You could request her. For your picture."

Ben nodded. An easy chance to make an ally.

"That picture? What voice-over?"

"One of the victims," Bunny said. "The voice-over tells her story."

Lasner stared at him for a second, then snorted. "You're going to tell Lou you want her to play a dead Jew? Let me know what he says."

He stood up, shaking his head. "That's some pair of balls you got on you," he said to Bunny, heading for the door.

Bunny picked up a clipboard. "Good night, Pete," he yelled to the projectionist, then turned to Ben. "Clever you," he said, his voice without edge, as if he were trying to decide how he felt.

"If it works."

"With Lou? He'll grab it. It gets his foot in the door." He sighed. "My new best friend," he said, then looked up. "It's hard for Sol to say no to Sam. They go back." He hesitated. "You don't have to use her. If she's not right for the picture."

"I can find something. Maybe buy myself a favor."

"I wonder what that could be."

Ben looked at him. It wouldn't be Ruth Harris, not even worth safety shots anymore. "You do any favors for Rosemary?"

"My whole life is doing favors for Rosemary," Bunny said. "Did you have a particular one in mind?"

His tone, a pretend innocence, drew a line, his eyes daring Ben to cross it. But what would be the point? Ben answered by saying nothing, a kind of standoff.

"I hope you're not still going on about people making calls. You don't want to be a nuisance." He paused. "Rosemary's been seeing Ty Power, since he got out of the Marines. She's been photographed seeing him. They make an attractive couple. She's going to keep seeing him. Until her picture comes out."

"A one-man woman."

Bunny tucked the clipboard under his arm and turned to the door, then stopped, looking back over his shoulder. "Why Rosemary?"

"She's Danny's type."

"Oh," Bunny said, his voice sliding an octave. "And here I thought you were just guessing."

"And she's important to the studio."

"Everybody's important. Until they're not." He turned fully, facing Ben. "Look, I don't know where you think you're going with this, but if I were you, I'd park it outside the gate. You don't want to be bothering people. Mr. L likes to keep things running. Anything interferes with production— Right now he likes you. He gets these little enthusiasms. You could have a future here. But he can blow hot and cold. You should know that. It's a studio. People come and go all the time."

"Except you."

Bunny nodded. "I keep things running."

SHE WAS in the pool when he got home. He followed the faint sounds of splashes through the quiet house and out onto the terrace, stopping for a second by the lemon tree near the door. Only the pool lights were on, a grotto effect, with blue light rising up, not spilling down, and he saw that she was naked, her body gliding through the water with a mermaid's freedom, alone in her own watery world. He knew he should make a sound but instead stood watching her, the smooth legs, the private dark patch in between when they opened out. When she became aware of him, a shadow at the end of the pool, she swam toward him without embarrassment, faintly amused at his own.

"I thought I was alone," she said smiling, glancing toward the crumpled bathing suit on the edge of the pool.

"Sorry, I didn't mean—" Still looking, only her head above water, but the rest of her clear in the pool lights.

"That's all right. I was getting out anyway." She reached for a towel, more of her out of the water now, her nipples hardening a little as the air touched them. "Quiet as a mouse."

She looked at him, still amused, then began to climb the shallow end steps so that he finally had to turn away, a show of modesty. Behind him he could hear the towel rubbing, another rustling as she put on a robe, watching her now by sound.

"Have a drink." She moved to the open wine bottle on the table, tying her belt. "Iris left something in the fridge, if you're hungry. I didn't know—"

"I should have called."

"No, don't feel that. Come and go as you like." She poured out two glasses from what he saw was an almost empty bottle. "Did you have a good day?" she said, handing him one.

He laughed, a reflex.

"What?"

"That's what people say in movies." What wives said.

"So how do I say it then?" She sat down on a chaise and lit a cigarette, turning to sit back but keeping one leg up, poking through the folds of the robe.

He shrugged. "Same way, I guess."

"Ha, art and life. Like my father's lectures. So, was it? A good day?"

He leaned back on the other chaise, taking a sip of the wine. "This is nice."

"Mm. Maybe I'll take to drink."

But he hadn't meant the wine: the warm night, the liquid light of the pool catching her bare leg, Danny's wonderful life. Is that how it had been? Comparing their days, listening to night sounds, the soft air rubbed with hints of chlorine and eucalyptus.

"Did you go to your father's?"

"No. He says it's too soon." She took another drink. "How long do people sit at home anyway? Do you know?"

"A week, I think."

"Two more days. Then what? Ciro's. Ha. Every night. *Das süsse Leben.*"

"How about dinner at Sol Lasner's? Saturday."

She turned to him, eyebrows raised.

"He said to bring someone," Ben said. "Who else do I know?"

She sat back, smiling. "Such an invitation. But you're in luck. I'm free. Every day, in fact. Well, not Sunday."

"What's Sunday?"

"My father's birthday. Salka makes a big lunch. Dieter comes and makes a toast—he writes it out before, a real speech. My father thanks him. Then *he* says something. It goes on like that, every year. Then chocolate cake."

"The one Danny liked."

"Yes," she said, a sudden punctuation mark. She stubbed out her cigarette, then got up and poured more wine in their glasses. "They sent the medical report you asked for. It's on the desk."

"What does it say?"

"He died," she said, sitting back down.

"I'll look at it later."

"Why?"

He said nothing for a minute, listening to the pool water hit against the drain flaps.

"I don't know. How he died. It's something we should know—it's part of it all."

She looked over at him for a second, about to speak, then let it go.

"If you say so," she said wearily. "So what do we wear to Lasner's? They dress up?"

"I'll ask Bunny."

She turned, a question.

"His right hand, his— I don't know what you'd call him. He used to be a child star."

"That's what happens to them? I never think of them grown up."

"Neither do they. Then they are and they have to do something else. But they look the same. Just older. Remember Wolf Breslau? The little boy in the Harz Mountain films? He became a Nazi. They put him on trial. For killing Poles. In open pits. The same baby face."

She was quiet for a minute. "Someone you saw in the *Kino*," she said to herself. "How can anybody go back?" She shook her head. "My father says Heinrich's making plans. To go back to that." She took a sip of wine. "And what about you? What are you going to do? Now that you're grown up. Make pictures?"

"No."

"No? Lasner must like you. Inviting you to dinner."

"He likes me this week. One in the family's enough." Was. "My father always expected Danny to—"

"But not you. So." Another sip, thinking. "Did you like him?"

"My father?"

"No. Daniel."

The question, never asked, took him by surprise, something tossed in the air that hung there, incapable of being answered.

"I mean, families, people don't always— So many years, you didn't see each other. I just wondered."

"That was the war."

"Ah," she said, the sound floating up to join the question, still suspended.

He looked out toward the city. "I wanted to be him," he said finally.

"When you were boys."

"Yes." When did that stop? Does it? He smiled, moving away from it. "He was good with girls."

"And not you?"

"I got better."

"They say in Germany now you can get a girl for a pack of cigarettes. One pack."

"That's not all you'd get."

"So it's not for you, the easy ones. I can see that. It wouldn't be— how do you say *schicklich*?"

"Proper. Seemly."

"Seemly," she said, trying it, then took another sip of wine. "The first time I met him—he'd undress you. Look right at you. He wanted you to know he was doing it. So people are different. You look at me from the side. You don't want me to know you're looking." She waved her hand at him before he could say anything. "It's all right. It's nice, someone looking. Don't be embarrassed." She paused. "I like you looking."

He turned to her, not sure how to respond.

"If it makes you uneasy, my being here—"

She shook her head. "No. It doesn't matter. That's not the way it would happen. I know you a little now. You look from the side. You'd wait. You'd wait for me to say. To start it. That's how it would happen." She looked at him. "Don't you think?"

A direct look, not from the side, holding his. He felt blood rise to his skin, as if she had touched him. Danny's wife.

"Maybe," he said. "And maybe you're having fun with me."

"No." She smiled, looking down at her glass. "Maybe the wine is." She sat up, a drowsy stretch, gathering the robe. "Anyway, it wouldn't be seemly, would it? Not yet."

"No."

"Not even cold. That's what they'd say, yes? Well, I'm going in." She picked up the bottle to take with her. "Have a swim if you like," she said, moving off, then smiled at him. "I won't look."

He sat for a while, his mind drifting but then, like the water, lapping back. *Schicklich.* The inside of a marriage was unknowable, curtained off. He listened for sounds of her inside, but only the crickets broke the quiet. Maybe she was already in bed, not at all uneasy because she knew the way it would happen.

On his way in, he stopped at the screening room to pick up some of the office papers Republic had sent over. Scripts, drafts. What had been in his mind those last weeks? Not that *Partners in Crime* was likely to be revealing—formula stuff, two brothers having fun, as frivolous as Otto's comedies.

He went over to an open film can. The film itself was still in the projector, not yet run through and put away, the last thing Danny had seen. Maybe a Continental picture with a young star, someone he wanted to watch over and over? Ben flicked the switch, half-expecting to see Ruth or Rosemary—any girl you'd want to spend an afternoon with at a residential hotel. Instead it was a Fox Movietone newsreel, men shaking hands right after Hiroshima. Ben rewound the film and started it again.

First, the usual opening montage with the water-skiers, then the airmen at Tinian Island, the ground crew loading the bomb, kneeling with the pilots in front of the plane, a picture everybody'd seen now, instant history according to the voice-over. But the camera had been there, too, recording it, making a movie. And in the plane, flying now through the clouds.

The flash and mushroom cloud, the whole city rolled up in smoke, the narrator excited by the scale of it, the most powerful thing the world has ever known. No voice, though, over the next segment, shot later, a silent sweeping pan of the charred, flattened city. A few figures picking their way through the landscape, otherwise no movement at all. More pan shots, the frame of a domed building by the river, the rest vaporized. Congratulations all around back home, scientists and generals shaking hands. They'd made a movie of it, sent cameras up, got flight crews to pose. But so had the Nazis, filming atrocities with smiling faces. That's how they'd identified Wolf Breslau, caught on film on the rim of the mass grave, smiling, unable to resist one last close-up.

The newsreel went on to the surrender scene on the *Missouri,* but even the narrator, booming with victory, couldn't lift the film from the streets of ashes. The voice wanted to celebrate, throw a hat in the air like the relieved sailors, but the words said one thing and the pictures showed another—this was the way it would be now, the way we would die. Kissing couples, the narrator announcing a world of hope. But it wasn't, Ben thought. Not now. Just an endless dread.

Ben took the reel off and put it in its canister. Not frivolous. Maybe *Partners* wasn't the whole of him, maybe the war had touched something deeper, just as Ben's life had been upturned by the camps, both of them alike under the skin.

He turned off the light and went into the house. On the desk in the study, just as she'd said, he found the autopsy report. He glanced through it. Medical English, not English at all, nearly incomprehensible. He heard a sound from her room, a turning perhaps, something dropped, meaningless in itself except as a sign of life. Just behind the door. He smiled to himself. *Schicklich.* How do we decide what's right? He looked down again at the sheet. Pulmonary—something to do with the lungs. But of course she was right. All it said was that Danny was dead.

. . .

"Was there some problem?" Dr. Walters said, caught on the run in the hall, not sure why Ben had come.

"I don't know the technical terms. I'm not sure what they actually mean."

"Simple language? He stopped breathing." He halted midstep. "I'm sorry. I know it sounds like a joke. All I mean is that there were no signs of stroke—that's the usual cause after a head trauma, edemal bleeding flooding the brain."

"But not in this case."

"No. Or heart damage. There are only a few ways to die. Of course, these are all connected." He paused, framing his hands, explaining to a classroom. "Think of the brain as a switchboard. The operator pulled a line connected to the lungs. Like being cut off on a call," he said, looking up, waiting to see if Ben was following. "The board controls everything. The lungs don't operate by themselves."

"Is that common?"

"Yes. Mr. Kohler, with a head injury like this, the surprising thing is that he didn't die instantly. I gather he was lucky in the response time—the ambulance got to him before he lost too much blood. So that bought him some time. I'm sorry."

"But if he regained consciousness—"

"We don't rule out miracles," he said patiently. "But I'm a doctor, you know, not a priest. This is what we expected to happen." He waited for Ben to reply.

"Was there anything—any sign that he may have been injured before he fell?"

"Before."

"Knocked out, anything like that."

"I'm not sure I understand."

"By someone else. Before."

Dr. Walters peered at him, disconcerted. "No. But I'm not a policeman, either. Is there any reason to think this happened?"

"I just wanted to look at everything. Every possibility."

Dr. Walters nodded. "I'm sorry, Mr. Kohler. These things can be hard to accept." He looked down at the paper in Ben's hand. "Maybe that's why we hide behind the language."

He had stopped by the hospital on his way to lunch and now found himself running late, caught in the traffic west to Fairfax. Kelly had suggested the Farmers Market, somewhere away from the studio, a pointless Dick Tracy feint, but not worth arguing about.

The market had started as a collection of produce stalls for Depression farmers, but now had the look of a small studio—permanent buildings for the stalls and restaurants, table seating on patios and its own logo clock tower, looking over the parking lot like the RKO globe. Everything was painted cream and light green and maroon, what Ben thought of as leftover colors, the same ones Lasner had used at Continental, maybe even from the same cheap supply. Kelly was already at a table under the trees, nursing a beer.

"So what have we got?" he said as Ben sat down, his eyes darting over Ben's shoulder.

"Not much. No matches from the building list." He pulled out a paper. "These are the top contract players, the ones they might want to protect, but that doesn't mean it's one of them. And they're not big names. Lasner doesn't—"

"Yeah, I know, the loan-out king. Who's he got borrowed, by the way. He'd want to take care of them, at least until the picture's out. Listen," he said abruptly. "You mention me to anyone? Tell them I'm looking at this?"

"No. You said—"

"You sure?"

Ben nodded. "Why?" he said, aware now of the look in Kelly's eyes, his quick movements.

"Maybe my imagination. Except it never is, is it? Don't turn around—no, don't, I mean it. People always do that. Take a look when we get up for the food. There's a guy over by the raw bar. I notice he's casing the place, and he looks familiar and then it comes to me—he was hanging around Republic. When I'm there checking the talent. This is before I hear about Continental. Some coincidence, if you believe in that. So maybe he's keeping an eye, you know? The guy's a cop—everything about him—and I'm thinking, what the hell, the cops enforce for the studios, so maybe someone—"

"I didn't say a word," Ben said, beginning to turn.

"No, don't. He'll pick up on it. Let's eat. You like seafood? They have a great Crab Louis."

They got up and walked across the patio to the sales counter. He spotted him immediately—the man in the gray suit reading a paper, almost hidden behind a tree but scanning the patio just as he had the crowd at the funeral, the reception afterward. Ben gave a don't-worry shake of his head to Kelly, and ordered the crab. A huge plate, enough for two.

"I know him," he said when they sat down again. "He works for Polly."

"No, he doesn't. He may feed her, but he doesn't work for her. I know all her runners. So what's he feed her. He's a cop. Maybe even Bureau. He's got that look. He could be Bureau."

"Calm down. You're—"

"Cop shows twice, something's up. You learn these things. So what the fuck does he want?"

"He came with Polly. To the funeral. That's all I can tell you. Your name never came up at the studio. You're sure he's a cop?"

"Some kind of cop. Has to be."

"I'm going to the head. See if he watches."

He walked to the men's room past piles of oranges, but the man in the gray suit seemed not to notice, his gaze still fixed toward the other end of the dining patio, an easier sight line than the side angle to Kelly. People in shirts having lunch, big California salads. A few suits. Liesl's father. Ben stopped. Ostermann saw him at the same time and nodded. Impossible now not to go over. Ben signaled to Kelly that he'd only be a minute, using the turn to check on the man in the gray suit, absorbed again in his paper. Meanwhile, Kaltenbach was waving him to their table.

"So, you know this place?" he said standing, playing host. "A coffee? You'll join us?"

Ben shook his head. "I'm with somebody. Just a hello."

"A little bit of Europe," Ostermann said, gesturing to the patio. "Not a real *Biergarten,* but still, trees. You can pretend."

Ben looked down at their plates—sausages and deli potato salad, what they might in fact have ordered at Hechinger's.

"That's what everyone does here," Kaltenbach said, waving his hands to take in the city. "Pretend." He looked over at Ben, excited. "Do you know that I am going to Berlin?"

"Berlin," Ben said, thinking of smashed bricks, jagged walls.

"Yes, I know, it's bad now, you hear it from everyone, but still, Berlin. Something survives. I thought I would never see it again. I thought I would die here." He gestured to the sunny patio, the healthy salad eaters, seeing something else. "And now—"

"How did you arrange it?" Ben said. "I thought nobody could get in, except the Army. A few reporters. You need a permit."

"Yes, yes, another exit visa. But Hans here will write a letter. Thomas Mann, too. Who would say no to them? Why would they keep me here? On relief. Eighteen dollars and fifty cents a week. A charity case. You don't think they'll be happy to see me go? One last visa and it's over. If Erika were still alive, think how happy."

"Maybe you should wait," Ben said, "until things are better. It's difficult now, just to live."

"No, they're giving me a flat."

"Who?"

"The university. I'm invited to accept a chair at the university."

"But it's in the Soviet sector."

"Yes, of course, that's who invites me."

Ben glanced at Ostermann, who met his eye but then looked deliberately away, toying with his fork.

"They are going to print my books again."

"The Soviets?"

"My friend, one conqueror or another, what's the difference? Germany lost the war. Do you think the Russians will leave now? How else can I do this? I can be a writer again. I can be in Berlin," he said in a kind of rush, emotional now, almost touching it. "Excuse me," he said, putting a fingertip to his eye. "So foolish. Old age. And now the bladder. I'll be right back."

Ben watched him head for the men's room.

"He's not a political man," Ostermann said quietly.

"He will be. The minute he gets off the plane. German writer returns. To the East. Which makes them look legitimate. They don't care about his books. They just want him for show."

"I know. They've asked some of the others. Even Brecht is reluctant and he—"

"They ask you?"

"No." He glanced up, a slightly impish smile. "Maybe they don't like my work. Too bourgeois."

"You can't let him do this. Do you know what it's like there?"

"What do I say to him? He lives in one room. On money we give him. His friends. Each handout a humiliation. His wife committed suicide. For her, it was too much. And now they come to him. A professor. With a flat. His books. What do we offer instead?"

"Not a prison. At least here—"

"Reuben," he said, using his full name as a kind of weight, "he doesn't even know he's here. He's somewhere else, waiting. So let him go."

"This isn't going to make him popular with the State Department. Or you. Writing letters."

"An act of friendship, not politics. Or isn't that possible anymore? I thought that time was over. Well, it doesn't matter for me. I don't want to go back. The conscience of Germany? I don't think they want that now. And maybe I don't want them, either."

Ben looked toward the other end of the patio. The man in the gray suit, paper down, was now sipping coffee. Just having lunch.

"A thousand apologies," Kaltenbach said, joining them at the table. "And after so many kindnesses. I'm not myself these days."

"Herr Kaltenbach," Ben said, a sudden thought, "how did the offer come, from the university. A letter? It's official?"

"Yes, yes. Hand delivered by the Soviet consul, all the way from San

Francisco. So I would know it was genuine. You know, you don't trust the mails for such an offer."

"Ah, the consul," Ben said. Someone who would certainly be watched everywhere, each contact another string to follow. "Well, I hope everything works out. Berlin—"

Kaltenbach nodded. "You don't have to say. I've seen the pictures. A wreck. But look at me. So maybe we'll suit each other."

There was another minute of bowing farewells, a European leave-taking, before Ben could go back across the patio. Kelly was waiting, smoking over the debris of his Crab Louis, but instead of turning to their table Ben kept going, an impulse, toward the gray suit.

"Excuse me. You were at my brother's funeral, but we weren't introduced," he said, extending his hand. "Ben Collier."

For a second, the man simply stared, as if the approach had violated some rule, then lifted his hand to shake Ben's.

"I didn't know who you were. They told me later. You had different names?" he said, keeping his eyes on Ben, reading him.

"My mother changed it. How did you know Danny?"

"We did some work together."

"You're in pictures?" Ben said, surprised.

"Technical advisor. To get the details right."

"On the series? Police details? My friend over there thought you might be. Maybe FBI." The man said nothing. "He thought you might be tailing him."

"Yeah? What'd he do?" he said, playing with it, then looked at Ben and shook his head. "I'm retired."

"From what?"

The man hesitated, thinking through a chess move, then nodded. "The Bureau."

"You don't look old enough to—"

"I took a bullet. That buys you a few years."

"So what do you do now?"

"Have lunch," he said, stretching his hand toward his finished plate, implying long afternoons.

"And work for Danny."

"I gave him advice, that's all. We helped each other out."

Ben looked up, an off phrase, but so innocuous there was nowhere to take it.

"Well, thanks for coming to the funeral. Funny running into you again."

"No, I'm here most days." He got up to go, taking his hat off the table. "I'm sorry about your brother. That was a hell of a thing."

"Whatever it was."

The man stopped, his eyes fixed on Ben. "What do you mean?"

"It's just a little fuzzy, wouldn't you say? What happened? You're the pro."

He waited. Finally the man looked away, putting on his hat.

"I wouldn't know. I'm retired." He paused. "It's tough to get over something like this. You should take it easy."

"Everyone says. Would you? Your brother?"

"Something worrying you? You were close? Maybe he said something to you."

Ben shook his head. "What would he say?" Now a cat and mouse game, but no longer sure who was which.

The man shrugged, then took out his wallet. "Sometimes you start something, you don't know what you're getting into. Here." He took out a card and handed it to Ben. "If you need any technical advice."

Ben looked at it. Dennis Riordan. No affiliation, just a telephone number.

"Technical advice," Ben repeated.

"Maybe he left something. Might explain it. Maybe I could help. Figure it out." He began to move off. "Anyway, tell your friend to keep his nose clean. Stop imagining things."

"What about German writers?"

Riordan turned. "You're a suspicious guy." He looked down at the table. "It was just lunch."

He crossed the patio to the exit near the vegetable stalls, unhurried, not even a backward glance.

"What the hell was that?" Kelly said at their table.

Ben handed him the business card. "What you thought. The Bureau. But retired."

"They never retire. They just find another pack of hyenas to sniff around with."

"Like Polly."

Kelly shook his head. "But somebody. I'll find out."

"You know people at Republic? Find out if he ever got a consultant fee. On Danny's pictures."

"What if he wasn't paid?"

"Then why do it?"

Kelly looked at the card again, memorizing the name, then handed it back.

"Christ, all I wanted was the girlfriend, an *item*, and now I've got the Bureau on my back."

"I don't think so. If he was tailing you, you'd never see him. Handing out cards. He wants something else."

"What?"

"I don't know. But think where we've seen him—Republic, the funeral. You weren't even at the funeral. He's not tailing you. It's like he's tailing Danny."

LASNER LIVED in a chateau near the top of Summit Drive with enough land for a full set of tennis courts and a formal garden. Danny's house flowed easily outside and back, the pool another room, but here the effect was moated, drawn up behind the gravel drive, the high view just something framed by picture windows. Teenagers in uniforms had been hired to park the cars so that arriving felt like stepping out of a liveried carriage, something Lubitsch might have shot.

The inside rooms were Du Barry French, high and ornate and formal, with gilded side tables and silk fire screens and ormolu footed chairs. Ben wondered what Lasner made of it all, passing through each morning on his way to coffee. Or did they have breakfast in bed, a proper *levée*? Still, Fay clearly loved playing chatelaine, greeting people just inside the door with real warmth, so where was the harm? The money, all those nickels, would have been spent somehow. Why not on a French dream? With a hostess once pretty enough to have been a Goldwyn Girl, far more attractive than any of the originals. Even Sol, beaming by her side, was an improvement, at least a bulldog jaw, not a weak Bourbon chin.

"My god, look at the jewels," Liesl said.

Bunny had said to dress, but Ben had expected country club cocktails in suits. Instead he felt he had walked into an A-picture party scene, everyone turned out by Makeup and Wardrobe, evening dresses and sparkling necklaces, the room like some velvet jewel case.

"Fake," he said, smiling.

"No, they're not." She put her fingers to her throat. "Anyway, the pearls are nothing to be ashamed of. My mother wouldn't sell them, not even in Paris when we—"

"Nothing to be ashamed of. The rest of you looks good, too."

"Oh yes, in a roomful of movie stars."

He glanced around, taking in what she'd already noticed, faces from covers, people you saw in magazine ads recommending soap. He thought of his mother's parties before the war, gaunt women with hats and fur trim, not beautiful, using their jewels to light up the room. Here the faces themselves were luminous. Paulette Goddard had come, looking even better than she had on the train. Alexis Smith was talking to the Lasners, her chin at a patrician tilt. He recognized Ann Sheridan by the fireplace, the full mouth not drawn in a glamour shot pout, but smiling, as down to earth as the girl next door, if she'd been beautiful. They were all beautiful. It seemed a kind of joke, an ancien régime room finally filled with glorious-looking people instead of pinched-faced heirs.

"There's Marion Wallace. I'd better say something to her. She sent a nice note."

"Let me buy you a drink first." He lifted two champagne flutes from a waiter's tray. "Who else is here?" he said, clinking her glass. "Do you know anyone?"

She smiled. "A few. There's Walter Reisch. Daniel used to play tennis with him. Paul Kohner. You know him, the agent? He handles Bruce Hudson. In the series." She took another sip. "It's a small town. Nobody ever believes that, but it is. They never see anyone else. If my father walked in, no one would know who he was. Alma used to complain about it. After *Bernadette,* when people asked Franz to parties." She giggled. "People thought she was a character actress."

"Ah, you're here," Lasner said, not really in a receiving line, but hovering near the door. "A clean shirt even. You know Fay."

"So glad you could come," she said. "Sol tells me everything's great with the picture."

"Well, the cutter is. Now all I have to do is listen to him."

"You think you're kidding, but I've seen it happen. So maybe you are as smart as he says." She smiled, rolling her eyes toward Lasner. "Hello," she said, extending her hand to Liesl.

"I'm sorry. Fay, Liesl Kohler."

"Talk about smart," Sol said quickly, missing the introduction but taking Liesl's hand. "One week in town, already a beautiful woman."

"Sol," Fay said, then to Liesl, "Pay no attention, he thinks he's a comedian."

"No, Jack thinks he's a comedian. He tells jokes to Jessel. The same jokes. You meet Jack?" he said to Ben. "When we were over in Europe? He was with the group."

"Jack Warner? Just to shake hands."

"You're lucky. He tells one tonight, it'll sound like the first time to you. Maybe even funny."

"Sol," Fay said, but with a glint, agreeing. She looked at Liesl. "Your pearls are lovely. I couldn't help noticing."

"My mother's."

"I knew it. The old ones have that rich tone. They say it comes from being worn next to the skin. All those years."

"Do me a favor," Lasner said to Ben. "I want to introduce you later. Fay's cousin. We just got her out. Over there. All along, we're thinking she must be dead and then the Red Cross calls and says she gave them our name, she's alive, would we send for her? So, we're crying, thinking, what are the odds? And now she's here, she just smokes."

"Sol, she has *been* through something."

"Did I say no? It's a miracle. She'll be interested—your picture."

"Sometimes, you know, it's the last thing they want to talk about. Where was she?"

"Poland. Not at first. They shipped her around. She doesn't say much."

"She told you, Sol. Oranienburg, then Poland." She turned to Ben. "She's getting used to things, that's all. She's only here two days. Big shot here wants— I don't know, what, she should be dancing."

"I'd like to meet her," Ben said politely.

"I figured," Lasner said. "You'll have something to talk about."

Is that why he'd been invited? To entertain survivors? But she'd only just arrived. Lasner was drawing him aside, keeping his hand on his arm.

"Listen," he said, low as a secret, "I just want you to know. I didn't want to say at the studio, but I appreciate—you know, on the train—"

"You feeling okay?"

"One hundred percent."

"Sol, it's Jack and Ann," Fay said, drawing him away.

The Warners were all smiles, Jack with a jaunty mustache and a tan so dark that it seemed to have shriveled his face, like a walnut. Ben remembered him from the Army tour, paler and in uniform, telling stories about Errol Flynn. They'd been on Hitler's boat, a brief day's outing on the Rhine, which reminded Warner of his own yacht, moored next to Flynn's at the marina, so close you could hear what happened in the master bedroom. "Not just every night, two, three *times* a night. Maybe different ones, I don't know. I said to him, you keep it up, it's going to fall off." Laughter from the others, watching the banks stream by. Now he shook Ben's hand without any hint of recognition, just a new face at Lasner's.

"So all I hear is Rosemary Miller," he said to Sol. "It's going to happen for her?"

"Your lips," Lasner said, raising his eyes.

"Get it in the can before the goddam union closes everybody down," Warner said, prompting a huddle, cutting Ben and Liesl loose to drift.

Waiters were still passing rich canapés—caviar and asparagus tips in puff pastry—so it would be a while before they sat down. Liesl had told him Hollywood ate early to get up early, but Saturday must be the exception. No one made any move to the several tables set up in the next room. Ben wondered how dinner would be announced. A gong? Meanwhile, more champagne was poured and the man at the grand piano in the corner, probably someone from Continental, kept playing show tunes.

All the talk, overheard in snippets as they walked around the room, was about pictures. An option picked up. Sturges's fight with Paramount. Disappointing grosses on *Wilson*. De Havilland taking Jack to court over her suspension. Would there be a strike? Paramount having a record year. But so was everybody. Knock wood. There seemed to be no one from the outside at all. The aircraft factories in Northridge, the oil companies downtown, shipping offices in Long Beach—all the rest of the new, rich city was somewhere else, at gentile dinners in Pasadena, maybe, or out at the movies. Rosemary Miller had just arrived, giving Sol a showy hug, careful not to muss her lipstick, then a broad smile to the rest of the group. Because it seemed to be her time—even Jack Warner had heard—and people were coming over to her, after all those parties where nobody had even noticed her.

"I'd better say something to Marion," Liesl said. "Who's that looking at you?"

Ben followed her gaze. "Bunny, the one I told you about. He runs things."

She patted his arm. "Then be nice. I won't be long."

She moved away before Bunny reached him.

"Who was that?" he said, his eyes following her, intrigued.

"Liesl Kohler."

"His wife?" he said, slightly addled. "You brought her? You might have said."

"She's allowed to go out. Why? Is there something wrong?"

"It's just that all the seating's been—well, never mind," he said, stopping. "I've put you next to Paulette. Since you're such old pals."

"Thanks."

"Well, that's your left. Right you've got a relative of Sol's. Fay's actually. Genia, hard g. Markowitz. Polish. But lived in Berlin. Sol asked. She doesn't speak much English, and I gather you can speak German," he said, his voice rising at the end, a question.

"I was brought up there. Partly, anyway."

"That's right, the father. Quite a life. More interesting by the day."

"And that's just my childhood."

Bunny smiled, enjoying the play, a kind of volley.

"Often the most interesting part," he said. "*Mine* was."

"God. Rex Morgan?" Ben said, distracted by a tall man near the corner. "I haven't seen him since I was a kid. He's not still a cowboy. He must be—"

"Real estate. Glendale. You'd be surprised how many people want to live there."

"His pictures were Continental?" Ben said, still trying to explain his being here.

"Every one. Locations out in Simi Valley. His ranch now. He bought it eventually."

"So he and Lasner are old friends."

"Well, that. And he owns a piece. Of the company. He came through in 'thirty when the banks wouldn't. Mr. L got through the crunch and Rex got eight percent," he said simply, the details of the business like a file at his fingertips.

There was a burst of laughter near the door.

"Wonderful. Jack's here. Telling jokes."

"You often have the competition over?"

"He's the reason for the party."

"It's not just dinner?"

"It's never just dinner."

"What's the occasion?"

"The Honorable Kenneth T. Minot." He looked at Ben. "Our congressman. He and Jack need to meet."

"Why?"

"His district takes in Burbank. Jack's in Burbank. They should know each other. Mr. L thinks he might be useful with the consent decree." He caught Ben's puzzled expression. "The Justice Department issued a consent decree, before the war, to separate the studios and the theaters. Force separate ownership. A disaster for us. Nobody wanted to do anything while the war was on—kick us while we were being so helpful—but now it's over, they're acting up again so we're trying to put a stop to it. Minot's been friendly."

"But Continental doesn't own theaters, does it?"

"But Jack *does*. And we have a distribution agreement with him. This goes through, everybody suffers."

"Warner doesn't know his own congressman?" Ben said. "A studio that size—"

"Wrong party. Jack's funny that way. After *Yankee Doodle*, he thought Roosevelt was a personal friend. But it's time he met more people."

"Across the aisle."

"We don't care where they sit as long as they get the decree squashed."

"And he gets?"

Bunny raised his eyebrows. "We'll have to see, won't we?"

Ben looked around the room again. All this extravagance to arrange a meeting. Rosemary was near the piano now, chatting with Alexis Smith. Ann Sheridan had gone over to greet the Warners. It occurred to Ben suddenly that the stars had been brought in to dress the room, like eye-catching centerpieces. They were all under contract to Continental or Warners—maybe Lasner and Jack had simply ordered them up. He wondered if there were a studio pecking order, Bette Davis having earned the right to pass, Cagney beyond this kind of thing. Only Paulette was with another studio, but she was a friend, happy to sparkle for old times' sake.

"Well, he's here," Bunny said, looking toward the door. "The Honorable. Ken to his friends."

Minot was sandy-haired, younger than Ben had expected, with an athlete's build already filling in, about to turn soft. There was a pleasant-looking woman on his arm, a little dismayed at the dazzle of the party about to swallow her up.

"His first term?" Ben said.

"War hero. Took out a Jap machine gun emplacement. Then caught shrapnel in the leg, enough to get him out. Just in time to start passing out flyers in Van Nuys. Well—oh god, the wife. Marie, I think. Marie?"

"Time to go to work."

"You think you're kidding. Sorry about the cousin, but I did give you Paulette. I just wish you'd told me— By the way, I talked to the boys in Publicity. And Security. Nobody made any calls about your brother. Nobody knew him, in fact. So I'd check your sources. They might have got mixed up. Another studio. That happens. Sometimes on purpose. A little game they play."

Taking the time to close the door on it. Ben started to say something, then let it go. Bunny was already moving away, on to more important things.

He made another circuit of the room, another glassful, then noticed Liesl listening to some man, her expression polite but a little pained, trapped. There had been a shift in the crowd, the people near her moving away, leaving her standing in a circle of space, like a fawn in a clearing, and he felt a sudden urge to wrap a coat around her shoulders. When he went over she smiled, a flicker of relief in her eyes. Marion had been replaced by a director who'd known Danny at Metro and was now offering his condolences. He took Ben as a convenient excuse to escape.

"Having fun?"

"I would be if I didn't have to talk. Be like her," she said, nodding toward a middle-aged woman staring out the picture window, smoking. "Just watch everybody."

"She's looking the other way."

"They all want to know what picture I'm working on. When I'm not, they walk away."

Ben's eye wandered back to the woman at the window, now moving to a coffee table to put out a cigarette and light another. She looked up, taking in the room, but blankly, as if she couldn't really see anything. A skeletal thinness, gray hair in short bangs, a velvet dress that seemed too big for her, borrowed. She turned back to the window, staring down at Los Angeles.

"I have a feeling that's my dinner partner," Ben said.

"No, it isn't," Paulette Goddard said, suddenly at his side. "I am. Hello again."

He introduced her to Liesl.

"Bunny told me," she said to Ben. "I don't suppose you brought any cards." Her smile and eyes bright, still carrying their own key light. Ben thought of her cross-legged on the Pullman bed, letting Sol win. A good sport.

"Hope you don't mind," he said.

"Mind? I usually get *Rex*. He likes me or something. I don't know why. He starts on his horses and I just nod off. Do you ride?" she said to Liesl, drawing her in.

"No."

"I can't imagine. The only ranch I've ever been to was the divorce ranch in *The Women*. At Metro." She glanced around. "Fay certainly knows how to go all out," she said, half-laughing. "I remember when it was soup and crackers." She reached for a canapé on a tray, showing a green flash of emerald bracelet.

"You're friends?" Liesl said, polite.

"Mm, from the good old days, and thank God they're over. Are you in pictures or—?"

"I translate books. From German," she said, with a sly glance to Ben, waiting for Paulette to bolt.

But Paulette was impressed. "Do you really? I wish I could. Anything like that. They say you're not supposed to regret anything, but when you don't have school— I started work so early, I don't know anything. You never catch up, really."

135

"Well, translation, it's not so brainy," Liesl said easily. "Just work. And they're my father's books, so I can always ask him what he meant. Then find the words."

"Your father?"

"Hans Ostermann. He's not so well known here—"

"*Central Station*," Paulette said immediately. "I read it. Warners made it. God, what a mess. Mary Astor. He must have hated it. But I read it in English, so that was you? I'd love to meet him sometime. Just coffee or something, if he sees people. Oh, there's Rosemary. Have you met? Rosemary," she said, drawing her to them, "come meet some people. Liesl Kohler," she said, remembering it, something they didn't teach in school. "My old friend Ben—we were on the Chief together."

Rosemary hesitated, staring at Liesl, that first appraisal women make at parties, seeing everything, then shook hands with them both.

"Are your ears burning?" Paulette said. "Everybody's talking about you."

"The picture isn't even finished yet," Rosemary said, glancing again at Liesl, then facing Paulette, a subtle ranking.

"That's the best time. When everybody still thinks it's wonderful. But I hear you *are*."

"Well, you know, everybody likes dailies and then it comes out and—"

"Just hit your marks and cross your fingers—that's all any of us can do."

Rosemary flushed, clearly pleased to be included in "us." In person, without the glow of backlighting, her features seemed sharper, everything less soft. She looked around, slightly nervous, perhaps still self-conscious about being the center of attention.

"I've never seen such a beautiful house," she said, apparently meaning it.

"Well, it's not my taste," Paulette said. "I can't even pronounce it. Louis Quinze?" she said to Liesl, saying it perfectly. "Liesl's a translator, so she can be mine tonight. Quinze," she said again, at Liesl's nod. "I always think about *dusting* it. But Fay loves it. She always had a good eye. I can't tell one vase from another. But Bunny says the Sèvres is museum quality." Again pronouncing it correctly. "So you see, she knows." She turned, seeing Bunny coming over to them. "Isn't that right?"

"Darling, I have to borrow you," Bunny said, ignoring the question. "Come meet the congressman. He loved *Standing Room Only*."

"God. And he got elected?"

"Nicey, nicey. Come on. You can talk to Ben at dinner. Rosemary, you know Irving Rapper's here. I'm sure he'd love to meet you." A firm do-yourself-some-good nudge, Liesl and Ben just table fillers.

"Now's your chance," Ben said to Liesl, nodding toward the woman at the window. "To join the wallflowers."

"Who is she? She hasn't talked to anyone."

"Fay's cousin. Has to be. I don't think she has any English."

"Then go rescue her. I'm going to the ladies', find out what people are really saying."

Fay's cousin didn't turn when he came up, her gaze still fixed out the window.

"*Entschuldigung. Pani Markowitz?*"

"*Pani?* So you speak Polish?" she said in German, finally turning.

Ben smiled. "No. A courtesy only. I was told you were Polish. I'm Ben Collier."

"I was born there, yes," she said, her voice flat.

It was then that he took in her eyes, the same faraway emptiness he'd seen in some of the others', a blind person's eyes, no longer needed, nothing more to see. Her collarbones stuck out, barely covered by the thin layer of skin.

"I thought I would die there, too, but no." She half turned to the window. "And now look. So many lights."

"You lived in Berlin?" Ben said, to say something. "I was there as a boy. A few years."

"Yes, Berlin."

"And you're Fay's cousin."

"Her father and my mother—but he came here. A long time ago, before the first war."

"Your mother stayed."

"My father—he did very well. There was no reason for us to leave. It was a different time then. My mother always said Max left for the adventure. They thought he was a no-good. To leave your family, your country. So who was right?" She turned fully to the room, the rich end of Max's gamble. "A daughter living like this. To think all this still exists."

"You were in a camp."

She raised her eyes, still not really looking. "We all were. My husband, my sister. Everyone."

"Are they—?"

She shook her head. "Now only me."

"I'm sorry."

She wrinkled her forehead, as if the words were not just inadequate but puzzling, irrelevant.

"I don't know why. I was not so strong. Leon was stronger, for the work. But they took him. To the gas. I don't know why. No reason. You survive, no reason. Or you don't."

"I knew you'd find each other," Lasner said in English, genial, putting his hand on Ben's shoulder.

"You speak English?" Ben asked her.

"A few words only."

"But now that you're here, you have to try. I tell her, if she gets every other word, she's at least halfway there, right? You tell her about the picture?"

"Not yet." Ben switched to German. "We're making a documentary for the Army, about the camps."

"You want to put this in a film?"

"So people will know. A record. Eisenhower ordered them to film it when we got there. He said no one would believe it otherwise. A kind of proof."

"A proof."

"That it happened." He looked at her. "We don't have to talk about this, if you'd rather not."

"Put her in the picture. You can tell your story," Lasner said.

"What would I say? I don't know the reason for any of it." She reached down to the coffee table for another cigarette.

"You ought to go easy on those things."

"I'm sorry. For me it's a luxury. A whole cigarette."

"I didn't mean— I just meant for your health. Your life is a gift now."

She stared at him, saying nothing until, slightly flustered, he changed the subject.

"You know who this is?" He nodded at Ben. "Otto Kohler's kid."

Now her eyes did move, suddenly alert, as if she'd heard another voice.

"Otto's? But—"

"You knew my father?"

"Otto," she said, the flat tone now a little agitated. "There was a boy, yes. But I don't understand. You're not—"

"My brother. I was in England."

"Your brother. Taller," she said, measuring. "What happened to him?"

"He's dead."

She drew on the cigarette and looked down. "Yes. Of course he would be dead." Her voice flat again. When she looked back up at him her eyes had retreated behind their blank wall. "So now this," she said aloud, but to herself. "Otto's son."

"I knew you two would have lots to talk about," Lasner said in English.

She turned to him, hesitating, translating in her head, then looked back at Ben, an almost wry expression on her lips.

"Yes, much to talk about," she said and then, suddenly skittish, "Excuse me."

She left before either of them could say anything. Lasner raised his eyebrows.

"So I was wrong?"

"She's grateful to you, you know," Ben said, an instinctive peacemaker. "It's just maybe too much for her." He opened his hand to the party. "So soon."

"You know what I think? Honest to God? I think Hitler won that one. I don't think she's here anymore."

"How did she know my father?"

"She was in pictures over there. They all knew each other. By that time, there's only one studio." He paused, taking a puff on his cigar. "She was a looker when she was young. What the hell, Fay's cousin." He looked down at the cigar. "Not now. To do that to someone—" He broke off, looking up at Ben. "Well, see if you can get her to talk a little. So she doesn't just sit there at dinner. Picking. Ask her about Otto."

"You think they were—"

"Christ, I don't know. I never thought. Otto? I wouldn't be surprised. You think that's what spooked her with you? Like seeing the kid walk in on you when you're— Oh, there goes Jack. Watch, he's going to take on Congress."

Ben followed him, intending to split off and not intrude, but the loose group around Minot seemed open to anyone passing by. Both Minot and Warner were used to audiences—even talking to each other, they were playing to the cluster around them, a public conversation. Ben noticed that they were already "Ken" and "Jack."

"I'll tell you what I see," Jack said. "I see the goddam unions at my throat and now this thing hanging over my head. Ready to chop. Consent decree. Whatever the hell that actually means. Except trouble. I look around, I see trouble. Here we are, knocking our brains out trying to make pictures and everybody wants a piece."

"Jack," Minot said smiling, "you're on top of the world. Top of the world." A soap box voice, resonant, his chest swelling. "The industry and this city grew up together." He gestured toward the lights outside the picture window. "Thirty years ago, that was bean fields. Now look at it. With lots more to come. This year the industry's revenues are going to hit one billion dollars. One billion."

"Revenues, not profits."

"Profits, estimate sixty-three million." He nodded again to the window. "It's not lima beans anymore."

"You just happen to have those numbers in your pocket."

"You like to come prepared," Minot said, almost winking. "Industry estimates, Jack, not some office in Washington doesn't know what it's talking about. Industry estimates. You're on top of the world."

"With a sword over my head."

"Jack's a worrier," Lasner said.

"Of course I can't predict what the Justice Department is going to do," Minot said. "With them you need a crystal ball. But I can tell you there're a lot of people in Washington grateful for all the fine work this industry did during the war."

"While they were earning those profits," someone said, a left jab.

"I don't begrudge profits. I'm not a socialist." He laughed, a stage chuckle. "Not even close. People buy your product, you ought to make a profit. And keep it. Not have the government reaching into your pocket every five minutes. But I'm not here to talk politics. All I'm saying," he said, looking directly at Jack, "is you treat your friends right and they'll treat you right. That's the way it works in Washington."

"That's the way it works here, too. Trick is knowing who your friends are."

"My job is to protect your interests. You do well, the district does well." Minot smiled. "And you know what I think? I think you're just getting started. The industry. Look what's ahead. No more war restrictions. No more price controls. Everybody wants what you make. You're just going to grow and grow. With this district, with California. You know why? Because it's our time. Right now. America's time. All through the war I kept thinking, win this thing and there's no stopping us. And we did win it. It's our time."

Lifted directly from a campaign speech, Ben thought, the rhetoric building, even Jack Warner listening now with full attention.

"Of course you've got somebody over there doesn't like that at all, and we all know who that is. No profits there," he said, nodding to

Warner. "No God, either. A country with no God. I think that says it all. You think the other guys were bad, the Japs, the Nazis, wait'll you see this one. But at least this time we're ready. The Commies want to fight, let them come. And all their helpers over here. Trying to bring this great country down. They don't like to fight in the open. Like to hide. But we'll find them, too. You know what a great job Jack Tenney's been doing up in Sacramento."

"I knew him when he wrote *Mexicali Rose*."

"Well, he's doing something a lot more important now. That state committee—they could use it as a model when they go national with this. And they will. A house has termites, you've got to get rid of them before the rot sets in. That's just common sense. Unless you want to see it fall down. Jack's been working this for years now. You know what he told me? How many files he's got? Reds and their pals and people too dumb to know any better? Over fourteen thousand. Just waiting for when we need them."

"Fourteen thousand subversives or fourteen thousand people he doesn't like?" The same man who'd made the crack about profits.

"Well, let's just say people he's not sure of," Minot said, deflecting this easily. "You'd want to be sure, something like this. When you're under attack. Not with guns—not yet anyway. But ideas, too, the wrong ideas. Slip them in every chance you get until people are confused. That's where you come in." He nodded to Warner. "Make sure it doesn't happen in pictures. There's nothing more powerful if you want to reach people. Not even radio. Hitler understood that. The power of film. These people, too."

"That's why we have the Breen Office," Jack said. "Try getting an idea past them." He laughed, a signal to the others, who joined in. After a second of hesitation, Minot did, too, playing a man who appreciates a good wisecrack.

"Now, Jack, I said wrong ideas," he said, still laughing.

"Congressman, you don't have to worry about that," Jack said seriously. "I've been in this business all my life and I don't think you could find a more patriotic group of people. We love this country."

"It gave us everything," Lasner said.

Jack waited, a twinkle in his eye. "And we're going to love it even more if you get this decree taken care of." More smiles all around.

"Jack, they told me you were a kidder," Minot said pleasantly. "They didn't tell me you were a politician. Next thing you know, you'll be running for my seat."

"You don't have to worry about that. I'm already running everything I want in Burbank. Sol, you going to give us something to eat tonight?" Cutting the scene before it ran too long, his point now made.

Minot's instincts weren't as sure—he missed Warner's cue and kept talking about the future, now of the Valley, but since none of his listeners actually lived there they became less attentive, darting glances around the room. He was saved by a waiter at his elbow quietly announcing dinner. Not a gong after all, servants discreetly guiding people into the dining room, a piece of social choreography.

Some attempt had been made to place the few German speakers at Genia's table, but, as her dinner partner, most of the caretaking still fell to Ben. Paul Henreid, no doubt another Warners draftee, was on her right but after a few pleasantries turned his attention, in English, to Rosemary. Liesl, an unexpected German speaker, was across the round table from them, too far for conversation. Paulette's other partner was Mike Curtiz, who might have helped but, head close, monopolized Paulette instead with studio gossip. Genia didn't seem to mind. She sat quietly, her own island, while the table talked around her. Since no one on either side was listening, when Ben spoke German to her it became oddly private, as if they were in another room, in no danger of being overheard. As Lasner predicted, she scarcely touched her food, moving pieces of the tournedos with her fork but not eating them.

"I can't, you know," she said, noticing his glance to her plate. "It's too rich for me."

Ben remembered the rescued inmates vomiting their first meal, their bodies no longer used to digesting anything but watery soup. He looked down at the deep burgundy glaze with its sliver of truffle.

"Such vegetables. This time of year."

"California," Ben said. "They grow all year round. Have you been able to get out? See anything?"

"The ocean. Fay took me for a drive. The rest, it's all houses, no—buildings. Not like Berlin."

"Liesl's father says it's still the first layer here. Before the Schinkels."

He smiled but she seemed not to understand this, at a loss. She looked over at Liesl.

"She's your wife?"

"No," he said, looking across with her, so that Liesl smiled back.

"Maybe one day. See how she looks at you."

"No," Ben said, flustered. "She's my brother's wife. Was."

"I don't understand. The same brother? He wasn't killed? Years ago."

"No, just this month. Why did you think—"

"Why? It was so dangerous. Back and forth. The courier. I never thought it was right—for your father to use a boy like that. Well, not a boy. Still, young. To risk his life. When you said he was dead, I thought, yes, it must be. Of course they killed him."

"Who?" Ben said, suddenly feeling light-headed.

"The Nazis," she said simply. "It was always a risk."

"For an American?"

"A Communist," she said, her voice steady, matter-of-fact.

"What?"

"You didn't know this?"

Involuntarily, Ben glanced toward Minot's table, apprehensive, the word itself now like a pointing finger. But no one in the room was paying attention, hearing anything more than a murmuring of German. Only Ben felt the words shouting in his ears. He shook his head slowly, barely moving.

"And he never told you? Well, that's right. We had to be secret to survive. The first enemy. Even before they started killing Jews. No one was safe from them. I said to Otto, how can you use your own? But of course it was important to him. And he was like you—an American passport would protect him, they wouldn't suspect. His mother's in England. Of course he travels. So, a courier."

"For the Communists," Ben said numbly, as if repeating the words would give a sense to them, steady the room.

"Yes, for your father. Anything for your father. For him it was like a religion, so maybe for the boy, too. I don't know."

"Like a religion," Ben said, still catching echoes.

"Yes. And he died for it."

"For being a Communist? That's why he stayed in Germany?" Not another woman, a career he couldn't leave behind, a misguided sense of safety.

"They didn't suspect him. He could do things the others couldn't. Goebbels liked him. All of them—they liked to watch those comedies. They thought he was like that. So he was useful to the Party. So close and they didn't suspect."

"They didn't protect him, either. He was still a Jew."

"That's what you think? All these years. That he was foolish? That he trusted them?" She shook her head. "They didn't kill him as a Jew. They killed him as a Communist." She paused. "He was betrayed," she said, her voice suddenly low, looking away, across the table.

Ben said nothing. He heard forks, people laughing, sound track noises from another movie. In this one, everything was still. He looked at Genia's hands, the bony fingers resting now on the table, pale, webbed with veins, the hands of an old woman.

"How do you know that?" he said finally.

For a minute she kept looking across the table, then turned to him. "Because it was me. I betrayed him," she said, her voice still detached, a confession without emotion or self-pity, something willed. He felt it like a hand on his arm, a restraint, making him look directly at her. "Why? Why else? To save myself." Staring back, the rest unsaid. Then she looked away, breaking the connection. "But I didn't. Not in the end." She picked up the small bag at her side. "Excuse me. I must have a cigarette. Apologies."

She stood up, catching Liesl's attention, who looked at Ben, first with casual curiosity, then, taking him in, with real alarm. Paulette was already putting her hand on his.

"I'm not ignoring you, really. Mike was just telling me about Selznick. You know, he's still in therapy. He believes in it. Since *Spellbound*. I said he could save a bundle and just give up the *pills*— Are you all right? You look as if you'd seen a ghost."

He tried to smile, shaking this off.

"Seriously. You're all white."

Finally the smile. "Just old war stories. I'm fine."

From the corner of his eye he could see the emerald bracelet covering his hand. At the next table Fay and Ann Sheridan were charming Minot, who wanted to get rid of termites. Bunny, apparently still worried about the seating, kept looking over at Liesl, watching her. Jack Warner was telling jokes. The waiters had begun to clear the tournedos, replacing it with floating island, puffy clouds of meringue. And Otto had risked Danny's life. The one Ben knew nothing about.

"I'd better check on her, make sure she's okay," he said to Paulette, getting up.

Liesl, still concerned, shot him a what? look, but he made a nothing movement with his head. As he crossed the room, still half in a daze, he noticed Bunny chatting with Marie Minot, keeping things going.

She was sitting behind the coffee table, tapping her cigarette on the rim of the ashtray.

"I thought I would never say that," she said, not even looking up, as if she'd expected him. "Not to anybody. And now his son. For years I thought, what if someone finds out? What if someone knows? And it doesn't matter. None of it matters."

"Everything matters."

She looked at him, then made a half smile. "To the living." She drew on the cigarette. "So, what do you want me to say to you? An apology? It's late for that."

"Tell me about Danny. What did he actually do? My father made him carry things?"

"In his mind only," she said, tapping the side of her head. "Messages he had to remember. No papers. If they had found papers, they would have arrested him. Killed him. So it was safer up here. Of course, if they tortured him, he would have told them—everybody did—but without papers there was no reason to suspect him. And an American passport. They couldn't arrest Americans so easily. So he was perfect for us."

"My father's idea?"

She nodded. "There was a problem. Before, we had a network with merchant seamen, for outside communications. You couldn't use the radio. By hand. By mouth. And then there was a roundup—one of the cells in Hamburg—and we knew they had been given away. An informer. We traced it to one of the sailors, so we couldn't use the network anymore. That's when your father had the idea. The one person he could really trust." She stopped. "Except me, he said. But he couldn't send me. So he was wrong about that, too."

"But what did he actually carry? What kind of messages."

She shrugged. "To help get people out. At that point, all we were trying to do was survive. Save ourselves. There weren't so many left. He would travel through Paris. There were people there who could make arrangements, to get people across. This was before the war. If we could get people to France—"

And later to Spain, Ben thought, helped across by someone with experience. By then you didn't have to be a Communist to be in danger.

"So we used him for that. Not a spy, not like in the films. Just messages, to help get people out."

"But he would have been hung just the same. If they'd caught him."

"Yes, naturally. That's why I thought it was too dangerous. But he wanted to do it. You know, at that age—no fear. It's exciting to them, everything a secret. They don't know yet what it's like to live that way, to live in secret." She rubbed out the cigarette. "But he survived, you said, so I'm glad for that. They never got him. Well, he stopped when Otto— He did it for Otto. He never came back to Germany after that. So maybe that saved him."

"Tell me what happened. With my father."

"It's not so much to know," she said, shrugging. "A familiar story. They caught me. My fault—I was careless. So, Prinz-Albrecht-Strasse. We used to talk about it, if the Gestapo— I knew what it would mean. Not just for me. My family. They didn't have to torture me. I already knew what they wanted, the names. Who was head of the cell? Well, Otto, Goebbels's friend." She looked up. "So I gave them your father."

"And they let you go? I thought—"

"Yes, usually they killed you, too. After you told them. We all knew that. They had no more use for you."

He looked at her, waiting.

"I agreed to give them names I didn't know yet. To be an informer. They thought I would do it—so weak, they hadn't even had to beat me. A coward. With blood on her hands. What they wanted."

"And did you?"

"Only to get out. To have a chance to escape. I knew they would watch. But we did it, my family. We went into hiding. The Party helped us, the ones who were left. They thought whoever had betrayed Otto had betrayed me, too, so they helped us. Safe houses. We lived like that, place to place. No one ever knew I'd given them Otto. Of course by that time it didn't matter if you were a Communist—it was enough to be a Jew. So we hid. Do you want to hear the rest?"

"How he died."

"I don't know that. Shot, I suppose. I hope it was that. No, what happened after. Not everything, don't worry, not all the horrors. Just enough to know why it's like this now. Why isn't she weeping? On her knees begging forgiveness—"

"You don't owe me any—"

"Doesn't she feel anything, facing me, Otto's son? What kind of person is this? That it doesn't matter to her. Can't even say she's sorry."

"Isn't that what you're doing now?" he said gently.

She shook her head. "It's too late for that. So, one story only. Something you can't put in a film. Never mind the hiding, the rest of it.

How you feel in the line, select one here for work, select him for the gas. Impossible to understand that, even when it's happening to you. So impossible for you." She took a breath. "We were back in Berlin then— the first big roundup. 1942, February. Cold. All of us in a basement, like rats, but still. Leon, my sister, her husband, all down there, but safe. Then not safe." She looked up. "We were betrayed. Maybe a justice. Anyway, Jews in the cellar, so they came for us. You don't fight, but they pull you out anyway. Poke the guns in your stomach. Yelling. I can hear them now, it never goes away, the yelling. And it frightens Rosa, my sister's baby. An infant. 'Shut it up,' he screams at her. The soldier. As if she could do something—all that noise, so terrifying. Terrifying to *us*. And she tries to quiet it, against her shoulder, you know, rocking, while they're pushing us out and it's not enough for him. 'Shut up!' he yells and then he grabs it, right out of her arms. A second, my heart stops. Now, too, I can see it. He takes Rosa by the feet and before my sister can move he smacks her against the wall, swinging her like a doll, once, that's all, because then it's quiet. He drops her like a rag, a piece of— I don't know. A thump, and then blood on the wall, a blotch, little streaks. There's nothing in his face. It doesn't matter to him. This takes—how long? How long can the heart stop? A second, less. And it's my whole life in that time. Then I hear my sister scream and I'm some-where else, another life."

She stopped, almost out of breath, shutting her eyes, then reached for another cigarette, something tangible, right now, and lit it.

"She brought it with us. She picked it up and brought it. They didn't care. On the train. Until Leon managed to get it away from her, get rid of it. By that time she didn't know. She was—not herself. So of course they selected her right away for the gas, a madwoman. Right on the platform." She looked up at him. "Tell me anything matters. Otto's son." She reached out and grazed his hand with her fingertips. "If it did matter, I would be sorry. Do you know that?"

She turned her head, distracted by the sound of doors opening.

"Here they come. They're going to watch a film." She stood, drawing him up with her. "Make some excuse for me, yes? Headache, whatever you like, it doesn't matter." She smiled to herself, a weak grimace. "That, either."

She slipped out behind the stream of people heading for the bathrooms before the movie started. It seemed a disorganized moment, an aimless milling, like the scattering pieces in his head.

"What's wrong? What was all that?" Liesl said.

He stared for a second, adjusting to the switch back to English, his mind elsewhere.

"Nothing. She's— I'll tell you later," he said, looking at her closely now. Had she known? How could she not? Unless Danny had kept this secret, too. "Can we cut out before the movie? What's the form?"

"We can't. It would be considered an insult," she said. "Listen, I have to talk to you. I think I know—"

"Later," he said, touching her arm. "Here's Bunny."

"Everything fine?" Bunny said, looking at Liesl. "Did you enjoy Dick?"

Her dinner partner had been Dick Marshall, out of his pilot uniform, a smile replacing the oxygen mask. More window dressing for the party.

"Yes, he was very funny."

"I'll bet," Bunny said, but relieved, as if he'd expected a different report. He turned to Ben. "And you. I thought it'd be pulling teeth, but there you were, nattering away."

Ben felt fuzzy, a diver decompressing too fast. Why were they talking about any of this? Floating on froth, like the meringues.

"Mr. L can't get two words out of her. Well, we'd better start the picture before the natives get restless. Glad you enjoyed yourself," he said to Liesl. "You've got a treat in store—Jack sent over something special."

"Ben," she said, when Bunny left, "at dinner—"

"She knew Otto," he said. "She knew Danny."

"Daniel?"

"In Berlin. When he was with my father. She thought the Nazis had killed him. He was getting people out. The way he helped you, later. It started then. Why didn't you tell me he was a Communist?"

"What are you talking about?" she said, nervous, unprepared for this.

"She told me. She was there. You must have known."

"Known what," she said, a quick dismissal. She looked toward the room, measuring their distance from the others, then back at him. "He never said. Everyone was a bit then. They were against the Nazis. Organized. There wouldn't have been a resistance if they hadn't—"

"You never asked?"

"I didn't care about that. Politics. When someone throws you a lifesaver, you take it."

"And marry him."

Her eyes flashed. "It wasn't important." She looked down, biting her lip. "I thought he was—sympathetic, that's all. So maybe he worked with them, everyone did. It was never official—you know, a Party member. Meetings. I would have known about that. It was a way of looking at things then, because of the Nazis. Years ago. Anyway, that was there. It was different after we came here."

"It's not something you stop, just like that."

"Things change. People change."

"Do they?"

"You think that? That's what you're looking for in his desk? A card? A letter from Stalin? I would have *known*." She looked away, hearing herself, yesterday's certainty. "He made movies here, that's all. Silly movies."

"So did my father. And he ran a cell. According to her."

"If you want to know, ask them. The Party."

"I don't think they're handing out membership lists these days."

"Ask Howard Stein. It's always in the papers about him. That he must be one. Polly says he is. Ask him. Why is it so important anyway?"

"Because we have to know everything about him. What he was doing. Why anyone would—"

"No. You have to know. I don't know why. Look, they're going in. No more about this. The way people talk. Who knows what's true. My father's applying for citizenship. How would it look? A Communist son."

"A dead one."

"Well, my father's alive. Talk like this—"

"We have to know. It might be important." He took her elbow. "Don't run away from this. Help me. We owe it to him."

"Owe it to him." She smiled to herself, then looked up. "I was trying to help. Before you started with all this. Politics. They don't kill you for that yet. Maybe not love, either. You want to know the girlfriend? Rosemary." She nodded. "Maybe not the only one, I don't know. So does that help? Does she look like—"

"How do you know?"

"I know. I knew at the table. The way she was with me. She wouldn't look at me. Not once. I could see her do it, not looking. And then she heard who you were and she was upset. She wasn't ready for that. The wife, that's one thing. But you—"

"That's it, the proof?"

"You can prove it any way you like. I already know. It's her," she said, turning away so that before he could say anything else she had already joined the people moving toward the screening room.

He followed, his mind darting again, his feet moving on their own, in another place. Around him people were talking about the movie, overheard but echoing, like voices in a train station.

Warner's treat turned out to be *Saratoga Trunk*, a Bergman not yet released.

"I've been sitting on this since over a year," Jack said.

"You're worried?" Sol said.

"Not worried. Sam Wood, you're always going to get an A product. Getting the time right. They put her in dark hair, in period, and I'm thinking, they want *Casablanca* again, not this. A totally different type. So I wait, we hold the picture. Then what? *The Bells of St. Mary's* for Christmas. Talk about timing. I figure after that they'll like her in anything. Put it out right after, you can't miss. Same season. You can't get into the Crosby, see the other."

"Well, the Crosby," Sol said. "They're already counting the money."

"Hundred bucks it grosses more than anything this year. The Catholics alone. You know how they come out for nuns."

"Jack."

"A hundred bucks."

There were no assigned seats in the theater, so Ben and Liesl sat together toward the back. Minot and his wife, still being charmed, were in the front row with the Lasners and the Warners. Bunny walked up the aisle like someone counting the house, making sure everything was in place. The lights dimmed, followed by a blast of music. When the Warner logo came on, people applauded, a jokey tribute to Jack.

Within minutes Ben saw why Warner had waited. Ingrid Bergman was in a bustle, pretending to be Creole. There was a dwarf and Flora Robeson in blackface as a maid who knew voodoo. Gary Cooper was Gary Cooper, a Texan. His name seemed to be Clint Maroon. None of it made sense, and Ben drifted, not really paying attention. Somewhere upstairs Fay's cousin was lying on a bed smoking, seeing a splotch of blood on a wall. He thought of her bony hand on his. How can you use your own? But Otto had. Like a religion to him. Abraham ready to sacrifice Isaac—by whose orders? The priests of the International? Wherever orders came from. Your own son. Who wanted to do it. Fearless. He went through the dinner again, trying to piece the parts of Danny's life together, looking for some clear thread that ran from Berlin to the Cherokee. But what? It seemed as patchy and unlikely as the movie, even without the dwarf.

Liesl wasn't watching, either. He could feel her beside him, restless in her seat, maybe looking for Rosemary. Knowing it was her, a feeling. The girl most likely. Someone Bunny would make a call for. Dating Ty Power while they built her up, not a B director on a B lot. But when Liesl leaned toward him to whisper, her mind was somewhere else.

"Why would he keep it secret? From me? Why that? I wouldn't have cared about that."

He felt her breath against him before he heard her, warm, reaching into him. When he turned her face was even closer, her eyes shiny, anxious. He sorted out the words. Not about Rosemary. But then he saw in her eyes that it was really the same question, another betrayal.

"I don't know," he said, less than a whisper, but feeling her breath again, the warmth coming off her skin with the last of the perfume, and suddenly, a trace memory, he was a teenager with a girl in a dark theater, so close, trying not to be overwhelmed by it. Wanting to lean forward, afraid to. In a second she would move back, the contact broken. But she didn't. The whispers became tactile, like a hand against the side of his face.

"Do you believe her, the cousin?"

"Yes."

"But why would he?"

"I don't know," he said again.

"Everything secret."

Now she did look away, dismayed, reminded of other secrets. She sat back, pretending to watch the movie, seemingly unaware that he didn't move, his head turned, as if her face were still next to his. Then someone coughed and he went back to the screen, wondering whether anyone had noticed, whether it showed on your face, the way he used to think it did when the lights came up, kids necking in the balcony.

Think about something else. Why had Danny kept it secret? Even from his wife. Politics were public, argued about. Unless there'd been a turning away, a new life that made the past embarrassing, something to put behind you. Howard Stein had said he'd even faded away from the union, no longer interested. You get to want other things. Which still didn't explain how he'd ended up in the alley at the Cherokee.

Saratoga Trunk was a hit with the party, ending to applause and pats on the back. Then everyone began to leave at once, pouring out of Lasner's chateau as if it were a downtown theater, without red trolley cars and taxis, just harried teenage parkers. The Warners and the Minots were the first to go, Bunny hovering nearby, followed by a halting line of impatient guests.

"Did you meet the Honorable Ken?" Bunny said, waiting with them.

"I heard him. That was good enough. Who voted for him anyway?"

"The same people who go to the movies." He looked up. "We don't make the world. Right now, he's what they like."

"Jack liked him anyway. That was the point, wasn't it?"

"Jack likes Jack. But it's a start. Glad you enjoyed the evening," he said to Liesl, another question mark, still working.

When she thanked him, a bland response, Ben noticed the quick flicker of relief in his eyes. Relieved about what? That she'd got on with Dick Marshall? Or that nothing more awkward had happened, placed at Rosemary's table? Something Bunny hadn't expected.

Another car left, the line moving forward. Bunny was looking at her again.

"Do you mind my asking? Are you a dancer?"

"A dancer?" Liesl said. "No. Why?"

"You move very well," he said, still looking at her.

"Oh," she said, not sure how to respond. A professional appraisal, not a pass.

"Maybe it's the theater," Ben said. "Same training."

"You're an actress?" Bunny said.

"Before, in Vienna. Not here."

Bunny tilted his head, taking her in at a slightly different angle. "But not in pictures. Would you make a test?"

"A test?"

"To see how you look," Bunny said simply. "People are different on film."

"Oh, and with my voice."

"Never mind about that. It's just—it gave me an idea, the way you moved. If you're interested."

Liesl nodded, still too surprised to answer.

"I'll send you some pages, then. Here we are," he said, opening the door as the car pulled up.

Liesl stood there for a second, hesitant, then got in, taking direction. Bunny bent forward, eye level with the window.

"Maybe nothing," he said. "Let's just see. We'll call you."

In the car she was quiet, looking out the open window at the dark hedges and driveways, Beverly Hills asleep.

"This place," she said, partly to herself. "Years. And then one night you walk into a party. So I should thank you for that."

"He's not doing it for me. You really interested?"

She shrugged. "It doesn't mean anything. They test everybody. Favors."

"Not Bunny."

"Ha. Place your bets. So maybe it comes up." She looked out again. "And maybe it doesn't. So let's see, what else am I going to do now?"

She pushed in the dashboard lighter, then rummaged in her purse for a cigarette.

"Do you think she's pretty?"

"Who?"

"Who," she said, waiting.

"I think she looks like you."

She stopped the lighter in midair, then put the red coiled tip to the cigarette.

"You do?"

"Maybe they were all you."

She went quiet again, smoking. "That's nice," she said softly. "To say that." She turned from the window. "Then why have them."

"I don't know," he said, keeping his eyes on the road. "Did you?"

"What, have others?" She turned up her lips slightly. "You mean since he did?" She shook her head. "Only before. You want to know how many?"

"I didn't mean—"

"I don't even remember. That life, it made you that way. You never knew when you'd have to leave. Go somewhere else. So you took what you could. I was no different. But not after."

"Why not?"

"I wasn't brought up that way. When you're married— You know I can cook? Sew. All those things. A good wife, for somebody. But not him."

They entered the house through the garage, turning off the driveway lights behind them.

"Do you want a swim?" she said, unclasping her pearls as they walked. "It's good after a party—for hangovers."

"You go ahead." He smiled. "Don't worry, I won't watch."

"Well, then good night. Thank you for the party. My evening with the stars."

She reached up and kissed his cheek, then stopped, her face as close as it had been in the theater, but this time looking at him, her eyes moving, as if she were reading him, deciphering. He stood still, feeling her breath again, then the graze of her hand behind his neck drawing him closer to kiss him on the mouth. He opened his, almost dizzy with surprise and the taste of her. They broke, a gasp for air, then kissed again, her mouth open to his, both of them eager.

"What are you doing?" he said, moving down to her neck, smelling perfume and warm skin.

She pulled back. "I wanted to know what it would be like."

He looked at her, their faces still close. "I'm not him."

She smiled, moving her hand to his forehead, gently brushing the hair away.

"No. Someone else."

He felt her hand, fingertips barely touching his skin but drawing him back, a kind of permission, then lowered his head to hers again, no longer thinking, all instinct. Her mouth was moist, all of her warm, rubbing against him so that his blood rushed, excited. She started unbuttoning his shirt, her mouth still on his, then pulled away, both of them panting, holding each other. Are we going to do this, a look, not words, and she answered by taking his hand, leading him into the bedroom, the furniture just shadows outlined by the pool lights outside. She turned her back to him so he could undo her zipper, move the dress off her shoulders, letting it slide down, then hold her there, kissing the back of her neck, no longer groping, smooth, wanting to kiss every part of her, this shoulder, that one.

She arched her back, an involuntary intake of breath, then a small sound, dropping her head so that he could kiss more of her neck, giving it to him. When he reached around to her breasts, holding them underneath, moving his thumbs against her nipples, her body came up again, pushing back against him, and he felt her bare behind, the soft round cheeks, press against the erection in his pants. They stood that way for a minute, her nipples growing hard, his groin tight against her, until he thought he would burst from it and he turned her around, kissing her mouth, then her breasts, faster, tearing off his clothes, then laying her on the bed and falling over her, his mouth covering hers, his hand moving down between her legs, feeling her wet, beginning to move against his hand.

There was no waiting, no drawn-out stroking, everything that might come later. Only an urgency, mindless. She pulled him into her, one thrust, a second to feel her wrapped around him, the wonderful fullness, and then they were moving again, not a steady rhythm, but a heedless plunging, impossible to wait, both of them grunting. He saw her in the pool, opening her legs to the patch of hair, where he was now, then he didn't see anything, could only hear her, next to his ear, breathing, then noises, little cries, as exciting as the slick feel of her pushing against him. When she came, a louder cry, broken, like a shuddering, he could feel her grip him inside and he wanted to shout, let something out before he exploded, and then the come shot out of him and he stopped, feeling the last jerks, his whole body emptying, then flooded with relief, inexplicable pleasure. He moved his elbow, falling on her, and it was only then that he felt the sweat, both of them shiny with it.

When he rolled away, she turned with him and they lay on their sides, heads touching, not saying anything, drained, then her body began to shake, not crying, a trembling.

"What?" he said quietly, touching her.

She shook her head. "Nothing. It's just—to feel something again." She put her hand on him.

He took her shoulder, drawing her closer and kissing her. "I'm sorry it was so fast."

"No, don't be sorry."

"Next time we won't have to hurry."

She propped herself up, looking down at him.

"Already a next time. You're so sure," she said lazily.

"Now I know you."

"You think that's true? You sleep with someone and you know her? All those girls before—you knew them? Every one?"

"I didn't want to know them."

"Just go to bed. Very nice. And now that you've seduced me—"

"Me?"

She smiled, moving her hand down his chest. "You're sweaty."

He moved his hand up to her breast, running the back along it.

"Come on," she said, getting off the bed.

"How can you move? Where?"

"Just come."

She pulled his hand and he followed, his eyes trailing her white skin, feeling illicit walking naked through the dark house. He put his hand on the smooth flesh of her behind, cupping it, and she laughed, then sprang away, opening the patio door and running across the tiles to the pool, looking over her shoulder once at him before she plunged in. He ran after her, the front of him flapping in the warm night air, then jumped in, too, and swam after her underwater, his testicles floating beneath him, everything free. When he caught up to her, they both rose to the surface.

"Isn't it wonderful?" she said, shaking her hair. "I never want to wear clothes again."

"All right," he said, kissing her.

She laughed. "And you'd like that?"

She swam a little toward the shallow end so they could hold each other without having to keep afloat in deep water.

"You know, my father says you can only seduce someone who wants to be seduced. Otherwise it can't work."

"When did he say that?" Ben said, kissing her again.

"In a story. *Die Verführung.*"

"*The Seduction.* He wrote a love story?"

She giggled. "Well, it was about Germany. How the country wanted to be seduced by Hitler. But I think it's the same with people. Like you," she said, touching his face.

"What about you?"

He drew her against him as they kissed, not playing anymore, aroused again, drawing one leg up around her.

"Everyone thinks it should be easy in the water," she said, "but it's hard. Maybe Esther Williams can."

"Who?"

"You don't know her? *Bathing Beauty?* With Cugat? Daniel did some Second Unit work on it." She stopped, looking away.

"We didn't get everything overseas," he said, trying to glide over it.

"Maybe it was like this for him," she said, distracted. "With the others. All like me. So now I'm one of them."

He let his leg drop, freeing her below, then turned her head with his fingers. "I'm not him."

She glanced up and moved her shoulder. "And you don't love me, either. So that's the same anyway. But I know it. So nobody gets hurt."

"Nobody gets hurt." Not wanting to go further, coaxing her back.

"Someone you meet at a party. Why not her?"

"Is that what it feels like to you?"

She looked at him for a second, her eyes opening wider, then pulled him closer, leaning her head into his.

"Make love to me," she said, her voice quick and raspy.

He glanced over the side of the pool. "The chaise," he said, kissing her.

"Yes, on the chaise," she said, amused. "Like an odalisque." She took his hand, urgent again, leading him up the shallow steps, shivering a little as the breeze touched them.

He held her to him, his body a blanket, then lay down next to her.

"Now you seduce me," she said.

"You have to want me to," he said, stroking her. "That's how it works."

She pulled herself up, her wet hair falling on him, then took his penis into her, straddling him. She closed her eyes, just feeling him there for a second, then slowly sat up, moving just a little, looking down on him. "This time we don't have to hurry."

This time it was slow enough to feel everything, every part, until they came again, gasping, and then fell back together, not talking, just breathing. Ben could see the city lights in the distance, hear the palm fronds overhead clicking in the soft air, the sound of paradise.

After a while it turned cooler, and he went over to the changing cabana and brought back two robes. She wrapped herself in one and reached for a cigarette pack on the table, then crunched it up.

"There are more in the house," she said. "Can I get you anything? A drink?"

He shook his head, then raised the back of the chaise to sit upright. He watched her go in, a blur of white through half-closed eyes, and leaned back, smelling the night flowers. A light went on in the house. In a minute, he knew, his body would start to go limp and he'd drift, the animal languor that came after sex. Everything else could wait until tomorrow—what had happened, what it would mean. Now there was just this.

"Ben." She was back at the door, her body tense, voice nervous. She waved him toward her, as if she were afraid of being overheard.

He crossed the patio, tilting his head in a question.

"Somebody's been in the house," she said, keeping her voice low.

"What?"

"In the office. Things were different. Moved. I could tell." She put her hand on his arm. "Maybe they're still here." Her eyes darting, upset.

"You're sure? You didn't lock the doors?"

"Of course I locked the doors. This one, too," she said, nodding to the patio door. "Sometimes Iris forgets."

He looked down at the door handle. No scratches or chipped paint, but an easy lock, he guessed, for someone who knew how.

"What if they're still *here*," she said, gripping his arm tighter.

"Calm down. There's no one here." He thought of them on the bed, grunting, someone watching—but they would have felt that, sensed anyone's presence, wouldn't they? "I'll walk through." He flicked on a light. "Is anything missing?"

"I don't know. I just went to the study, for cigarettes."

"What was moved?"

"Little things. On the desk."

"Maybe Iris—"

"No. It didn't seem right. I could feel it."

"Another feeling?"

"Don't laugh at me," she said, almost snapping. "Someone was here. In the house." She clutched the top of her robe tighter, her voice rising a pitch.

"All right, I'll look. Where do you keep your valuables?"

She looked at him blankly.

"Jewels," he said. "Cash."

"Jewels? Just the pearls—in the bedroom."

But the bedroom was untouched, except for the bed, the spread twisted and still damp from sex. Nobody had taken anything from the bureau drawer, the velvet box with earrings and a clip. There was still money under the handkerchiefs.

He went through the rest of the house, turning on lights, Liesl close to him, still anxious, fear bobbing just beneath the surface. Not just an intruder, a more general violation.

"Ever have any trouble before?" Ben said.

"No, it was safe. I was safe here."

"You're still safe," he said, taking her by the shoulders. "Stop."

"You don't know what it's like," she said, not really hearing him. "Every knock. Always looking back. I thought it was different here."

"Liesl, nothing's missing. So, just in here?" he said, turning in to the study.

162

She nodded. "The desk. Somebody went through the desk."

"How do you know?"

"It's different. Look at the blotter—see the one end out? To look under. See for yourself. You know his drawers."

She picked up the cigarettes, lighting one now, her hand shaking, then stood watching him go through the drawer. Everything seemed the same. Until the second drawer, the folders of personal papers. The police accident report, jammed at the end, not where he'd put it.

"What?" she said, seeing him hesitate.

"Something's out of place."

He went through the envelope, flipping through the photos.

"Everything's here. Probably where I put it, just looked different."

"No, you noticed."

"Liesl, why would someone break into the house and not take money—anything—just go through a desk?"

"His desk."

"All right, his desk."

She inhaled smoke, then folded her arms across her chest, holding herself in. "It's what you said. I didn't believe you. Why would anybody do that? I thought it was just your way of—" She broke off, hearing herself, racing. "But it's true, isn't it? Maybe I always knew it. That he wouldn't. I didn't want to be afraid. And now they're in my house. Somebody killed him and they're still not finished. What do they want?"

"I don't know," he said, coming over to her.

"Maybe they think I have it—whatever they want."

"They didn't go through your things. Just his."

"I can't stay here. Listening. Any noise. I'll go to my father's."

He took her by the shoulders, as if he were holding her down before she could fly away.

"I'm here. You're just nervous, that's all. I'll be right next to you. All night."

"Oh, next to me, and what will Iris think?" An automatic response.

He smiled at her. "The worst, probably."

"How can you joke?"

"I'll check the doors. Nothing is going to happen to you. I promise." He kissed her forehead. "If you're worried about the house, I'll talk to somebody. Make it safe."

"Who?"

"Guy I met. He'd know."

She dropped her head to his chest. "When is it going to be over? The phone rings—your husband's in—when was that? And it's still not over. What did he do? Go with Rosemary? And he's dead for that? It's crazy. And now you. What am I doing? His brother." She raised her head. "Maybe that's crazy, too. My lover."

"Say that again," he said, brushing her hair.

She looked away. "Oh, that doesn't make it any better."

"It doesn't have to make sense. It happens. We wanted it to." He paused. "We seduced each other."

"So nothing makes sense."

"What happened to him. We have to make sense of that." He touched her hair again. "Just that."

LIESL'S FATHER'S birthday went exactly as predicted. Dieter read a long prepared toast, then Ostermann stood up for his own prepared thank-you. The others were more spontaneous, but none of them brief. "The Conscience of Germany," a glib phrase from *Time,* had now become a kind of honorary title, his own *von*. The toasts ran to form: the books, the humanitarian concerns, the early courage in speaking out, all noted before and repeated now, familiar as myth.

The dinner itself followed a prescribed pattern. It had been called for late afternoon, a throwback to the curfew days when aliens had to be home by eight, and the food, according to Liesl, was unvarying—steaming bowls of chicken soup with liver dumplings, boiled beef with horseradish, potatoes, and red cabbage, followed finally by Salka's chocolate cake, a menu that seemed designed to weigh people down in their chairs for the toasts. Later, after the brandies, there would be coffee and mohn cookies, more winter food as the California sun poured through the window.

Salka's house, on a steep wooded road dropping down into Santa Monica Canyon, was modest, a doll's house compared to Lasner's. The guests were many of the same people who'd come to Danny's funeral, and they greeted Ben like an old friend with the fast hospitality of exiles. Brecht was there again and spent most of the time arguing with someone in a corner. Lion Feuchtwanger, interrupting, playing peacemaker; Fritz Lang, with a monocle. Thomas Mann had not come this time, a social deference, not wanting to eclipse the birthday honoree. Kaltenbach wore a suit that needed cleaning.

Ben noticed scarcely any of it, preoccupied, the German toasts droning in the background, Liesl down the table, her face half-hidden by one of Salka's flower arrangements. Did she look different? Did he? Could anyone tell? If he looked down at the lace tablecloth, blotting out the rest, he could see her last night, riding him, her breasts bobbing, and he smiled to himself because no one else knew, their secret. Maybe this was the excitement spies felt, sitting down with the enemy, knowing something, holding it to themselves, while no one else had the faintest idea. What was more secretive than sex? Kaltenbach stood up to make his toast. Ben glanced down again at Liesl, this time meeting her eyes, amused, talking to him in code, just the two of them.

When he went out to the kitchen to open more wine she followed, standing behind as he pulled the corkscrew, putting her hand on his waist. He turned, their faces close.

"Somebody'll see," he said quietly, glancing toward the dining room, the angle of the table.

She pulled at his shirt, moving them away from the sink, the open door.

"No, they won't," she said, urgent, her eyes darting with excitement. "Not here." Kissing him then, her lips warm, unexpected, alive with risk. From the dining room there was the tinkle of glass, and they kissed harder, racing ahead of it.

JOSEPH KANON

He pulled away, breathless. "They'll see," he said, already hard, his face red with it, unmistakable.

"I don't care," she said, eyes shiny, still moving, then leaned forward again. "I don't care."

Not really meaning it, playing, but the words flooding into him like sex itself, rushing, wonderful. Then there was the scrape of a chair and he turned back to the counter, grasping the wine bottle, and she slipped over to the refrigerator, opening it with a faint suppressed giggle, kids stealing cookies, waiting to be found out. He took a breath to calm himself and started in with the wine. But when he saw that the chair belonged to Ostermann, standing to respond to a toast, he glanced back at Liesl, a complicit smile, something they'd got away with after all.

After dinner Salka led the party down Mabery Road to the beach to watch the sunset. Ben had volunteered to drive Feuchtwanger home, a cliffside house on a twisting Palisades road that would be treacherous in the dark, so he was late joining the others on the broad beach. People who'd come earlier for the day were still in bathing suits or sweatshirts and stared openly at Salka's group in suits and ties. Liesl took her shoes off, but the men didn't bother, formal even in the sand. The light on the water had already begun to turn the deep gold just before orange.

"You know I was twelve before I saw the ocean?" Ostermann said to Ben. They were walking with Dieter, the others straggling behind. "Fifty years ago. More now. The *Nordsee*. Absolutely gray. Freezing. Rocks for beaches. But my father had paid for the week, so we had to stay." He made a mock shudder at the memory.

"So, something else good here," Dieter said, indicating the white sand.

"Yes, but shallow. You have to walk far before you can swim. That's why they build the piers." He nodded to the amusement pier farther down the beach. "Me, I prefer lakes. Of course, it's what I knew. The *Wannsee*. Anyway, Liesl's the swimmer, not me. From a child, always in the water."

"Yes. She loves the pool," Ben said, seeing her gliding underwater, parting her legs. Everyone thinks it would be easy in the water, but it's not. Preferring a chaise.

He looked over at Ostermann, suddenly embarrassed. Change the subject.

"She told me about *Die Verführung*," he said. "I've never read it. Is it in a collection?"

"No, alone. Quieros did it in Holland. A small edition. It was not so popular, you know. Not even the émigrés liked it. Anti-German. Me, anti-German."

"It's a German failing," Dieter said. "Thin skin."

"And thick boots," Ostermann said. "A wonderful combination. Anyway, no one read it. I thought they might buy it for the title," he said, teasing. "They would think it's something else. But no one did."

"You always write about Germany," Dieter said. "Everybody knows that. And this time—be fair—a fatal flaw in the blood, an insult."

"No, not in the blood. That's what the Nazis believed, things in the blood. Destiny. It wasn't like that. A whole country seduced. Led into a dream. You have to make that happen." He raised his finger, a classroom gesture. "But they have to want the dream. The master race. Imagine—to believe that. If it's German, it's better. Well, the French, too. Maybe everyone. Look at them here. 'The Greatest Country in the World.' What does that mean? Great how? But they believe it."

"It's not the same," Dieter said. "What happened there was unique."

"You think so? Well, let's hope. It's not so hard, you know. Give them something to be afraid of. Someone else. The process is the same."

"Did Danny ever talk to you about this?" Ben said. "Liesl said he liked to talk to you."

"About this?" Ostermann said, confused. "The story? He said it was different here." He nodded to Dieter, a point. "He said they were already seduced. By the movies."

"Ha," Dieter said. "He was serious?"

Ostermann shrugged. "Well, an idea. To make talk. That was his world, not politics."

"He never talked to you about politics?" Ben said.

"Maybe I talked enough for both of us," Ostermann said wryly. "Of course you know he worked against the Nazis. To get people out of France. But I think that was for the adventure. He had that spirit. But here—"

"But someone told me last night he was a Communist. You'd think—"

"People are always saying such things now," Dieter said. "Every day in the papers. How many could there be? Just for signing a petition." A glance to Ostermann.

"No, the woman knew him. In Berlin. She said he worked for them."

"In Berlin?" Ostermann said. "But he must have been a boy."

"Old enough. He helped my father."

"What woman?"

"Fay Lasner's cousin. Genia. She was in the camps."

"To survive that," Dieter said, impressed. "Genia. A Polish name?"

"Originally. But she knew him in Berlin."

"But saying such things at dinner. To accuse—"

"She wasn't accusing him of anything. She was one, too."

"And he never said anything to you?" Dieter said. "His brother? It's her imagination, I think."

"What did you think when you were eighteen?" Ostermann said gently, putting a hand on Ben's shoulder. "Do you remember? I was for the Kaiser. A young man's ideas. Things change. Maybe he changed, too. A flirtation and then you want to put it behind you."

"Especially now," Dieter said. "The way things are. Even at the school. Checking on everybody. So strict. What do they think we write on the blackboards?" He nodded toward Ostermann. "Maybe you can help me persuade The Conscience of Germany to keep his conscience to himself a little. It's not a good time to show these opinions."

"When was the good time, 'thirty-three?"

Dieter gave Ben a see-what-I-mean? look, then turned to the water. "Look, it's setting. At the end, so fast."

"Do you know why?" Liesl said, coming up to them, slipping her arm through Dieter's.

"Of course," he said, affectionate. "When the horizon line—"

She reached up and kissed him on the cheek. "I'm teasing. Of course you know everything. When are you going to show us the stars? I thought you were going to take us up the mountain."

"You're serious, you're interested to go?" he said, including Ben. "Whenever you like. You have to stay overnight, you know."

"Yes, I know," she said, turning to Ben, her eyes meeting his in code again. "I'll pack something warm." Smiling now, handing him a room key. He smiled back, then toward the sunset before anyone could notice, feeling the color in his face.

"You know, I don't think it can be true," Ostermann said quietly to Ben, reassuring again. "The ones I knew—they talked about it. They liked to tell you. For them it was—the truth. It explained everything. Children. Daniel wasn't like that. More—elastic. Anyway, does it matter so much now, what he thought?"

"YOU'VE GOT a hell of a nerve. How would I know?"

Howard Stein pushed back from his desk, as if he'd been touched by a cattle prod.

"I thought you were in the Party. That's what I heard."

"What are you, working for that fuck Tenney? Or did the studio send you? Lasner doesn't like the pickets? He wants to nail us this way?"

"It's a simple question."

"Get a subpoena, you might get an answer. That's how it works now." He looked across the desk. "You have any idea what you're getting into with this?"

"I just want to know about Danny. Somebody told me he was. So, was he? It's not a crime, last time I heard."

"Yeah, and it's a free country."

"He was a friend of yours."

"That doesn't make him anything." He looked up. "It doesn't make me anything, either." He kept looking at Ben, hesitating, then stood up, taking his hat off the stand, his manner deliberately lighter. "But I'll buy you a cup of coffee, you want some stories for your scrapbook." He jerked his head toward the door, more than a suggestion. "He could be a funny guy."

Before Ben could say anything more, they were heading down the stairs and into the glare of the street. Stein's office was over a car showroom on Wilshire, not far from the Tar Pits, and the closest diner was empty at this hour, still waiting for school groups.

"You think I'm crazy, maybe you're right, but I think they got the office wired. You talk about stuff like this, the board starts lighting up. Don't bother," he said, catching Ben's look. "I know. Paranoid. I even know how to spell it. But I'm still walking around. It never hurt anybody, be a little careful. You, either." He nodded to the waitress to bring the coffee pot. "First of all, I'm *not* in the Party. I left the Party. That's for you, all right? Not the water cooler. Just something you heard around."

"So was he?"

"You want him to be? Everybody else is running away from this and you want to hand him a card?"

"I just want to know."

Stein waited until the waitress had poured their cups.

"The god's truth? No. Not that I ever heard of. Or saw. Not one meeting. I'd swear to it. At least him I won't have to. He's dead. It's the others they'll want to get. Fuck 'em. It's a funny thing about age—the memory goes. Not a goddam thing you can do about it."

"Even under oath?"

"What, with Tenney? Up in Sacramento? What's he going to do, put me away? I've been there, I'm not afraid of it."

"You were in prison?"

"You didn't know? I'm a tough guy. Fucking George Raft." He stirred some sugar in his coffee. "Aggravated assault. That was hitting back when they broke up a picket line. Teach me a lesson. Which it did, but not the one they thought." He looked up. "No, he wasn't. Like I said, he was a friend to the union, that's all. And then not even that. Five years ago, there were lots of shades of red here. Like a fucking lipstick counter. Now, there's one. And it's too bright for most people."

"Then why would she say he was—the woman who knew him."

"Make trouble, maybe. This is someone in the Hollywood group?"

"No, from before. In Germany."

"Germany? That's years ago. He was a member or just—?"

"He was a courier for them. Would they have trusted an outsider? Then?"

Stein thought for a minute. "All right. But that's still years ago."

"It doesn't expire, does it? It's not like a library card."

"Maybe he quit."

"I thought you couldn't."

"No, that's what they think. The Tenneys, the Minots. You're never clean. Unless you confess. Help them throw a few other people on the fire. You can quit. I did."

"Why did you?" Ben asked, suddenly curious. He sipped his coffee.

"No one thing. Maybe I got tired of taking orders. Party discipline. All the goddam meetings. It wears you out. And this place. You got a bunch of people sitting around, beating themselves up, part of the *dialectic,* and they're bringing home five hundred a week, more. I didn't sign on for that. And you know what? I got more done outside than in. My little time away kept me out of the service so I went to work for the union, the last thing they expected when they put on the cuffs."

"When was this?"

Stein glanced up. "Late, if that's what you mean. It's a funny thing. After the Hitler pact, 'thirty-nine, everyone here's bailing, and I stick. Maybe stubborn. But I figure maybe there's something I don't know. Then it all turns around and I see there wasn't. Just what's good for Russia. It takes a while, you know, to see where it's going. Then we get in the war, and now everybody's friends again—some people here came back in, you believe it?—but it has the opposite effect on me. I don't care anymore. The Party line, keep the movement alive. Help Russia. What about this country? What are we doing for us?" He shrugged.

"Maybe it was all the patriotic movies, what the hell. Me, waving flags. I know what it's like here." He touched the top of his head. "I got the bruises. But I figure if we can get rid of the fucking golfers we still have a shot at something here."

Ben smiled. "But the golfers have the money."

"Yeah, they do," Stein said, smiling a little. "Right on top, where they like to be. Now, anyway. You ever go across the street, see the Pits? It's interesting. You see these bones, the dinosaurs, and you think, there they were, walking around, fucking *owned* the place, top of the world. And then the next thing—they're gone. Just bones in a pit. It's something to think about. You drive out to the Valley, past Warners, you see those big sound stages, sitting there like the whole thing's theirs, and for all they know a tar pit's going to open up on them."

"Then your pickets go, too."

Stein grinned. "Jack would like that. He'd throw them in first—buy a little time." He looked down. "You want pie or something with that?" he said, a signal to wrap things up.

Ben shook his head.

"This is so important to you? Whether he was a Red?"

"Did he ever talk about my father?"

"Some big-time director over there, right? The Nazis killed him. He didn't get out in time or something."

"Or something."

Stein waited.

"That's who Danny was working for."

"He used his own kid?"

"What does that tell you?"

"That's a trick question?" he said, flustered. "Listen, I knew your brother. The family, that's something else. He didn't talk about that—just your father once in a while. Not the mother. He never mentioned you, for instance."

"No," Ben said, feeling it anyway, a sharp point going in.

"So I don't know. What does it tell me? He must have thought it was important. To do that."

"It was. To them. They helped smuggle people out. Then, after they got my father, Danny kept doing it. Getting people out of France. Probably using the same network, wouldn't you say? It's not the kind of thing you can do freelance. You need some—comrades in place. So he still must have been a Red. And then he gets on a boat to come home and throws his card over the side. Does that seem like Danny to you?"

"Not on a boat," Stein said quietly.

"What?"

"He came on the Clipper. The boats weren't running then."

Something else he didn't know. A meaningless detail with the same sharp end.

"So does it?" Ben said.

Stein thought for a minute, playing with his spoon.

"You ask his wife?"

"She says no. He didn't tell her, either," Ben said, including Stein.

"But you believe the other woman. The one who said he was."

"She survived the camps. People like that don't have to make anything up."

"They could make a mistake."

Ben shook his head. "Not her. It cost her to tell me."

Stein looked at him, uncomfortable, then went back to his spoon. "Sometimes it's better, keeping things quiet. Let's say he gets here, first thing he sees is you don't want to advertise. Lie low. We were never popular here, you know, even before this craziness began. So he goes unofficial."

"Unofficial."

"Part of a closed chapter."

"You mean secret?"

"Don't get excited. Not like that. Just off the books. To protect their jobs. Some places, this can get you fired. Flash a card at Hearst, see how long you last. You go unofficial to protect yourself."

"There's a chapter like that here?"

Stein shrugged. "You're in pictures, you can't afford to offend the public. My group, it was mostly writers—they don't have to care."

"But they must answer to somebody in the Party. They wouldn't just be left on their own, would they?"

"No."

"So who would it be here?"

"I wouldn't know."

Ben looked at him. "Even if you did."

"I left the Party. Not everybody did. And I don't know you from Adam." He paused. "Look, I liked your brother, so I'm telling you. Maybe he was unofficial. But I never heard that. And it doesn't matter a damn now anyway. Leave it. You don't want to get somebody else in trouble. They put me under oath? There are no unofficials. Never heard of them. The rest of us, the dues payers?—it's open season on us. But we don't have to give them anyone else. All right?"

"Take a look at this," Hal said, head leaning over the Moviola viewer. His jaw, even in the morning, had traces of beard. "Birkenau—we haven't seen this before."

Ben looked with him. Silent film, with card titles in Cyrillic. Stacks of corpses. He felt his stomach slide, the way it always did. Open oven doors with mounds of ashes.

"Lasner won't like using Russian footage."

"Cut away from the soldiers. It doesn't matter who's holding the camera. We just want to see the place. Look, the guards are still there. This must be just after they went in."

On the small screen, men in uniforms were being led away, hands up, their collars open, disheveled.

"What do they look like to you?" Ben said, watching them.

"Anybody."

Ben nodded. "Anybody. You wonder what went through their heads. The ovens going night and day. The smell."

There were people in bunks, too weak to move, hollow-eyed, and Ben realized, going down the line with the film, that he was looking for Genia. An outside shot now, prisoners standing around, disoriented, waiting for another roll call. The wire fence, the ovens again, bodies everywhere. What she must have seen every day, unable to turn away like the guards. He thought of her in the big Louis XV room, her dead eyes still seeing what was in the film. After a while, it would be the only thing you knew. And then you were here, in the sunshine with people drinking milkshakes, and you saw that it must have been going on at the same time, while the doctors made selections on the platform, and there was no reason at all why you were in one place or the other, reality itself become something random, inexplicable.

"This is pretty rough," Hal was saying. "Worse than the other stuff. We're going to have to be careful. You don't want to chase the audience away."

"We want them to see it. That's the point."

"Look at the Russians." Soldiers carrying inmates to carts. "They've all got their heads turned. You don't want the audience doing that." He glanced up at Ben. "Let me work on it. You want anything back, we'll put it back."

"But keep the guards. The way they look."

They watched the rest of the film, then another, absorbed, not even making notes, letting it run. A pan shot across bodies, the genitals just smudges, as if they had retreated inside, the women oddly neutered, without sex. Open mouths.

"Bastards," Hal said, almost a whisper, and then neither of them said anything.

When it was over, they went outside for a cigarette, wanting distance, even a few feet. Hal leaned back against the wall, looking toward the Admin building on Gower.

"How'd you get him to do it?" he said. "Lasner."

"He saw it—one of the camps. I didn't have to do anything."

"Well, whatever you did. I never thought I'd get to do something like this. At Continental. Piece of history. Fort Roach. *Enemies to Friends.* How to bow to a Jap. What not to say to the women. Put in your time, go home at night. That's all I've done. Nothing like this." He cocked his head, taking in Ben from a new angle. "What are you going to do after?"

"What, the Army?" Ben shrugged. "Maybe go back overseas. There's a newsreel job if I want it."

"Most people, they get on the lot, they never want to leave."

"I just want to get this one done."

"You saw it for real. That's why?"

Ben dropped his cigarette and rubbed it out with his foot.

"I'm still trying to figure it out. The guards. How do you get to that point? When you can do that. What makes it all right? Do you know? I don't."

"You're never going to know that. A wife shoots her husband, that you can know. This—"

"There has to be something. What makes them think it's the right thing to do? There's no money in it, nothing—personal. Like the wife. Some other reason."

For ending up in a mound of ashes. Or in an alley with your blood running out. At least he could know the reason for that. As blameless as the ash heaps? The question that was always there. What had he done?

RIORDAN'S TELEPHONE voice was all business, as if he were sitting behind a desk.

"What kind of technical advice? For a picture?"

"No. Someone broke into the house last night."

"So call the cops."

"Nothing's missing. I can't prove anyone was there."

"Then why do you think—"

"Some things were rearranged."

"Rearranged."

"Look, the point is it made Liesl nervous. I don't want it to happen again. I figured you'd have some ideas. The Bureau must—"

"What? Train us in breaking and entering? I'll tell you this much, somebody wants to get in, he'll get in. Get better locks. Alarms will run you money, and anybody who knows what he's doing can get in anyway. Get dead bolts. That's for free."

"I was thinking about surveillance."

There was a pause as Riordan took this in.

"You're asking me to babysit?"

"I figured you'd know somebody."

"What makes you think they're coming back."

"They didn't take anything. Even stuff just lying around. So they must have been after something in particular. If they didn't find it, maybe they'll try again. Look, I'm just asking you to recommend somebody."

Another pause. "All right, I'll have a look around. Anybody home today?"

"Iris, the housekeeper. Liesl probably. Tell whoever's there I sent you, to check the locks. Got a pencil?"

"I know where it is."

"That's right. The funeral."

"What was rearranged? So you knew somebody had been there."

"A file. In the desk."

"That was careless. What's in the desk?"

"Nothing. Papers. Desk stuff."

"No idea what they were looking for?"

"That's why I called the Bureau."

"Yeah. All right. I'll take care of it. Where are you, the studio? That's Gower. You know Lucey's on Melrose? By Paramount. Six? But I'm telling you now, it's locks."

THE RED light was on so Ben waited, leaning against the sound stage wall, his head still full of the Artkino footage. In the street, two Japanese pilots were sharing a smoke, probably on their way to dive-bomb Dick Marshall. The casually surreal world Hal thought everyone wanted. "What, have you got a girl back over there or something?" he'd said, not able to let it go. No, here. Ben smiled to himself. A mermaid. Waiting at home. Danny's home.

The red light flicked off and he heard the buzzer inside, unlocking the doors. What would Rosemary say? Why would she say anything? A girl on her way up, dancing with Ty Power at the Mocambo. She'd want to shed Danny, any B-list affair, like molted skin.

Ben stepped in, facing the backs of some painted flats, then walked around to the interior of the set, still drenched in hot light. A nightclub with an orchestra stage and a bar at the side, now being set up for a tracking shot. Gaffers were making adjustments in the over-heads, angling away from the mirror behind the bar. The extras, in suits and evening dresses, were still sitting at the club tables, waiting to be told to start talking again. Rosemary, in a tight dress, was leaning back against a slant board to keep the skirt from creasing, while a makeup girl ran a comb over her hair, patting it gently into place. Rosemary didn't move. When the girl stepped aside, leaving her alone against the board, she seemed for a minute like an oil painting propped on an easel.

"I hope you don't mind," he said, coming up to her. "We didn't get a chance to talk at dinner."

"No," she said, wary, but not surprised to see him.

"Ready in two, darling," the assistant director said, passing them.

"We're in the middle of a scene," she said to Ben.

"You all right with the gun?" the AD said.

She nodded, glancing at the gun on the table beside her. Make a leap, before she can react.

"Danny told me a lot about you."

Eyes cornered now, but meeting his, not backing away.

"Yes?" Noncommittal, waiting.

"We were close. He could tell me things," he said, wondering if a lie showed in your face.

She looked at him, still waiting.

"Just me," he said, a reassurance.

She stared for another second, then raised her eyebrow. "Well, that puts you one up. He never told me anything. It turns out," she said, her voice sarcastic but warm, as if bad behavior were a bond between them, something they should have expected.

"How do you mean?"

"I always believe it. I always think, okay, this time I'm not going to listen, and then I do. I guess you like to think—you're the only one. So that's what you hear."

"He never told me about anyone else," Ben said, trying it, another fly cast.

"Just me, huh? Well, so there's that. Look, I don't know what to say to you. Is there a script for this? I mean—his brother. It's a relief in a way, I guess. That somebody knows. One day you think you're—" She stopped, looking down. "And the next day you're not supposed to exist. You can't go to the funeral. Upset anyone. So what do I say? I'm sorry for your loss? Well, I'm sorry for mine, too, but nobody's going to say it to me."

"I'll say it to you."

"Thanks," she said, stopped by this. "Well. So now what?"

"I want to talk to you about him."

"Why? Warn me off? Before it gets out of hand? Before the wife finds out? A little late now. Anyway, she knows. I could tell. Was that you?"

He shook his head. "Not Danny, either. A hunch, I guess. Maybe you told her, the way you acted with her."

"Yeah, and maybe it was that big A on my back." She looked up at him, amused. "Your face. I played the part in stock. You're right, though. I never read the book. So what do you want to talk about?"

"Were you there the night he fell?"

"What?" she said, a place holder, caught off guard.

"With him."

"With him? You think he'd do that with me there? It's the kind of thing you do alone."

"Somebody was there. Or expected. Maybe you were on your way?"

She looked at him carefully. "What's this all about?"

"Nothing. I'm just trying to find out how it happened."

"Who to blame, you mean. You think I wanted this?" She shook her head. "Why would I? I thought we were— I was silly about him.

Huh. That's the first time I've said that. Even to myself." She looked away. "Whatever it means. He said it, and it turns out it didn't mean much. No, I wasn't there. Must have been somebody else on the call sheet." She turned back to him. "You think it was because of me? Is that what you want to know? Maybe I should be flattered. But I wasn't anything special to him. I know that now. What did he tell you, when you were so buddy-buddy? What did he say about me? Besides being an easy lay."

"Places!" the AD yelled.

"He said you were nice."

"Oh," she said softly, surprised, her eyes suddenly moist. "If you ruin this scene for me, I'll kill you." She got off the slant board, checking her dress, and picked up the gun, then turned to him. "Nice? That's not a word he'd use."

"Maybe I said it." He nodded to the gun. "Who are you going to shoot?"

The makeup girl came back for a last brush of powder.

"My lover. I'm jealous." She met his eyes.

"People! Are we going to wrap today or not? Places. Monica, stick that puff somewhere. All right, here we go."

The buzzer sounded. The director, looking through the viewfinder on the tracking camera, signaled for the clapper. Rosemary's lover, an actor Ben didn't know, turned from his drink and started walking down the length of the bar into the moving camera.

"You think you can, but you can't," he said, looking from her to the gun.

Rosemary's hand shook, her eyes beginning to tear up.

"You love me," the actor said with a sneer.

"I hate you," Rosemary said, the words pulled out of her.

"Then shoot," he said easily, still coming toward her.

He froze as the shot exploded, then grabbed his stomach in astonishment and dropped to the floor. Rosemary kept holding the gun out, then lowered her arm, her shoulders shaking.

"Cut," the director said. "Nice. Let's get one for safety."

They did it twice more, then broke to change the set-ups for Rosemary's reaction shots.

"We're almost there," the director said to Rosemary. "The payoff shot. Remember, you still love him."

"Even while I'm plugging him," she said wryly.

"And I want to see it right here," he said, pointing to her eyes. "Watch the dress."

She stepped back against the slant board.

"That was good," Ben said.

"It's always good until you see it."

"We can talk later if you—"

"They'll be ten minutes," she said. "You want to know why he did it? So do I. Don't you think I've asked myself a million times? I never thought there was anything wrong. Maybe one of his other friends didn't show and he got all upset. I don't know. Me? All he'd have had to do was pick up the phone."

"He was seeing someone else?"

"He must have been. Why else would he have the place? We never went there. Well, once—I had somebody staying with me. We used mine. Sometimes little trips. Santa Barbara, the Biltmore. He was romantic like that." Her voice thickened. "La Valencia, down in La Jolla. Places."

"But not the Cherokee."

"Just the once. He said it was a friend's place. He borrowed it because we couldn't use any of the hotels—the columns watch. And then I read in the paper that it was his. So there must have been somebody else, without a place. Maybe more than one, who knows? That hurt a little. You like to think— But why should I be surprised? What did I think I was? Someone he saw like that. On the side. Call it romantic— oh, La Valencia. But you know what it is. It didn't seem that way, though, at the time. It was—nice."

"How long were you—?"

"A few months. Last spring. V-E Day. I was on loan-out at Republic and they stopped work. All-day party. So I guess I could blame the booze. But it wasn't."

"And he wasn't breaking it off?"

"Not that he told me," she said, a little sharp. "Maybe he told you." Ben shook his head. "Then why do you ask?"

"Because he gave notice at the Cherokee. End of the month. I just assumed—he didn't need it anymore."

She took this in. "You think someone gave him the brush?"

"I don't know. Any idea who it might have been?"

"I never even suspected. Why would I? We were good together. You look at it now, and I guess I was a fool, but I never thought— When I first heard, I thought maybe he'd been sick. Some condition. He had a lot of doctor appointments. Then I read the place was his and I thought, oh, that's where the doctor was. Those kind of appointments."

"How did you hear?"

"In the papers. I was on the set, and it's in the papers and I had to pretend it didn't mean anything. It didn't say how bad he was. Not that I could go to the hospital anyway."

"You had no idea he was in a coma?"

"You call and they say 'stable.'"

"They didn't know who you were, when you called?"

"What do you think? I'm not supposed to exist, remember?"

"And you weren't at the Cherokee that night."

"I told you. Why do you keep asking that?"

"Because if you weren't—if there was nothing to connect you to him—why would Bunny get the police to file it as an accident?"

She started, then pushed herself away from the slant board, no longer caring about the dress.

"What are you talking about? You think Bunny would fix something for me? I'm not important enough."

"Did he know about you and Danny?"

"I don't know. He knows everything. He's like that. But what if he did? You think the studio's going to fall apart because somebody sees us necking in La Jolla?"

"With Danny. Not Ty Power. He wouldn't like that."

"Then he'd tell me about it. Not go flying around town playing Mr. Fixit. You think he'd do that for me? You don't know what it's like here. He can trade me in for a new model any time he likes."

"Not if you're a star."

"That's something to look forward to then, isn't it? Bunny cleaning up after you. But he's not doing it now. I'm just a big 'maybe' to him. You know how many chances you get in this town?"

"One?"

"Not even. Half, maybe. And nobody gives it to you. You just keep working and one day you get lucky." She opened her hand to the set. "This is mine. If the picture works, maybe I get the other half, a real chance. That's after ten years. A Greyhound from Newark. Nobody fixes anything for me. Anyway, fix what?"

"You close a file, nobody asks any questions. Nobody's embarrassed. That's all."

"And I'm the embarrassment."

"Maybe Danny was. A married man. They have plans for you."

The buzzer sounded.

"Ro?"

"One sec." She turned to Ben. "Look, what happened—this business about giving somebody the brush. He wasn't planning to do that, was he? I mean to me. He didn't tell you that."

"No."

She nodded, holding on to it. "Thanks. This is a funny kind of conversation to be having. I never thought of him as dead. I knew it wouldn't last—but not like this."

"Why wouldn't it last?"

"Well, they don't, do they? These things." She shrugged. "They're all still in love with their wives, I think." She brushed the front of her skirt, smoothing it for the shot. "Anyway, they don't leave them."

• • •

HE HAD lunch with Hal, taking in the pecking order of the commissary. Lasner had nodded to them when they came in, a sign of favor from the head table, but nobody got up to ask them to join the group, sober gray and pinstripe suits except for Bunny in his camel hair jacket. The writers were more casual, hound's tooth checks and plaids, noisy with laughter, as if they'd just moved the table over from the Derby on Vine. The actors stayed with their production units, eating salads in period dress and seating themselves by salary levels. Otherwise, technicians talked shop with each other. The room itself seemed the one place on the lot where Lasner, or Bunny, had been willing to spend money—chair backs of curved chromium tubes, lacquered tables and sleek sconces, a Cedric Gibbons set.

"Who's that with Sam Pilcer?" Hal said, nodding to a table near the window where Julie Sherman was huddled with a short man in a double-breasted suit.

"That was fast. The ink can't even be dry on the contract yet. You want me to introduce you?"

"Later. Not in front of Sam."

Ben smiled but looked over again uneasily. Julie was leaning forward, her full attention on Pilcer. Is this how Danny had done it? A drink and a promise? Then a quick trip to the Cherokee—except they'd never gone there, only the once. A place paid for by the month.

"They're wrapping today," Hal was saying. "Maybe I'll run into her at the party. Without Sam."

"Rosemary's picture? What about her?"

"What about?"

"Chances with her."

Hal shook his head, protective. "She's not— She's got talent."

Ben looked at him, surprised he'd made the distinction. "Talent."

"Watch her on the set. A pro. On time, knows her lines. No high-hatting, ever. Knows your name. She does the job." He looked at Ben. "Then she goes home."

But not always. Sometimes she went to La Jolla.

"The papers have her out with Ty Power."

"Yeah, well," Hal said. "You know these pictures they put her in, she's got the figure for it, but she's not like that." He looked again toward Julie's table. "You want to get something going, ask her if she has a friend. What?"

"Just thinking," Ben said, then gathered up his tray. "I have to make a call."

On his way out he couldn't resist another sidelong glance—Pilcer even closer now, smiling, telling her all the things he could do for her. What men must have said to Rosemary, too, while she waited for half a chance. But she'd believed Danny.

Kelly was in a rush, claiming to be on deadline.

"Quick question," Ben said. "One sec."

"Long time no hear."

"Nothing to tell."

"Yeah, I know. This one's heading for the fridge. So what do you want to know?"

"When did Danny take up the lease at the Cherokee? Did anybody ever say? Last spring?"

"No, first of the year. They didn't say, I asked. I'm a reporter." A cheeky Dick Powell. "Why do you want to know?"

Why would he?

"I'm checking the loan-outs. Helps to have a time, when she might have been here."

"First of the year. You're still on this, huh?"

"Aren't you?"

"I'll tell you something. The way it works? At a certain point you think, I'm just spinning wheels. It's getting late. I can feel the chill on this one already. How many weeks now? And all I got is one girlfriend who wasn't there."

"What? Who?"

"The Miller kid. On your contract list," he said, a tiny delay, making a point.

"How do you figure that?"

"I showed glossies to the night clerk, the real one, not Joel. He ID'd her. But not Joel. Never saw her. So I checked her out. And he's right, she wasn't there that night. So, nothing."

"You never told me."

"Keep your pants on. Tell what? We don't have anything if she wasn't there, a hit and run. If I ran an item on everyone who got laid, there wouldn't be enough paper. So they screwed around and he's dead, but where's the connection? No story."

"But you ran it down anyway."

"It's always nice to know. Something to put on the layaway plan. Might come in handy, you never know."

"If she makes it," Ben said. "Then you can give it to Polly."

"Tch, tch, is that nice? Anyway, what's in it for Polly? He's dead. Sorry, I didn't mean—but he is. And not a star. So the only way it plays now is if she *is* and he was the secret love of her life. Which doesn't sound like it was. The clerk saw her once. You can't do much with a one-nighter, not even Polly."

Ben said nothing. One night. La Jolla, the Biltmore, all the others still hers, not tucked away in anyone's file.

"Hey, speaking of which, you know the Fed at the Market you asked me to check out?"

"Riordan."

"Yeah, the Technical Consultant. Turns out he was. Republic paid him. Worked for your brother on the series, just like he said. So."

"Why speaking of which," Ben said, trying to follow.

"Oh, Polly's secretary. You said he came to the funeral with Polly, so I figured she'd know him."

"And?"

"Well, I told you, they never retire, they just find other garbage to go through. He's been freelancing for Tenney—you know the one with the committee. A bunch of old hands from the Bureau dig around for him. He sends stuff over to Polly, and sometimes Riordan takes it. That's how Polly knows him. Tenney stays clear, so nobody figures where the stuff is coming from."

"So he's a messenger?"

"More like a supplier. Anyway, he's who he says he is. And a little more. Christ, there's the ME, I have to go."

"Wait, one more thing. The clerk who ID'd Rosemary? He saw her? They didn't go through the back?"

"No, he saw her. They must have come in the front. I gotta run. You want, I'll keep poking around, but this is already going away. What I can't figure is the studio. But maybe they got trigger happy—grabbed the phone before there was anything to cover up. It happens, you get nervous about people. Maybe they don't like Rosemary screwing around. But that doesn't get us anywhere. We need someone there that night. Or every night—the romance that broke his heart. But all we've got is a jump. Yesterday."

Check the loan-outs. Danny had rented the Cherokee months before Rosemary. Maybe for someone he didn't bring through the front door. He started out for Personnel to get the monthly lists, but got sidetracked by Hal instead, excited about something.

"I was thinking about the guards," he said, leading Ben to the cutting room. "You know the faces are hard to see. Medium pan shots, nothing closer."

"It's newsreel film. Army. They don't do close-ups." Heads tilted up to the light, long lashes making shadows.

"Right. But take a look at this." At the Moviola, a frozen frame of the guards being led away. "Just for the idea. It's a work print. But they should have the camera originals in Culver City. Now look."

He took a lens and held it over a section of the viewer so that a single face leapt out of the frame.

"Blow up the negative here. Show his face."

Ben looked at the spot enlargement, the guard's eyes caught forever on a piece of film. In the full running shot he'd be turning away from the camera, a close-up of shame itself.

"It'll cost, though, the lab work. You're not just splicing."

"What if the quality's not good enough? The stock's grainy."

"Wet-gate print it."

"What?"

"Before you transfer. It takes out the scratches. We always do it with a sixteen-millimeter transfer. Come back here, I'll show you."

Ben followed him, not really wanting to take the time but feeling obligated. He had felt in Hal's eyes the line worker's mild contempt for the foreman still learning the fundamentals. The whole technical side of film-making—the developing tanks, the chemical emulsions, the synchronized sprockets—were things handled by someone else. They went through heavy double doors to a big factory space of drying rooms and machines that made the transfer from light to image, Merlin's workshop.

"See, the transfer's clear," Hal said, leading him to a machine. "But you couldn't close in on this. Depends on the exposure, what light was retained." He pointed to the sample, an indoor shot of people lying in bunks. "You blow up these faces, you don't have enough resolution. Like a night shot. See what I mean?"

Ben looked at the faces, visible now as individuals, but slightly blurred, not good enough for full-scale projection.

"I tried printing with more light, but you can't get the background up. Too dark in the first place."

He reversed the process, the faces slipping back into a formless crowd.

"But the other stock we can work with."

Shadowy faces in a crowd. Ben stood still, eyes fixed on the enlarging mechanism.

"Hal," he said, not looking at him, thinking. "You can do this with any picture, right? Bring up the background."

"Depends how it was printed. If you can work from the negative, you can pretty much get whatever's there."

"The negative," Ben said, elsewhere.

"That's right. Then you control the printing, kind of coax it out."

Ben looked at his wristwatch. "How long would it take? Blow up some negatives? Stills?"

"No time. What stills?"

Ben touched his upper arm. "I'll be back. Keep the machine free, okay?"

"What stills?"

In the car he tried to remember the lighting in the pictures, windows shining down on the Cherokee alley, the glare of a police flashbulb, a few people standing near the body, the rest outside the circle of light, like dots in an afterimage. He tried to remember the women—a distraught neighbor, anyone from the studio, maybe even Rosemary herself, who hadn't been there—but all he'd really looked at before was the body.

Iris's car was in the driveway so he parked on the street and walked around to the back of the house, the French doors wide open, another invitation to rifle through Danny's desk. Liesl was in the kitchen grating potatoes, her face pink from the work, wisps of hair spilling down out of the pile on top.

"Oh! What are you doing here?"

"Just picking something up." Wanting to go over to her, touch her arm, but aware of Iris at her ironing board. "I thought you were going to keep the doors locked."

"Well, at night. Oh, now you won't be surprised." She waved the knife. "I wanted to surprise you. My roast chicken."

He nodded to the mixing bowl. "What's that?"

"Kartoffelpuffer." A hesitant smile. "I told you I could cook."

"What did Riordan say? About the locks."

"Who?"

"The man I sent over to check the house."

"No one's been here."

Ben looked at his watch. Cutting it close or not coming. Or maybe he'd been there without announcing himself, playing burglar.

"That's a lot of food. Are people coming?"

"No, just us," she said, looking at him, her eyes soft. "It's going to rain, I think. So it's cozy, eating in."

He held her stare for a second, trying not to smile in front of Iris, then headed to the study.

The photographs were just as he'd remembered, Danny lying with a dark smear around his head, people huddled at the edge of the flash. Two angles with two backgrounds, one of the parking area, the other leading to the street. He looked carefully at the faces in front but still didn't recognize anybody. They'd be neighbors, rushing out at the sudden sound, then the police lights, something more exciting than the radio. But who were the people right behind them? He slipped out the written reports, leaving the prints and negatives in the envelope.

"When will you be home?" Liesl said, then flushed, the simplest domestic question now somehow suggestive. "I only ask because of the chicken."

"I'm supposed to see Riordan after work. If he shows. Eight, eight-thirty?"

"Yes, all right. But you'll call if you'll be late? So I know."

This time he did smile, not caring whether Iris saw. Something any couple might say.

HAL LOOKED at the pictures, waiting for Ben to explain.

"What exactly are we looking for?"

"People you can't see clearly in the prints."

"They're dark." He held up one of the negatives to the light, then turned it on its side, looking at the numbers in the margin. "These are police? Where'd you—?" He stopped, still waiting. "Who's the victim?"

"My brother."

"I thought—"

Ben nodded. "I want to see who was there. Somebody from the building, maybe. Anybody I could talk to."

Hal looked at him, skeptical, then took up the negatives. "Okay, let's go to work."

Ben watched, fascinated, as Hal manipulated the negatives, enlarging, then disappearing into the darkroom with its trays of solutions. But even the studio couldn't produce a miracle. In the shot looking toward the parking lot, faces were barely visible, even blown up. The alley angle was better, street lamps at the end providing a kind of backlight. They looked at the enlargements together, Ben hoping that Hal, familiar with everyone on the lot, might suddenly recognize somebody. But they were all anonymous, caught unexpectedly in suspenders and house dresses, one woman in curlers, hand over her mouth.

"You can tell the cops by the hats," Hal said, examining a new print. "Everyone else just rushed out, I guess. Look, back there in the alley. You can always tell, can't you?"

"So why is he in the alley, not with the others? He's just someone off the street. Who's the woman next to him? Can we get in closer on her?"

"Closer? Not much. A few more degrees, you'll get a blotch. But let's try one."

When the print was done, it was just clear enough. Ben looked, then went rigid, stunned.

"She looked better in the dark," Hal said. "But the hat—pure cop. You still think he's in off the street?"

"No, he's a cop," Ben said slowly. "Ex-FBI."

HIS PARKING space was behind Admin B, but when he got there he put the keys back in his pocket. He could use the walk to clear his head. He passed the choked line of cars at the gate, all heading home at once, then the small knot of picketers, and turned down Gower. Where they used to shoot Westerns, under roofs of cheesecloth. Today they wouldn't need to filter the light—the day, cloudy before, was overcast and thick, already growing faint. How long had Riordan been in the alley? In the picture, he'd been craning his neck to see, just another curious bystander. But how could he have been? Someone Danny knew. Who had never made himself known, not on any of the reports, a hat in the crowd. Wanting to see, maybe wanting to make sure.

Lucey's was more than a few blocks, a longer walk than he expected, so he was late when he pushed open the door and took a second to adjust to the dim light inside. The after-work drinkers had already piled in from Paramount, but Riordan had managed to get a table and he signaled Ben through the crowd with a two-finger wave.

"I went ahead and ordered," he said, pointing to two glasses. "Try getting a waitress in this. Beer okay?"

Ben sat down, putting the envelope next to Riordan's hat. "So," he said, letting Riordan take the lead.

"So you need to do something about the pool doors."

"Oh," Ben said, looking over at him, the same military short hair, steady eyes, but everything different now, someone who'd been in the alley. "Is that how you got in?"

"They'd be easy to jimmy," he said, not picking up on this. "I noticed at the funeral."

"And that's why you didn't bother going over today."

Riordan said nothing.

"Or because you already knew how he got in Saturday. Did you do it yourself, or did you send someone else? In case."

Riordan picked up his glass, staring at Ben over the rim as he drank, buying a minute.

"If I'd done it, you wouldn't have known anybody was there," he said finally.

"So someone else. But you'd tell him what to look for. Now you want to tell me?"

"You think I knocked over your place? What for?"

"For something you didn't get. Maybe I can help."

"You're going in circles."

"And I keep coming back here. You were tailing him. You're *still* tailing him. A dead man. What do you want? Didn't you have enough on him already? A nice big file down in Tenney's office."

"You don't know what you're talking about."

"I know you work for Tenney. Take love notes to Polly. God knows what else. Keep tabs on Liesl's father, dangerous characters like him. So we can sleep safe at night. While you're breaking into the house."

"I don't work for Tenney."

"Were you getting stuff on Danny while he was paying you? Maybe little notes on his love life. Tenney likes that, I hear."

"Where is this coming from?" Riordan said evenly. "Your information's old. I don't work for Tenney. I did. A while ago. But that's a while ago. And by the way, I'm not tailing Ostermann."

"You just like having lunch at the Farmers Market."

Riordan sat back, his eyes steady on Ben.

"You going to tell me what this is all about?"

Ben slid the envelope to Riordan. "Have a look."

Ben watched him open the envelope and take out the picture, his face registering no emotion at all, a practiced blank. But when he did raise his eyes, they had a new directness.

"Where did you get this?"

"The police had it. They just didn't know what they had."

"What did they have?"

"Someone he knew, right at the scene, who didn't identify himself. Just stood there watching him bleed out. They might be interested in that. I was."

"And?"

"And they might want to know more. Show your picture around—do those things the police do. To see what connection there might be."

"They have any reason to do that?"

Ben shrugged. "A courtesy to the family. After they start making noise. Plus interfering with police procedures. Getting a report changed. They really don't like that. Unless they're the ones doing it, but that can't be all of them, can it?"

"And I'm supposed to be the one asking."

"Continental asked. But the studio had to get a call from somebody who was there. Otherwise it's too late, the time doesn't fit. I've been looking for the girlfriend, whoever he must have been meeting. But the girlfriend wasn't there. You were. The meeting was with you?"

Riordan said nothing.

"So we're back in the circle again—what were you doing there?"

"Maybe I happened to be passing by."

"Passing by."

"Who can say different?"

"Well, there's the call. Why call Bunny if you're just passing by."

"He told you this?"

"Not a word. Loose lips sink ships. Your secret's safe with him. I just figured. But put him under oath and he's not going to keep ducking and weaving—he'll have other things to think about. So will you. The police might want to change the accident report again. Make it a criminal case this time."

"What are you saying? You think I killed him?"

"Somebody did."

Riordan looked at him sharply. "Nobody else thinks so."

"Just the two of us, huh?"

Riordan paused for a minute, staring at him, then nodded. "But I don't know it. Neither do you."

"Then you won't mind if the police give us a hand. So we'll all know." Ben slid the picture back. "I can get more made, if you'd like one."

Riordan sat forward, his shoulders hunched. "We need to talk."

"Start."

"You think you know something, but you have things a little confused. So let's put them straight. First, I didn't kill your brother. And you don't think so either or you wouldn't be sitting here. Kind of a dangerous thing to say to somebody if it were true."

"Why? Because you'd plug me here in Lucey's?"

"You won't always be in Lucey's," Riordan said calmly. "And you can save the tough guy talk. I know people who really are tough."

"What are they like? You?"

"They don't talk much at all. Second, you're not going to the cops. You don't have anything to give them except a picture that doesn't mean much. And you start anything, they'll mess it up. You don't want any mess with this. They closed it out as an accident, keep it that way."

"Thanks to you."

Riordan opened his hand, conceding the point.

"You don't want anybody nosing around. Trust me on that."

"I know what Danny was. You must, too, or you wouldn't have been hounding him. More Red meat. Is that why you didn't want it as a suicide? They'd blame you for hounding him?"

"I wasn't hounding him."

"Then what were you doing at the Cherokee? We're back there again," he said, tapping his finger on the photo.

"I was keeping an eye."

"Jesus," Ben said, turning his head in disgust. "And what did you think when you saw him there? What was in your head? One less Red? Keeping an eye."

"You want to listen to this or just get up on a soapbox? I was keeping an eye because something was wrong. I knew your brother. We did business together. And then all of a sudden he was acting funny. Upset. And I thought, which? Is he upsetting himself or is somebody upsetting him? So I started keeping an eye, friendly, to see what was going on. That night I'm sitting in the car on Cherokee. No idea what he was doing there. A woman? Maybe. I see him go in, but I don't see anyone else. So somebody who lives there. Then the crash. People come running out. I go take a look. And there he is." He pointed to the picture. "The police come right away. Everybody's talking in the alley, he's a jumper. That fairy night clerk, carrying on. And I get that he rents there, it's *his* place. And I think, this is going to be a mess."

"So you decide to be the janitor."

"You know what happens? A suicide, anything suspicious? They're going to seal the place. Make an investigation. That's not going to do anybody good."

"Not you anyway. How does it look? You go after somebody and he finally runs so hard he jumps. That's not the kind of press Tenney needs. What his files are really doing to people."

Riordan sat back. "Whoa," he said, putting up his hand in a stop gesture. "Look, you're not playing with a full deck here. That's not how it was."

"No?"

"Nobody was chasing him. He was working with me. He was a source."

For a second, even the sounds of Lucey's seemed to fall away, his head stopped up with a cotton numbness.

"What kind of source," he said quietly.

"A source. He gave me names. Things to follow up. You've got this backwards. He helped *make* the files."

"I don't believe that," Ben said, suddenly chilled, his blood stopped for a minute.

Riordan shrugged. "That doesn't change anything."

"He wouldn't do that."

"I can show you reports. In the files."

Ben said nothing, still digesting this. Then he looked down to the photo.

"You bastard," he said. "That's why you thought he jumped. That he couldn't live with himself anymore."

Riordan looked away, embarrassed. "People are unpredictable."

"Especially informers. They turn on everybody. Then themselves. Is that it?"

"What are you talking about? Informer. He was a patriot."

"Jesus Fucking Christ. A patriot. What did you do to make him do it? What club did you use."

"You've got this wrong. Nobody made him do anything. We were all on the same side in this."

"He was a Communist."

"In Germany. Was. He saw what it meant. Right here." He held his hand close to his face. "You see it that clear, you want to do something."

"Like shop people to you."

Riordan took a breath. "Sometimes, you stop believing in something, you go the other way. You hate it."

"And hate yourself."

"No, not like that."

"Then why did you think he'd jumped?"

Riordan looked away again. "People get ideas. You never know how they're going to—" He stopped, leaning forward. "But that's why. It didn't make sense to me, the way I knew him. So I thought, what if it wasn't? Just the way you did. I thought, what if he had help? Someone who knew. Wanted him stopped."

"Communists, you mean. At it again. Is that the way you think Party discipline works? Throw people out of windows. You should go to work for Minot."

Riordan looked at him. "I do."

"You work for Minot?"

"It's not a secret."

Ben studied him again, as if he were moving pieces of his face, seeing him new, rearranged. "And that's why Bunny made the call," he said, half to himself. "Not for you."

"Ken doesn't forget a favor."

"And nobody would know Danny was feeding you. Minot's own Bureau."

"Just one of the field agents," Riordan said smoothly. "Tenney recommended me."

"After all your good work there."

"You want to be a wiseass, go ahead. I don't care. Your brother knew what was what. Maybe you will, too, someday. Everybody will. Minot's going to take this national."

"Take what national?"

"The threat in the industry." He held out his hand, stopping a passing waitress. "You want another?"

Ben looked at his beer, scarcely touched, then sat back, staring at the picture. Riordan waited, letting him catch his breath.

"You're surprised."

"Why would he do it?"

"Why wouldn't he? It's the right thing to do."

Ben looked up at him. "To fight the threat. Which one? Betty Grable taking over the government?"

"You think it's a joke. It's not. This is a war of ideas."

"What's the last idea you saw in the movies?"

Riordan said nothing, not wanting to quarrel.

"How long was all this?" Ben said. "How long did you know him?"

"Couple of years. Since the Bureau. He was a friend to the Bureau."

"What kind of friend?"

"We asked for some help, he gave it."

"You asked for help? What, go through Herb Yates's mail?"

"We don't need people for that. We know what people say, what they write to each other. What we need to know is what they think. Your brother had special access."

"To whom?" Ben said, chilled again, apprehensive.

"He did us a service. But I think he did them a service, too. Wartime, the Bureau has to keep an eye on enemy aliens. It's our job. But you don't want to make people uncomfortable. Not if they're what they say they are."

"He spied on his friends?" Ben said, suddenly seeing the exile faces at the funeral, Heinrich and Alma and Feuchtwanger. Hans and Liesl. Family.

"I wouldn't use that term. He reassured us, that's closer. That they were all right. Well, Brecht I still wouldn't trust as far as I could throw. But we got nothing yet, so we can't touch him. Eisler we already knew. And the Mann kid's a fruit, that's always a risk. The others, harmless, more or less. But we had to know that. So like I say, he did everybody a service."

"The Bureau spied on them? These people risked their lives. Fighting Nazis."

"So they say. That doesn't necessarily mean they're good for America. They have a different idea of politics over there. You ask me to tell you the difference between a Nazi and a Communist and what would I say? This much?" He held up two fingers, a tiny space apart. "At the Bureau we call them Communazis—they're both on the same side, so why not put them together? We needed to keep tabs. Your brother saw it. How the Reds tried to use them—small stuff, innocent, put your name on a letter, then maybe not so innocent. He was worried about them being used. We knew how he felt."

"How? You tap his phone?"

Riordan ignored this. "So we asked him to help. You know, the Bureau, it's hard to say no. Wartime, it's a patriotic duty."

"And then you kept asking."

"He saw how it was going in the industry. So he gave me a hand."

"Real pals." Ben looked again at the alley picture. "But you couldn't even go over to the body, see if you could help. Just stood there thinking how to cover your ass."

"He was dead. I thought he was dead."

"How's that feel? Having someone's blood on your hands?"

Riordan glanced up at the returning waitress, but she seemed not to have overheard, smiling as she put down his glass and moved on. He took a sip of his beer.

"How do you figure that?"

"First you think he jumped because he got disgusted with himself. For what? The work he was doing for you. That's what you thought, isn't it?"

Riordan said nothing.

"But what if somebody killed him. Who would that be? Who'd hate him that much? How about somebody he sold out to you?" He picked up the photo, both of them glancing at it again, back in the alley, then slid it into the envelope. "Either way it comes back to you," he said, his voice lower, drained.

Behind him he heard the tinkle of glasses, then a roll of thunder. He turned to the window, even darker now, and suddenly thought of the window on the Chief, looking out at the endless bright fields, everything getting bigger and more open, golden, the way he imagined Danny's life had become, not shadowy and squalid.

"I don't see it that way," Riordan said. "He did what he thought was right. I didn't kill him. But somebody did. You're his brother. If you'd stop spitting at me for two minutes, maybe we could help each other out."

Ben stared for a second, hearing the voice, steady and reasonable, then separating it from the words. What he might have said to Danny, help each other out, while he wrapped the coil around him. Ben stood up.

"It's still on them," he said, nodding to Riordan's hands. He reached into his pocket to pull out some money, then stopped. "I'll let you get this one."

He didn't turn until he was at the door, seeing Riordan drop some change on the table.

Outside it had finally begun to rain, heavy sheets of it, so that he was trapped under the small awning. The Mediterranean hills had disappeared, even the Paramount water tower, leaving a few flat streets with running gutters and a tangle of overhead wires.

"Christ," Riordan said, coming out. "Where's your car?"

"I walked."

Riordan looked at him, puzzled, a joke he didn't quite get. "I'm there," he said, pointing to a car. "Come on, I'll drop you."

"I'll wait it out."

Riordan gave him a suit-yourself shrug, then turned up the back of his collar, ready to dart to the car. "By the way," he said. "You're going in circles again. You think it's somebody he gave me. If he'd already done that, it'd be too late, wouldn't it? No point then. Right?"

He dashed out into the rain, fumbling with his keys, and got into his car. The rain was blowing in under the awning. In a real city there'd be taxis or a bus rumbling along. Ben watched Riordan's car move into the street. Circles. No point then. Right?

Riordan pulled up in front and rolled down his window. "Don't be a jerk. Get in."

Ben looked at the rain again, feeling the bottom of his pants already wet, and sprinted to the passenger door.

"You've got a short fuse," Riordan said, pulling out into traffic.

Ben brushed the front of his jacket, damp in patches.

"I liked him, you know. Whatever you think."

"Yeah," Ben said. He took out a cigarette and lit it. They were passing RKO. Only a few blocks, the windshield wipers keeping rhythm. "Everybody did."

Even as a kid, friends clung to him, following him home. Jokes about the teachers, plans for later. But what had he felt about them? Nothing can lie like a smile. Kaltenbach spoke of him as a hero. But Danny must have filed reports on him, too. Long talks with Liesl's father—taken down later? Bedtime reading for Riordan. Who must have supplied the lever. Maybe not blackmail, a plot out of *Partners,* just a soft pressure point, and then he was in it. But at least part of him must have wanted to be. Sometimes you stop believing, you go the other way. But when had it happened? Had he enjoyed it? Even justified it to himself—keeping the wolf away from innocent people? But not from everybody. How did it feel, giving Riordan a name?

"I'll tell you one thing," Riordan was saying. "It's a funny thing to say, but I'm glad it's this way. That he didn't do it to himself. I'd hate to think that."

"Just as long as everybody else does."

Riordan was quiet for a minute. "You've got some mouth on you. That's not even fair. I got it changed."

Ben rolled down the window and tossed the cigarette. The quick storm had slowed to a light drizzle. "Just up here," he said.

At the Continental gate they idled behind a white convertible with a canvas top, its tail lights bathing the trunk in neon red. Even the cars were different here, bright pieces of color, not gray jeeps and flatbed convoys. Like waking up in Oz. Maybe it had been that simple, not some blinding light on the road to Damascus. Maybe Danny had just seen a red convertible, an aqua swimming pool, and decided to leave the old world behind.

"Why Bunny?" Ben said suddenly. "Why ask Bunny? Doesn't Minot know anybody downtown?"

"Picture people. Call comes from the studio, they figure the usual, a dame, maybe high on weed. Something. A congressman calls, they wonder. People talk. And word gets out." He looked at Ben. "How'd you hear, by the way?"

Ben said nothing, turning back to the gate.

"Right," Riordan said slowly, doing a sum in his head. "Your pal at the Market. Little Jimmy Olsen."

"Did Bunny know why?"

Riordan shook his head. "Just a favor."

"So Danny's a drunk. Another studio mess. But not a snitch."

"Snitch. He was your brother. What do you want to beat him up like that for?"

"I beat him up?" Ben said, looking over at Riordan.

"You're doing it now. What he did—"

"You're right," Ben said, tired of it. "Maybe you didn't, either. Maybe he beat himself up."

"He didn't do anything to himself. That's the point. Somebody else did. So who?"

"Check your files."

"You didn't listen before. If I know, it's too late. Somebody wanted to stop him. It's somebody he hadn't told me about yet."

Ben watched the tail lights pass through.

"We could help each other out," Riordan said.

Ben turned to him, meeting his eyes.

"That's what you were looking for in his desk," he said finally. "Another name."

"It's the same one you want, isn't it?"

He walked through the gate and heard music, people singing around a piano. The door of Sound Stage 4 was open, light pouring out onto the wet pavement. To one side, holding an umbrella, Bunny stood watching, his figure oddly poignant, like one of the waifs he used to play, nose pressed against the glass.

He was in a belted raincoat, dressed to go—where? Ben had never imagined him off the lot. But he must have a life somewhere, maybe a house on the beach, a bungalow in one of the canyons. Where he took phone calls at night, doing favors. Something he must have done a dozen times, just putting things right. A call the police understood, coming from him—studio business, another embarrassment to keep out of the papers. Not asking Riordan why, just holding the favor in his hand like an IOU. Not talking about it, either, certainly not to the un-expected brother, who kept poking at it.

Ben stopped. According to Riordan. It was still a call to the police, not something Bunny would do without knowing why. What had Riordan said to him? Or didn't he have to say anything?

"It's stopped raining," Ben said, coming up to him.

He looked at Ben, distracted, then up at the dark sky and closed the umbrella. "So it has."

"You're not going in?"

On the nightclub set everything was still in place, but the gowns had been traded in for ordinary skirts, the men back in casual trousers and V-neck sweaters, even the cocktail glasses replaced by bottles of beer. Platters of food had been set up along the bar.

"No, you don't want to barge in on a wrap party. Breaks the mood."

The piano player shifted to a new song, the small knot of singers laughing as they picked it up.

"No fun with the boss around?"

Bunny shook his head. "Ever work on a picture?" he said, smiling a little, his voice distant. "For six weeks, eight weeks, whatever the shoot is—the minute this door closes everything else goes away. Everything. There's just the crew, what you're doing that day, getting the take right. That's all. Like family. Closer. Then it's over." He nodded to the set where Rosemary was being lifted onto the bar next to the piano. "And you pretend you're relieved, but—now what? You don't want outsiders, not at the end. Well," he said, catching himself, "listen to me."

"You must miss it."

"Well, of course you *miss* it. It's the whole point. All the rest of it—" He waved his hand. "Remember *Castaway*? My first picture. A hundred years ago. We opened at the Pantages. My first time. I'd never seen anything like it before—the flashbulbs, people yelling your name. I was on the *radio*. And I thought, well, this is all right, this is it. But it wasn't. This was it," he said, looking at the set. "You can get things right. Perfect, sometimes. A perfect take. You can never get things right out here." He looked down at his watch. "Still, here we are. And I'm late, I'm late," he said, doing the White Rabbit.

"No rushes tonight?"

"Not tonight," he said, closing down, moving back into the life Ben knew nothing about, as secret as Danny's. Ben looked over at him. The one Riordan had called.

"You're all wet, by the way," Bunny said, starting to move. "Better get dried off."

"I got caught. I was having a drink at Lucey's with a friend of yours."

Bunny stopped.

"Dennis Riordan."

Bunny turned, trying to read his face.

"What a busy little bee it is. Buzz, buzz," he said slowly. "And what did he have to say?"

"Not much. He knew my brother."

"Oh yes? His nickel or yours?"

"His. A condolence call."

Bunny took a second, fiddling with the umbrella. "You want to have a care there. You know who he is?"

Ben nodded. "One of Minot's field hands. Don't worry, I told him you said the Pledge of Allegiance every morning."

"That's not funny. What did he ask you?"

"About you? You didn't come up."

"Then why did you say he was a friend of mine?"

Ben shrugged. "I figured you'd know everybody on Minot's staff."

"Not everybody."

"We just talked about Danny."

"Was this after your chat with Rosemary?" Not making a point, just letting him know. "Quite a day for old times."

Ben hesitated. "Why didn't you tell me? Why the big mystery? You knew what I was looking for—"

"Tell you what?" Bunny said, then looked away, switching gears. "It wasn't mine to tell. Yours, either."

"You said you didn't know him."

"I said I'd never met him. I knew who he was. Hard not to, considering."

"So it must have been a relief."

Bunny peered at him. "Are you trying to get me to say something unpleasant? Why? I'm sorry for your loss, all right? Let's leave it at that."

"All I wanted was to talk to her. I knew there'd been someone."

"And do you feel better now? Any more skeletons in the closet or are we ready to move on?"

"I don't know, are there?"

But Bunny didn't rise to this. "Usually. People are disappointing once you get to know them. I find. You'd do better remembering the good times. I assume there were?"

"A few."

"Well, hold on to those," he said archly, patting Ben's upper arm. He glanced through the door. "Now let's let her have her party in peace. Anyway, I'm late." He began to move away again.

"Why'd you make the call?"

Bunny was quiet for a second. "*Les frères Kohler,*" he said finally, rhyming. "One was trouble. Now two."

"You didn't answer."

"All right. What call?"

"The one you made to the police."

"Again? You're like a record with a skip. Back and back."

"The one Riordan asked you to make. Why you?"

"Did he? Tell you what, now that you're chums, why don't you ask him?" he said, an end move. He let out a breath with an audible weariness. "Look, we're stuck with each other for a while. Mr. L insists. Let's make the best of it." He nodded toward the sound stage. "For a start, we'll keep Rosemary to ourselves, shall we? What's done is done. No need to upset anyone. There's the grieving widow to consider."

"Is that why the screen test? Something for the wronged party?"

"Don't be ridiculous," Bunny said, genuinely put out. "Screen tests aren't favors. Not mine. You think we're all Sam Pilcer?" He looked up, feeling the drizzle begin again, cooling his mood. "I think she has something."

"Besides an accent."

"So did Bergman, when she started. You can work with an accent, if there's something there." He looked again at the sound stage. "Whatever it is. Some quality."

"And you think she has that?"

"Haven't the faintest. She moves well, that's what I noticed. But you can't know anything until you see film. It's not what you see, it's what the camera sees. What quality it brings out. You have to have that."

"What was yours?" Ben said.

Bunny looked at him, then smiled, amused. "Innocence, I think."

AFTER BUNNY left, Ben stood for a while watching the party, invisible in the dark outside. There was a cake, somebody's birthday, with candles to blow, then whoops and applause. He wondered if Bunny had had a cake on his set, eleven candles, surrounded by beaming grips and the family closer than family. Years like that, closing the world out with a door, until he was outside, too.

He darted back to Admin B, then sat at his desk looking at the photos in the manila envelope. Riordan peering over someone's shoulder, maybe already planning how to clean up. Not a stranger to it. You'd see things at the Bureau, maybe another informer, tired of it. Except Danny had stayed with Riordan, not yet tired, wanting to—what? Protect the country? From whom? What names had he actually given? It was possible, wasn't it, that he'd just told them things they already knew, some nimble card shuffle to protect his own flanks and bank a favor or two. But there he was, lying facedown in the alley, evidently not harmless. The same boy who'd been in the bed across the room, talking late into the night. Ben looked at the pictures again, feeling a heaviness in his chest. An informer.

And what about the boy in the other bed? No longer all ears, the eager audience. Now he'd seen things himself, stacks of bodies, a shocked face watching blood gush out. Not a boy anymore, either. Someone who knew the camp guards might be anybody, might be us— and where did we go from there? Now that we were capable of anything? They'd both done things they'd never imagined they'd do. Who was he to blame Danny, making love now to his wife? Maybe he would have helped Riordan, too, done the same thing under the circumstances—which were what exactly?

He shoved the pictures back in the envelope and put them in the drawer. Who knows what Danny's reasons had been, some twisted apostasy. The point was he'd ended up in the alley. Nothing he could have told Riordan deserved that. A career jeopardized, a reputation? Not a real war, with real casualties. You didn't kill people yet for name-calling.

Hal had asked him to stop by the cutting room on his way out, a quick check-in, he assumed, but some of the enlarged clips had come back from the lab, so a few minutes became an hour, then two. By the time he headed out to his car, he was already late for the roast chicken, the sort of absentmindedness they wrote into the Blondie series, cut to a scolding or an exasperated sigh at the door. He opened the car door. What were they doing? It's too soon, she'd said, but done it anyway, gasping. If he thought about it, things flooded in, all the awkward questions. But if you didn't think about it, it was simple again—the feel of skin. He wanted her because he wanted her. And she clutched him when she came, him, not someone else. No need to go deeper than skin. You could feel alive in it.

"Thank god." An out-of-breath Lasner, upset, his eyes slightly frantic. "Where the hell's Bunny?"

"He went off the lot."

"Where? There's nobody home. I tried. What, does he have a *date* for chrissake? Henry took Fay to her cards. So now what? Call a cab?"

"What's wrong?"

"Your car?" Lasner said, eyeing it. "You mind? I appreciate it."

"You need a lift?"

"Hurry," Lasner said, opening the passenger door. "Come to think of it, you can talk to her. If she can talk. They didn't say."

"Who?" Ben said, getting in.

"The cops called. There's a crash. The Buick. Lorna said Genia took it out. I didn't even know she could *drive*."

Ben started the car and backed it out. "Where?"

"Go out Sunset. The Palisades. So who does she know out there? She doesn't know anybody. What's she doing there?"

At the gate, Lasner leaned over Ben to talk to the guard.

"Carl? Henry comes, tell him I got a lift home, will you?"

"Sure thing, Mr. Lasner," he said, saluting, a Dick Marshall–army gesture.

"He takes Fay to the cards," Lasner said to Ben, "and then she likes him to stay. I'm here late anyway, so what the hell. Then something like this happens."

They went up Gower and made a left on Sunset.

"They got the name off the registration. Lucky Fay's not home— you imagine, she gets the call? So Lorna says call here. Now the car's a wreck, I guess. Not that you mind the car. I mean, family. I don't know, you try to do something nice for somebody and she just sits there. Then it rains, she takes the car out. A night like this."

"Maybe she was going to see somebody."

"Who does she know?"

They had passed through Hollywood, then the long featureless stretch before Fairfax, slowing now as they came to the heavier traffic on the Strip, bright from the neon signs over the clubs.

"Who knew she could drive? Who has cars over there? Look at this," he said, indicating the slick street. "She goes tonight, roads like this."

"What about the other car?"

"They didn't say. Maybe she went into a tree, I don't know. Just come. It's serious."

Lasner was quiet for a minute.

"It's a hell of a thing, isn't it? You get through all that business, survive *Hitler*, and then you come here and—bam."

"They didn't say she was dead, did they?"

"No. Just there was an accident. But they don't on the phone, do they? Christ, imagine how Fay's going to feel—"

"Let's wait till we get there."

Lasner fidgeted as they snaked around miles of houses. When they climbed into the Palisades, he pulled a note out of his pocket.

"Paseo Miramar. On the north side, they said. After Palisades Drive, into Topanga."

"I know it."

"What do you mean, you know it? You just got here."

"Feuchtwanger lives there. A friend of Liesl's father. I had to drop him off there."

A Mediterranean villa spilling three stories down the cliff.

"And that's where she goes for a drive? Christ, look at it." They had started up the narrow, twisting road, slowing on the sharp curves. "And they put houses here."

"For the views. That's the ocean." He nodded to the string of highway lights in the distance, the dark sea beyond.

They passed Feuchtwanger's house, dark except for a single light in the study, not expecting visitors. But why even suppose they knew each other? A convenient turnoff up into the hills, maybe even picked at random. He imagined her at the wheel, deliberate, her eyes still blank, the light left somewhere in Poland.

"She comes up here? You know what I'm thinking?" Lasner said, a kind of echo. "It's a hell of a thing. To do that." He looked over at Ben, suddenly embarrassed. "Well, I don't have to tell you."

"No."

At the top there was another turn, then a swarm of lights at the end of a stretch, just before the road looped back. Ben saw an ambulance and a cluster of police cars, lights trained on a splintered section of a wooden barrier fence at the edge of the cliff. One of the policemen was holding back a group of curious neighbors, the same extras, Ben thought, who'd appeared in the Cherokee alley. A flashbulb went off—maybe even the same police photographer. Now a few more shots, catching the group of ambulance workers carrying a litter up the side of the hill and onto the road.

"I made the call," the policeman in charge said. "Sorry to bring you out, but we need an ID on her. It's your car."

Another cop drew back the sheet. Lasner looked down at the body, his face growing slack, then turned away, squeamish.

"A friend?"

"Cousin," Lasner said, almost inaudible.

"You're next of kin?"

"My wife."

"Close enough. You'll need to see the ME over there, make the ID. I'm sorry, but we need to do it."

"What happened?" Ben said, staring at her face, torn by shards of glass where she must have hit the windshield, her hair matted with blood. Her eyes were closed but her mouth was open, as if it were still saying "oh."

"She went through there," the cop said, pointing to the broken fence. "Into the canyon. The car didn't catch fire, so that's one thing, but a drop like that, be a miracle you survive it. You just get knocked to hell." He looked up at Lasner. "Sorry."

Ben looked at the length of road, almost straight after the hairpins coming up.

"What do you think?" he said. "She swerved to avoid another car?"

The cop shook his head. "No sign of that. No skid marks either side. Course the rain didn't help there. But you get a slippery patch here, you take it a little fast—" He raised his hand, letting them fill in the rest. "We had a hell of a time getting her out. The door stuck."

But the curve wasn't sharp, a gradual arc that anyone should have handled easily—unless you hadn't driven a car in years, or never intended to turn. He looked down at the body again, trying to imagine the last minute, through the fence and then suspended in nothing, waiting for it to be over. Something no one else ever knows, the desperation for release. But what prompts it? Ben wondered, an awkward second, whether he had been part of it, the unexpected reminder, ghosts coming back.

"Reuben, it's you?"

He turned to find Feuchtwanger, a raincoat over his jacket and tie, the slicked-back hair and wireless glasses formally in place.

"Herr Feuchtwanger."

"Such a commotion. We saw the lights." He looked over at Genia's body, clearly not recognizing her. "Poor woman. Oh, these roads. Marta says it's no worse than the corniche but me, I think a death trap." He paused. "But what are you doing here?"

"She's a cousin," Ben said, indicating Lasner, huddled now with the ME.

"I'm sorry," he said. "Would you like to come back to the house? Some coffee?" A ritual courtesy.

"No, no, thank you. We have to—" He spread his hand to the accident scene, policemen still moving idly around. "Stay with the body. Sign things." He looked down at her. "She survived the camps," he said, perhaps a memory trigger.

But Feuchtwanger still didn't know her. The sorrow on his face was impersonal, another victim.

"The camps, but not this road," he said, shaking his head. "Well, what am I doing here? They say in English a rubberneck—it's amusing, a rubberneck. So." He looked toward the group of neighbors, still gawking. "Marta wanted to know—all the lights. If you need to telephone, please come to the house."

Ben nodded a thank-you.

"And coffee one day. Tell Liesl to bring you, we'll talk. She looked well. So strong. I thought it would kill her, too—the way she felt about him. But no, strong. The father's daughter." He looked down at the stretcher. "But so much death."

Ben stood in the road, watching him walk away. The way she felt about him. But Lion was a romantic, his books filled with duchesses and men in wigs and undying love. He didn't know she could lean her head into your shoulder, soft, not strong at all. Everybody saw what he wanted to see.

Lasner was almost finished with the police. Once the ID had been made there was little either of them could do except arrange for the car to be towed. He looked again at the road. No skid marks, the policeman had said, but you didn't need to slam on the brakes to have an accident here. Another car, with its lights in your eyes. The inky darkness of the canyon beyond, making the guard rail hard to see. The slide effect of wet pavement. There were lots of ways it could have happened, all of them easy to believe, unless you had sat with her at dinner and seen her eyes.

Still, why this road? The next turnoff would have taken her up over the coast highway itself, a more dramatic plunge off the cliff into the traffic, a spectacular end. But the etiquette of suicide could be peculiar, oddly discreet. Maybe she hadn't wanted to make a point, just go quietly, no trouble to anyone.

"Who found her?" Ben said suddenly to the cop. They had pulled the sheet back over her face. "I mean, anybody see it happen? Stop?"

"No. Some kids. See the shoulder over there? It's a view point, daytime anyway. Sometimes they park there—it's away from the houses. Nights you don't get many cars, so it's—anyway, they're there, going at it, and when they leave they spot the fence. They take a look and there's the car, her in it. So they call it in."

"This was when?"

"Hour ago, maybe. Couldn't have been too long after she went over. No rigor. Tire marks still fresh. Must have been a quickie." He caught Ben's look. "The kids, I mean."

"Nobody heard the crash?"

"Nobody said. Pretty quiet up here. She'd have the place to herself. Till morning anyway. Then you get the dog walkers." Hours later, not an instant attraction on the highway. "It's just lucky it didn't burn. A few weeks ago, all you'd need is one spark and—*woof.*"

But she would burn now, finally the ashes the Germans had wanted.

Unless Sol decided to have her buried. He looked over to where Lasner was standing, a little lost. He was avoiding the stretcher, still shaken. But Sol had scarcely known her. It occurred to Ben that their talk at dinner may have been the only real connection she'd made in California, that he had known her better than anyone. Not buried. She'd want to go up in smoke, erasing herself.

Another car had pulled up, with a noisy greeting to the police photographer. Kelly. Ben, not yet seen, went quickly over to Lasner.

"Get in the car," he said.

"What?"

"Now. Don't let him see you, the guy over there—he's press. If he thinks there's a studio connection, he'll do a story. You don't need that."

"You're looking after me now?" he said.

"I know him, I'll take care of it. Just don't let him see you. He'll recognize you. Not her."

"Another Bunny," Lasner said, but moved to the car, his face turned away.

Kelly was already at the stretcher with the cop.

"Hey, Kelly," Ben said. "Chasing ambulances?"

"Hey," Kelly said, surprised to see him. "It's a living." He nodded to the stretcher. "More trouble in the family?"

"Just visiting down the street. We heard the sirens."

"Visiting," Kelly said, taking in the neighborhood, an open question.

"If you need to call you could use their phone."

Kelly turned back to the cop. "Who is it? Anybody?"

The cop passed over a clipboard. "Here," he said, "I can't even pronounce it. Copy it if you want. Polish or something. Slid in the rain and went through the fence."

Ben looked nervously at the form on the clipboard. They'd have the Summit Drive address, a Crestview phone exchange, easy for Kelly to spot. But Kelly didn't bother to look.

"Polish," he said, a code for no story. "Anybody else hurt?"

"If so, they took off. Just her." He lifted the sheet off her face.

"Christ, she did a job on herself, didn't she? What's with the head, in the back? You get banged up there, you're the driver?"

The cop nodded to the cars. "Take one and find out. I'll give you a push."

"I'm just saying. A wound like that, it's consistent with a crash?"

"Kelly, for chrissake, anything's consistent with a crash. You know that."

"Yeah."

"It's always got to be something," he said, taking the clipboard away. "It's not enough she's dead. She's got to be somebody dead." Ben waited for him to mention Lasner, but evidently the name hadn't meant anything to him. "If it was Lana Turner, I'd be on the phone to you."

"If it was Lana, you'd be fucking the corpse. I wouldn't put it past you."

"Nice. And all those years in school. You going to write this up or what?"

"A Polack goes in the ditch? My Pulitzer." He turned back to Ben. "Funny seeing you here."

"Friend lives down there," Ben said, cocking his head toward the houses. "Another refugee."

"Some refugee. You know what these go for?"

"I guess he got his money out." Ben moved slightly to the left, blocking Kelly's view of his car.

"I was going to call you."

"Yes?" Ben said, alarmed. Now what? A new scent? Maybe not just some gossip this time. Now there were worse secrets, the kind that could spread like a stain, touching other people. Things he wouldn't want Kelly to overhear at Lucey's.

"Get anywhere with the loan-outs?"

Ben shook his head. "I thought you were giving up on it."

"Yeah," said Kelly. "Too bad, though. You hate to leave it, there's a studio angle. Sometimes it's like this with a story. It goes and then it comes back. Never close a door." He held up a finger and smiled. "You know where I got that? *Partners in Crime.* Remember how Frank always said that?"

Otto's pet phrase. After he started working for Goebbels.

"Which one were you?" Kelly said. "The younger one?"

"Neither. It's a movie."

Kelly nodded, unconvinced. "Well, you hear anything, you know where to reach me."

"You're the first call."

He put the car in a U-turn away from the accident and started back down the hill.

"What was that all about? He's going to write this up?" Lasner said.

"The only story was, she was related to you, so there's no story."

"You forgot to mention it, huh?"

"Mrs. Lasner doesn't need to see this in the papers. I know what it's like."

Lasner looked over at him. "You're a piece of work. You're here, what, five minutes? And already you know guys on the paper. Not to mention the goddam Palisades." They were passing Feuchtwanger's house, dark now. "Thanks for this," Lasner said, serious. He was quiet for a minute as they turned onto Sunset, heading back. "It's a hell of a life, when you think about it. Hiding like an animal. The camp. Now this. To do something like this."

"There was nothing you could have done," Ben said quietly.

"I don't know."

"What she went through, it breaks something. You can't fix it. Not just like that."

"What did she say to you? At dinner. She talk about it?"

"No," Ben said, avoiding it. "She was sad, Sol. Nothing was going to change that."

"You give her all this," Lasner said, glancing out the window, brooding. "You know the best thing that ever happened to me? Getting the hell out. Everybody should have got out. Even now, you want to kiss the ground here. What kind of life could you have there? This country—"

He broke off, as if the thought had overwhelmed him. Ben followed his gaze out the side window, trying to see what he was seeing, the big, sleepy houses and palms and hedges of paradise.

"She asks, tell Fay it was an accident."

But he didn't have to say anything. When they pulled into the driveway Fay came running out of the house, and Ben could tell from her face that calls had been made and nothing needed to be explained. Behind her, like a shadow, Bunny stood in the doorway, evidently summoned to wait with her. She hugged Lasner, then put her hands on his chest, smoothing his jacket, a hovering gesture.

"Are you all right?" she said. "Did you eat anything?" she said, her hands still on his jacket. "Come on, I'll get you something."

"I'm not hungry."

"And then you're weak. It puts a strain." She patted his chest. "Come on. It was bad?"

Lasner said nothing, moving one of his shoulders.

"Her face, too?"

"No."

She shook her head a little, relieved. "You know she was beautiful. Before everything started. You can't see it now, but she was." She took his arm to lead him into the house. Bunny stepped aside.

"And where the hell were you?" Lasner said, not really angry.

"Out."

"Out."

"Even the maid gets a night off. I'll make the arrangements tomorrow. Fay said cremation?"

Lasner nodded.

"What shape's the car in?"

"Scrap, probably." He pulled a receipt out of his pocket. "Here's where they tow it."

"Anybody there from the papers? You want me to—?"

"Ben took care of it," Lasner said, giving him a thank-you wave.

Bunny hesitated for a moment. "Ah. See you tomorrow then. You want an obit?"

"Who would read it? Who did she know?"

"It's a question of respect," Fay said, then to Bunny, "I'll get you the dates. She was in a few pictures over there. You think they'd be interested in those?"

"They always cut something," Bunny said, evasive. "But we'll see."

He watched them go in, then came over to Ben.

"German silents. From the 'twenties. Just what the papers want." He looked at Ben. "Who'd you talk to?"

"Kelly from the *Examiner*. Don't worry, they already had this one as an accident. You don't have to make any calls."

Bunny held his stare, not answering, then said, "How's Mr. L doing?"

"He's all right. It's more the idea of it. He scarcely knew her."

"Neither of them. I don't think she said ten words. Except to you."

Ben glanced up at the big picture window where she'd looked out over what had been bean fields. "She knew my father. It took her back."

He drove to the Hollywood Hills, his head filled with the grainy clips in Hal's cutting room. Why did some survive and some break? But maybe it was only a matter of degree. Nobody was the same after. Only the mindless, or the callous, could pretend nothing had happened. The others would feel the weight of it, pressing on them, until they accepted it, part of the air, or it got worse and they drove away from it. Still, why the car? Maybe because it was the one way it wouldn't have happened there—not gas or starvation, what they used, your own choice.

Liesl was on the couch, smoking, her legs drawn up under her, a script in her lap. When he walked in, she drew on the cigarette, deliberately not saying anything.

"I'm sorry. I couldn't call."

"I play a daughter," she said, picking up the script. "So it's good for me. Something I know." Not asking where he'd been.

He went over to the tray on the side table and poured a drink.

"She takes care of him, but now she has to go away. So I can just think of my father. What that would be like."

"You didn't wait, I hope."

"No. Daniel would do it sometimes—not come. So I know, don't wait." She put out the cigarette. "Of course I thought he was working. That's all I thought then."

"There was an accident. I had to take Lasner. Remember the cousin at dinner?"

"What happened?"

"Car crash. Near Lion's, in fact. I saw him. When they pulled her out."

"You mean she's dead?"

Ben nodded. "She went into the canyon. Probably killed when she hit, that kind of drop."

"Oh," she said, a sound standing in for everything else.

"They're listing it as an accident."

She raised her eyebrows.

"No other car. She drove herself off."

"Oh," she said again, taking this in. "She did that?"

"It happens, with the survivors. It's hard to come back."

"And here I am, thinking about— You're not surprised at this."

"No. Neither was Lasner."

"It's terrible for them. To be the ones left. It doesn't end—" she said, her voice private, interior.

He looked over at her. "He didn't do that to you. That's not what happened."

"It feels the same. You can't put it away somewhere. It's in your head. Tonight I sat here, I thought, it's just like before. So foolish—a roast chicken, something as foolish as that. Waiting, just like before. And I thought, it's happening again. I'm waiting again."

He went over to the couch, reaching out to put a hand on her shoulder, but she shrank from it, moving away.

"No. Don't."

She stood up and moved toward the French windows, clutching the sides of her arms, guarded.

"We can't do this. What happened—all right, it happened. But to keep—" She turned. "You know what I was thinking about tonight?

Maybe I'm still angry, that's why. Like a child, hitting back. You can, I can, too, something like that, I don't know."

"It's not like that."

"Not for you. I don't know what it is for you. Maybe something of his. Something crazy like that."

"Why does it have to be anything?"

"Because he's still in my head. How can you want me like that?"

"I don't care."

"Oh. And that makes it all right." She shook her head, then moved toward the kitchen, a distraction. "Are you hungry?"

"No. I want to talk."

"About this? There's nothing to say. We have to stop. Before something happens."

"Like what?"

"We went to bed. I don't know why, maybe just to do it."

"You enjoyed it."

"Yes, all right. Do you want to hear that? I enjoyed it. But now it's not so easy."

Ben was quiet for a second, taking another sip of his drink, waiting for her, a look to get them over it.

"Do you want me to leave?"

"Leave. Where would you go?"

"The Cherokee. I still have the key."

"Ha. To take women there. Then you can really be him. It's what you wanted."

"Not anymore."

"No, why not?"

"He's not who I thought he was."

She looked at him, disconcerted, then turned back to the window, not wanting to pursue it.

"You can't go to that place. It's—what's *schaurig*?"

"Ghoulish. Creepy."

"Ghoulish." She fingered the handle on the window, testing it. "Anyway, I'm afraid here now. The man never came. About the locks."

"I know. You don't have to worry. Turns out it was him. Or someone he sent."

"What?"

"He wanted to look through Danny's desk."

"Like a thief? Why?"

"They used to work together. He wanted some information Danny didn't get to pass on," he said, his voice taut.

"I don't understand. Worked how?"

"You don't want to know."

"Know what?"

"You can stop waiting for him," he said, cocking his head toward the couch. "He wasn't who you thought he was, either."

"What's wrong?" she said, her hands fluttery, nervous. "What's happened?"

"I had a drink. A real eye-opener. With Dennis Riordan. Mean anything to you?"

She shook her head.

"Ex-FBI. They worked together. Danny was keeping an eye on all of you for the Bureau." He gulped down the rest of the drink, angry at the sound of his own voice.

"All of who?"

"The Germans. All of you. Your father, I suppose. I don't have the exact list. I'd like to get it, see how far he went. What do you think he told them about Alma? Talk about suspicious characters." He looked up at her. "You really had no idea?"

"What, that people watched us? Of course, all during the war. My father always said. We had to be careful on the phone. They listened. You had to expect that."

"But not from your husband. But who better? He was practically a refugee himself. He'd know everyone in the German community—he married into it. Be the most natural thing in the world for him to know what everyone was up to. Just not so natural telling the FBI about it."

"I don't believe you. It's a lie."

"Riordan told me himself. Why would he lie? What for? Why would I?"

"A man who breaks into the house—you believe him?"

"They got together again later. After the Bureau. Riordan catches Reds for Minot and Danny helped him with that, too. A name here and there—I don't know how many. But enough to keep Riordan interested. Partners in crime."

"It's not true."

"But he thinks there must be one more name. Somebody Danny didn't get to tell him about. Whoever killed him. So he had the desk searched. A little clumsy, but he wanted to know. He sends apologies if it frightened you."

"No, you," she said, suddenly white, her face drained. "You frighten me."

"Me?"

"You'll say anything now, to make me hate him. Any lie. Daniel wouldn't do that."

"Yes, he would. He just wouldn't tell you about it. Like a lot of things."

She glared at him. "That makes it easier for you? If he was like that. Then it doesn't matter what we do?" She went over to him, putting her fists on his chest. "Stop it."

"You think I'd make all this up to go to bed with you? I didn't have to, remember? I didn't have to force you, either."

He took her hands, holding them, close enough to feel her breathing, until she pulled them away. She looked at him, then slumped onto the couch, half-sitting on the back.

"No, you didn't," she said quietly. "So it's another thing I've done in my life."

He touched the side of her face, tentative, waiting for her to turn away, but she leaned into it, letting him work down to her neck.

"I'll never force you to do anything," he said.

"No?" she said, staring at the carpet.

"No."

"No," she said wearily. "That wouldn't be—seemly." She looked up at him. "The good brother. But not always."

He took his hand away.

She said nothing, then got up and went over to the window again, pacing.

"And the bad one, who was supposed to do all these things—who was that? I didn't know anybody like that."

"Riordan saw the reports."

"Your friend."

"For the moment. He wants to know who killed Danny, too. His own reasons, but so what? He can help. He's—"

"Expedient," she said, a test answer.

"A chance. A lead."

"It was better when it was Rosemary," she said, picking nervously now at her fingers. "One push. You could believe it." She paused. "What did he say about my father?"

"I don't know yet."

"Yet?"

"I don't know what he said about anybody. But we need to, now," he said, including her, still together. "We need to know what he gave them. See who might have been next."

"Oh, and they'll tell you. How are you going to do that?"

"I thought, the way he did."

She looked over at him.

"Work with them. Be like Danny. The one we didn't know."

POSSE

Minot had suggested Chasen's for lunch and Dave Chasen himself took them to the table, one of the front booths reserved for regulars and recognizable faces. Greer Garson, near the door, seemed not to know who Minot was, but most of the others parading past the table did, and the lunch was interrupted by a series of hellos and handshakes. A surprisingly public place for such a meeting, but what had he expected? Raincoats in an alley? A murky room, drapes drawn? In real life you talked at Chasen's, hoping for a mention in the columns.

"The chili here is great," Minot said, ordering it. "Some people never have anything else."

"Best in L.A.," Riordan said, a chorus.

"You notice how good Dave is? Smooth. You're in, he's gone. He lets you get on with it. Romanoff, he's all over you, you can't get rid of him. The Russian prince. Harry Gerguson, Brooklyn." He had leaned his football shoulders forward, confiding. "That's the real name." He shook his head. "There's a lot of that element here."

"What element is that?" Ben said, on guard, as if someone had just stamped a J in his passport.

"Phonies. I like to know who people are."

"You picked the wrong town then," Ben said, easier. "Half the people in Hollywood have changed names."

"Well, in the industry sure. That's just part of the territory, isn't it? But a waiter pretending to be—"

"A waiter," Riordan said, amused.

"Anyway, I didn't pick this town, you know, I was born here. Native Californian, one of the few. I've seen it change. A small town in those days—well, small compared—then the phonies and smart guys start coming in. Spoilers. A couple of years ago it was still just oranges here. Like a Garden of Eden. Now you have to be careful you don't step on the snakes." He smiled, pleased at the turn of phrase, something he could use again.

"A big city's bound to have crime."

"Not crime. Police can handle that. But what do we do with the others? They want to spoil what we've got here, where we're *going,* and I still don't know why. Some idea. Have you been down to Long Beach? You see what's happened there since the war? We can have the biggest port in America, big as New York, and I'll be goddamned if we're going to let somebody like Harry Bridges close it down. San Francisco, all he's got to do is snap his fingers and nothing moves. We don't want that here. Man's not even a citizen and he can push a whole city around."

"He's not a citizen?"

"Australian. A break for us. You can't bust a union, but you can sure as hell deport troublemakers. Cheryl, dear." He rose to greet a gray-haired woman in a feathery hat and fur stole. "How's George?"

"The flowers meant so much to him, Ken, thank you."

"Never mind about that, you just get him home. You get the best at Cedars but it's still not home." He patted her hand.

"At least they keep him in bed. You know what he's like. He'll be a *bear.*"

"You'll have a nurse?"

"He says he wants Laraine Day, so I guess he's getting better," she said, almost winking. "Well, enjoy your lunch. I'll tell him you asked."

"A massive heart attack," Minot said after she'd gone. "Richfield Petroleum. Not everyone here's in the movies. Just the ones everybody knows about." He took a drink from his water glass. "That makes them special. People are interested in the movies. You can get their attention."

Ben said nothing, waiting for him.

"Dennis here tells me we might have some mutual interests."

Ben nodded.

"I like the sound of that. That's how I like to work. What government's all about. Mutual interests. I don't believe in isms. Any of them. Just getting things done. But you've got people out there, they have a different idea. Not to your face. A fair fight, they know they'd lose. They get underneath. Hide. That's the way they work. We need to know who they are, get them out into the open."

"Congressman," Ben said, stopping him. "A Communist killed my brother. They're not my favorite people, either."

"Ken," Minot said automatically. "And now they want this country." Unable to let it go. "Your brother did us a great service. Dennis says we can count on you, too."

"I want to find out who did it." He nodded to Riordan. "We think it's somebody he was going to give you, so I figure we both want to know."

"Like I said." Minot smiled. "A mutual interest. I have to say, when Dennis told me about this, I was—well, relieved isn't the right word. It's a tragedy, what happened, however it happened. A man's dead. But you hate to think people you work with might be—unreliable. A lot of what we get is hearsay. You'd be surprised how much time we have to spend just making sure information's worth something. Now with your brother we never had that. If he told us to take a look at somebody, we'd find it all right. He didn't shoot from the hip, he got it right. So you learn to trust that. Then this happens and you have to wonder. You're going to have people saying your sources are unstable. And that makes it all suspect. They'd like people to think that, it's one of their tactics."

"So it was better as an accident," Ben said, interrupting the flow.

"That's right," Minot said, hesitating, not sure what Ben knew. "But this, this is a whole new game. If it's true, we could make some real noise. Most of the time it's hard to get people excited. They think it's just about union business, organizing the coloreds. Politics. But a trial, that's something else. A Red kills somebody working for the Bureau—everybody's going to jump on that."

"If it's true?"

"Well, I mean you have to prove it. Otherwise, it's still just 'a man fell.' Dennis here says it's not going to be easy. Police never took it up, so we're not long on evidence. We can get some help from the Bureau, on the quiet, but even they can't make a miracle. Far as I can see, the best chance we have is you."

"Me."

"You're in his house, you know everybody he knows. And it has to be somebody he knows. You don't name strangers."

"I've already looked through his things. If he was keeping notes, something like that, he wasn't keeping them there. But sometimes one name leads to another, so it would be useful to see the files."

"What files would those be?" Minot said, wary.

"What he gave you."

"Look, let me explain how this works. Your brother never gave us any paper. He liked to play things close to the vest. He didn't want anything traced back to him. Limits you, once that's out. People don't confide in you. No, he'd just give Dennis a name, a little information if he had it, and then it was up to us. Like I said, they were the right names—once we knew where to look."

"You said there were reports," Ben said to Riordan.

"With the Bureau, you talk and somebody types it up. That's how it worked with us. He'd talk to me and I'd memo the file. You don't have to see them—just ask me."

"Who did he talk about? Can you give me a list?"

"How this started? The Bureau wanted to know what Ostermann was up to."

"You thought he was a Communist?"

"We didn't know what he was. All we knew was when he spoke—wrote an article or something—people listened. There's a war on, it's important to know what somebody like that is going to say. And your brother—well, who was in a better position to know?"

"So he agreed to report on him," Ben said, hoping to be contradicted.

"Tell you the truth, it kind of surprised me, too. I mean, what if the wife found out? How would she feel? But I think maybe he thought he could do him some good. He liked Ostermann. He said we never had to worry about him. And you know, we didn't. No funny business there at all. Wants to be a citizen now."

"Maybe you should write him a character reference," Ben said, more sourly than he'd intended.

"Don't get touchy. You got an important German figure and we're at war with Germany, of course the Bureau has to be interested. Nobody ever interfered with him. He went right on making those speeches, all that. I doubt he ever knew."

"So that's how it started," Ben said, leading him. "Who else?"

"We asked about Brecht. No surprises there—we already knew. But that was a kind of test, see if your brother was pulling his punches."

"And he wasn't."

"The important thing, see, was whether somebody was actually in the Party or just had lefty sympathies. Like Feuchtwanger. Your brother'd been inside, so he knew the difference. People approached him, tried to recruit him back in."

"How? At lunch?" Ben said, opening his hand to Chasen's.

Minot peered at him. "We don't recruit. People come to us. Like you."

"Not to inform on my family."

"Informing," Riordan said, waving this off. "Nobody's *informing*."

"He didn't see it that way," Minot said calmly. "It was—part of the war effort."

"And now?"

"It's a different war."

"I just want to be clear. Not Ostermann. Not—family. I won't do that."

"Nobody gives a rat's ass what Ostermann says now," Riordan said, a little exasperated.

"As long as it's pro-American."

"But he *is* pro-American," Minot said patiently. "And Feuchtwanger writes—what do you call them? Like *Anthony Adverse*. Kaltenbach can't get work at the studios so he's flirting with the East Germans, but he's not going anywhere."

"He's not."

"I think he'd find it hard to leave the country. We're not going to give him a passport so he can be some propaganda stunt. The point is, nobody's asking about the Germans. That's how it started, with your brother, but that's not what he did for me. I'm not interested in that."

"What are you interested in?"

Minot leaned back against the booth, playing with his fork.

"I'm interested in getting people's attention. This country is under attack and it doesn't even know it. How do you get them to see it? And here we are, sitting in a district with the most popular thing on earth. You want something to make people sit up and notice, nothing even comes close to the industry. They've already got people's attention. If we show what's happening here—"

"In the industry? You mean in the unions?"

Minot smiled. "Well, the unions. Nobody would be very surprised at that, would they? Howard Stein, he's practically got a Party number on his back." He looked up. "Your brother was helpful about that. Information we can use when the time comes."

"I thought everybody already knew," Ben said, his stomach turning over. "At least they assume—"

"And he can deny it. But not under oath. Then you're looking at perjury."

"He's going on trial?"

Minot made another half smile. "No. The industry is."

Ben looked at the broad, handsome face, remembering his hand on

Jack Warner's shoulder, Bunny eager to please, everyone taking up positions in the chess game of the consent decree. Minot leaned forward.

"I assume all this is in confidence?"

Ben nodded, fascinated, a different game board.

"Hollywood has done a lot for this city," Minot said. "Nobody knows better than I do. I even know the figures, which is more than you can say for most of them. And the figures are big. Since the war—" He trailed off, letting the obvious finish itself. "So now it's like a rich widow—everyone wants something out of her. The unions want their piece. The East Coast bankers. Let's not even think about the payoffs, let's just pretend they don't happen. But the Commies want something else, they want to use her to get *ideas* across." He caught Ben's skeptical expression. "They don't have to be blatant. Nobody's making *Battleship Potemkin* here. Good thing," he said, flashing a smile. "Who the hell would go see it? Nothing that obvious. You don't attack America. You just chip away at it. Some doubt here. Suspicion. But how do you stop them? First you have to find them." He nodded, somehow including Ben with Danny. "Then you get them to lie. Actually show them lying. Not even their fans are going to trust them after that. You know, you can't put someone away just for being a Commie. Conspiracy to overthrow? You spend years making a case like that. But perjury's quick, and it's right there. They're lying or they're not." He paused. "As long as you have evidence. So you get some. You ask about files, Tenney's got files. And Jack can be a little hasty, so god knows what he's got in them. But we have to be more careful. We're not just some committee in Sacramento. We're a congressional committee. Subpoena power. You lie at the hearing, you just bought a ticket inside."

"And if they do come across," Riordan said, "you still have a shot at contempt."

Ben raised his eyebrow, waiting.

"Nobody's a Red alone," Riordan said. "But they're usually reluctant to say who their friends are. Even under oath."

"So either way," Ben said.

"Assuming we've got the goods on them in the first place."

"And that's what Danny was doing for you? Giving you movie stars for show trials?"

"No, we're a little shy in the star department," Minot said with a stage modesty, not catching the Moscow reference, something that had happened far away. "But any kind of friendly witness here can be something—you still get the press. There's lots of ways you can use information. Your brother wasn't going to testify, anything like that. I told you, he liked to play things close to the vest. Of course, if I'd really had to, I could have subpoenaed him, but why would I do that? He played fair with me. He gave me background. And you can use background in different ways. Sometimes, like I say, to set up a perjury charge. But sometimes to get people to cooperate, lead you somewhere else."

"Give you other names."

"That, or help in other ways. Be a friend to the committee. You know, we don't want to hurt the industry. We want to help it protect itself."

His voice earnest, without a trace of irony. Was it possible he really believed this? Saw himself as a savior, not just another of the rich widow's cynical suitors, borrowing her limelight?

"So, are you going to be a friend to the committee?" he said casually, bringing his hands together, fingers touching, putting a question.

But when he looked at Ben, not smiling, his whole body seemed to tense, expectant, as if he were waiting for the snap of the ball, and Ben saw that the rest of the lunch didn't matter, just this moment. He sat fixed by Minot's gaze, in a kind of quiet panic, feeling exposed, like the second before you leaned forward to a woman, crossing a line. He thought, wildly, of the first night with Liesl, being drawn in, no going back.

"He was my brother," he said finally, hoping his voice sounded steady, plausible. "I want to know who did it. I think we both owe him that."

Minot said nothing, assessing, then nodded, the bargain struck, that easy.

"Everything goes through Dennis, understand? Not through my office. When we're ready for subpoenas, we want them to come as a surprise."

"Like an ambush."

Minot hesitated for a second, then smiled. "That's right. By the good guys this time."

"Ben, how nice. You're *every*where."

Paulette Goddard on her way in. He stood up, taking her offered hand.

"Paulette. You remember Congressman Minot?"

"Of course, at the Lasners'. Nice to see you again." An efficient smile, not overlong.

"Dennis Riordan."

"Mr. Riordan," she said. "Goodness, you all look so *serious*."

"That's what happens with just Dennis to look at," Minot joked, a compliment to her. She was wearing lunch jewels, a solitary drop and a diamond bracelet, everything about her shiny.

"I'm here to eat humble pie with Polly," she said. "Apparently I owed her a train interview and she's been seething. Nice if they had told *me*. But I'm the one in the doghouse."

"Not for long, I'll bet," Minot said, smiling.

"My god, is that chili? At this hour. Men." She rolled her eyes. "I don't suppose you have anything I can give her," she said to Ben. "Otherwise she'll just go on about Charlie again, and what am I supposed to say?"

"Just kiss and make up," Ben said.

She giggled. "In Chasen's. Wouldn't they be surprised. Well, I'll let you get back to business. Three men, it's always business. Don't sign anything," she said, putting a finger on Ben's chest. "That's my motto. Ken." She nodded to Minot, remembering his name. When she left, there was a trace of perfume.

"That's some good-looking woman," Riordan said.

"Hard to believe she was married to him," Minot said.

"Chaplin?" Ben said. "That was a while ago."

"When he wanted to open a second front. Just a little earlier than

Ike did. I'd like to get him in front of a microphone now. Tell us all about his Russian friends."

"I can't help you there," Ben said, moving him away from it. "Never met him. Anyway, I doubt they ever talked politics. Would you? With her?"

"Not me," Riordan said, grinning.

"I don't want you to expect too much," Ben said to Minot. "I don't know the people Danny knew."

"They'll know you," Minot said. "They'll want to know if you're sympathetic. His brother. They'll come to you."

"But I'll have no way of knowing whether they're really— How far it goes."

"Leave that to Dennis. We're just looking for background. Sympathies."

"It would help if I knew who he'd already—"

Minot nodded. "Dennis can help you with that, too. Keep in mind, some of those people agreed to be friends. Protected friends. Even from you. We promised them that."

Ben looked at his smooth, untroubled face, the careful eyes. What had those conversations been like? No one will know if—not blackmail, just a sensible arrangement to keep information coming. A friend to the committee. What he'd promised now, too. He shifted in the booth, feeling suddenly hemmed in. You can do business with anyone, Otto had said. Until he couldn't. Across the room, Paulette was ordering a drink. Don't sign anything. He could still say no, go over to her table, stay in the bright world.

"You understand," Minot said.

"What you want to do," Riordan said, "now that we think it's like this, is go through everything again, calendars, things like that, who he was seeing. He's not going to pick a name out of the blue. What you want are the contacts. Who'd he take to that room, anyway? Any idea?"

Ben shook his head, surprised at how easy it was to lie. Just another move on the board, protecting your pawn.

"You take a room, it's somebody to you. You'd talk."

"You know," Minot said, slowing them down, "to kill someone, you'd have to have an awful lot at stake. Something important to protect. The people we know about—they're writers, studio people who wrote a few checks to send an ambulance to Spain, people like that. So who else?" His voice more excited now. "Who had a reputation so big you'd kill to protect it?"

A reputation, Ben thought, you could showcase in a hearing room, newsreel cameras turning while you pounded a gavel.

"You mean a star," Ben said.

"It's possible."

"But everyone thinks his reputation's important. If somebody's threatening you, everything you have. Something like this, exposing people—you set up conditions." He looked at Minot. "You have to be careful."

"Do you mean me?"

"I meant Danny. But let's face it, Congressman, you keep going, a few people might think they had a reason to kill you."

"What kind of talk is this?" Riordan said.

"Just making a point."

Minot reached over to sign the check, a house account. "Some point. Are we done here, gentlemen?"

They made their way out the door, through another round of nods and waves, and almost collided with Polly rushing in. She was tottering in her heels, the way she had been that morning at Union Station, but came to a dead stop when she saw Minot.

"Congressman," she said, flustered, a hesitation Ben took as a sign of respect.

"Polly, I've been meaning to call you."

"Me?" she said, almost girlish.

"That piece Sunday. I just hope everybody reads it. Stars still in the service. You know my office gets calls every day—the war's over, when is he coming home? Now we can say, look at this. Did you read Polly Marks? Is Bob Montgomery home yet? Movie stars. But they're not bellyaching. They're doing what we all need to do, hang in there till the job's done."

Ben watched, fascinated, as this rolled out in what seemed to be one breath, effortless.

"Congressman—"

"I take my hat off to you. What's Winchell say? Orchids? An orchid for that one. You know Dennis, I think. My friend Ben Collier here? He's still in the service, come to think of it. Still working for Uncle Sam. Making one of those great pictures the WAC's been putting out this year. It's not over for them."

"Yes, at Continental. Of course. Good to see you again," she said, her eyes almost doing a double take. Someone she hadn't quite got the measure of before, a friend of Minot's. "I hear Sol Lasner thinks the world of you."

Ben shrugged, not knowing how to respond.

"Awful about Fay's cousin, isn't it? I heard you were there."

"Terrible," he agreed, noncommittal, avoiding her eyes.

"You'd think they could've met at Sol's, not have her drive way out there. Road like that. Probably feels terrible about it now."

"Who?"

"Whoever she was meeting. The one who called."

"What?" he said, everything stopping for a second, his whole body rooted.

"Somebody called her, that afternoon. They think that's why she went out."

"I hadn't heard that."

How had she? Fay? Lorna? The Hollywood switchboard.

"And in the rain. You'd think—but you never know about people, do you?"

"Well, you do," Minot said, "that's for sure. There's not much Polly misses, or so they tell me." A wrapping-up voice, ready to leave. Riordan, hearing it, handed a stub to the parking attendant.

"I get paid not to miss anything," Polly said, smiling again, flattered.

"Well, you keep writing pieces like Sunday's, they'd better give you a raise. You can tell them I said so, too," he said, a verbal wink. "That was fine work. Nice to run into you." Moving her through the door before she could say anything else.

Ben stood still, only vaguely aware of them. Who would she have been meeting? Not Feuchtwanger. Had she been peering through the rain, looking for house numbers? But the houses stopped and she had gone on. But not necessarily lost, or alone.

"That's a powerful lady," Minot was saying. "Do you know how many people—first thing they do in the morning, turn to Polly? Millions."

"One hundred twenty-three newspapers," Ben said dully, still preoccupied.

Minot looked at him, surprised, then let it pass. "And the radio," he said. "A good friend to have." His car was being brought up. "I'm glad we could do this," he said to Ben. "I think we can do some good work. You know the MPC?"

Ben shook his head.

"Motion Picture Council. For the First Amendment."

"Pinks," Riordan said.

"But not a front group. Legitimate. You might think about joining it. Show them where your heart is. What you might be ready for. Let them approach you." He paused, an interior debate. "How well do you know Kaltenbach?"

"I've met him. He's close to Ostermann. I thought you weren't interested in the Germans."

"Only if they're in the industry."

"He had a lifesaver contract at Warners in 'forty-one. One year. He hasn't worked since."

"At a hundred dollars a week. That still sounds like a lot of money to some people. Hollywood money."

"He's nobody."

"The Germans don't seem to think so. The East Germans."

"He's a famous writer there. Nobody's heard of him here."

"Maybe he'll be better known."

Ben watched him hand some money to the attendant.

"How?" he said, apprehensive.

"Be a help to us if you could let us know what his plans are."

"I thought you said—"

"The State Department's unreliable. People write them—influential people—and they do things they shouldn't. If it were me, there wouldn't be a hope in hell he could go anywhere, but it's not up to me. So we need to keep an eye on him. I don't want him taking any trips. Not before the hearings."

"You're going to call him? He's a Communist?"

Minot shook his head. "No, just two meetings. A little window shopping. But we can put him at the meetings. That means he can tell us who else was there."

"I don't think he'll do that."

"He'll have a lot of incentive under oath."

"Who put him at the meetings?" Ben said, queasy, already knowing.

Minot looked at him, not saying anything.

"Danny saved his life, in France."

"I'm trying to save this country," Minot said. He put his hand on Ben's shoulder, about to move to his car. "Nice to have you with us."

FAY ASSUMED it was a condolence call and insisted they have coffee on the back patio. The day was mild but overcast, fall on Summit Drive, and she put a light cardigan over her shoulders as they went out. After Lorna brought the tray, Fay poured from the silver pot, fluttering like Billie Burke, then sat back and lit a cigarette, crossing her still-good Goldwyn Girl legs.

"It was nice of you to come. There's no one to talk to—who knew her, I mean."

"It was only the once. But I liked her."

"The language was a problem. People don't make the effort."

"The friend who called—he was German?"

"Well, Lorna didn't think so at first. She thought it was Bunny, somebody from the studio, you know. But then Genia spoke German to him, so it must have been."

"A man, then?"

"Mm hmm. Why?"

"I just wondered. He never called again?"

"No, isn't it the strangest thing? Maybe he doesn't *know*. Thinks he was stood up or something. The notice in the papers—if you blinked, you missed it. I can't imagine who it was. She never talked to anybody."

"Maybe someone she knew before. Over there."

"But she never went out. Where would she—?"

"At the party, maybe. She met people then."

"You, mostly. Of course, Bunny can talk to a stone, so she knew him. Maybe somebody through the Red Cross. I don't know. None of it makes sense to me. I mean, you call to meet somebody, it's usually a hotel, a bar, someplace like that."

"Maybe she was going to his house."

"And never got there. Or maybe she did. I never thought of that. Maybe it was after." She frowned, turning this over. "Well, he has the number."

"Let me know if he calls, will you?"

She looked at him, surprised, her cigarette in midair.

"Just curious. It's like a mystery."

"Everything about her was a mystery." She inhaled some smoke. "Look, we don't have to pretend. She didn't slide off the road, did she?"

Ben said nothing.

"I thought it would help, all this," she said, stretching her hand toward the sloping lawn. "Well, you do what you can. She liked the garden. So that's one thing."

"You've put a lot of work into it," he said, taking in the lush rose beds, the perennial borders.

"Me? I wouldn't know a weed from—well, whatever the opposite is. Miguel does everything. Filipino, but with a Mex name, don't ask me why."

"It was a Spanish colony. So lots of Spanish names."

"Is that right? Ha. Wait till I tell Sol." She looked over at him. "That's something everybody knows, right? About it being a colony?"

"No. It was a while ago."

"But people know." She laughed. "Who am I kidding? Sitting here with a teapot, la-di-da, like I ever made it past ninth grade. Bunny likes me with all this high-tone stuff, and fine, I like it, too, because Sol likes it, but I know. I like the roses, though, to look at. Sometimes I look at this place and I think, who would have imagined? All those years on the road, washing out things in the sink, and now you've got your own roses, not just what some guy brings backstage. A gardener with a fancy name." She stopped and looked away. "But I guess she didn't see it that way."

"You ever miss it?" he said, steering them away. "The business?"

"That life? Not for two seconds. What's to miss? One town after another with nothing to do—someplace in the sticks, you couldn't wait to get back to New York. It's the same here, you ask me, but don't, because Sol loves it. At least it's not the road, schlepping around, worrying are you losing your looks. What kind of life is that? Oh, at first, you're young, you think there isn't anything else. I never saw myself like this. Married. Mrs. Lasner. And all right, he's a handful, but you know what? He's crazy about me. The rest," she said, waving her hand, "it's nothing." She put out the cigarette, looking straight at him. "Would you tell me something? He almost died on the train, didn't he? Don't worry, I didn't get it from you."

"He had an attack. I don't know how serious. I'm not a doctor."

"He almost died," she said flatly. "He thinks I don't know. How can you live with somebody and not know these things?"

"What did the doctor say?"

"Rosen? What does he ever say? Retire. And do what? Watch birds? Anyway, he wasn't there, only later when Sol's better. You were. You know how I know? How he is with you."

"What do you mean?"

"Close. You almost die, there's a closeness."

"I think you're imagin—"

But she was shaking her head. "He watches you at the studio, how you're doing."

"He watches everybody," Ben said.

"But he tells me about you. How you are with Hal. Other things. He thinks you have a feel for the business. A family thing."

"Only my father. My mother hated it."

"Why? Oh, the girls? He got distracted?"

Ben smiled at the word. "Over and over."

"People say I should worry about Sol, and you know I never do. I figure, if it happens, who'd want to know?"

"She did."

Fay smiled. "So maybe I'm not telling the truth, either. I'd kill him. Bare hands. But I'll tell you something, he doesn't even look. I know. I was on the lot, for years. I know what to look for. The thing about Sol, nobody gets this, he's a gentleman. They see the rough spots, not here." She tapped her heart. "Here he's not so tough." She looked down, flustered. "I don't mean the real one. A figure of speech."

"I know."

"But that's right, too, isn't it? The real one's not so tough, either. Then what? You know what he thinks about, all the time? What happens to the studio. Me, I guess he figures I can take care of myself. But what happens to the studio. Who could do it? You know we never had children. He said it didn't matter to him, but now I think it does. You build something, you want to pass it on, not just hand it over to the banks. I said to him once, maybe it's better, look at the Laemmles, Junior almost took it down with him, and I could tell he's not even listening. So that's part of it, I think. Why he watches people."

"What about Bunny?"

"Bunny's not a son."

"I'm not, either."

"But he likes you. So maybe it was the train, I don't know. All the sudden you feel you're running out of time. Maybe this is it. Did you ever wonder how much time you have left? I've been thinking about

that, because of Sol. But I guess that's one thing nobody can know."
She paused. "Unless it's like with her. You decide," she said, her face
softer. "You were nice to come. It's good somebody came." She lifted
her head, a visual pulling up. "It's funny, she's the one contacted the
Red Cross. She wanted to come over. You wonder. But you know what I
think? It came to me this morning. Does this make sense to you? I
think she was already gone. She just didn't want to die over there—give
those bastards the satisfaction."

THERE WAS still a police marker by the broken fence, so Ben stopped
short, pulling the car over to the lookout shoulder where couples parked.
The drive up Feuchtwanger's corniche had been no easier in daylight, an
ordeal even for anybody familiar with the road. Ben imagined it dark,
headlights shining on the wet surface. He got out, not even sure what he
was looking for. Something left carelessly behind? But the place seemed
undisturbed, even the smashed car removed now, any tire marks or
shoe prints washed away. He walked to the fence, looking over into the
canyon. A steep drop. All you'd have to do was put the car in gear and
let it go. Gravity and a soft skull would do the rest.

Ben went down the slope. There were ruts gouged out of the
ground, probably made by the tow truck or whatever kind of winch
they'd used to haul the wreck up. The tree that had stopped it had some
bark scraped away, but was still standing. Given the angle of descent,
the impact must have been violent, a thudding crash, enough to throw
a body into the windshield. So why hadn't there been more blood? He
tried to remember the body, his brief look when the sheet was pulled
back. Lacerations, the matted wound on the head, but not drenched in
blood. But it wouldn't have been if she'd died instantly. A dead body
doesn't pump blood. Still, the blow on the head had caused a bloody
welling. Ben looked up to the broken fence. Unless she'd been hit before the crash, maybe already dead when the car began plunging.

He hiked back to the road and walked along the shoulder to the
turnoff. Big enough for two cars, even more, somewhere to meet,

marked by the curve. Ben turned back again to the fence, searching the ground. He'd wanted to come back to the site, show himself how it was possible, but he'd known outside Chasen's that she hadn't been alone. A phone call, a hasty meeting, dead or almost dead before she went over. The ground falling into Topanga told him nothing. He thought of her at the Lasner party, unafraid to tell him things he shouldn't know. No more whispers and shadows, not after everything. A German voice on the phone. Who else was at the party, what other ghost? Who recognized her.

He drove back to Feuchtwanger's house, parking near the other cars along the steep patch of road, one of them, he noticed, Ostermann's.

"Come in, come in," Feuchtwanger said, bubbling, his rimless glasses catching the afternoon light.

"I didn't mean to interrupt."

"No. Brecht is starting to make speeches. Please interrupt. What, were you just passing by? Nobody passes by up here."

He led Ben into a large living room with a spectacular view of the Pacific through the picture window. Couches were arranged to face it, but the group sat instead at the end of the room, away from the light, clustered around a coffee table littered with half-finished cups and hazy with smoke, as intimate as a Ku'damm café. Everyone was speaking German.

"So, you can decide," Feuchtwanger said. "I'm thinking about a play and of course Brecht doesn't want me to write a play, so he doesn't like anything about it."

"Write the play," Brecht said, deadpan, drawing on his cigar.

"Do you like *The Devil in Boston*? For a title?"

"The title tells you what's wrong," Brecht said. "All right, so witch trials. Yes, everyone sees, a metaphor for what is happening here, what is going to happen, but it's not exact. It was then about belief, the *devil* in Boston, a religious phenomenon, not political persecution."

"It felt the same to the witches," Feuchtwanger said.

Brecht waved this aside. "It confuses the issue."

"But the *process* is exactly the same, the psychology."

"Oh, psychology," Brecht said, dismissive.

"Why do you think it's going to happen," Ben said, back at Chasen's, Minot's hand on his shoulder.

"Because I've seen it happen before."

"Precisely," Feuchtwanger said. "The process is the same, always. Make the fear, then the fear feeds on itself. That's the devil. Hitler made the Jew the devil, but it was the fear."

"The motivations are different," Brecht said. "Hitler wanted to go to war, that's what he always wanted. From the first. Not religious hysteria."

"And the rallies?" Feuchtwanger said. "What do you call that?"

Brecht drew on his cigar with a little smile. "Show business," he said in English.

"Ach," Feuchtwanger said, a mock exasperation, but enjoying the joke. "And here?"

"Politics," Brecht said. "Not even serious politics. Foolishness. It's a country of children." He turned to Ben. "You know what his inspiration is? For a play about witches? They refused his application. To be a citizen. Of this place. Why he wants such a thing—"

"Why not gratitude?" Ostermann said. "They took us in. They took you in, too."

"Yes, and they'll spit me out. Watch." He took a drink from a small glass. "We have no place now. Only here," he said, touching his temple.

"Hah. I'm not such a poet," Feuchtwanger said. "I live here." He pointed his finger to the floor.

"But not as an American."

"Why? What did they say?" Ben asked Feuchtwanger.

"I can appeal. The time isn't right maybe. With what's going on."

"The reason? 'Premature antifascism,'" Brecht said, rolling out the phrase slowly, savoring it. "What can it mean? There must have been a time when it was good to be a fascist. Then not. It's a trick, finding the right moment. You can be against the fascists, but not too soon. Then you're—well, what exactly?"

Feuchtwanger shrugged, nodding with him. "A socialist. A pacifist.

Before, when you wrote against the Nazis, where could you do it? The places they suspect now. Too left, too this, too that. So it's not the best time here."

"Thomas Mann had no problem," Brecht said, puckish.

"Oh, Saint Thomas."

They laughed softly, a café murmur. Ben looked at them, slumped against cushions, holding cigars, easy with each other. Was this the sort of meeting Danny had described, Riordan scribbling notes? The author of *Josephus* is preparing a play about the Salem witch trials, drawing analogies to contemporary events. The author of *Galileo* made remarks critical of the U.S. Hans Ostermann, my father-in-law, said— All typed up for the files, smoky, idle talk, a harmless report. But no betrayal was harmless.

"What brings you here?" Ostermann said suddenly.

What did?

"Just a quick hello. Lasner wanted me to check on the car, whether they'd towed it."

"Yes, the accident," Feuchtwanger said. "I told you about it," he said to Ostermann. "Terrible."

"But on this road not a surprise," Ostermann said. "Someone you knew?"

"A relative of Lasner's." Ben turned to Feuchtwanger. "Are there any Germans living here, up on the hill? Besides you?"

"Oh no. We're famous, Marta and me—the foreigners. Of course Mann is also in the Palisades. Vicki Baum. But not here, nearer the village."

"Why do you ask?" Ostermann said.

Ben looked up, at a loss. "Maybe this, hearing German. It would be so nice for you if there were someone else nearby."

"Only Lion has the courage," Brecht said. "These roads. In Santa Monica it's safe, all flat. Even Salka, in the canyon, it's not so bad."

"But the views," Feuchtwanger said, extending his hand toward the window and the fading afternoon, copper glints on the water and lights beginning to come on.

"But we always have to drive you," Ostermann said. "The courageous Lion."

Another easy laugh, the road familiar to all of them. You didn't have to live here to know it. Even Lion's guests, German speakers.

"So how was it at Alma's?" Brecht asked Feuchtwanger.

"You know she had Schoenberg and Stravinsky? Both. The same dinner."

"Another play for you," Brecht said, mischievous.

"No, it was dull. They wouldn't talk about music. Out of respect. Anything but music—so nothing, really."

"And Alma talked about herself."

Ben drank his coffee, half-listening, talk that could go on for hours. No other Germans on the road. Just a place to meet, then, out of the way. He stood up.

"But you've just come," Feuchtwanger said.

"I know. But I have to get back to the studio."

"Ah, the studio," Brecht said airily. "Back to the assembly line." He moved his arms in a pincer, like Chaplin working the wrenches in *Modern Times*. "More dreams. More dreams."

"And me," Ostermann said, standing, too. "No, no, don't get up. A nice afternoon, Lion. Like before."

"Nothing's like before," Brecht said. "Even before."

Outside Ostermann walked Ben to his car.

"I thought when you came, it was for me. That you had news."

"News?"

"About the screen test."

Almost forgotten. Liesl playing a daughter.

"No, not yet."

"I don't want her to be disappointed. After everything. Although to wish such a life for your child— Still, I can hear it in her voice, how she wants it. I was worried, after the funeral. I remembered how it feels, how lonely. But now look. Screen tests. It was good not being alone in the house, I think. So thank you for that."

Ben looked away.

"They really refused Lion?" he said.

"He's a socialist. It's very well known, even here."

All you had to do was check a file, information from a well-placed source.

"But that's not—"

"Not before. Now it's different. His lawyer said, be patient. Now he gets his publisher to write for him. How distinguished he is. He does very well here, you know. The translations. Not like poor Heinrich."

Is this how it was done? You didn't have to ask, just let the conversation run, listening for Riordan, a sponge.

"And now there are difficulties. It's ironic, yes? They didn't want Heinrich to leave Europe. Now they don't want him to leave here. This time, no Daniel to arrange the escape. So he goes to offices and waits. For a piece of paper. Just like his script."

"Why not leave without it?"

"Cross the Pyrenees again? You forget, he had papers then. That's what Daniel arranged. It's not so easy without that, a passport. Brecht doesn't understand, living in his head," he said with a sarcastic smile. "Why Lion wants his piece of paper. If he leaves, he can't come back. He's not a refugee anymore, but not a citizen, either. Of anywhere. So all he can do is stay here, as he is. Yes, it's very comfortable for him." He gestured toward the house. "But now a cage also."

"But Kaltenbach doesn't want to come back."

"So he thinks. I wonder what he will say after. When those doors close." He sighed. "But first he has to get there."

With Minot watching. With Ben watching for him.

"What about you? Are you having any trouble?"

"Me? Oh, I'm not such a dangerous person as Lion. I wasn't premature." He looked down. "Maybe too late. How we waited, hoping it would go away. Thinking a catastrophe would go away."

There was traffic on Sunset so that by the time Ben got back to Gower the lot had taken on the after-work quiet of skeleton crews and empty sound stages, only a few cars left in their reserved spaces.

"Screening room with Mr. L," said one of Bunny's secretaries, anticipating his question. She was putting folders in drawers, evidently working late to catch up on the filing.

"How'd the test go, do you know? Liesl Kohler." Or had they changed her name?

"When was this, today? Maybe they're looking at it now. The only way I know is, he writes a memo."

"On a screen test?"

"Everything," she said, with a nod to the wall of filing cabinets. What Tenney's office must look like. Fourteen thousand files, rumors on paper.

"How about the guest list for Lasner's party Saturday?"

Her head went up, immediately protective.

"I was there," he explained, "and I talked to somebody and I can't remember her name. I thought if I could go through the list, you know, it might come back to me. Does he keep them, the lists?"

"Uh huh."

"Don't worry. I'm sure it'll be okay with him."

She said nothing.

"I could go down to the screening room, have him phone up."

She hesitated, trying to guess what Bunny's reaction would be to either course.

"No, it's here," she said finally, turning to a drawer. "I just filed it, in fact." She got it out and handed it to him.

"You mind? I'll bring it back?"

"You want to take it?" she said, suspicious again.

He began to read down the list. Everyone there, with marks next to the Warners people. Seating plans, names on spokes around a circle, everything thought out. Liesl listed as Ben Collier guest. Rex Morgan, who owned 8 percent. But who had talked to Genia, spotted her across the room? A German speaker, so not Ann Sheridan or one of the starlets. Maybe not at the party at all, just someone who knew she was in town. But it would be easy enough to come up with a short list of possibilities, then use Dennis to check them, routine for a Bureau man. Start somewhere. She hadn't taken a random turn off Sunset. Someone had told her where to go.

He looked up to find the secretary watching him. "He doesn't like things to leave the office," she said, expecting trouble.

"It's a party list," he said, folding it. "I'll tell him downstairs."

They had already started running the dailies, so Ben slipped into the screening room quietly and took a seat at the back. Bunny was in his usual watching posture, chin resting on a pyramid of fingers, while Lasner made running comments to the directors. It was Dick Marshall again, out of the fighter plane, making a sentimental visit to another pilot in the hospital.

"Why a profile," Lasner said. "They're paying to see the face."

"Watch the eyes when he turns," the director said. "Now you see the tears. He's been holding them back."

"Why? He saw the picture?"

"Sol."

"The buddy dies? Wonderful. Something upbeat."

"What can I tell you, Sol? It's a war picture."

"All right, all right."

"He looks good, Jamie," Bunny said to the director, placating. "Think you can wrap this week?"

There was another clip, Lasner quiet, his silence acting like a sigh, then the directors left.

"Jesus Christ, Bunny," Lasner said.

The room was still dim, Ben invisible in the back shadows.

"I know. It'll be okay if we can get it out fast. We can book it with Rosemary's picture, recover the costs."

"We're supposed to be making money, not recovering costs."

"Sol, you're the one who taught me. Pay the overhead with these, your wins are twice as big."

"And what about Dick? We got an investment there, too. Another war picture—"

"I had an idea about that. I want you to see this test." Bunny picked up the phone. "Could you run the test now? The first one."

This would have been the moment, Ben knew, to cough, declare himself, but he sat still, too interested to move.

It was the same scene they'd used with Julie, the young girl getting up from the piano and saying good-bye to the older man—her father? her teacher?—who was sending her away, better for everyone for some reason. Liesl was wearing a simple white blouse and skirt, her hair brushed straight, the whole effect young, on the brink. When she lifted her face at the piano, it seemed to draw the key light to it, a sudden radiance. Ben knew that it was framing and makeup and well-placed arcs, that it was Liesl playing the piano, but knowing all of it made no difference. Film transformed everything. Even the piano gleamed. She smiled now at the keyboard, slightly wistful, a girl he had never seen before.

"Watch this?" Bunny said.

"What am I watching?" Lasner said.

"The way she moves. It's the first thing I noticed. Like a dancer. Watch how she gets up. You know who does that? Cary Grant."

"He was an acrobat," Lasner said, "not a dancer."

"Same thing," Bunny said, still fixed on the screen. "Now the hands. Watch her with his arm, she just *grazes* it."

The way she might have touched Ostermann, a gesture Ben had seen her make, protective.

"Listen," Bunny said.

"I'm hearing?"

"Someone who went to school."

The clip ended.

"With an accent," Lasner said.

"Never mind. That's part of it. Stay with me. Watch it again."

He asked the projectionist to rerun it. This time neither of them spoke, paying attention. Lasner was quiet afterward.

"A nice girl," he said finally.

Bunny nodded. "Exactly. She looks like she could actually *play* the piano."

"So? What was with the piano, by the way?"

"You don't miss much, do you? Vegetable oil. You spray it on and the lights pick it up."

Lasner shook his head, delighted, another magic trick.

"They don't line up for nice."

"This is something else, Sol. Maybe another Bergman."

"You're serious about this?"

Bunny picked up the phone. "Run the other one."

"You made two tests?"

"Nice with something behind it. Watch."

Liesl was on a terrace now, outside a pair of French windows, about to kiss Dick Marshall. It was a night scene, their faces lit by moonlight, her white skin glowing in a low-cut dress.

"You used Dick in a test?"

"Watch."

Marshall kissed her and she responded, then began kissing his face all over, devouring it, an eruption of kisses that seemed to well up out of her control. When Dick pulled back, breathless, the camera went to her, leaning forward, still eager, her eyes darting all over his face, as if she were kissing him now with her eyes.

"Somebody'll see," Marshall whispered.

"I don't care," she said, her breath a gasp, moving up to kiss him again.

Ben's own breathing stopped for a minute, hair bristling on the back of his neck. Not just the same words, the same face.

"Turner does that with her eyes," Lasner was saying.

No, Ben thought, Liesl does that, a look printed in the back of his head, just for him. When her lips reached Dick Marshall, he knew how they would open, the same soft yielding. He felt his hand tighten on the armrest. An actress borrowed from life. The look in her eyes now was real, as real as it had been with him. But what if it hadn't been? Maybe it was just the way she played the scene, with him, with Dick, acting both times. How had she played it with Danny? Something he hadn't allowed himself to think about before. The same expression, the same eyes all over his face? Or had it been different with him, a different acting, or not acting at all. The way they felt about each other.

"How do you like her with Dick?" Bunny said as the clip ended.

Ben scarcely heard him, his mind flooding with scenes—in the pool, on the chaise, her hand reaching up to his neck. Had any of them been real? None of them? Didn't everybody react this way when they saw someone they knew on film? They seemed the same because the gestures came from the same place—a protective pat on a father's arm. But not the eyes. Intimacy wasn't something you could carry away with you, turn into a character touch.

"That's why you used him?"

"It works, the two of them."

"So she can kiss. There's still the accent. You know what it would take? Smooth that out?"

Bunny nodded. "But not yet. The accent's part of it. Remember *Dearly Beloved?*"

"The Klausner script. He brings the wife home and the mother makes trouble. I thought you didn't like it for Dick."

"I didn't. Too light for him—a meringue."

"And with her a strudel. Give it to Rosemary."

Bunny shook his head. "The problem's always been, why does she put up with it? Why doesn't she get wise to the mother? Rosemary'd be onto her in a minute. But if she were foreign—"

"A Kraut."

"Dutch, whatever. The accent'll pass for anything. A war bride. Dick brings her home."

"Now it's okay for Dick?"

"It's time to get him out of uniform. He marries her over there. She's crazy about him. Why not? He saves her. He's taking her out of there. To heaven, she thinks. Then she gets here, and there's mom. Before it's a B about newlyweds. Now you've got GIs coming home, it's *about* something. Dick can handle that. And she'd be perfect. A nice girl, you're on her side when the mother starts in. And she gets him back in the end because he's nuts about her—which you can believe," he said, flipping his hand to the screen, the remembered kiss. He paused. "We need to get him into something right away."

"With an unknown. The biggest name we've got."

"She won't *be* unknown when the picture opens. She'll be his new friend. First time they meet on the set, sparks. Then the brush fire. You can see it on the screen, before your eyes. Polly will eat it up."

Lasner looked down, thinking. "How soon? To get it fixed?"

"Get Ben Hecht to do a polish."

"A polish. He's five thousand a week."

"That's all he'd need. We could put it into production right away. A Dick Marshall for the holidays." He paused. "We own it and it's sitting there."

Lasner looked over at Bunny. "You really have a feeling about her?"

Ben sat still, fascinated, the moment suddenly important. A feeling about her. Not Brecht's factory, a casino, as imprecise as a white ball spinning round a wheel. Lasner sighed, a moment of theater, then lowered his voice.

"Standard options. And you have to do something about the name. What are you going to call her?"

"Linda. It's close. You like 'Linda Eastman'? Her name means Eastman in German."

"Now you speak German?"

"Enough to know that."

Ben sat up. Enough to make a telephone call? But why would he?

"Where'd you find her?"

"At your house. She was at the dinner for Minot. With Ben Collier."

"Collier? Oh, Otto's kid. What, he's screwing her?"

"His brother's wife."

"The one who—"

Ben cleared his throat, announcing himself. Both men turned. Bunny touched a switch on his armrest console to raise the lights.

"You're there all this time?" Lasner said. "Like a spook?"

"I didn't want to interrupt. I just wanted to see how she did."

"Dailies are by invitation," Bunny said, frosty. "Anything you hear stays in this room, understood?"

"It's all right," Lasner said, patting Bunny's arm. "He's with the studio."

"He's also a relative."

"So when's that a crime? This whole business is relatives." He got up, facing Ben. "What's the matter? You look funny."

"Nothing," Ben said, also getting up. "Just seeing someone you know up there."

"What did you think?" Lasner said, walking up the aisle.

"Don't ask me—I'm family. Bunny's the expert," he said, a peace offering. "The scene with Marshall. Did they improvise the lines or—"

"Improvise," Bunny said, rolling his eyes. "On a test."

The words a coincidence, then, but not the face.

"Bunny's looking for a nice girl," Lasner said, a tease. "A Bergman."

"She's the biggest thing in pictures, Sol. Nice, but something underneath."

"What, underneath? She's playing a *nun*."

"One picture. You want to borrow her for Dick? It's a fortune and you won't even notice him. Somebody new, it looks like he's pulling *her*. And we go into production right away." Making a case.

Lasner hesitated, for effect, then nodded. "One week for Hecht. And no color."

"No color," Bunny agreed. "It's not a musical."

Lasner glanced up. "Sam come to you yet? About the musical? Now he's telling me she can sing, the new skirt. As if he would know—another Pasternak. He hears her humming on his dick, he thinks it's a musical. A Bar Mitzvah coming up and he's playing around with that. Well, Sam."

Bunny had been watching Lasner's face, scanning a page.

"You want me to put her in something right away," he said flatly.

"She's busy, maybe Sam doesn't think we're Metro."

Bunny looked at him, then put a folder of notes under his arm. "I'll find something."

"How long does it last with Sam anyway?" Lasner said, but Bunny had begun to usher them out, moving on.

"The first contract's always boiler plate," he said to Ben.

"Don't worry, she'll sign. She wants this."

"Everybody wants this," Bunny said simply, turning to him, explaining something to a child. "Everybody in the world."

By the time Ben had finished copying the guest list, Bunny's secretary had finally gone. He put the list back on her desk, then, an impulse, went through to Bunny's office and glanced around the room, a more careful look than on that first rushed morning. Wood paneling, barrel chairs with metal trim, but none of the personal effects that usually filled shelves, no photographs of Bunny as a child star, no leather-bound favorite scripts—nothing, in fact, but the business of Continental, filing cabinets and in-boxes filled with waiting papers. It was as if his former life had receded with his hairline, leaving the front office to Mr. Jenkins.

He walked over to the desk and ran his eye down the open calendar, tomorrow's page crowded with appointments and reminders, as detailed and inflexible as a shooting schedule. He glanced up quickly to make sure he was still alone, then flipped back to Monday. Another full page, ending with Rosemary's wrap party and *Rushes with L,* the usual last entry. Except he hadn't stayed to watch them. Ben remembered him standing outside the sound stage, on his way somewhere, Lasner annoyed later when he couldn't be found. Where? Just out of curiosity, Ben estimated the time between Bunny's leaving and Lasner getting the police call. How long to the Palisades? Forty minutes, even with the wet roads, maybe less. He could easily have been there. But why would he be? He wasn't someone in her past, like Danny. He'd probably helped arrange to bring her over. Why ask now for a secret meeting? Still, hadn't Lorna thought at first the call was from the studio?

When he got home he found Liesl in the screening room, watching one of the *Partners* movies. The light pouring through the open door had startled her, someone caught in a guilty pleasure.

"You know this one?" she said. "*Car Trouble*? It's from life, when our car broke down. In Laguna. They're all from life. I never realized before. I never paid attention. The premiere, all you can think about is the audience, do they like it? But he took everything from life."

Their life, the one they had together.

"I'll let you finish," he said, backing away.

"No, turn it off. It's enough. I just wanted to see you. What you were like. Well, what he thought you were like," she said, her voice offhand, plausible.

"And how was I?" he said, moving to the projection room.

"Serious. A great believer in justice," she said, playing with it.

He switched off the projector and raised the lights.

"What made you run it?" he said, coming back. "You weren't trying to see me. Eddie's not me."

"You don't think so?" she said, an evasive shrug. "I don't know. Maybe for Daniel. Maybe I wanted to see what was on his mind. You tell me things—you make me think I never knew him. So who was he?"

"Any answers?"

"No. Maybe in the one he didn't make." She nodded to the box Republic had sent over.

He picked a script out of the box.

"You're late again," she said.

"I've been watching you," he said with a sly smile. "They liked the test."

"Yes?" she said, lifting her head, alert.

"Lasner, Bunny. They liked it."

"Tell me," she said, excited. "What did they say?"

"Get an agent."

"Yes? They want to make a contract? Well, Kohner, I can call him," she said, suddenly practical. "He knows my father. They really liked it?"

"Bunny wants to give you a buildup."

"A buildup," she said, translating it.

"Publicity."

"Oh, to make me a movie star," she said, skeptical. "With my accent. Daniel said it was impossible. With my accent."

"Times change. He sees you as a war bride. Dick Marshall's."

Her eyes widened. "His wife? It's a real part?"

Ben nodded. "Also his girlfriend. Off screen. At least at Ciro's, places they take pictures."

"They can do that?"

"It's a personal services contract. That's part of the service."

"Oh, will you be jealous?" she said, coming over to him, putting her hands on his arms.

"That depends what happens after," he said, playing along.

"That's not in the contract, too, is it?"

"No."

"Good," she said, reaching her hand up to his neck. "Then there's nothing to worry about."

She smiled, her whole body warm against him, eyes darting across his face, just the way they had when she said, "I don't care." And suddenly he didn't care, either. Maybe it was always acting. He thought of the girls in Germany—there'd been no pretense there, a warm mouth for a few cigarettes. No one thought of sex in the back of a jeep as making love, just something you did while you waited to go home, to real intimacy, a cry that wasn't fake. Her eyes moved over him now, the way they had in the test, but did that make it any less real? He was already hard, wanting to be seduced, wanting the touch that reached inside you, when the eyes were only for you, the way it was in the movies.

Liesl became Linda Eastman, suddenly swept up in a storm of wardrobe fittings and blocking rehearsals, and Ben moved out of the house. It wasn't a question of propriety. He was family, easily explainable to the photographers, but why raise questions at all? She was supposed to be lonely, waiting for someone like Dick to come along.

He wasn't superstitious about the Cherokee. Danny may have died there, but he had never actually stayed there, and there was still part of a month already paid for, with the next now paid in advance to Joel. It was convenient, just a few blocks' walk to drugstore counters on Hollywood Boulevard if he didn't want to eat in. Still, there was a haunted feeling to the place, especially at night when the thin sound of a radio playing downstairs came in through the window, like smoke. He never saw his neighbors and after a while he began to feel that no one really lived there—they were all just passing through, drinking or washing out nylons or memorizing lines, all waiting, the way they did in Hollywood, for the phone to ring.

Even with his things hung in the closet and books and papers in a small heap on the desk, the room seemed empty. He paced through it, door to kitchen counter to balcony, an animal staking out territory to make it his own. The balcony especially needed to be claimed, swept free of ghosts. He looked down, seeing the body in the photograph again, the huddled neighbors, Riordan hanging back, surprised. If he had been. If he hadn't been upstairs, racing down with the others to gape. The photograph was real, but everything else was a story you chose to believe. You couldn't be certain, not of anybody.

Even someone you thought you knew. He'd seen that going through Danny's reports in Minot's office, a paper trail of little betrayals, no one ever suspecting. Just listening and passing on, but violating, too. As Ben flipped through folder after folder, he felt he was no longer looking for leads, but for something else, a reason.

At first Riordan hadn't wanted Ben in the files at all. "It's not somebody we know, it's somebody we don't know, remember?" But Ben had insisted—it was his bargaining chip, a matter of trust—and Riordan finally agreed, but only at night, after everyone had gone. He steered Ben to files that used Danny's reports—Ostermann, Brecht, the émigré circle. There were even notes on Werfel and Salka and Thomas Mann. Everyone. Danny appeared simply as the initial K in the margins, identifying him as a source on the memos Riordan had written up, Bureau style.

"Subject [Ostermann] requested sign position paper Latin American Committee for Free Germany sponsored by exile group, Mexico City (see Seghers, et al.)." Brecht's sexual relations with secretary Ruth Berlau were known to wife, Helene Weigel. "Guest Viertel home Santa

Monica (arranged Brecht). Numerous visits Brecht." Kaltenbach had met with Kranzler, *Aufbau*. "Kranzler under Bureau surveillance after visit Eisler (known CP). Purpose: discuss English translation of subject's works. No decision reached (K)." According to the files, Kranzler visited other German writers, then the Highland Lounge, "popular with deviants. Entertained US serviceman overnight at Roosevelt Hotel."

There were more. Brecht's arguments with Fritz Lang on *Hangmen Also Die*, Kaltenbach's finances, Ostermann's intention to apply for citizenship after the five-year waiting period. Could anyone have taken these seriously? Written down, recorded, sources put into code so that the files themselves became secrets about secrets. Were they all like this? Ben thought of the FBI, the GPU, any of them, with their archives and hundreds of legmen, filling folders with items no more damaging than onions in Winchell. But there were other items, too, from other sources, requests for surveillance, possible new informants, now vulnerable to approach, everyone caught in a fun house hall of mirrors. In Germany files like these had killed.

"None of these are recent," Ben said.

"That's what he used to give the Bureau—it's just there as backup. You know, in case we ever need it. The congressman's more interested in the industry."

Riordan pulled another file.

"Subject [Schaeffer] suspected CP, Hollywood branch. K suggests verify with source G, ex-CP."

"Who's Schaeffer?"

"A writer. Fox. But you get one, you have a lead to someone else."

"Did G verify?"

Riordan nodded.

"What happens to Schaeffer?"

"That depends what he says under oath, doesn't it? When he testifies. How cooperative he is."

"Who else?"

Riordan looked to the filing cabinets. "I told you, he's not going to be here. Bring me a suggestion, a name in his desk. We can check that out. But here, it's a needle in a— What's that?"

"A guest list. People Danny knew. I thought—" He stopped. What could he tell Riordan? Another crime, with no connection except a shared past? Something Genia must have known. "Look, we're flying blind here, I know. But I think he was going to put one of these names in here." He pointed to the files. "Let's see who's already there."

Riordan looked at him, then at his watch, then back again.

"Can I say something to you? I know this is personal with you. But make it too personal, you're not going to get anywhere. You want to know everything he told us. What's the point?"

"I want to know where he was looking. If there was a pattern. You think he just pulled names out of a hat?"

"Tell you the truth, I didn't give it a thought. As long as the names checked out."

"And they did. So where was he getting them?"

"His memory box, I always thought," Riordan said, tapping his head. "These are people he knew, some of them."

"But not all. So there's another source, not just him. Someone else."

Riordan stared at him, then got up, a weary shuffling.

"All right, you got an itch about this, scratch it. But—I don't have to say, anything in here stays here. You know that, right?"

"You think I care whether Schaeffer's Red or not? There's only one Communist I'm interested in. You and Minot can have all the rest. I never even saw these, all right?"

Riordan said nothing for a moment, then picked up his hat. "The door locks behind you. I'm just saying, there's a lot of privileged stuff here."

"And I'm trying to get you more. One more friendly witness."

"Just don't do it solo."

"Don't worry. I'll give him to you."

"I didn't mean that."

"What?"

"You get too close, all by yourself, you could get hurt. He'd have to, wouldn't he? Like before. Wouldn't think twice." He put on his hat. "Safety in numbers."

When he'd gone, the room turned eerily silent, and Ben found himself moving quietly, too, as if he had broken in and had to make sure no noise reached the night watchman. He slid the file drawer out carefully, guest list in his other hand. The easiest way would be to eliminate the obvious names first, then move on to the ones he didn't know, but it was hard to be methodical. Even when a name had no file he would bump up against another one, not on the list, that seemed vaguely familiar. Paulette Goddard was there, but only as an ex-wife cross-reference to the thick Chaplin file. Ben flipped through this—every speech he'd ever made, every interview, anonymous evaluations of his opinions, a full dossier of meaningless paper, flecked with little drops of professional envy. But someone had taken the time to compile it. Out of curiosity, he looked for his own name, but neither he nor Liesl had attracted anyone's attention—nor Danny, for that matter, unless the sources had a special file drawer of their own. A Warners director had solicited contributions for the Abraham Lincoln Brigade, and his films had been reviewed for left-wing sentiments. Feldman, a front office crony Ben knew only by sight, had attended an Anti-Fascist League fund-raiser 1938, Ambassador Hotel, with Gail Simco, ex-CP, 1940. His girlfriend? A party seven years ago. It was when he found a file on Warner himself—production decisions made on *Mission to Moscow*—that the full craziness of it all struck him. He looked around Minot's silent office, drawer after drawer of trivia and innuendo, put together during the war, consuming time and expense, to prepare for the war in their imaginations. And Danny a willing part of it. Had his sense by then been blunted, too? Crazy wasn't necessarily harmless. The files were an arsenal. They were getting ready.

His fingers stopped, surprised, at the tab with Rosemary's name on it.

"Subject (real name Risa Meyer) raised CP household. Father (Jacob) arrested NYC 1933 strike action, later official ILGWU. Mother

(Irene) seamstress, also ILGWU. Both CP 1927–1939, membership on record. Resignation 1939. No evidence subsequent membership but source (G) believes remained socialist. Subject attended Pine Hill, Monticello, NY, children's summer camp known for CP indoctrination. No known official CP affiliation, but background suggests further investigation."

Attached were supporting documents, even a camp roster, a list of her magazine subscriptions—obtained how?—SAG membership date, a copy of the police report of her father's arrest, none of it important or secret, yet sitting in a file, available. He looked at it again, feeling squeamish, as if he'd opened a lingerie drawer, a private place where he wasn't supposed to be. No K source, at least. He'd reported on Ostermann, on friends. Why not jottings after a weekend at the Biltmore? But he wouldn't have, one fine line he wouldn't have crossed. As if Ben knew any longer what he wouldn't have done.

He came back to her again after he'd checked more names off the list. Had Rosemary known? He thought of her at the party, enjoying her moment, not meeting Liesl's eyes. Suggests further investigation. What if that had been Danny, listening closely?

The click of the key in the door startled him. He looked up, frozen, at Minot coming in, his hand still on the door, even more surprised. For a second neither of them moved.

"What are you doing?" Minot said finally, his voice flat, waiting to hear. He was in black tie, evidently on his way home from a formal evening.

"Checking files," Ben said, trying to sound calm. "Riordan had to leave."

"An eager beaver," Minot said, squeezing out a small smile. "Dennis shouldn't have done that." He went over to his desk and took an envelope out of his in-box. "The files are private."

"I was just checking my brother's reports."

"No offense." He stopped, taking in the stack in front of Ben. "You understand, we promise people, when they help us. Well, like yourself. You wouldn't want everyone—"

"The sources are coded."

Minot nodded, his eyes darting involuntarily toward the bottom drawer, a quick check to see if it had been opened.

"But not impossible. To guess, I mean. We need to protect them. You'd want that, wouldn't you? Your brother was very particular on that point. And even so. Well, it's late. Need a lift? I've got a car waiting downstairs."

"I'll just put these back."

"No, leave them," Minot said firmly. "Sally can get them in the morning."

He was moving to the door now, opening it, expecting Ben to follow.

"Anything for us yet?" he said pleasantly.

"No. I was hoping—" He opened his hand to the files.

"I think you'd find it easier with someone around. Help you navigate." He switched off the light, closing the door behind them, testing the knob to make sure it had locked.

"What did you mean, even so?" Ben said. "About Danny. You said, 'and even so.'"

"Oh. Well, you know things happen. Even when you're careful. Your brother was very careful. I don't think anybody ever knew—that he gave us information about them. But somebody did find out. I can't even remember how—Dennis, I suppose. Your brother chewed him out for it. Said it cost him a job."

"Who found out?"

Minot slowed, looking at him. "Oh, I see. No, it's not what you're thinking. No grudges."

"But if the guy—"

"It wouldn't be," he said evenly. "He became a friend of ours."

"*After* Danny—"

"A friend," Minot said, cutting him off. "Like you. We trust our friends." He glanced over. "Be a hell of a world if we didn't, wouldn't it?" He waved to the night watchman, his tone suddenly genial. "Frank, where've you been keeping yourself?"

"Right here. Not out on the town like some people," the guard said, smiling at the tuxedo.

"Well, somebody's got to do it. How's the wife—better?" A politician's memory, better than a room of files.

"Like new. I'll tell her you asked," he said, pleased, taking in Ben now.

Minot handed him the envelope from his in-box. "Somebody'll be by for this. Sorry about the hour."

"I'm here anyway," Frank said, propping it on the fire extinguisher while he opened the door for them.

Outside a car was waiting, the driver idling the motor. Ben caught a glimpse of a woman's crossed leg in the backseat, patient Mrs. Minot.

"Sure I can't give you a lift?"

"No, my car's over there," Ben said, nodding to the dark parking lot.

Minot reached out for the door handle then hesitated, turning. "Have you seen Kaltenbach?" he said, lowering his voice. "I keep hearing things. We don't want to have to move too early, tip our hand. One subpoena too soon, it's like scaring birds, they start flying all over the place. You want to get the timing right." He hesitated again. "I'd appreciate it if you spent a little time with him. I know you've got something else on your mind and that's fine, but right now we could use someone inside. I'd think of it as a favor."

Ben watched his car go, then started over to his own, thinking. A friend of ours. But how willing? Danny said it had cost him a job. He looked toward the dark building then suddenly, with a wheel click, he was back on the Chief. Something that hadn't worked out. Sol couldn't remember why.

Frank looked up from a magazine when Ben tapped on the glass.

"Like a dummy, I forgot something and Ken took the key. Do you have a pass? Take me a second."

The first name did it. A man who'd asked about his wife. Frank led him down the hall and found the key on his ring.

"Thanks. Appreciate it," Ben said, but Frank stayed with him, just inside the door.

He went over to the bottom drawer and flipped through the tabs. There might have been other jobs, not necessarily— But there it was, Jenkins, so thin he almost missed it. He slipped the file under his arm.

"I owe you one," he said to Frank, putting on a relieved expression, his homework safe in hand.

In the car he flicked on the overhead light. A studio bio sheet, innocuous, presumably there for reference, and a single report sheet.

"Subject JENKINS attended discussion group 1940, CP Westwood, guest of J. MacDonald."

Source initial K in the margin. One meeting. Not enough to suggest any serious political window shopping, much less something to use against him later. Maybe it had been nothing more than a courtesy drop-in for MacDonald's sake. Why even bother to keep the report, now that he was a friend? But why look for logic in any of it? Why report that Kranzler had asked a GI up to his room, that Brecht had arranged trysts at Salka's, that Rosemary read *Collier's*? The peeping, like any compulsion, was an end in itself. No information was useless if the point was the gathering. A brief word from Danny, now permanently on file. To hold over Bunny's head, keep him friendly? But Bunny had reasons of his own to get close to Minot. Why would he care about this?

Still, he had—enough to be angry with Danny. Maybe it was nothing more than the startled, uneasy feeling of someone who realizes he's being watched through the window, anger a natural reflex. Maybe it had to do with MacDonald, a name to check the next time he got into the files. But not angry enough to kill. A job denied, no more. I knew who he was, he'd said to Ben. No explanation necessary when Riordan asked him to make the call. Maybe even a touch of satisfaction, bringing source K to an end.

Ben switched off the light and lit a cigarette. Rosemary's file was more damaging—not a summer camp the studio would want to see written up in *Photoplay*. Ben wondered if Bunny knew about the report—more interesting, if Rosemary knew about it. Her moment, with everything at stake. There was nothing to indicate that Danny had ever betrayed her. What if she'd thought he had? But Bunny hadn't made the call for her, he'd made it for Riordan.

He looked up, his eyes caught by the headlights sweeping into the parking lot. Not Minot again, a smaller car. It pulled up to the door, and the driver ran up the steps, tapping on the glass. It was only when Frank turned on another light that the driver became more than a shadow. For a minute Ben still didn't recognize him—a natural lag, seeing something unexpected, out of place. Frank opened the door and handed over Minot's envelope, then Kelly started back down the stairs. Ben watched, moving pieces around in his head. Kelly playing messenger. For Minot? But at the Farmers Market he hadn't known Riordan. The connection must be at the other end.

There wasn't time to sort it out. Kelly's lights came on again, the car starting for the street. Almost without thinking, Ben turned the key. Kelly. Getting something for the paper? But at Wilshire he was turning away from downtown, heading toward Beverly Hills. Just keep a few lengths behind. No one ever noticed a tail if he wasn't looking for it. Kelly was leaning forward to turn the radio knob, just going about his business, whatever it was.

After El Camino, Kelly turned right, passing blocks of stores and then crossing Santa Monica to the horseshoe-curve streets of the flats below Sunset. Ben slowed, dropping farther behind. The streets were empty, dark between the corner lights, half-asleep. Just stop signs now, not enough traffic for lights. Another right turn.

The house was halfway up the block. Ben parked a little way down and across, killing his lights, the car swallowed up in the shade of a big pepper tree. Kelly was walking up the curved pavement. He rang the bell, waited, looking up at the fanlight. A brighter light, then the door opened and Polly Marks stepped out, a drink in one hand. Running an errand for Polly. Not for the first time. A few familiar words, the envelope delivered, and she was turning back to her drink, all in one gliding movement, something they'd done before. In time to get it into the typewriter, a leak from the files. More kindling. He watched Kelly drive away, then sat for a minute looking at the quiet street—shrubs and lawns and even a trellis of flowers. No sound but crickets, peaceful and unaware, not a flame in sight.

HE WAS surprised when Riordan answered the phone.

"You're there early."

"Ken likes it. Navy hours or some shit," Riordan said, his voice husky, only half-awake.

"Studio hours, too," Ben said, looking at the pile of paper already on his desk. Outside, technicians with coffee cups were heading for the sound stages. "Anyway, I'm glad I caught you."

"What I hear, Ken caught you. You don't want to surprise him like that. He gets riled up."

"I was just checking names."

"Not anymore," he said, a thud in his voice. "Files are closed."

"Great. Open one for me then, will you? See if you have anything on a J. MacDonald. M-a-c. Even a cross-reference."

"Who is he?"

"That's what I'm asking you. His name came up, that's all."

"Came up how?"

"Dennis, are you going to do this or not? Just see what you have."

A hesitation, then an exaggerated sigh. "Give me a sec."

Ben heard the receiver being laid on the desk, the sharp metallic scrape of a file drawer opening. A meeting five years ago.

"Music department. Universal," Riordan said, reading.

"CP?"

"Not in here. Fellow traveler, though. Lots of organizations, the usual pink. Went into the Army 'forty-two. That's the last thing we have. Want me to check some more?"

"Check what?"

"Army records. Friend of mine has access. See if he was discharged. Died, maybe."

"Who was the source on the file?"

"No source, just a general. Stuff you can pull from the papers. This goes back some, nothing recent. You think your brother knew him?"

"Maybe just a loose end. I mean, if there's been nothing for years—" But he must have known his name. At least well enough to mention it in Bunny's file. "You have an old address?"

"Uh uh. Nobody ever wrote him up. He's just a guy on some lists, so they made a file. Strictly what he joined. Anti-Fascist League, things like that. How'd you say he came up?"

Ben glanced at Bunny's thin file. How long before anyone missed it?

"On a list. Probably nothing. Let me know about the Army though, okay? So I can scratch him off. Do I need to do anything about Ken? I don't want him to think—"

"He'll calm down. You're the only one he's got now, with the Krauts."

"I thought he wasn't interested in them."

"They meet people. It all connects."

Like a web, one strand to another. And who else was present, Mr. Kaltenbach? To the best of your recollection. Heinrich must have met people. If he was sympathetic enough to be approached now, invited to return, why not then? A gathering over coffee. One name, then another, until they found one for the newsreels. And who else was at the meeting, Mr. MacDonald? But Bunny would be protected, a friend to the committee. Until it began to eat its own, too hungry to stop.

Ben walked over to the window, looking out at the sunny lot. Cowboys and showgirls coming out of Makeup. Grips moving scenery. Everyone busy, unconcerned. Did any of them know what Minot was planning, what it would mean? For a second he saw the street in a freeze frame, a stopped moment before it all began. They'd turn on each other, running for cover, right into Minot's hands.

At the gate, there was a commotion as some grips crossed the picket line. More pickets had come out today, not just the usual handful, and the guards had seemed jittery when Ben drove through earlier. Shouts now, instead of breezy catcalls. One of the grips shouted back, then had to be pulled away. Two of the picketers lunged toward him, then stopped, posturing. More shouts, name-calling. But no sticks or stones. A jurisdictional dispute.

He turned back to the paperwork, then saw her coming out of Makeup. She was in the same kind of white blouse and simple skirt they'd used in the test, but now wore heels, so that her legs stretched up. His eyes followed her toward the actors' trailers, hair catching the morning light, watching the way she moved, the easy glide Bunny had noticed. But Ben had noticed other things, a leg in a mirror, eyes that darted across your face. He missed the swimming pool, sitting on the chaise still wet in terry robes, then the smell of chlorine on her skin, her thigh half open to its soft side.

She looked up into the mirror of her dressing table when the door opened.

"I saw you pass. Going over lines?"

She nodded to the script in front of her. "Today I meet the sister. She's jealous."

He closed the door behind him.

"Don't. People will notice."

"I'm family."

"In my dressing room. What if Connie comes? It's hers, too."

"You share? You're the star."

She smiled. "Not yet." She held up both hands to the mirror, wriggling them. "I haven't put my hands in cement. Why do they do that?"

He shrugged. "Why do they do anything?"

"You think it's all foolish. Only newsreels."

He walked over to the chair, standing behind her.

"Next week we do the scenes in Germany," she said to the mirror. "Did you see what they're building? I live in a house that was bombed. In a cellar. It's strange, you know? Where I'd be if I'd never come here."

"Or dead."

"Yes. You know my name, the character? Maria. No Saras here, either. Like Goebbels."

"I thought they were making you Dutch," he said back to the mirror.

"No, they want the ruins. So when I see his mother's house—"

He put his hands on her shoulders, leaning down to kiss her neck.

"Don't," she said, moving forward. "I'll have to do the makeup all over again. It took hours."

"To look like this? Not even lipstick?"

"It's the hardest, Connie says. To look natural."

He brushed his hand down the back of her hair. "It's good to see you."

She looked down. "Maybe it's good. It gives us time to think."

"About what?"

She looked at him in the mirror for a moment, then let it go.

"I don't know," she said, getting up and turning, so that now they were facing each other.

"How's Dick Marshall?"

"The perfect gentleman." She put her hand on his chest, holding him in place. "Not like you."

"How about I come for a swim?"

She shook her head, still holding him back, their faces close. "He's taking me to the Grove."

"After."

"After I sleep. The camera picks it up. If your skin—"

"There's nothing wrong with your skin," he said, moving closer.

"Not here," she said, pushing her hand against him.

"I can come late. Leave early," he said, his face almost on hers.

"Don't," she said again.

"No one would know." When she didn't answer, he waited for another second, then stepped back. "If that's it," he said, his voice ironic. He moved away, leaving it, but she reached for his arm, pulling him back.

"Maybe it's best. For now."

He stopped still, just looking, trying to read her expression. Could eyes be trained, like voices?

"I wish I knew what you wanted," he said quietly.

She returned his look, then let her hand drop, moving away from him.

"I wish I knew that, too." She went back over to the mirror, a final check. "I have to go. They'll be ready. You, too. Before anyone sees." She patted her hair. "I have to meet the sister."

He glanced at his watch, shifting moods with her. "And I have a meeting. Lasner keeps asking me to meetings."

"He likes you."

"I think he does it to needle Bunny. All right," he said, moving to the door. "Do I go first or do you want me to sneak out after you've gone?"

"You think it's a joke. People look for that."

"By the way, what I came for? Did Danny know a man called Mac-Donald?"

She thought for a second. "I don't think so. Why?"

"I came across his name in some papers."

"What papers?"

"It doesn't matter. Papers. He never mentioned a MacDonald?"

"No. That's what you came for? More Daniel."

"You're sure?" he said, ignoring this.

"I don't know. One name, all those years. How would I remember? MacDonald? Like the man on the farm?"

Ben nodded, waiting.

"I don't think so." She looked up. "I wish you would stop with this business."

"When I know."

"How? Who's going to tell you? Daniel?"

"Maybe."

"From the grave. You keep him alive, with all this. Here," she said, touching her head, then turned and closed the script, her back to him. "It feels like cheating."

He said nothing, looking into the mirror.

"Maybe that's what I want," she said. "Two in the room, not three."

"I only see two," Ben said.

HE WAS early for the scheduling meeting. With only one project to manage there was no real need for him to be there at all, but Lasner had insisted, another mark of favor the other line producers took in with nervous wait-and-see glances. Only Sam Pilcer, an old hand at musical chairs, seemed not to care. They were waiting in the conference room next to Lasner's office, where Bunny had set up a television, the first Ben had actually seen outside magazines. On the small glass screen a clown was performing.

"Again with this," Lasner said to Bunny.

"Just look at it."

"Look at what?"

"Found money."

Lasner waved this off. "You're like Freeman at Paramount. Remember he set up that Kraut? Right before the war?"

"Klaus Landsberg," Bunny said. "And what? Two years, minimal investment, and he takes it on the air. W6XYZ. What you're watching now," he said, catching Lasner's puzzled expression. "It's not an experiment anymore, Sol. The only question is how fast they can make them. Last four years, they've all been working for the government. Every electronics company in the country. Army contracts. Now watch. They can start turning these out."

"To watch this? Clowns."

"No, Rex Morgan. The Silver Bullet series."

"That's ten, fifteen years old."

"And just sitting there in the warehouse. Pictures nobody's going to run again. And here's a new exhibitor. With all day to fill. Why not with Rex? I'm telling you, found money. No prints. No advertising. No overhead. Aunt Tillie just died and left you a little something. Say thank you and cash the check."

"What kind of money can something like that pay?"

"Not much now," Bunny said. "But it's bottom line to us, all of it. Right now we're making nothing on Rex, just paying storage."

But Lasner was only half listening, staring at the wooden box, eyes narrowing in thought, and Ben wondered for a moment if he was back in the dry goods store on Fourteenth Street, the fuzzy lines behind the glass just like the jerky figures of light on the tacked-up sheet.

"Of course, the real money," Bunny was saying, "is going to be in production. But that's down the road."

"This is going to be the new pictures?"

"Nobody's saying that."

"People say it—I hear it. And we're going to hand over Continental product for a few bucks? Cut our own throats? Let them stick with the clowns, see how far they get."

"B product. *Old* B product."

"And you said production."

"It's getting harder with the B's, Sol, you know that. If they take away the block booking, we're going to have a problem on our hands. We're not Metro."

"And you don't see Mayer making clown shows, either." He looked again at the set. "Where are the kids going to neck?"

"In the balcony. At the movies. That's not going to change. Not with A product anyway."

"I know, I know. More A's. You keep saying."

Bunny made a little nod, backing away, familiar ground. "It'll never be pictures," he said. "But maybe the new radio."

"We're not in the radio business."

"No, the hotel business. It's about turning over rooms," Bunny said, spreading his arm to take in the lot outside. "Every time one of those stages is empty, we're losing money. Sam's going to wrap next week. Stage Seven," he said, including Pilcer. "Then we're dark two weeks until Greg does the interiors on *Abilene*."

"Move *River House* from Five," Lasner said. "They haven't built the porch set yet. Then you've got Five for a longer shoot. Harry, you wanted six weeks, right?"

Ben listened, interested, the whole scheduling meeting already worked out in their heads.

"We can, yes," Bunny said to Sol. "But the point is, you're going to have *some* off weeks. So why not use the room, not waste it?"

"Bunny, we're not just talking square feet here." He looked again at the television. "The money's not there yet," he said flatly, as if he'd just run through the expense sheet.

"No, not yet."

"And I should set up a new Second Unit," Lasner said to Pilcer. "I think he enjoys it, giving me grief." He turned to Bunny. "You got something, though, with the *Silver Bullets*. What the hell. Get one of these for Rex, he can watch himself all day. Fees, right? Not sales. Just another exhibitor."

"Fees," Bunny said, a handshake.

"He keeps an eye out for you, Sol," Pilcer said.

Bunny dipped his head to Pilcer, self-deprecating, like a courtier in one of his boy prince films.

Sol smiled, touching Bunny's shoulder. "Who else could squeeze another nickel out of Rex? Christ."

"All right, shall we start?" Bunny said, pulling out some papers with time graphs. "We're looking at a two-week overrun on *River House* and that's before the retakes, so we're going to have to move things around. *Abilene* we're still okay."

"Nobody ever lost money on a Western," Lasner said, about to take a seat. "What the hell's that?"

They all looked toward the window. Lasner went over, following the shouting coming from below. On Gower Street, the pickets had swarmed around a car trying to go through the gate, yelling, a few of them banging on the fender.

"What the hell—?"

"Why so many today?" Pilcer said, joining him, everyone else following.

"Change of tactics," one of the producers said. "What I heard," he said when they all looked at him. "Pick one or two studios to make a point. Instead of spreading themselves thin."

"So they pick us?" Lasner said.

"And Warners. They've got a whole army out on Olive. I heard," he said when they looked again. "We're the pick in town. One gate. Paramount, you'd need three times the people."

Below, the studio police had rushed out and were now pushing people away from the car with clubs. Just night watchmen, Bunny had said.

"I thought this wasn't supposed to happen," Lasner said to Bunny.

"With our people, no. You can't pay off two sides, Sol."

The car had begun to move, but now the strikers were squaring off against the studio cops, shouting in their faces, still a ritual, not an actual fight.

"There's that fuck Stein," a producer said.

Ben followed the pointing finger. Howard was near the edge of the crowd, apparently trying to quiet things down as he made his way through. A technician heading for the gate was stopped by picketers, then surrounded by studio police, pushing the strikers away. One shoved back, grabbing the cop, who raised his stick. Two other pickets rushed over and the cop, alarmed, stuck the club into the striker's chest to hold him off. The striker, taking it as an attack, swung at the cop and then, in an instant, like a fire catching, everyone seemed to be shoving, pushing chests, the line breaking up, people spilling into each other.

Bunny picked up the phone and dialed an extension. "Carl, get the police. Ask for Healy. Tell him we've got a street fight here. And tell Charlie to keep his men out of there. Away from the gate."

The shouting was now a roar, and Ben felt his neck stiffen, a startled animal's reaction. Violence was always sudden. A fistfight in a cellar bar, drunk GIs smashing bottles, jeeps pulling up, white helmets and billy clubs. Combat. The same adrenaline fear, your whole body flushed with it, everything happening fast. It was nothing like the movies, no sound-effect punches, choreographed swings. Clumsy, pulling at shirts, gouging, falling down, like the studio cop below, covering his face to ward off a kick. Ben saw Howard Stein, still trying to pull people away, putting out a brush fire.

"Jesus Christ," Lasner said, but quietly, his face pale, eyes fixed on Gower Street.

Then Ben saw Hal trying to skirt around the crowd to reach the gate. Strikers swerved around to block his way, the crowd now moving by instinct. More shouts, grabbing him as he tried to rush in, the studio police shrinking back. Someone landed a punch, maybe unintentional, and Hal swung back, drawing the others on him. A lucky hit to the face, suddenly a spurt of blood, so startling that everything stopped for a second, a freeze before crossing the line, then a blur of rushing hands. Ben looked down the street. A siren wailing, squad cars. Not one, a stream of them. Like MPs with clubs. Now there wouldn't be any sides. Just bodies in the way.

He ran out of the conference room, clumping down the stairs and tearing through the gate. A small group of studio workers had clustered behind it, watching.

"Help me get Hal," he shouted at one of them, but didn't wait, pushing his way into the crowd.

"What the fuck do you want?"

"The cops are coming. Get out of here. Everybody."

"Yeah? Friends of yours?"

He kept going. Hal and the striker were now in a kind of wrestling lock, too close to get any punches in, pounding each other's back.

"Get the fuck out," the striker said as Ben tried to separate them.

"Let go. The cops are coming. Want to get your head cracked?"

Hal stepped away, the opening the picket had been waiting for. A quick jab to the face, Hal's nose running blood, then another punch as Hal held his hand to his nose, stunned and reeling now.

"You stupid fuck!" Ben yelled, jumping on the picket, hitting him hard enough to knock him down, then dropping to his chest, another hard punch, so that the striker turned on his side, cowering, trying to cover his head.

Ben pushed himself up and grabbed Hal by the shoulders, herding him toward the gate, his hand throbbing. A studio cop stopped Hal with his stick, anyone bleeding now suspect, and Hal swung back at him. The cop weaved, clutching Hal's shirt until Hal managed to pry him loose, flinging his arms away. A flashbulb went off somewhere to the side. The cop fell, taking one of the strikers down with him. But people had begun pulling away, looking toward the sirens, the street jumping with sound. Ben got Hal through the gate.

"Call the infirmary," he said to Carl. "He's not going to be the only one."

He pulled Hal over to a low wall, sitting him down, and handed him a handkerchief to wipe the blood. "How's the nose? Broken?"

"I don't know. What's that feel like?"

"Squishy."

"My head," Hal said, touching it. "Son of a bitch actually kicked me."

A studio cop staggered in, blood streaming down the side of his head. One of the infirmary nurses, rushing to the gate, intercepted him, making him sit.

"You know the good part?" Hal said. "I'm on their side." He looked at the clotted handkerchief. "We never get blood right. It processes too red."

"You dizzy, anything like that?"

"No, the posse got there in time." He looked over at Ben. "Thanks. Where'd that come from?"

The police were wading in with clubs, swinging indiscriminately at everyone. Bodies in the way. Even the studio cops were shrinking back, out of range. Some press had arrived, trailing after the squad cars, and more flashbulbs went off around the edges of the fight. Tomorrow the picture would be a mob out of control, a breakdown, not a confused, spontaneous fight, overwhelmed by police clubs. People were falling down, crawling away before they could be trampled. One of the cops bent over to hit a striker again, not finished, drawing some blood before they began the arrests.

"Jesus Christ. Hal," Lasner said, his voice shaking. Most of the other producers had followed, drawn like gawkers at a highway wreck.

"I'm okay."

"What the hell is happening?" Lasner said, not really a question, looking out through the gate, his face bewildered.

Some press photographers raced past. Out to the left, two cops had zeroed in on Howard Stein, who had begun with his hands outstretched in a stop signal but now had thrown them on top of his head, trying to wrench himself away as the cops grabbed his shirt, dragging him. A flashbulb. A club whacked his arm. Another striker came to help but the police ignored him, interested only in Stein, pummeling him now.

"Do you need help to the infirmary?" Bunny was saying to Hal.

"Our own people," Lasner said to himself, still looking out.

They hit Stein again, this time in the head, and he staggered, falling as a second blow got him on the neck, and Ben saw that they weren't going to stop, a storm trooper kind of frenzy. Another club, raised high, then swung hard. He glanced quickly at Hal, now being swabbed by a nurse, and rushed through the gate again, grabbing some of the others.

"Get Stein! They'll kill him."

At first no one seemed to have heard, then one of them looked toward Stein, the swinging clubs.

"Fuck," he said, dragging another picket and racing over with Ben.

They came up behind the police, jabbing at them with picket sticks, a quick thrust to the knee that brought one down. The other swung around, his club whacking Ben on the arm. Ben lunged for his throat, a surprise, the cop's face drawn back in a snarl. Then one of the pickets threw a kidney punch and the cop teetered backward, falling against the strikers. More men came over, blocking the cops from Stein. Ben looked down, winded for a second. Stein was lying on the pavement, a pool of blood spreading under his head, Danny in the police photo, his body flung in the same angle. Or did all bodies fall that way, arms awkward, twisted? He knelt down and felt his neck. Not dead. But now the police would have him, resisting arrest the least of it. Legal clubs this time.

"Help me," he said to one of the pickets. "We have to get him out of here."

"You shouldn't move him."

"Just fucking give me a hand," he said, a command, lifting Stein from underneath and waiting for the picket to take the other side.

"Fuck," the man said, grunting as he lifted.

"Howard, can you walk at all? We can't do deadweight."

"Not dead." Almost indistinct, a growl.

"Just try to walk. We've got you. Put your arm there. Hold on."

They went a few steps, Stein dragging, then pulling himself up, putting weight on his feet. Blood was still running from his head, staining Ben's shoulders.

"Who called the cops?" Stein said, another mumble.

"Just keep walking. There's a doctor. Not far."

Stein opened his eyes, squinting at the Continental gate.

"A doctor," he said, trying to make sense of this.

"Just inside. Keep moving."

He swiveled his head to check on the two cops, still down, the others not near enough to help. The crowd was a blur of hand fighting. Some people had begun to run away, yelling curses, but retreating. A flashbulb went off in front of them, the photographer probably recognizing Stein. Another siren. Reinforcements. Ben was straining under the weight, sweaty now, his shirt bloody.

"Almost there. Not far," he said again, trying to move faster, before the police noticed and could cut them off.

At the gate the crowd of employees were still watching, looking dazed. A battle scene on Gower Street. Casualties. Real blood. Ben realized then that they were looking at him, wet with it. But he'd made it to Carl's booth.

"You can't bring him in here," Bunny said. "Do you know who that is?"

"So what? He's hurt."

Stein opened his eyes again, looking at Bunny, then Lasner, and began to smile, as if they were acting out a surreal joke.

"You have a stretcher?" Ben said to the nurse. "He's heavy."

She hesitated, uncertain, waiting to be told what to do.

"You can't be serious," Bunny said.

"You want the cops to finish him off?" Ben said. "He's hurt."

"He's picketing *us*," Bunny said.

"Get the stretcher," Ben said to the nurse, then turned to Bunny. "Look at his head. You can't just leave him in the street."

He looked at Lasner, still sitting next to Hal, a vacant expression on his face, like someone after a house fire.

"Fucking Stein," one of the producers said.

"He could be dying," Ben said to Bunny. "You want the papers to see Continental throw him back in the street?" He jerked his head, motioning to the photographers outside the gate. "How would you fix that?"

For a moment no one said anything, then Lasner got up, his eyes on Ben. "Get a stretcher," he said to the nurse. "And the doc." He turned to one of the studio cops. "Tell Charlie to get the men back in. That's it."

They waited together for a few seconds, an awkward silence, louder than the yells and sirens behind them, then Lasner patted Hal on the shoulder and turned to go. "See if anybody else needs an ambulance," he said to Carl. "Before they start throwing them in the wagon." He looked at Bunny, expressionless. "The cops stay off the lot."

The nurse was running toward them, bringing two aides with a stretcher.

"Get him to Cedars," Lasner said to her. "When the doc says it's okay." Then, his face drained, almost vacant, he started back to the Admin building.

"I suppose you know what's going to happen when our people see him," Bunny said to Ben.

"Maybe you should switch unions. Or would it cost you?"

"You don't know the first thing about it."

"I don't care," Ben said, helping the aides lift Stein onto the stretcher. Stein groaned, eyes half-open.

"Right. Leave it to me to explain. Make a mess and hand somebody else a mop. And when the police come looking for him? Not exactly Mr. X, is he? They know him."

Ben stood. "And went at him. I saw it. And I have a good memory for faces. Tell them anybody comes after him with cuffs, I'll ID *them*. The ones who clobbered him when he was down. And me." He touched his arm. "Beating up soldiers. I'm still in the Army, remember?"

"Out of uniform."

"Not when I testify. We can play it that way, if you want. You think this is a mess? You wouldn't have a mop big enough." He turned to the aides. "Got him? On two."

Bunny watched them lift the stretcher. "Why are you doing this?" he said.

"I owe him a favor."

Stein opened his eyes, watching them both as the group moved past the Admin building toward the infirmary.

"A favor," Bunny said.

"Plus he's bleeding." He turned. "I'd do the same for you."

In the infirmary, the aides transferred Stein to an examination table, high enough to do stitches. As the nurse swiped his head, stanching blood, Stein reached out his hand, grabbing Ben's wrist.

"Don't leave me," he said.

Ben started, back in the other hospital, another hand on his wrist, a stopped moment.

"You'll be all right," the nurse said, reassuring.

A hand with the same urgency, but it was Stein, not Danny, a different meaning.

"Not with them," he said, looking at Bunny and one of the aides.

Bunny rolled his eyes. "Wonderful. Now I'm Chester Morris. Where did I put my gun?"

"You'd all better scoot," the doctor said, "while we patch him up. This is going to sting. We can't use anesthetics until we know what's going on in there." He gestured to Stein's head. "Here, hold on to these." He put one of Stein's hands on the gurney frame.

Ben moved the other hand off his wrist. "I'll be just outside." He looked toward Bunny, already at the door. "They're going."

"What favor?" Stein said, his voice raspy. "Why do you owe me a favor?"

"I figure Danny owes you something. A little payback."

"Payback?" Stein said, vague.

"He should have been a better friend."

"Well," Stein said, shrugging this off, then winced at the antiseptic.

"One more," the doctor said. "Just a sting."

"I'll be right outside," Ben said.

In the hallway a nurse was wrapping an Ace bandage around a studio cop's wrist while another lay on a gurney, holding a pad to a cut on his forehead. The aide had gone but Bunny was still there, smoking just outside the screen door. He stepped aside as another stretcher was brought in.

"Christ, Scarlett down at the rail yard," he said, offering Ben a cigarette. "Looking for Dr. Meade."

"Thanks," Ben said, lighting it.

Bunny nodded at the splotch of blood on Ben's shirt. "Yours?"

"No. Carrying him."

"How's the hand?"

Ben made a fist and opened it. "Nothing broken."

"All very *Boy's Own*, I must say. Wading in like that. Who'd have thought?" He looked toward the gate. "The problem is, it won't solve anything. They'll be out there again tomorrow. And now we've got this little situation here." He looked back to Stein's room.

"He'll be out of here in an hour. What situation."

"The unions are a little prickly at the moment. Or hadn't you noticed?"

"Nobody'll accuse you of switching sides. Act of mercy. The papers got some pictures, by the way. You might want to see what they're planning to run."

"Right," he said, making a mental note. "It wouldn't do to have Charlie's boys looking—well, looking unfriendly. Just the big Boy

282

Scouts they are." He drew on the cigarette. "God, I hate this. IATSE, all of them. We're supposed to be making pictures, not—whatever they think they're doing. I suppose you know your new best friend in there is a Red. Just to make things that little bit more complicated."

"Does it?"

Bunny circled around, not rising to this, then looked over at Ben. "I hear you've been talking to Minot."

"Where did you hear that?"

"Just listening to the drums. Lunch at Chasen's. Hardly a secret."

"It was just lunch."

"What did you talk about?"

"My brother, mostly."

"Your brother?"

"He worked for Minot. One of his legmen. You know that. You made the call for him. Can we stop this? All the cat and mouse?"

Bunny said nothing for a second, drawing on his cigarette. "All right. I don't like Tom and Jerry much, either. Dennis asked, I called. Nothing earthshaking. It was an easy favor to put in the piggy bank, that's all."

"For someone you'd never met."

"I didn't do it for him. I wouldn't have lifted a finger for him."

"But Minot—"

"Is important. We need him on the consent decree."

"So why not help him—what? Tidy up?"

Bunny shrugged. "Very scrupulous they are. Afraid a little of the soot would rub off, I suppose. But who cares? So let's just say he tripped. Nicer for them. And the family. For you, come to that. Much nicer. And you keep hounding me about it." He paused. "Now Ken. You're not hounding him, I hope. He could have you for breakfast before you noticed."

"And that's why you jump when—"

"I don't jump. The studio needs him."

"For the studio. Not because he has something on you. That's his specialty, isn't it?"

"Don't be ridiculous."

"If he does, he didn't get it from Danny. If that's what you think. I checked. All he ever did was put you at a meeting. As a tourist. That's it."

"Well, there's a comfort. He doesn't 'have' anything. There's nothing to have."

"Only a meeting? You scare easy. How did Danny know, by the way? Who told him about it?"

"Nobody told him," Bunny said, dismissive. "He was there."

Ben looked up, caught off guard. "I thought you said you never met him."

"I didn't. We were never introduced. People weren't. Not exactly a garden party. But I knew who he was."

"And he knew you."

"He must have. And, think, to remember all those years. Just store it up here and wait till you need a little mud to throw."

"So it wasn't MacDonald."

Bunny hesitated for a second, either rattled or genuinely confused. "Who?"

"He was at the meeting, too."

Bunny shook his head. "I told you, nobody was introduced."

"Danny said you were with him."

"With him?" Bunny said, wrinkling his brow, acting out thinking. He dropped the cigarette and started rubbing it out. "Oh, *Jack*. It's been years. He was in the Pasternak unit, over at Universal. An arranger. He worked on some of the Durbin pictures."

"A friend?"

"Just someone around."

"Who took you to meetings."

"Once. I didn't know—well, we all say that now, don't we? Anyway, I didn't. Not really my idea of a good time."

"Where is he now?"

"No idea. We're talking about years—"

"He went into the Army."

"Did he? I didn't know." He looked up. "How did you? Oh, Brother Tell All. What else did he say?"

"Nothing. Just the one meeting."

"Then what's this all about?"

"A loose end. I just wanted to know."

"A loose end of what? You want to hound him, too? Sorry to disappoint. I don't have the faintest. I expect if the Army got him, he's probably dead. Not much of a fighter." He paused, checking himself. "You don't want to get mixed up with Minot. They don't fight like this," he said, waving at Ben's shirt. "You won't even see it coming. I don't want Continental involved in any of his—" He stopped again. "Not one person on this lot."

"I don't work for him. I'm not Danny."

He looked at Ben, then backed off. "Better get a shirt from Wardrobe. Before you start scaring people. I'll see what's happening outside. I suppose they're arresting people." He sighed. "But they won't *stay* arrested." He started to move off, then stopped. "How much does she know? About all this. I mean, married to him."

Ben shook his head.

"You'd want to keep this to yourself, then. Not clutter things up." He tapped a finger against his temple. "You don't want anything here now but the part."

Before Ben could answer, the doctor came through the screen door.

"Is he going to be all right?" Ben said.

The doctor nodded. "Just a little agitated. About being on the lot."

"While we're so tickled pink," Bunny said. "So to speak."

"I'll go in," Ben said.

Stein, his head now bandaged, opened his eyes when Ben approached the bed.

"We'll get you to a hospital. Just take it easy."

"This wasn't supposed to happen. Now they'll say we started it."

"Probably."

Stein grimaced. "So thanks for—"

Ben nodded, cutting him off. "We'll get you an ambulance."

"You know, with your brother? That was all right. A lot of people lose interest."

Ben said nothing, confused for a minute, until he realized Stein meant the union.

"I don't want you to think—he wasn't a friend. People lose touch, that's all."

After Stein was taken away, Ben stopped by the cutting room to check on Hal, already back splicing film, as if nothing very much had happened. But something had. The lot had a hospital quiet, and, even though the police had now cleared the street, people kept looking toward the gate, an accident after the tow truck had pulled away.

"On Gower," Hal said. "Lasner—it's like somebody knocked the wind out of him."

"Nobody's had a raise since wage controls. He had to expect—"

"It's not the money. It's his studio. He knows everybody's name."

ROSEMARY WAS in Post-Production, recording, the red light on. Why did he have to know? To salvage one piece of decent behavior? Find one line Danny hadn't crossed, after crossing all the others?

When she came out on break she was in street clothes, her skin pale, not made up for the camera.

"I heard you got beat up," she said, noticing the cut on his forehead.

"You should see the other guy." He smiled. "Cheap line. How's it going? I thought you wrapped."

"Dubbing. They want to sneak it and the sound's still not finished."

"I need to ask you something. I hope you don't mind."

"About Daniel?"

"Yes. Well, about you."

"Me."

"Did you ever tell him about Pine Hill? When you were with him, I mean, did you ever mention it?"

She stared at him, clearly thrown. "You have a great way of coming up from behind," she said finally.

"Sorry. I didn't mean—"

"Sure you did."

"Did you? Talk about it?"

"No." She took out a cigarette and let him light it for her. "Why, did he?"

"No," he said, a relief audible only to him.

"How do you know about it, then?"

"I read something. It said you'd been there as a kid. I wondered if he knew."

"Why? Am I supposed to be ashamed of it? Eight years old? Read something where?"

Ben shrugged.

"Or are we going to? Is that what this is, a shakedown? 'Rosemary Miller: Red Diaper Baby.'" She moved her hand through the air, a headline.

"No."

She looked at him sharply. "I always knew somebody would some-day. You never see it coming, though, do you?"

"It's not coming now. This is just between us."

"You think I'm afraid of this? There are pictures. Me and Aaron Sil-ber, who later went on to—who knows? His father was a button sup-plier, he's probably running that now. Anyway, we're on a raft. In the lake. Cute. They ran it in the *Daily Worker*. My parents still have a copy, if that's what you're after."

"I'm not after anything."

"No, just curious. Want to know what it was like? Nice. We had a lake. Campfires. No running water in the bunks, but that was all right. Everything looks good when you're eight. Eight." She looked directly at him. "A child. Who didn't know it was any different from the other places in the mountains. I felt lucky to go. The classes with the lessons? Only one a day and who listened in class anyway? Not with Aaron

Silber around. Shows, too. I was on the stage. My parents came up for it. They thought it was wonderful. They thought the whole *thing* was wonderful. What the future would be like. One big Pine Hill." She looked down, her voice lower. "Maybe I would have thought so, too. If I'd had that life. You see these fingers?" She held up her index and middle fingers. "My mother has no feeling in them. Ever operate a sewing machine?" She held her hands in front of her, mimicking pushing material toward a bobbing needle. "Sometimes it slips, you get your fingers caught under the needle. It hurts. Not like a saw or anything. You don't lose them. But after a while, it happens enough, it kills the nerves, so you lose feeling. My father, with him it's the cough. From the fabrics, the dust. It gets in your lungs, you never get it out, just keep coughing. So maybe they were right, what they thought. If you have that life." She looked up at him. "But I don't. I have this life. But there's always somebody looking to dump you right back, isn't there?"

"I'm not—"

"What did they do anyway, that was so wrong? Send me to camp. I'm supposed to apologize for that?"

"No. Stop," he said, raising his hand a little.

"They're my parents—"

He raised it higher, a halt. "My father was a Communist, Rosemary." He looked at her. "So was Danny."

"What?" Her head tilted, as if it had been literally jarred, hit by something.

"He never said?"

"No," she said, still off balance.

"I thought he might have talked about it, that's all. That's the only reason I asked." He trailed off, letting them both take a breath. "I'm not trying to—"

"Never. He never said anything like that," she said, her voice vague, groping. "It's true? He was?"

"In Germany. Then he changed. That's what I'm trying to understand. What made him change."

"But all this time," she said, moving, her body restless, unsettled.

She dropped the cigarette with a willed half smile. "What my parents always wanted. A boy from—well, but not married." She shook her head, a physical clearing out. "But how could it be true? He wasn't like them. He wasn't even interested."

"It was a while ago. He was younger."

"My parents never changed. Every time my father read the paper— But not Daniel. Not even that, what was in the paper. Or maybe he just never talked about it with me. Anything he cared about. Not with the girlfriend."

"It wasn't like that."

"Oh, you know that, too? What he was thinking. Tell me. I don't understand any of it. Why would he—?"

"I'll tell you this. If he never asked you, it means he cared about you."

"I don't understand that, either."

"He was protecting you."

She looked at him quizzically, then smiled to herself. "Protecting me. It sounds better, anyway. Or maybe you like making him look good. What's next? Maybe he was in love with me, too."

"Maybe he was."

She glanced up, her eyes suddenly moist, but her voice still edged. "Well, that's something to hold on to."

RIORDAN CALLED late in the afternoon while Ben was drafting the last of the voice-overs.

"You're going to love this."

"What?"

"John MacDonald."

"You found him?"

"Army records. Once you're in—"

"He's alive?"

"Wounded. Discharged 'forty-four," he said, reading from notes. "VA Hospital over by Sepulveda until May. Then you follow the disability checks. They thought he was dead because they started coming back for a while, then the change of address came through."

"So where is he?"

Riordan paused, a delivery line. "Care of Continental Pictures."

"What?"

"But that's not the part you're going to love."

Ben waited.

"Previous address?" Riordan said, teasing him with it. "Cherokee Arms."

Ben sat for a minute afterward, his mind racing, then reached for the studio directory. No MacDonald. But had he really expected to find him there?

The mailroom was in the basement of the Admin building, filled with sorting boxes and the deep canvas bins for fan mail, hundreds of envelopes waiting to hear back from Dick Marshall, with his own signature on the photograph. One of the mail boys pushed an empty cart through the door.

"Help you?"

"I'm trying to find somebody. He's not in the directory, but he gets mail here. So where does it go? You have a list or something like that? MacDonald."

"Sure. Give me a sec."

He went over to a clipboard hanging beneath the rows of pigeonholes and started flipping pages. An eternity of minutes, everything in slow motion. Or maybe it was just that Ben already knew what he would say.

"That goes to Mr. Jenkins's office."

Joel had only been working at the Cherokee since winter and had never heard of MacDonald, but the name was there on the rent rolls. A few months and then gone, no forwarding address. Danny hadn't taken 5C until later, so there was nothing to connect them but coincidence. And Danny's source entry in Minot's file, familiar. And now Bunny collecting his checks.

But what did he do with them? Bunny got to the studio a little after the first makeup call and usually stayed late to watch the dailies. He took scripts home to an apartment on Ivar, handy to the studio, and seemed to have no personal life at all. According to his calendar, he spent Sundays making the rounds of tennis parties and open houses, and since he organized most of the Lasner dinners, there were frequent entries for Summit Drive, but otherwise the schedule was a long list of business appointments and business in disguise: a premiere, a night at Perino's with an agent, a producer's birthday. He was invited to Cukor's for dinner about once a month and appeared to have standing dates with Marion Davies and Billy Haines, presumably old friends. He never saw Jack MacDonald.

Ben had actually followed him home a few nights, stopping short of his building, but Bunny had stayed in, the reading lamp burning in the corner window. A working Hollywood life, none of the samba bands and white furs that twinkled in Polly's column every morning.

At the studio, Ben began staying closer to him, spending more time at Admin. Stein had pulled his pickets, which Bunny assumed was a favor to Ben, and a quiet Gower Street was worth an uneasy truce. He even included Ben in the sneak-preview car, usually restricted to the line producer.

"Always Glendale," Lasner said.

"It's anywhere."

"This hour, it's going to be kids."

"We want kids," Bunny said.

"With all the wiseass response cards. Go on the Boulevard, later, you get the swing shift, it's a better crowd."

"That was during the war, Sol. They're not staying open late anymore."

"They liked everything," Lasner said stubbornly.

The Glendale audience, as young as predicted, seemed to like it well enough. There was the usual surprise when the unannounced movie came on, but no groans or jokey demands for the regular feature, and they clapped at Rosemary's name in the credits, a good sign. The Continental group, sitting in the back, had already seen the picture so they watched the audience instead, a kind of seismic reading, alert to rustlings and murmurs and pockets of quiet. On the screen sequined women were dancing in a nightclub, the set of the wrap party, but Ben drifted, more interested in the men around him, seriously at work, one of whom had lied to him. A name he hadn't heard in years, whose mail came to his office. It would be useless to ask him why. He'd already ducked once. Another question would be a warning, drive him further away.

Ben looked down the row. Bunny sat slumped in his viewing posture, hands tipped, the bald patch on top of his head gleaming slightly. How many pictures had he seen? Half a lifetime sitting in the dark. It was hard to imagine him anywhere else. Not on a balcony at the Cherokee. Ben tried to run the scene in his head, Bunny in one of his soft sport jackets, the fawn eyes narrowing as he pushed—but it kept slipping away, impossible. Besides, he'd been home when Dennis called, hadn't he? A fixer. Fixing something else now.

Only half the audience bothered to fill out the comment cards, but Lasner ignored these anyway, scanning faces as they came out during the break before the regular feature. He stood near the balcony stairs in his suit, watching the lobby, not looking directly at anybody, just taking in the air. The publicity assistants, who'd been collecting the cards, were sorting them in stacks and handing a few to Bunny. Al Shulman, the producer, had already gone outside to smoke, unable to stand still.

"They're okay," Bunny said in the car, riffling through the cards.

"Just okay," Lasner said.

"It'll do business."

"With 'okay.'"

"A million."

"Seven hundred. Eight," Lasner said. "And that's with South America. Eight."

"We can recut," Shulman said.

"There's nothing wrong with the picture," Lasner said. "Harry did a good job. What's to recut?"

"Rosemary," Bunny said. "They like her." He held up one of the cards. "Women, too. They just could like her more. She needs this picture, Sol. It's time." He turned to Shulman. "Can you soften the bar scene? Maybe cut to her when he leaves? How it hits her?"

"Sure. From the two shot. Take a day."

Ben looked at Bunny, hunched forward, calculating, ready to do what had to be done. Another scene, this one easier to imagine: releasing a hand brake, letting gravity do the work, a quick fix. But why? Lasner said nothing, looking out the car window, and after a while his silence became a noise of its own, something audible underneath the talk around him. Ben thought of him looking down at the fighting on Gower Street, distant, thinking something through.

"It's too late to change the dress," Bunny was saying. "Anyway, it looks great."

"You wanted soft."

"Her *face*. Not the dress. We'll keep the heat on the trades. They don't like to back away—the early word was good."

Even Paulette had said so, flocking around Rosemary with the others, her moment.

Lasner turned to Bunny. "What did they say?" He nodded to the cards. "The ones that weren't okay."

Bunny met his eyes, then picked up one of the cards. "'Didn't I see this last year? But I liked Dana Andrews. Yes, I'd recommend.'" Then another. "'Usual hard to believe junk.'" He looked up. "One of the kids. This one says the picture's okay, but why not in color." He looked at Lasner. "I've seen worse, Sol. It'll do business."

Lasner said nothing, then went back to the window. The car was through the pass now, heading west on Fountain. "You feel it in the lobby? We didn't have the audience," he said, still looking out. "We used to have the audience."

The rest of the trip back was dispiriting, Shulman worried, everyone staring at the half-lit billboards, a funeral quiet. Bunny had tried putting a pragmatic good face on things. Seven or eight, even with South America, was respectable and nobody had been expecting *Going My Way*. But they'd been hoping for something more.

When he got back to the Cherokee, Ben walked down to Hollywood Boulevard to get a sandwich at the Rexall, still brooding. He looked at his reflection in the glare of one of the storefronts, a disembodied image, as if he were not actually there, invisible to the people passing behind him. Why couldn't Danny, another shade now, appear in the glass beside him, tell him what had happened? Or just talk? Tell one of his jokes.

At the lunch counter, while dishes and coffee cups slammed around him, he took the family picture out of his wallet. All of them together in the Tiergarten, his mother in the cloche hat, Danny grinning, him smiling, held next to each other by Otto, one hand on each shoulder. How could they have changed so much? He looked at his father, holding his boys tight against his coat. Not putting them at risk. His mother leaning against him, eyes laughing, before the bitterness. And Danny, mischievous and daring, who got him into trouble, but protected him, too, who never told on him, gave him away. Partners in crime. None of them the same. But they had been like that once. Maybe you always carried it with you, what you used to be. Danny hadn't told on Rosemary. Then why the others? Put yourself in his place. But he couldn't. He was still the boy in the picture, too, wanting to be his brother, before they changed.

The night clerk barely looked up when Ben got back, fixed instead on the crossword he was filling in, his voice lazy, almost a drawl.

"Any luck finding that mail key? Management was asking."

"No."

"They'll charge you, get another one made."

"Don't bother, then. I'm not expecting any mail."

Officially that would still go through the APO, sent on by Fort Roach. But who would write, now that Danny was gone?

"You've got some in there now."

Ben looked at his box, the see-through holes backed white with an open piece of paper, another Current Resident flyer.

"It'll keep."

"You have to turn one in when you leave, so you'll still have the charge."

"Maybe I won't leave."

The clerk didn't rise to this, his hand still moving across the puzzle. "I'll order it," he said indifferently. "Here's a message."

He reached over to a box and handed Ben a slip. Liesl. Out tonight, talk tomorrow. Another evening with Dick, the perfect gentleman. And then sleep, because the camera sees everything. But she'd called, hoping to catch him in. He felt a warm stirring on his skin. Just from a message slip.

Upstairs, he poured a drink of the brandy and sat up on the bed with one of Danny's scripts. The partners were foiling a blackmail scheme. The victim, someone Rosemary might have played, was a woman with a past who was about to marry into society. Danny was coming to her rescue, flirting, and Ben was doggedly following leads. He smiled to himself. There was some business with post office boxes— maybe the lost key downstairs put to use here—and a confrontation in a gambling club. Danny and the blackmailer play cards. "You give yourself away." What Danny used to say when they played cards, Ben's eyes apparently acting like mirrors into his hand. But unlike Ben, the blackmailer wasn't intimidated. He tosses a chip. "You're wasting your money. That's all right with me. I own the place. But don't waste your time, too. You work for her, what have you got? Be a friend to the house, you'll come out ahead." Ben sat up straighter, hearing Minot's voice. He flipped back. Even the physical description fit, an athlete's swagger. Would he have recognized himself? Was this how Danny saw him, a blackmailer? But why risk offending him? An actor might read it differently, but the likeness underneath would be unmistakable. If you saw yourself that way. And of course Minot didn't.

What else? Ben kept reading, looking for anything real, the stray detail that might lead somehow to the balcony outside. But *Partners* ran to formula. After a few kisses, Danny sends the girl back to her rich suitor—better for her and better for the series. The blackmailer goes to jail. Danny remains uncompromised. The brothers drive off together. Everything that didn't happen. Ben closed the script. But the way he'd wanted it to happen. That was something at least, wasn't it?

He got up, restless. She'd be home now, before the second set started at the Grove. Talk tomorrow. But there was still tonight, a drink by the pool, his hand idling on her leg, no files with coded sources, scripts with Minot. Just the soft air. Afterward, when she slept, he'd lie next to her, the scent of her still on him.

The driveway was empty. Should he wait? But maybe the car had already been put in the garage, tucked away for the night. There was a faint light coming from around back and he got out and followed it. The way Riordan's man had come, slipping through the French windows to look for a name. He heard her before he reached the corner of the house, still awake, an easy murmur, leaving part of it behind in her throat. Now a laugh, louder, maybe reading something by the pool. He should call out, not startle her, coming out of the dark. He turned the corner and stopped.

She was kneeling on the chaise, someone beneath her, lowering her face to his. Another murmur, playful, the light catching her bare back now, naked, moving gently, like pool water. Ben felt his stomach clench, punched in. Her hair came up again, white shoulders. He stared, unable to move, step away. Now he took in the rest, the robes lying on the ground, the wine on the table, the blue light coming from the pool. She dipped her head again, then raised it, her face visible over the back of the chaise. His breath was coming back a little, blood rushing to his head. In a second, his face would be flush with it, surprise replaced by something else. She arched her neck back, and her face came up, eyes closed, then opening, then locked on his.

For a second there seemed to be no sound at all, no gasp, not even crickets. They looked at each other, too shaken to react. Then her eyes moved, one thought chasing another, and she reached for her robe, her breasts showing. She said something to the man in the chaise as she put it on, presumably an excuse, improvised, keeping him there as she got up to go into the house, any excuse, moving steadily, not alarmed, not seeing anybody standing by the house. An arm dropped over the side of the chaise and picked up cigarettes. Then a head leaned down, lighting one. Dick Marshall. Liesl stood between him and Ben, but Dick wasn't looking. He lay back on the chaise, a bare arm flung out. The rest of him would be naked too, waiting for her. Liesl started across the patio, belting the robe, her eyes on Ben again, a flicker of panic. He turned away, heading back to the driveway.

"Wait," she said, a whisper, no louder than a hiss. Then she was past the patio, following him down the flagstone steps, out of earshot. "Wait," she said again.

Ben turned, his body still tingling, everything mixed up.

"I guess I should have called," he said, his voice neutral.

"It's not what you think," she said, no longer whispering, but soft, conspiratorial.

"What is it, then?"

"It doesn't mean anything."

He looked at her for a second. "Does he know that? I didn't."

She stared back, biting her lip. "Don't."

Silence again, the air churning, any words likely to wound.

"Talk to me," she said finally.

He kept looking at her, not speaking, things still shifting inside, falling. "You'd better get back," he said, turning to the car.

She reached out and they both looked down at her hand on his arm, something out of place. She pulled it back, the movement opening the top of her robe, so that she had to clutch the lapel, covering herself.

"Did you swim first?" he said, nodding to the robe.

Her eyes flashed, then looked away. "You've no right."

"I guess not. What was it? Just one of those things."

"No," she said quietly. "You know that."

"Getting back at him? Something like that?"

"Don't be—"

"Not that I didn't enjoy it. Just next time, let me in on it."

"We can't talk now. You're so—"

He waited. "So what?"

"I don't know. Angry."

"Ah," he said, exhaling it.

She looked down. "How could we go on like that? Him always there."

"Instead of like this?" he said, motioning toward the pool.

"It doesn't mean anything," she said again.

"It does to me."

"We have to talk later. Now it's—"

He shook his head. "You don't owe me an explanation. Let's just— not." He turned to go.

"It's nothing," she said, her head down.

"You must have had a good laugh. Me being so—"

She leaned forward, her head close to his chest.

"No. I wasn't laughing."

He could feel the robe near him, aware of her. He stepped back.

"You better go finish him off. Before he starts playing with himself. You should have him about halfway there by now. If I remember it right."

She looked up, her eyes suddenly filling, stung. "Go to hell."

He took out his car keys, flipping them, about to say something more, but instead just nodded and held one up, a kind of wave, and got into the car. He turned his head backing out, not wanting to see her standing there in her robe, a good-bye glimpse.

In a few minutes, twisting down, he was out of the hills. He stopped for a red light and sat staring out, jumpy, afraid for a second he might be sick. The light changed, then went red again, unnoticed, no one behind him to make him move. Staring, no longer queasy, his mind blank. When he finally turned onto Hollywood Boulevard, the Rexall, the theaters, all of it was still lit up, as if nothing had happened. But he felt that if he got out and walked by the plate glass windows again his reflection wouldn't be there, that his heart was still beating but the rest of him had disappeared.

SAM PILCER invited most of the studio to his son's Bar Mitzvah. The list had begun modestly, just the commissary head table, but then he felt he had to include people in his unit and after that it became impossible to draw the line. People would feel slighted, and why leave yourself open to resentment? Besides, it was the kind of occasion that wanted a crowd.

He canceled the small ballroom he'd booked at the Ambassador and took over the Grove instead.

By midmorning there was already a line of cars in front of Wilshire Boulevard Temple. The lot behind was full, but Ben circled around and finally found a spot two blocks in on Hobart. The temple was Byzantine inspired, a scaled-down Hagia Sophia, and the crowd gathering outside made it feel a little like one of the big movie theaters downtown. Ben stopped for a minute, watching people being helped out of black Packards and hugging each other on the sidewalk, another premiere. There were photographers and even the usual cluster of fringe people who'd come to see stars, held away from the entrance doors by ushers. Sam and his younger wife stood at the top of the stairs, hemmed in by well-wishers. Women were in dressy day clothes, navy set off with a diamond brooch, peach silk with pearls, everyone in hats and a few in fur stoles, in spite of the bright autumn sun.

Ben thought, looking at the guests, that all weddings and family parties were the same, everyone falling into predictable place. Rosemary stepped out of her car all ready for the camera, but the beefy middle-aged man off to the side, looking slightly lost, was probably Uncle Al, who ran a linen supply business in Inglewood. Sam's mother-in-law, on a cane, was being escorted by an older grandchild—Jonathan, the Bar Mitzvah boy, would already be inside looking over the Hebrew passage. Al's daughter, the pretty one, had brought a new man. Aunt Rose, whom nobody ever knew what to do with, was beaming at a photographer. Happy families, all alike.

The front office people were now arriving, the Lasners first, then everyone else in a quick jumble so that they all reached the steps at once, swarming around Sol the way they had at Grand Central. Fay teetered on high heels, holding on to his arm.

"What are you, walking?" Sol said, seeing Ben.

"I parked behind."

"Yourself? What if people see?"

"What people?" Ben said, laughing.

"People. There's always people. You should know that."

"Just saving the studio money," Ben said, brushing it off.

"You and who else?"

But he dropped it, tugged by Fay to start up the stairs.

"Rabbi Magnin's doing it himself," she said to him, leaning in. "Say something to Esther. She's thrilled."

Lasner turned slightly to Ben. "Come sit with us," he said.

But Ben held back, already imagining Bunny's scowl, Fay's appraising glances. Liesl was getting out of a car with Dick Marshall, a little excitement running through the spectators.

"Dick! Over here!" Almost a squeal as he waved, flashing the Marshall grin.

Ben kissed Liesl on both cheeks, a European family greeting.

"You look nice."

She smiled, relieved, but still tentative. "Wardrobe. I think from the Wehrmacht," she said, touching one of the padded shoulders. "You know Dick?"

But Dick was flashing the grin again for one of the photographers.

"Save me a dance later."

"What?" she said, slightly thrown, not sure if it was a double-entendre.

"At the Grove. Sam hired the band, too."

"Oh. Yes, that would be nice." Letting her eyes stay on him, talking.

More car doors were slamming, voices getting louder, rising like heat waves.

"Better get inside. There's Polly," he said, spying her farther down the row of cars.

"No, we're supposed to talk to her."

Dick, seeing her, put his arm around Liesl. "Hey," he said to Ben, drawing a blank.

Liesl put on a public smile and started to turn.

"Have fun," Ben said, sliding away, heading for the stairs.

"So glad you could come," Pilcer said as they shook hands. "You know Esther?"

"Congratulations. You must be proud."

"Ask me after," she said pleasantly. "It's still touch and go with the Hebrew."

"It'll be fine," he said, a meaningless reassurance. But wasn't it always? How many had he seen—struggling through their readings, rabbis at their sides, but always ending with elated grins. He remembered a whole season of them, the year Danny was thirteen, dreading the boredom of the service, all of it alien to them, who weren't being instructed, who weren't in their friends' eyes even Jews. Otto had been indifferent and their mother gentile, so they'd escaped the Hebrew lessons, the tedious weeks of preparation. The services themselves were exotic, a series of risings and sitting downs and words repeated phonetically, just to go along. Most of the boys used the synagogue in Fasanenstrasse and afterward there would be a formal lunch across the street at the Kempinski, all good manners and politely smiling grown-ups. Years later, after they had left, it had been torched on Kristallnacht. Now there was nothing, a few shell-like walls.

"He's reading from Esther," Sam was saying. "For his mother. It's a nice touch, don't you think? What did you read? I'll bet you don't even remember."

Ben shook his head. "I didn't. My father wasn't observant."

"Like Sam," Esther said, nodding to him. "'A lot of work and who remembers?' But I think it's important. Now, I mean." She faltered a little, embarrassed. "You know, after—"

"Yes," Ben said, helping her.

"Of course, you would," Sam said. "You know what he's making at the studio?" But someone had taken his elbow. "Abe. Wonderful to see you. Esther, you remember Abe Lastfogel. The Morris office."

"Congratulations again," Ben said to Esther, letting her go. "He'll be fine."

"It's just, you know, it's important to have a sense now," she said, still making a case to herself.

"Yes," Ben said, moving inside. But was it? Had it mattered before? Even *Mischling*s had been taken, one parent, people who'd had no teaching at all.

He picked up a yarmulke from a pile on a sideboard. Inside, through the marble arches, people were settling in, waving to friends, the hum before a show. All religion was a kind of theater. He smiled to himself as he walked in. At least here they knew their audience. The whole vaulted ceiling, a night sky, was covered with stars.

He sat with Hal Jasper behind the Lasners, close enough to be in the party without taking anyone's place. Bunny, who'd also put on a yarmulke, was next to Fay and took his cues from her, rising when she did, mumbling during the unison response. Rabbi Magnin, in wire-rimmed glasses, led the Shabbat service in one of those pleased-with-itself oratorical voices Ben remembered from his childhood. Jonathan sat waiting on the bema, dwarfed in a chair that made him look no older than eight. All of it just as expected. In a few minutes they'd open the ark and walk the Torah through the congregation, letting people reach out to touch it, then finally open it for Jonathan to read and then they'd all go to the Ambassador.

Fasanenstrasse. Otto hadn't believed in any of it, only allowed them to go because it would have been impolite to refuse the invitations. *Drehkopf*s, he called the rabbis, head spinners. A hostility that Ben had never really understood until now. No room for two religions. But he would have been killed for either. As a Communist, Genia had said, not as a Jew. But that had only been a matter of time. Ben looked around— all these well-dressed lucky people, faintly bored, waiting to congratulate Sam and go to lunch. It could have been any of them, except they'd been here, out of the way. And Otto had stayed.

He shifted in his seat, uncomfortable. It always came back to that. Why make Danny run the same risk? They knew what would happen if they were caught. What did happen, at least to Otto, denounced. And now his denouncer gone, connected somehow to Danny, the link he couldn't understand but must be there. Could Otto really have believed in it that much, when he didn't believe in anything else? Or did he know, somehow sense, that he'd left it too late, that he could only help save the others now, before he became one of the millions, no matter what he believed. Somebody Ben had seen standing on the platform and then never saw again.

On the bema Magnin had finished and the cantor got up and walked to the lectern. Another endless wail, Ben thought, another thing he'd hated about the services. He looked at Bunny, wondering how he was reacting, one of the few there for whom this wouldn't even be a memory, the yarmulke just a prop of respect. Thinking about the studio maybe, or how Polly's talk had gone with Liesl, a hundred things. How to protect Jack MacDonald.

The first note, high and clear, wavered in the air, dropped, then rose again, a call reaching out. Ben felt his head go up, as if the note were lifting it. A second phrase without a breath, lonely, the voice its own music, but so beautiful that it filled the great room, hushing it. It hung there for a minute, a pure abstraction, and then the imagination rushed in around it, adding color and suggestion as the music began to float, a haunting stream of notes. A few heads nodded, familiar with it, but Ben couldn't move. A sadness so knowing that it felt like an actual fingertip on his heart. Not a wail, not even a lamentation, but an endless sorrow. He imagined it vibrating through thin air, over bleached rocks, stretches of dry waste, desert music, meant to carry long distances, across emptiness. Had it really been written there, a tribal heirloom, or much later in some Polish village, the desert by then more a story than a memory. There were notes in Gershwin like this, bent midway in a kind of ache. He didn't know the words—it might have been a simple hymn of praise—but what he saw were figures wrapping a body in linen, laying it into a shallow ditch, rocks and sand. And the body, he knew, was Otto. The day, the temple, had triggered the memories, all the old questions. There hadn't been a service for him. No details of the death itself, so that it seemed not to have really happened, the official letter a kind of missing persons report. But now here he was in the music, everything he'd denied being, the string that connected Ben to this room of survivors, not lessons but blood.

The music might have meant anything, but in the stillness of the room he saw that it now meant everyone who had gone. It was important to have a sense, Esther had thought. He noticed that Lasner had lowered his head, a tear running down his cheek, overwhelmed by some loss of his own. Or perhaps a sign of age, easily moved. Ben remembered him at the camp, actually sobbing. The first thing Ben had liked about him. Who was it now? The same vast number, a lost father? How long before a blood tie finally dissolved? Never. He was still Otto's son, after everything. Danny even more so. Ben sat up. Even more so. Otto wasn't someone he would ever deny, no matter how much his politics had changed. Otto had died for his. You didn't honor the memory of that by feeding gossip to a Minot. He wouldn't have done it. But there were the files.

Hal leaned toward his ear. "This is it," he said softly. "The music. For the pan shot."

For a moment Ben was confused, still lost in his own thoughts. He needed to think it through, about Otto, and Danny. But the music was moving on and he began to move with it, like a wind, out of the desert, across the steppes to a stretch of cold, flat land. He knew the shot Hal meant. Taken high, from on top of the cab of an Army truck, panning slowly, left to right, over the endless reach of the camp. And as he listened, he saw the finished film, the plain mournful sound passing over the miles of barracks, a perfect match, as if the writer of the song, from its first clear note, had known all along it would end this way.

When the cantor finished there was a stillness. Fay put her hand over Sol's, bringing him back, the tear discreetly brushed away. Then another piece of music began, the ark was opened, and everything went on.

"You know what it's called?" Hal whispered.

Ben shook his head and Hal made a note to himself, jotting something on the program.

"You think we could get him?" He nodded to the cantor.

Ben didn't bother to answer. Did anyone ever say no? But the mood was broken, the haunting music of the dead now just sound to be scored, used. But isn't that why they were making the film, for them?

"Make it the last shot," he said. "Use it at the end."

Jonathan read well, his young boy's voice surprisingly clear and precise, pitched to his family in the first row. Esther looked side to side, pleased, but Sam kept his eyes on the bema, his face soft with unguarded affection. Around them people were nodding, one of them patting Sam on the arm. A few rows behind, Liesl was following with polite attention, her blond hair hanging back, grazing her shoulders. Another *Mischling*. Was the hair from Hans, the mother another dark Sara? She turned, meeting his gaze, then looked down, a smile forming at the corners of her mouth, and Ben realized she had misinterpreted. When she looked back again, just a moment between them, she was answering something else, not what had been in his mind at all, and he felt his face answer her, another layer. It could go on this way, he thought, one response building on the next, all begun with a mistake. Maybe that's how we all talked, not knowing each other, a verbal house of cards.

They were seated at lunch with studio people, away from the family table down front. The Cocoanut Grove was usually lit softly to suggest evening, and the bright daylights now made the prop palms look slightly tawdry, like an island beach that unexpectedly turns out to be littered. The band had already been playing when they arrived and the floor beyond the Moorish arches had been kept clear for dancing, just a few extra tables laid along the side. Waiters had held out trays of drinks as they arrived.

"A little early in the day, don't you think?" Dick Marshall said, taking one.

"Not for champagne," Liesl said.

They were playing a couple, moving through the room together. Only a few people were actually sitting down. After they found their place cards, they circled the room, seeing everybody.

"How long is this going to last?" Rosemary said to Ben.

"You have to stay for the speeches. After that—"

"All day, then."

They had reached the buffet table of canapés, elaborately laid out, with ice sculpture centerpieces.

"They sneaked the picture," she said suddenly. "You were there."

"The cards were good."

"So why is Al so nervous. Level with me."

"They liked it. They didn't love it."

She flinched a little, a jab to the stomach.

"They liked you. It wasn't you."

"And that'll make a difference."

"Nobody's saying—"

"Nobody's saying anything. That's the trouble. You think I don't know how to read the tea leaves?"

"You're overreacting."

"You think so?" She touched her forehead. "You know what that is, what they call it in the theater? Flop sweat. In a refrigerator like this. Do they always keep it so cold? It's like a banana boat."

"Coconuts," he said, smiling, looking up at the trees, then back at her. "Don't worry. It's one sneak. Kids in Glendale."

"You haven't been here very long, have you? Don't worry. How? You stop worrying, you're dead."

"I just meant—"

"I know what you meant. My option gets picked up in January. So we have to talk now, and all they're thinking about is the kids in Glendale."

"You're the biggest star on the lot."

"After Dick. And nobody's hiring Ben Hecht to do rewrites for me." She looked across the room to where Liesl was standing with Marshall.

"One week."

"So, one week. They just shot ours. Every lousy line. For her, Hecht." She stopped, lowering her head. "They're rushing her picture. She's all they're thinking about now. Funny, isn't it? That it's her. After everything."

The early cocktail hour went on, but the waiters had begun to put out the fruit cups so people slowly gravitated to the tables. It was then that the bandleader announced a special treat and introduced Julie Sherman. She was dressed modestly, a blue jersey with a big pin, but the dress was formfitting, clinging and folding, showing her off. Ben thought of her on the train, drawing eyes. But she'd done the voice-over in a day, professional, and the surprise now was that she was good, one of those performers who comes alive with music, warm and easy, comfortable with herself. They were doing "Let Me Off Uptown," and while she wasn't as throaty as Anita O'Day she had the same swinging assurance, fronting the band, too distinctive to be background. A few people turned to look as they made their way to the tables. Bunny, not expecting this, was watching her carefully, evaluating. The up tempo seemed designed to move people to their seats and the band kept it up with "Riding High," the bright Porter lyrics an even better showcase for her voice.

"Do you believe this?" Lasner said, annoyed. He'd been coming back from the men's room and stopped midway, next to Ben. "He has her at his kid's Bar Mitzvah? A piece he's banging? What the hell is he thinking? What's Esther supposed to think?"

But Esther, oblivious, seemed happy, the entertainment just another benefit of being a studio wife.

"She knows?"

"It's the idea of it. Where's the sense? Anyway, who has a Bar Mitzvah in a nightclub?" He flung his arm to take in the room. "Downstairs in the temple. Some cakes, coffee, maybe lunch somewhere after. No, that's not enough, he has to have a floor show. With her yet. It's a question of respect. A nightclub." He looked around the oasis room. "You know where they got the palms? *The Sheik.* Off the set. It was Valentino's idea. Well, that was a while ago. Maybe they're not the same ones anymore, who knows? Here he brings his kid. You know we go back. Sam, he was an extra, in the Gulch. Waiting around. I pick him one day and he tells me the picture's a piece of shit. Oh yeah, so what would you do? And he tells me and you know what? He's right. So I give him a shot. Fix it and we'll do some business. That's twenty-five, thirty years now. He never lost me a nickel, not once. Still, all this— You want to chase something, all right, but you don't bring it home."

There was applause as Julie finished, followed by a dinner gong, one of those handheld xylophones they used on ships.

"Let's see where she goes," Lasner said, his eyes following her off the stage. "She's going to sit with the family? No, so at least he's not that crazy. Look at Esther. She's thanking her, like she's the help." He shook his head and turned to Ben. "Hal tells me you're almost finished with the picture."

"Almost."

"So we should talk sometime. What you're going to do next."

"That's up to the Army."

"Don't be a schmuck. I talked to Arnold. They're doing the papers. Maybe a week, two."

Ben nodded a thank-you.

"My only question is, are you tough enough for this business."

"How tough do you have to be?"

Lasner smiled, pleased with this, then put a finger on Ben's chest. "We'll talk. There's Fay. Go keep an eye on your sister. Dick's all over her."

"He's supposed to be. That's the idea. It builds her. For the picture."

"Yeah, I know all about that. I still say, somebody tell Dick. He's god's gift—he likes to be reminded. Any chance he gets. I know. I'm the one had to pay off the paternity suit. So keep an eye." He tapped Ben's chest again. "I tell Bunny, these things get out of hand, you've got a mess to deal with, but he doesn't listen. Like he knows. Dames always think it's real. Besides she's supposed to be *fresh*. Right off the boat. Not another chippie. Look at that." He nodded to the table, where Dick had put his arm around Liesl.

"They're talking to Polly. It's for her."

"Five bucks it's for him, too."

Ben joined them after Polly had gone, sitting between Liesl and Julie, Dick still drawing a blank as they were introduced again. Wine was served with lunch, but instead of feeling logy he was more alert than before, Lasner's bet planted in his head now, watching Dick touch her, all the usual little moves, claiming territory. She smiled back at him, a public smile, but Ben suddenly saw them on pillows, talking lazily about nothing, smoking. He turned his head, cutting away from it. Julie, who'd been talking to Hal, turned at the same time.

"That was terrific before," he said.

"You're nice."

"No, you were good. You should do a musical."

"From your lips," she said, laughing, rolling her eyes upward. "Mr. Pilcer's trying to fix something."

"At Continental?"

"I know, no musicals. But maybe a first time. If he can get Mr. Lasner to go for it."

Ben looked at her, lips glistening, her pretty face still young, going places. Did she really believe this?

"But that's probably not going to happen," she said, sensible after all. "I mean, the studio's not really set up for musicals. At Fox—I was there for about five minutes—they had a whole building, all these rooms with pianos. Arrangers. Voice coaches. You know, the whole thing. Maybe I should have done a party, like this. Sang for Zanuck. Anyway, now I'm here."

"Where they don't do musicals."

"But here's the thing—a loan-out? Mr. Pilcer knows people at Metro. He can get a test over to the Freed Unit. You never know. It could happen that way." Her voice had got faster, a little breathy. "That would be my dream." Said plainly, too important for irony.

Ben smiled at her, trying not to look dismayed. The hunger that moved everything here. Did Liesl feel it now, too? Pretending not to care, a European reserve, but there every day at dawn. Maybe, like Julie, doing whatever it took.

"I hope it works out," he said blandly. What else did one say?

"Something will. Mr. Pilcer's helped lots of people," she said, looking at him directly, without embarrassment.

Sam and Esther had got up to dance, a signal to everyone else, and now Liesl and Dick followed, as much an attraction as Julie had been on the bandstand. Wardrobe had done a good job. Beneath the military padded shoulders her dress was soft and flowing, swaying against her long legs. Dick held her in the small of her back, just close enough to brush against her but far enough away to talk. About what? Evening after evening.

When Sam made a welcoming toast during the first course, Esther at his side, Ben glanced at Julie, curious to see her reaction, but her face gave nothing away, a polite guest. He looked around the rest of the table, imagining for a minute all the invisible ties between them, and it occurred to him that Julie might be the only one who knew exactly where she stood, not measuring love, somebody else's real feelings, not even wondering. Mr. Pilcer helped people, a simple transaction. But was it ever? What did she feel when she saw him beaming with Jonathan and Esther? People came with strings attached. When you touched someone's skin, you always touched something else.

He looked at Liesl, who was skittish, aware of him, aware of Dick, and he thought of that first night, how easy it had been, unplanned. Not calculated, not for a chance at a song, just because it happened. Dick was standing now and leading the woman on his right to the dance floor.

"Careful with that," Al Shulman said, joking, apparently his wife.

"Back in one piece," Dick said pleasantly.

"Stop staring at him," Liesl said in a low voice, even though they were alone. "He'll think you're angry with him. Something."

"Why would I be? When everybody's so happy."

"Do you think I'm enjoying this? I didn't make up the tables."

"Come and dance."

"No."

"For old times' sake." He looked at her. "Otherwise Al Shulman'll think he has to. Come on, before he gets up."

On the dance floor, only half-crowded, he put his hand on her waist, then moved it slowly to her back, drawing her to him with the music. "Easy to Love." She put her hand in his, making contact, their heads still far apart.

"I've never danced with you before," she said.

"No," he said, feeling her.

"We never did normal things."

"Like what?"

"Go dancing. Meet in a café. Well, that was all before the war." She looked up at him. "I wonder. If it had been you. In France. If I'd met you. How different everything would have been."

They moved together, easier, his hand resting higher now on her back. She came nearer, lowering her head. He touched the back of her neck, just one finger, stroking it gently.

"Can anyone see?" she said, shivering a little.

"No."

"Don't," she said, pulling away a little. "Like dancing class." She looked at him. "*Schicklich.*"

Another minute, just moving.

"What do I say to you? I don't know what to say."

"You don't have to say anything. We already did that."

"And now what? My father was asking about you. Why he never sees you anymore."

"What did you tell him?"

She shrugged. "You're busy. Both of us. Anyway, he'll see you to-night."

"Tonight?"

"At the Observatory. With Dieter. You forgot it's tonight? But you're coming, yes? He planned it for you."

"All of us?"

"Yes, all. You want me to stay home? What would I say? That it's awkward now? Just to be in the same room. We have to learn how to do this." She looked away. "What a mess we've made for ourselves. If we'd never started this."

"But we did," he said. "Why did we?" Not really a question, then looking at her, wanting to know. "Why did you?"

The words hung there for a second, waiting, and he saw something change in her eyes, a flicker of hesitation, then a softening, familiar, the way they'd known each other before.

"Because I wanted to," she said, her voice low, like a hook, drawing him closer. "And you. We wanted to."

He drew a breath, remembering the dress slipping off her shoulders, his mouth on her back, excited, both of them wanting it. He felt his lower body now against hers. The same. Not the same. But still drawn in.

He leaned forward, whispering. "Come with me. Now. Just come."

She pulled her head back. "Are you crazy?" she said, barely audible. "We can't." A little breathless, panicky, everything happening on the dance floor, people around them.

"Just for a minute. Come outside."

"How can—?"

"Go to the ladies' room. Take the door out to the courts. Just for a minute."

Her eyes were shining, excited now too, catching his eagerness, stealing just a minute.

"Now. I'll tell him. A minute."

"My purse. I can't go to the ladies' without my purse." Complicit.

She drew him by the hand, hurrying to the table before the others, picking up her bag.

"The door out to the courts. Down the hall," he said, but she had already gone, both of them caught up in a rush, not caring, as if they were throwing off clothes.

Dick returned with Mrs. Shulman.

"Liesl's gone to the ladies'," Ben said casually. "Can I bring you something from the bar?"

When Dick said no, Ben started across. You always ran into somebody at the bar, it was bound to take a while to pick up a drink. Minutes, longer. He disappeared behind the crowd and out of the Grove.

The Ambassador had courts and a pool behind the main wing, country club grounds. As he went through the side door he saw, in a blink, the studio cars grouped near the driveway, their drivers smoking in the shade, prepared to wait all day, like coachmen in a period picture, but then he saw her waiting for him, there first, and he took her arm without thinking, pressing her against the wall, and kissed her, his mouth already open.

"We can't. Not here," she said.

Without leaving her mouth, he moved her away against the adjoining wall behind a tree.

"Jonathan has to light candles," he said into her neck, moving back to another kiss. "Name all the relatives." His mouth on hers again. "It'll take hours."

"How do you know?"

"It always does. Ssh." An open kiss now, no time for talking, excited by the wet, by knowing she was here, wanting to. He leaned closer, pressing against her breasts.

"Oh," she said, finally breaking the kiss, gulping air. "I hate this."

"No you don't," he said, sure now, nuzzling her, feeling her respond.

"Not this," she said, moving her neck with him.

"What?"

She pulled her head back, breathing hard. "I don't know what I'm doing. I used to know what I was doing. Now I—" She looked down. "One minute—now look at us. I'm not like this."

"Everybody's like this."

"I don't mean that. I don't know myself anymore. I used to know—" She broke off. "But I was wrong, wasn't I? All those years, I thought I knew and it wasn't true."

He leaned forward again, but she put her hand up.

"No, we have to go back." She took a breath, calming herself, then smiled. "Tonight. Come tonight."

"Too many people," he said, his face close.

She moved her hand up to his cheek. "Not after. When they go to bed," she said. "Not then. It's what you want, isn't it?"

"If you do."

She nodded. "Yes," she said, then looked down. "Another mess. I don't know what I'm doing, and I want to do it anyway." She brought up her purse and took out a handkerchief, reaching over and wiping lipstick from the corner of his mouth, then stopped, looking at him for a minute.

The door slammed open. They both turned, Ben shielding her. Bunny. Her eyes widened, her fingers clutching him. But Bunny was preoccupied, never glancing to the side, heading straight for the studio cars.

"He didn't see," Ben whispered. "Just stay still. What do you think happened? He's running."

"I don't care. If he looks—"

"He'll just see the tree. Why come out this way?"

Bunny summoned one of the drivers with his fingers, then jumped into the backseat.

"It's early to leave," Ben said as the car began to start down the driveway. He turned to Liesl. "Make some excuse for me. I'll be back later."

"What excuse?"

"Don't say anything then. They'll think I got lucky at the bar." He touched her shoulder. "Later."

"But where—?"

He ran out from behind the trees and darted into the lot, looking down the driveway to see which way Bunny turned on Wilshire, then raced back to his car, taking his keys out as he ran. It took two blocks before he got Bunny's car in sight, hemmed in by Saturday traffic headed for the department stores. Maybe he was going back to the studio, a minor crisis to settle, but they passed all the logical turnoffs for Continental and after a turn on Sunset, Ben knew they must be heading for Bunny's apartment on Ivar. Maybe he'd just had enough and decided to go home.

Ben parked at the bottom of the block as Bunny got out, thanked the driver, and headed down into the basement garage. Why change cars? A Continental driver would take Bunny anywhere he wanted to go. Ben waited for a few minutes, watching the street, empty and sunny. Then Bunny's car appeared up out of the driveway and turned back toward Sunset. Ben ducked. When he sat up again Bunny's car was already at the next corner.

The first blocks on Ivar were tricky because there were no other cars, but on Sunset Ben managed to put a few between them, staying far enough back to avoid being seen. Still heading west, past Highland and Hollywood High, commercial blocks of drive-ins and offices with blinds. Ben anticipated a turning somewhere, but Bunny stayed on Sunset, past Fairfax and then through the Strip, where Dick Marshall took Liesl dancing. I don't know what I'm doing. But she wanted him to come. And how would he explain this, tracking Bunny? But he wouldn't have just left in the middle of lunch. Sam would notice.

There was a close moment in Beverly Hills, at the light before the hotel, when the car ahead turned and Ben found himself just behind. He pulled down the sun visor so that Bunny would only see the bottom of his face, then waited until someone had cut in before following again. The streets were quieter here and they picked up some time, Bunny actually running one of the lights. Still heading west, past UCLA, then down the hill past the Bel-Air gates. This endless city—where was he going? In a while they'd be in the Palisades. One of the émigrés' houses, on the steep slopes of the canyon? Why not Paseo Miramar? They were through the village now. If he didn't turn soon, they'd be at the ocean. Ben imagined him making the hard right and climbing the cliff, past Feuchtwanger's, past the lonely turn where Genia's car had gone straight. Did MacDonald live up there, one of the neighbors Lion hadn't met? He slowed a little, ready to make the turn.

But Bunny didn't stop, sailing past Paseo Miramar, all the way to the Pacific, and turning north on the coast highway, the sun flashing off the flat blue water. Ben kept following, confused now. They had reached the end, joining the steady stream of traffic going out of town. Ventura? Who lived this far away, where Bunny didn't want to take a studio car? Ben checked his gas gauge—they could be going anywhere. Then suddenly Bunny's turning signal started flashing, just before a narrow opening in the cliffs. Not a major road, not even signposted. Ben slowed, watching Bunny turn, but then drove past. Impossible to miss a car behind you on that road. He continued until a break in the traffic let him pull left in a U-turn and double back to Bunny's road.

What if it were a private driveway, Bunny's car already invisible in a

garage? At first there seemed to be no houses at all, just tall, wild grass.
The road switched back as it climbed, the guard rail just like the one
Genia had crashed through. A first house, with two cars in front, neither of them Bunny's, then a modern, glass-fronted house, looking
empty. Ben climbed again, another switchback, and the land leveled
out, a straight stretch and then a clump of trees and a huge building,
stucco with balconies, one of the big Mediterranean beach houses
they'd built in the twenties, this one stuck on top of the hill for the
views. In the white gravel forecourt there was a half circle of parked cars,
Bunny's at the end. Ben hesitated for a second, not sure what to do
next, then pulled in beside it. The checks came to the studio. He had to
be somewhere.

Ben got out and looked around. Why so many cars? But he remembered Iris's car at the house, a city where even maids drove. The morning fog had burned off and there was a breeze. He walked around to the
side. The back of the house faced the water, with balconies large enough
for outdoor furniture, a chaise to lie on in the salt air. Walking trails had
been cut into the bluff. He went back to the forecourt. Someone was
coming out, a girl with a sweater over a white blouse—no, over a white
uniform, with white shoes.

"The desk is just inside. If you're looking for somebody," she said,
helping.

He nodded a thank-you and watched her get into her car. Not a private house, but not really a hospital, either, not up this secondary road.
He was still standing there, thinking, when Bunny came out and lit a
cigarette. He saw Ben and froze, neither of them moving, then hurried
over, throwing the cigarette away.

"What are you doing here?" he said, his voice almost a growl. "Are
you following me?"

"You said you hadn't seen him in years, but you get his checks. He
lived at the Cherokee. So did Danny. I have a right to know."

"A right."

"Is he here?"

"What do you want?"

"Was he there that night? Is that what you were really trying to fix?"

He looked at Ben, his eyes flashing, moving from fury to contempt, his whole body tense, unsettled. And then he quieted, a giving way, and Ben noticed what he'd missed before, the pale skin, the eyes close to brimming, face haunted, like someone after an accident.

"You want to see Jack, is that it?"

"What is this place?"

"It's where he lives now. Come and see," he said, turning, his voice sharp.

Ben grabbed his arm, stopping him. "Just tell me one thing. Was he there that night?"

"Take your hand off me," Bunny said, a stage line, haughty, then he switched, unexpectedly breezy, almost malicious. "Come and see."

Inside there were more people in white coats, attendants in loose pajama-like uniforms.

"Is this a hospital?"

"It's a private facility. For people who can't manage on their own."

"What's wrong with him?"

"He's been coming along nicely," Bunny said, Laraine Day for a second. "But today we've had a little setback, I'm afraid. Still, since you've come all this way."

A man holding a clipboard looked up, concerned, but Bunny made a little hand motion that seemed to vouch for Ben. They walked down a hall of polished Mexican tile.

"He'll be sleeping. So just a look today. I suppose you wanted to talk, have a heart-to-heart about the brother, but that'll have to wait."

"Is something wrong. I'm not trying to—"

Bunny turned. "What are you trying to do? Just in here."

He opened the door to a large bright room facing the sea, what must have been the master bedroom in the old house. It was not a hospital room. There were reading chairs and tables with books and magazines, a small dining area, an ordinary bed, but Ben noticed a pull cord next to a nightstand covered with pill boxes and medicines. MacDonald was lying half propped up, his face away from the light pouring in from the terrace. His bare shoulders and the top of his chest were visible over the sheet, but one of the shoulders ended in a stump, the arm gone. The other arm was lying out on the sheet, the wrist wrapped in a white bandage.

"This is Jack," Bunny said.

"What happened?" Ben said, almost a whisper.

"He can't hear," Bunny said, a normal voice. "They gave him something earlier." He looked down at the bandage. "He gets sad sometimes. Oh, you mean the arm. A grenade. They took it off over there—New Guinea. God knows what the place must have been like. Probably some tent. Butchers. *Next.* Anyway, not Cedars, but maybe it wouldn't have made any difference. It was shattered. You knew he was a pianist?"

"At Universal," Ben said quietly. "An arranger."

"Helpful, aren't they, those files? Not just an arranger. A pianist." He was looking down at him now. "The lightest touch. Chopin, especially. Like night sounds. He was very gifted." He touched the sleeping man's hair. "Of course, there's nothing we can do about the hand now. He can use that to get around," he said, nodding to a corner where a prosthetic arm rested on an end table, "but not for the piano. The face, though—there's a surgeon at UCLA who's been doing wonders with grafts, so we might get that back." Ben now saw that the side of his face away from the window was a blotch, what must be a burn scar from the same explosion. "He was so good-looking." He brushed the hair back again, a sleeping child.

"I'm sorry."

Bunny took his hand away. "Yes. But there's no bottom to sorry, is there? Down and down. So one of us has to keep things going. It's just—I wish he didn't get so sad sometimes."

There was a knock on the door, then a white coat halfway through.

"Mr. Jenkins? Oh, I'm sorry," he said, noticing Ben.

"No, it's all right. Please. Dr. Owen. You wanted to see me."

"It's just that—" He glanced again at Ben, uneasy. "It's just, we can't take the responsibility."

"I'll take the responsibility."

"We can't be with him all the time."

"I know. And accidents will happen." He looked at the doctor. "But not again. I'll talk to him. He has to be more careful, that's all."

"But Mr. Jenkins, we can't—" He looked to the terrace. "We can't be building fences on the balconies. We're not a—"

"I'll talk to him," Bunny said firmly. "All these medicines, you have to be extra careful. So disorienting. But thank you for everything," he said, coming over, as if he were seeing someone out after a party. "The stitches. It seemed like a nasty cut."

"Yes, nasty. Mr. Jenkins—"

"He may need a little extra help at meals for a while. You know, with both arms not really— There won't be any problem with that, will there?"

The doctor faced him down, a moment, then looked away. "No, there shouldn't be a problem. Mr. Jenkins—"

"I'll talk to him. I know this will be a warning to him. To be more careful."

"Yes, a warning," the doctor said, a last shot, then nodded to Ben and left.

"I'm sorry," Ben said.

"So you said. So everybody says. Well, they would if they knew. But no one does, except you. The Grand Inquisitor. So let me ask you something. What would you do? Leave him to rot in that Veterans Hospital, everyone walking around on crutches, missing this, missing that, bedpans and people leaking—imagine living there, all the time, looking at who you are, all those people like you. Sad? You might as well—" He stopped and reached into his pocket for a cigarette.

"Is that allowed?"

"Darling, I don't give a shit. It's my nickel. Nickel. Thousands. And not even a fucking ashtray. All right, let's go out there. Better for him, anyway. And no doubt you'll want to chat, now that you're here. About that wonderful brother of yours." He looked at the bed. "Sometimes I think they can hear when they're under. They come to looking like they know everything." They were moving out onto the balcony.

"Or maybe he'll look surprised. That he's here. Until the next time. They're right, you know. They shouldn't have to worry about this— give the place a bad name. He's right about these, too," he said, touching the balcony wall. "Why not just slip right over? Quite a drop. No, he had to do it that way, all messy and— So maybe he didn't really mean it. Not finally, anyway. If you really mean it, why not jump? Easier. Yours did."

"Danny didn't jump."

"No, he tripped," he said, sarcastic, then looked up. "Oh, Jack gave him a push, is that it? With his good arm, no doubt. Really, even you—"

"He lived there. At the Cherokee."

"For a while. I thought it would be better for him. But he kept running into people."

"Danny, you mean."

"Mm. Old comrades. I wasn't having that."

"Tell me. Please."

Bunny looked over at him, then put out the cigarette on the rail.

"You put him there?" Ben said.

"I had to get him out of the hospital. I couldn't face it. All those boys, trying to come back. Clomping around. They'd fall sometimes and they'd have to wait for someone to pick them up. You could see it in their faces, what it did to them. It was making him worse, being there. So I hired somebody to be with him. Found a place."

"Why didn't you bring him home?"

"Home. Where have you been living?" He caught himself and looked away, toward the Pacific. "You don't know how it is, do you? That really wouldn't have been on. Sharing. There's a certain standard you have to keep up here. Not startle the horses. Unless you're a set dresser, something like that." He turned to Ben. "And I'm not. So I found him a place. One of the contract players used to live there—"

"Who?" Ben said, thinking of the lists he'd gone through.

"Does it matter? The boy who played the gunner on Dick Marshall's bombing raid. Dick Marshall," he said, partly to himself. "That's the war we gave them. Not the one in there. Well, why not? Dick killing Japs—you'd pay to see that. Who'd pay to see this?" He took a breath. "*Any*way, he was at the Cherokee for a while, and I knew about the phone there. That was essential, having the phone, but still private, not the Roosevelt or something, so I moved him in, with Robert to look after him. And I think he liked it. So much better than the hospital. Like being on your own, in a way. That was before the leg got better, so he was still in a wheelchair, but even so. Not as—sad."

"And Danny was there?"

"No. That was all an accident—a meet cute. Robert was wheeling him, doing errands, I suppose, just getting out, and your brother was— well, I don't know what he was doing, actually. Make something up— lunch at Musso's. Who knows? Who cares. Anyway, on the street and wouldn't you know? Long-lost Jack, it's been years, what happened to you—like that. Robert probably thought they were old *Army* buddies, not comrades. Anyway, it cheered Jack up, seeing somebody from the old days, so come back and have a drink. And they did. A lot to catch up on."

"So that's how Danny knew about the Cherokee."

Bunny shrugged. "I must say, it never would have occurred to me to use it for— But I didn't have his imagination."

"You saw him there?"

"No. I never knew he took a place there until Dennis called. I guess he liked the look of it. All the possibilities. But he saw Jack there. The second time I thought, that's it, I'm getting him out of here. The re-union's over. Anyway, Robert really wasn't enough. He couldn't be with him all the time. Jack needed somewhere like this. Where they can watch him." He glanced again into the bedroom.

"Why didn't you want him to see Danny? I mean, if they knew each other."

"Well, it's *how*, isn't it? I knew what your brother was doing. I've done Minot a favor or two myself. But not like that. Jack left that life a long time ago—well, the war left it for him. It was only his good nature, you know. Always for the underdog. But try to tell anybody that now.

He's been through a lot. He doesn't need to go through anything more. Not one more thing."

"You think Danny was going to give him to Minot? A crippled war hero? What for?"

"To see who else he remembers, from those Fuller Brush parties they used to have. Very sinister characters they were. How can we help Paul *Robeson*? Christ." He looked up. "His arm's gone, but his memory's there. No, thank you."

"He has a Silver Star."

Bunny raised his eyebrows, a question.

"Army records," Ben said.

Bunny said nothing for a second, taking this in. "I always underestimate you."

"They're not going to go after somebody with a Silver Star. How would that make them look?"

"They don't have to play to the gallery. Nobody sees friendly witnesses in closed sessions. I'm not putting him through that, either. I'm not."

"But Danny didn't do that—I've seen the files. He wouldn't have."

"Touching, your faith in him. He was an *informer*. You don't want to face that, don't. I had to. I had someone else to think about. One time, how've you been? Fine. Two, he's after something. So I moved him."

"What would Danny have said? We went to a meeting five years ago—bring him in? They're after more than that. Headlines."

"And they'll get them. But not here. Not from me. And not from you, either," he said, leveling his gaze. "Not here."

"You don't have to worry about that."

"Then what are you doing, running errands for Dennis?"

"I'm trying to find out what Danny was doing, that's all. So I'm friendly. Just like you. To get something."

"And what was your brother trying to get?"

Ben said nothing, his own question come back at him. He leaned against the rail.

"You're wrong about him, though," he said quietly. "He never gave

MacDonald away, where he was, even if he's alive. There's nothing there. I checked."

"You forget—he stopped reporting."

"He wouldn't have."

Bunny looked at him, then let it go, taking out another cigarette instead and sitting on the chaise.

"Do you know how it works?" he said, not angry, a resigned patience. "Ever been to the zoo? Watch them feed? The big cats, animals like that? Give them a piece of meat, then another. It only stops when you stop feeding them. The cats just keep eating. You think they can't be hungry anymore, but they'll still take the meat. It's what they do. No matter how much you give them, it's never enough. You think you know these people? I knew Tenney. That same hunger—I don't know where it comes from—he could never get enough. But a crackpot. You didn't have to take all that carrying-on seriously. Look good in Sacramento and he's satisfied. But Minot's not a crackpot. You stick your hand through the bars, he'd take it with the meat. Get out of this before it turns on you. Once you're part of it, you're expected to *supply*. Just to prove you're with them. So you throw them anything. Maybe even Jack. To stay in. Your brother would have done it. But now Jack's safe. Except from you."

"I told you, you don't have to worry about that."

"I just want to be clear. How unwise that would be. Oh, I know, little Brian, not very scary. But you know who is? Somebody with nothing to lose. And I'm going to lose. Everything I want. I know it." He looked back to the bedroom. "One of these times it's going to work. So all I can do is hold on till it does." He looked back at Ben. "You were never here."

Ben held his stare. "That's right."

Bunny nodded, then drew on the cigarette. "But you were, weren't you? So now you're part of it. My confidante. So what do I do? Tell me. I don't know anymore. He's going to do it again. I don't know what to do."

"Give him time. Even here," he said, holding his hand to the view. "It takes time."

"Darling, *time*. Does it get any hoarier? I suppose I deserve that. Wallowing like this." He sat up. "Mustn't grumble. As they used to say in the Blitz. My mother was like that. Mustn't grumble. Mustn't grumble." He covered his eyes with his hand. "Why the fuck not? That's what I'd like to know." He paused. "What if it works next time? You'd think I'd be enough. Even with all the rest. You'd think it would be enough—not to want to, for me. But it isn't."

Ben was quiet for a minute, then moved away from the railing. "I'd better go."

"Am I embarrassing you? Or just me," Bunny said, moving his hands over his cheeks, a quick-change. "What do I say when he wakes up? The last time—"

"Last Monday," Ben said, trying it.

Bunny's head jerked up. "How do you know that? Why would you?"

"You left the studio in a hurry. You never leave early. I figured—just now, I mean."

Bunny stood up, a willed change of mood. "My every move. I didn't realize I was so fascinating. I still don't know why. What do you want, exactly? Coming here."

"Just following a name. I didn't know." He looked toward the bed.

"What, all this because he knew your brother?"

"I think somebody tried to stop Danny before he could—"

"Rat on them? I don't blame him. I'd do it myself." He raised an eyebrow. "Or did you think that I did? Ben," he said, drawing the word out. "Well, sorry to disappoint. Dennis called me. At *home*. I may have picked up a phone from time to time, but my activities don't extend to—oh, never mind. Think what you like. You might scratch Jack's name off the list, though, don't you think? He really wouldn't have been up to it. Anyway, he was here. Ask anybody." He waved his hand to the house.

"I had to be sure, that's all."

"Well, now you are. So fuck off." He looked down. "Sorry. Not very nice, was it? What a hard case I have become," he said, giving it a hint of a Southern accent. "You get that way when you stop telling yourself stories. You can't change things. No matter how many stories. I remember standing in front of the mirror, looking at my hair go, just crying and crying because I knew everything was coming to an end, and my face just stared right back at me. There it was. Like it or not." He turned away. "Like it or not."

From the bed there was a soft rustling, Jack's head moving slowly, still asleep. Bunny went over and watched for a second. The side of Jack's face with the purple splotch was more visible now. He made a sound without opening his eyes, some fragment line in a dream. Bunny touched his forehead. "Ssh," he said, calming him. Ben stood in the room, not moving, afraid any sound would wake him, watching Bunny's hand stroking Jack's hair. When he finally turned, satisfied Jack was still asleep, his eyes were squinting, in pain.

"Oh, go ahead and look," he said, then glanced back at the bed. "He was a hero, did you know? A real war hero. He saved someone's life. From that grenade. Just—not his. Well," he said, raising his head. "Mustn't grumble." Then he looked at Ben, his eyes brimming. "Do you know what it's like? When you feel everything slipping away?" He held out his hand, as if it were actually happening. "Like water, right through your fingers."

THERE WAS no point going back to the Ambassador so he drove to the Cherokee to change and throw a sweater in an overnight bag. Weather was vertical here: Mt. Wilson would be chilly at night. First tea, an excuse to see the campus in Pasadena, and then by convoy up the mountain. An evening with the émigrés, the last thing he wanted, his head filled now with Bunny and Danny and the unknowability of people.

He parked in back and was about to take the stairs when he remembered the key and went to the front desk instead.

"You have a mail key for me yet?"

"You 5C?" A new clerk, the staff as transient as the guests. He reached under the desk and handed Ben an envelope. "There's a charge."

"Put it on the bill."

"Can't."

Ben, exasperated, put a few dollars on the counter and went over to the mailboxes, opening his. For a second he just stared. Empty. But there'd been something there, a flyer for Current Resident, something. The mailman wouldn't have arbitrarily cleaned out the box.

"Mail's late today," the clerk said, helpful. "Should be here soon."

"But I thought—" He closed the box. No white paper visible through the holes. But there had been.

Upstairs, he packed his small bag, then looked at the key again. If the box had been opened, then someone else must have one. From Danny. He noticed the script on the night stand. Bits of business about post office boxes, something that had been on his mind. Ben glanced at his watch again. Think about it in the car.

When he got to the lobby, he saw the mailman filling the tilted wall of boxes.

"Anything for 5C?" he asked.

The mailman flipped through the stack in his hand. "John Collins, that you?"

Ben held up his key, an ID tag, and took the envelope, staring at it. John Collins, what Danny had called himself here. He went out the back, threw his bag into the car and stood there, holding the letter. John Collins. A name for hotel registers, hiding out. Who knew him as John Collins? A San Francisco postmark. He opened it carefully, as if he were prying. But wasn't he John Collins now?

Not a letter. A sheet with a list of names, grouped, not boxed like an organizational chart but arranged in clusters, some kind of order. He looked down the list. No one he recognized from the Continental list. Men, not starlets. But a list Danny evidently had wanted. Ben studied the names again, wondering whether any of them were already in Minot's files or whether they were new. More names to feed him. At the bottom of the list there was a group of numbers, also arranged by some unknown scheme. Army serial numbers? He counted one off against his own—no, wrong number of digits. Some other number then, maybe file references. Sent by some friend in San Francisco. He looked at the building, half-expecting to see people watching him. Why would Danny get mail here? Where he'd brought his women. Except he hadn't. Stained sheets in the afternoon—but the maid hadn't seen any. Rented months before Rosemary. Then used once. But why drive up to Santa Barbara when you had a secret place in town? Ben looked at the list again, then folded it and put the envelope in his pocket. Unless it hadn't been used for that. No personal items in the bath, no toiletries or leftover boxes of powder. Maybe the point all along had been the mail, not girls. Ben saw him walking Jack MacDonald home, taking in the barely supervised lobby, the anonymous rooms upstairs. Ideal for sex, what everyone would think. Not noticing the boxes. But letters from whom? Not whoever had killed him—he'd have stopped sending them. Someone still unaware that Danny was gone.

Ben looked at the time. Minot's office would be closed Saturdays—he'd need Riordan to let him in. And he was already running late. Anyway, why suppose the names were already in the files? Danny's new list. Maybe with the one who'd thought he'd acted in time, before his name was in the mail.

He headed east on Hollywood Boulevard, storefronts slipping by in a blur. There had been a flyer in the box. So someone had opened it recently, maybe looking for the envelope now in his pocket. How long would he wait? And why set it up this way? Why not pass a list in a bar? Call from a pay phone. Unless the source couldn't be too careful.

He cut down through Silver Lake then crossed the river and followed the winding road through the Arroyo Seco. The old commuter route from downtown, businessmen in starched collars driving home to their Midwestern houses and flowering gardens, what the city had been like before the movies came. Turn-of-the-century lampposts and rows of trees, the streets empty in the yellow afternoon light. He'd expected Cal Tech to be utilitarian, but the look was residential, cloistered quadrangles, the buildings larger versions of the houses down the street. The faculty lounge was even more traditional, dark wood paneling and oil portraits. Dieter was already pouring tea for Liesl and her father. To Ben's surprise, Kaltenbach rounded out the table.

"I didn't realize you were coming," he said.

"Yes, maybe a last chance," Kaltenbach said in German. "To see heaven."

"English here, Heinrich," Dieter said and Ben saw that the purpose of the party had been to show off the lounge, Dieter's assimilated life.

"I'm sorry I'm late."

"What happened?" Liesl said, not looking at him directly. "You left so suddenly." Sprinting across a parking lot.

"I had to see someone in the hospital."

"The hospital?"

"It's all right. Just a long drive."

"Everywhere is far here," Kaltenbach said.

"A mission of mercy," Dieter said. "So now you're here. Some tea?"

Liesl looked over at Ben, curious, but caught his signal to wait. They talked idly for a few minutes, Dieter at one point introducing them to a passing colleague. Ostermann, a folded newspaper near his place, seemed preoccupied. Around the room men sat talking quietly or reading papers, formal in jackets and ties, all moving slowly, like people under water.

"Did you see any of the campus as you came in?" Dieter said to Ben.

"Just a glimpse."

"The grounds are handsome. Of course everything grows so well here. In Europe—you remember the university? Tram lines outside the door."

"Another reason to prefer it here," Ostermann said deadpan, teasing him.

"You admit, it's more pleasant." He turned to Ben. "You're still anxious about him? Your friend?"

"No," Ben said. Did he look nervous? The rest of the room seemed to be moving at a different rhythm, almost placid. "But is there a phone? If I could call—"

"Downstairs," Dieter said. "Near the toilets. You have nickels?"

Ben hesitated for a second, as if he hadn't heard, then nodded. Of course they'd be pay phones. Not Chasen's, phones plugged in at the tables. He was back in the real world, where no one cared about the Crosby grosses or who was being fed to Minot. Or who hadn't been. One name. He stood up, the envelope almost pounding in his pocket.

"Right back," he said, hurrying to the stairs.

Riordan might recognize someone, just hearing the name. The top group, Ben guessed, was the most important. But Riordan wasn't home. Ben hung up the receiver. How did you find people? Phone books. He took out the list, reading the top names to himself, then started leafing through the flimsy pages. Not in Los Angeles. But why give them to Danny, to Minot, if they weren't local? San Francisco. He picked up the receiver again and asked for long distance information. The top two names, just to check. It took a few minutes. But they weren't in San Francisco, either.

"He's all right, I hope?" Dieter, on his way to the men's room.

"Yes," Ben said, startled, sticking the letter back in his pocket. "Fine."

"We should leave soon. After the light goes, the road—"

"Meet you upstairs," Ben said, already moving.

Why not just rent a post office box if all you wanted was mail? Wouldn't it have been safe there? But in the script the partners get the police to search the boxes. A court order. Ostermann said his mail was read. Not at his front door, intercepted at the post office, one branch helping another. Maybe something the FBI did all the time, a consulting tip from Dennis. But who had sent the letter? Danny hadn't just filed reports from scraps of memory. There'd been a source, someone who might be traced. He thought of the paper in his pocket, any fingerprints now smudged by his own. But the police had ways of finding things, paper and postmarks and typewriter strokes, clues invisible to anyone else. Riordan's friends could tell him. A rush job, a small favor for Congressman Minot.

Upstairs they had gathered near the door.

"You can imagine my relief when it came," Kaltenbach was saying in German.

"Yes, but will you use it?" Ostermann said.

"Heinrich, I told you, English here," Dieter said, joining them.

"Yes, no German," Ostermann said. He held out the paper. "What would people think?"

Ben looked at the news picture—the first group of defendants at Nuremberg, sitting erect in uniforms and proper suits.

"Don't be foolish," Dieter said. "It's nothing to do with us."

"Do they know that?" Ostermann said, nodding to the room. "It's the language of criminals now, our German."

"Criminals. Who, everybody? Are we supposed to be guilty, too? I don't feel that. Do you?"

"No, not guilt." He glanced down at the newspaper. "Shame."

"Ach. A literary position." Dieter arched his eyebrows at Liesl, a what-do-you-expect gesture. "All right, Ben, you take the criminals. Speak all the German you like, nobody will hear. Liesl, darling, come with me." He held up a finger. "English only."

She smiled and put her arm through his. "My car. You still drive in German."

Before Ben could say anything, they had paired off, Dieter leading everyone to the lot.

"All-American," Ostermann said wryly, watching him. "So he doesn't feel German anymore. Just like that. When does that happen? Take an oath and—"

"Any news on your citizenship papers?"

"Not yet. But my lawyer says it's a question of time only. I have 'good moral character,'" he said, amused. "How dull I must be."

"You?" Heinrich said. "'The most provocative writer today.' They used to say that, all the critics."

"Well, now just dull," Ostermann said, smiling. "You heard the good news?" he said to Ben. "Heinrich's passport came."

"An American passport?" Ben said, confused.

"With my moral character?" Kaltenbach laughed. "No, Czech. You know, before the war they would help us, a passport of convenience, so we could leave. And then, no Czechoslovakia. So after the war it was a question, would the new government honor the old passports? Give us new ones. And, yes! So it came, from the consulate."

"But do you want to be Czech? I thought—"

"I must be something. To travel. You can't, without a passport. So now I can go anywhere. Not like a prisoner. It's a wonderful thing."

They had reached the parking lot, Liesl fiddling with her keys.

Dieter looked at Ben's car. "Daniel's," he said, then looked up. "Yes, of course, I forgot. You're at the house."

"Not anymore. Now it's on Lend-Lease."

"You've moved? I didn't know."

"Hm. To the Cherokee."

"You're living there?"

"It's convenient. To the studio."

"Yes, but—" He stopped, slightly flustered. "You don't mind that—"

"He never really lived there," Ben said. "It's just a room."

Dieter looked at him, not sure how to respond, then at Liesl to see her reaction. "Well, that's right," he said finally, uncomfortable. "Just a room."

"Ready?" Liesl said.

"Would you show me on the map?" Ben said. "Just in case."

"Yes, all right. It's very direct." She brought a map over to him and opened it.

"This isn't going to be so easy," he said to her out of earshot of the others. "Tonight."

"No. Maybe not. Was that true, about the hospital?"

Ben nodded. "He was visiting someone. It was nothing," he said, suddenly protective. "But I need to ask you something. The mail key for the Cherokee. You never found it in Danny's things?"

"Again? You asked me that before. No. Look for yourself. Why is it so important? Get them to give you another one."

"I want to know where his is."

"Maybe he never had one. Why would he? 'He never really lived there,'" she said, quoting, then looked down. "Just sometimes."

"I don't think he used the place for that."

"What, then? To write scripts?" She folded the map. "Why are we talking about this? Always Daniel. Right here," she said, motioning with her hand to the space between them. She stopped and exhaled, collecting herself. "They're waiting. Now Dieter will want to know. Why you didn't stay. Family should stay. What do I tell him?"

"That I couldn't keep my hands off you."

"A nice conversation for an uncle." She paused. "The key. What does it mean?"

"If you don't have it, someone else does."

"Yes?"

"So how did he get it?"

They drove through the suburbs in the foothills and then started the steep climb on the Angeles Crest Highway, a two-lane road that twisted high into the San Gabriels, the low grassy hills giving way to dry chaparral, clumps of sage and prickly pear cactus and dwarf oaks.

"Like a Western," Ostermann said, gazing out the window.

"*Ja*, a stagecoach," Kaltenbach said from the backseat. "It's an agony back here. I feel sick."

"Look straight ahead, not out the side."

"All these twists and turns," Heinrich said as they cut sharply into another hairpin curve. "Look at Liesl, she can't slow down?" Ahead of them, Liesl's car kept darting out of sight. "And look how close to the edge. It can't be safe. Just like Lion's street. I have to close my eyes when she takes me there. So fast. I don't know how he can live there."

"For the views."

"Views. We had views in Berlin and it was *flat*. Views everywhere."

"Not so many now," Ostermann said gently.

They kept climbing, skirting a sheer drop beyond the chiseled boulders lining the shoulder.

"You know someone went over the edge?" Heinrich said, back at

Feuchtwanger's. "Near Lion's house. So you see it's not safe. I always said."

"And yet you go."

And so had Genia, Ben thought, but not to see Feuchtwanger. Someone else, familiar with the road.

"A friendship," Kaltenbach said. Up ahead, Liesl turned sharply. "My god."

"Dieter says the old road was worse. From the south. In the beginning, not even paved. They had to bring everything up in wagons, with mules. All the pieces of the telescopes. Imagine what that was like."

The turnoff road for Mt. Wilson seemed narrower, not intended for highway traffic. They had had the sun behind them and now the slopes were becoming shadowy, gathering dark at the bottom. Ben, hunched over the wheel to concentrate on the road, saw what it must be like at night, even headlights swallowed up in the pitch black. Kaltenbach had actually closed his eyes, not wanting to look anymore. There were more trees, forests of conifers.

"Like Germany," Ostermann said. "So many pines. The Harz Mountains. Well, a long time ago. Heinrich thinks it's the same."

"What are you saying?" Kaltenbach said from the back, hearing his name.

"That you should stay here."

"Another flag-waver. Like Dieter. Even the oranges are better. It's easy for him. Numbers. You can do that in any language." He was quiet for a minute. "I'd have a post. At the university. A professor, like him."

"But you're still here."

"You know Dolner, at RKO, is giving *Exit Visa* to Koerner—he's the head."

"You think they would make it now?" Ostermann said politely. "A war story?"

"No, an escape story. That has an appeal anytime. Dolner thinks it's possible. Even now," Kaltenbach said stubbornly, a man clutching a lottery ticket.

"Dieter's fond of Liesl," Ben said, to change the subject.

"He sees her mother."

"Were they alike?"

"A physical resemblance. Anna was not so strong. It was hard for her, to live like that, new places. Liesl, maybe she was always an actress. German, now Austrian, French—you learn to adapt. But Anna never did. It killed her, I think. Of course Dieter says it was me, waiting too long. He never saw the nerves, the worry. Not like Liesl that way. To escape with Daniel. The danger. Anna could never have done it."

Ben saw the solar towers first, poking up through the trees like radio antennas. Beyond them was the dome for the telescope and even farther, on the other side of the complex, another, much larger dome. Scattered between, on side paths, were wooden frame buildings where the staff lived, like a permanent summer camp under the pines. Liesl's car was turning left to one of these, a long white building with green trim. A man came out to greet Dieter, signaling Ben to park on the side.

"There's been a little mix-up about the rooms," Dieter said when they joined him, annoyed but trying to be pleasant. "Professor Davis brought some graduate students, so we'll have to double-up. They won't be in the way—they're working with the sixty-inch—but it does mean sharing. Ben, how about you and Hans? Then Heinrich with me. John will show you where you are."

Professor Davis, full of dates and statistics, showed them the grounds, a visitor talk he'd obviously given before. The first tower in 1904, then the sixty-inch telescope, finally the one-hundred-inch in 1917, still the largest in the world. The dome was on its own promontory, reached by footbridge over a shallow chasm and a reservoir pond. It was getting dark now, flashlights needed on the path.

"The site is remarkable," Davis was saying. "It has the best 'seeing' in the country."

"Seeing?" Kaltenbach said.

"The best conditions. Very little atmospheric turbulence."

"But so close to the city," Ostermann said. "The lights."

"Yes, but even so. It's the turbulence that matters. You know if you stand in a swimming pool and look down, the water moves, your feet seem to move. Turbulence is like that. We see the stars twinkle but they don't—it's just air moving across their light. But up here, with the good seeing, they're steady. Well, you'll see later. Shall we have some dinner now?"

"They don't twinkle?" Ostermann said. "It's a little disappointing."

Davis looked at him, puzzled.

"All the poems," Ostermann added lamely. "Songs."

"Well, songs," Davis said, at a loss.

Ben hung back as they got near the dining room.

"Now what?" he said to Liesl. "Am I supposed to sneak out while he's sleeping?"

She smiled. "Like a teenager." She touched his arm. "Maybe it's enough for now. To know we want to. Don't look like that. What are you thinking?"

"Ever hear of Arnold Wallace?" he said, his head still in the letter.

"No," she said, an abrupt change of mood.

He went down the sheet in his mind, one typed name after another. "Raymond Gilbert?"

"Who are these people?"

"I don't know yet."

"More friends of Daniel."

"People he might have mentioned."

She looked away. "Not to me."

The graduate students left as soon as they'd finished eating, but the émigré group lingered, talking with Eric, Professor Davis's assistant, who had now taken charge of them. Eric was tall and gawky, but eager to please, consumed by astronomy. It seemed to Ben a conversation from another world, beamed in from one of the stars, not nine miles up the slope from Pasadena.

"The hundred-inch is really the point now. Mt. Wilson began as a solar observatory but after Professor Hubble's work, there was a shift to nighttime research. Without the hundred-inch, modern cosmology—"

Ben drifted and he could see the others were having trouble keeping up. Dieter, to whom all this was familiar, seemed to be monitoring their response, glancing at each of them, ready to interrupt if things became hopelessly tangled. Ben felt the envelope in his pocket. Maybe the names were arranged by studios. How many groups had there been? Five majors, maybe a few Poverty Row companies. But none of the names were familiar. Technicians, screenwriters? He hadn't heard of Schaeffer at Fox until Minot's files. But not in the phone book. They couldn't all be unlisted, not technicians.

"The key was proving that spiral nebulae are distant galaxies. Outside the Milky Way. In other words, the universe is expanding."

"Expanding," Ostermann said thoughtfully. "What does it mean? Oh, I know," he said, waving off Eric, "there's an explanation, of course. But how do we imagine such a thing? The universe expanding. How do we even imagine the universe?"

"You don't have to imagine it. You can see it," Eric said, getting up.

Outside they trailed behind him to the big dome, the sky all lit up.

"If you look that way," he said, pointing, "you'll see the section we're studying at the moment. There. Keep it in mind when we go inside. You'll see how much more the telescope picks up."

It seemed impossible there could be more, the stars already too numerous to count, much less name. As Davis had predicted, they were steady lights, not twinkling.

The telescope was more than just the giant shaft that shot out through the dome's opening. There was the heavy platform with its gears, the series of reflectors and magnifying properties to explain, and Eric grew more excited as he talked, a boy with his wonderful toy. Ben smiled to himself, thinking of the Hal Jaspers at the Moviola, both mechanics at heart. But why would Minot want technicians? Recognizable faces. Nobody cared about the Hal Jaspers. Maybe these weren't the intended names, just ways to get to them. Sources, like Danny.

They had made an adjustment to one of the mirrors that brought the sky into sharp focus, a swath of stars leaping out of the black. Ben stared at it for a minute, as silent as the others, dazzled. He felt himself getting smaller, a speck, reduced to nothing by a vast indifference. The universe expanded without us. None of it mattered—not the preview audience's reaction or whether Julie Sherman could sing or whether Danny had filed reports. They were just frames flying by in a movie we'd made to keep us awake in the dark.

"You see the dust to the right of the star we're measuring?" Eric said, pointing again. "We're not sure yet, it's early, but the gap there might be another star forming."

"When will you know?" Liesl said.

Eric smiled. "Not for years. The dust has to fuse, a long process. But we can track the movement."

"It's real dust? Not just light?"

"Real dust. And gas. Particles of elements. But we *see* it as light. Sometimes it's what's in the way. But with this, you see beyond, what's really there."

"I wonder," Ostermann said, "do we want to see everything so clearly."

"Well, you want to see this clearly or you won't get the measurements right," Eric said, no poet.

Ostermann smiled. "Yes, that's right. A distraction, if we want to know. But beautiful, I think, all the same."

"Well, yes," Eric said, not sure what he meant. "You have to be careful. You see the star there on the right, two o'clock? That was mine, my project. I knew it, all its properties. And then there was movement, some dust, and it confused everything. I began to doubt it, what I already knew. But that was with the sixty-inch. With this it was clear again, the same properties. Which was lucky for me. My whole dissertation was based on it. Years of work."

But nothing was clear yet. The names had to mean something, people Minot would be interested in. Focus. Who interested him? Ben turned to Dieter.

"Is there a phone up here?"

"In the director's office. You're still worried about your friend? Come, I'll show you."

They walked back across the bridge, stars everywhere, a whole sky of them. There were other phone books. Follow the logic. Dieter turned on the light in the office.

"Thanks. Don't wait. I can find my way back."

Dieter hesitated, but then made a polite nod and backed out, pointing to the light, a reminder.

It was late but Kelly was still at his desk.

"See? Something always turns up. You got a body or just a tip?"

"I need a favor."

"Last time I looked, you owed *me*."

"Now I'll owe you two. You've got all the studio phone listings, right?"

"Maybe."

"You'd have to. They'd be your favorite bedtime reading. I want you to look up a few names—just tell me which studio."

"I should do this why?" Kelly said, playing with him, a wiseguy line.

"Does your paper know you're moonlighting for Polly?"

There was a silence. "I don't know what you're talking about."

"Then you'd have a tough time explaining it to them, wouldn't you? If they ever asked. Come on, Kelly, there's nothing to this. Just pull the lists out of the drawer, and we're done in two minutes."

"There goes one," Kelly said.

"Wallace, first name Arnold. You'll find it near the bottom of the list."

"Ha ha."

Ben could hear a shuffling of papers.

"Nope."

"Not at Fox?"

"Not anywhere."

"Try Gilbert, Raymond."

Another shuffle.

"Gilbert, Allen, at Republic. No Raymond. Who are these guys supposed to be?"

"Friends of my brother. I found them in his book and I'm trying to get in touch." The lie said easily, a little wave of turbulence over the wire. "Try Friedman, Alfred."

But Friedman wasn't there, either, nor three others. Ben looked at the list, stymied. Minot was going after the industry, but Danny was feeding him someone else.

"So who could they be?" he said aloud, but really to himself.

"Bookies. IOUs. Muscle. All guys, right?" Kelly's world.

"Okay, thanks. Sorry to bother you."

"How about a little payback? Something on Dick Marshall and the sister."

"How would I know?"

"You live there. Give me an item. I could sell anything on them."

"I'm not there anymore. I'm at the Cherokee."

"What, his room? Talk about sick."

"I haven't run into any ghosts yet."

"Maybe he'll talk to you in the night. Tell you who he was banging."

"I'll let you know."

"About that other thing. Polly. How'd you happen to come up with that?"

"A shot in the dark. Thanks for the favor."

"A shot in the dark."

"Now I owe you two."

He stared at the list again, then put it back in his pocket, out of ideas. Maybe he'll talk to you in the night.

He walked back to the dome smelling the night moisture on the pines, fresh, something to wipe away Kelly. I could sell anything on them. Inside, Eric was demonstrating a spectroscopic binary, the guests following attentively, as if it made sense.

"He's all right?" Dieter said.

"Yes, thanks. What have I missed?"

Dieter smiled. "Advanced Astronomy 205—his course. Do you think they'll pass the exam?" he said, nodding to the others.

They adjusted the mirror again, a new perspective, larger than the last, but Dieter noticed that people had begun to tire.

"Eric, I promised the guests a nightcap, so I'm going to steal them from you."

"Yes, I'll just finish with this magnification. Now see those very small points there? Outside, they'd be invisible. The eye simply can't take them in. But they're out there. We have no idea what we're going to see when we build the new scope down at Palomar. Two-hundred-inch. Things in there we can't see now," he said, pointing to the image, his voice excited.

What wasn't he seeing? A San Francisco postmark. Someone who didn't know Danny had died. And no way of telling him, no return address. But they must have communicated somehow. The letter hadn't dropped out of the sky. Was some response expected? What if he hadn't taken it, just let it sit there? He held the thought for a minute, like a breath. But it wouldn't just sit there. Somebody else would have picked it up.

Eric finally finished, to a chorus of thank-yous. Outside, the sky seemed less full, limited by the unaided eye to only a sampling of stars, like the ceiling of the Wilshire Temple. Could it only have been this morning? Gazing up while the music tugged at him, back to Otto, an invisible chord. Suddenly he felt tired, light-headed, as if he had climbed up to this thin air on foot. Good seeing. But how could you do it below? You had to wait for a flash, something that broke through all the obscuring dust. Sam Pilcer looking at his son, his heart suddenly visible. Bunny gazing at a bandage, finally without irony. This wasn't all they were—the other parts were still there—but without the glimpse you couldn't really see them, take some kind of measure. Maybe the letter, if he could explain it, was a flash, a way to see Danny.

He stopped, looking up again. But he already knew him. The way Eric had known his star, before all the dust got in the way. The same properties, the same constant light. And if you knew that, you could explain the rest. He hadn't mentioned Jack MacDonald after he'd seen him, an easy bone to toss. He hadn't mentioned Rosemary, either. He never stopped writing to Ben, stayed with Otto to the end. Got Liesl out, a dangerous trip. Who he really was.

Back at the lodge, they spoke German for Heinrich's sake and Ben, already tired, found himself sitting back, not really listening. They were huddled around the table drinking, and for an instant he saw them as Danny might have, refugees in a mountain hut waiting to be smuggled across. But now they were here, at the end of another continent, and Heinrich was talking about going back.

"But you don't consider the rest of us," Dieter said. "The effect it might have." He waved his hand in a circle. "A decision like this—it will draw attention to all of us."

"But only I would be going."

"And then they think, who else? Who's next? Remember during the war, how they watched us?"

"The war's over."

"That one, yes. Now a new one. And look where you'd go. The other side. You think it's so pleasant there now? At least wait a little."

"I'm an old man, Dieter. How long should I wait?"

"You make yourself old." Dieter poured more brandy in the glasses. "You talk to him," he said to Ostermann.

"Maybe we're a little selfish," Ostermann said. "We don't want to see you go."

"You want to speak German, go to Switzerland," Dieter said. "Lion is thinking about that. Zurich."

"Lion has money. No one is asking me to come to Zurich."

"There's no rush," Liesl said to Heinrich. "You can stay with me for a while if you like. The room just sits there."

"But what about—" Heinrich looked at Ben.

"I'm not there anymore."

"No. In that apartment," Dieter said. "You know, where Daniel—" He shook his head. "It seems so strange to me. You don't feel—"

"He didn't die there," Liesl said into her glass. "He died at the hospital."

Ben looked up, jarred, as if he had just heard a skip on a record, a needle scratch. The hospital, those awful last minutes, people racing, Liesl's face as she stood in the doorway, "Don't leave me," the last thing he'd ever say. But Ben had.

"A technicality," Dieter said.

"I still wonder to myself, what was on his mind?" Kaltenbach said, then looked at Liesl. "Forgive me. An intrusion. It's just—someone with so much courage."

Liesl drew on her cigarette, as if she hadn't heard, then tamped it on the ashtray, preoccupied.

"You think it's an act of weakness," Ostermann said. "I don't know, maybe it's the hardest. The rest—you can do anything if you have to."

"You? With your good moral character?"

"Is there such a thing? I used to think so. Very clear. The Nazis are here," he said, putting his hand at one end of the table. "And we're here?" Bookending the other. He moved both to the middle. "No, here somewhere. Mixed together. We know that now. We can cross any line. But that last one—"

"Such talk," Liesl said, rubbing out the cigarette.

"Any line?" Ben said. "Not killing someone."

"Look how often we do it. It's only ourselves we can't."

Kaltenbach nodded, settling in for a longer discussion. Ben stood up.

"I want to get an early start back," he said, an apology.

"But the studios are closed Sunday," Dieter said. "Even Continental. Well, a last one for me. Liesl? Another brandy?"

"No, no," she said, picking up her glass and finishing it.

Another skip on the record, watching her drink. He felt the back of his neck go still, the way it had watching the screen test. Except this time he saw Ruth Harris on the penthouse terrace. Easy enough for a woman to do. He shook his head. More interference, dust.

"And you come, too," she said to her father. "You'll be up all night, the two of you."

Outside they all looked up again. Ben tilted his head to where Eric's star would be—bright and clear, if you knew how to find it. The letter,

he thought, was a kind of telescope. The names were out there somewhere, in a bigger file.

No entries turned up at Minot's office.

"You got me down here on a Sunday morning?" Riordan said, eyes
still a little puffy with sleep. Ben had gone straight to his apartment,
waking him with drugstore coffee.

"I wanted to make sure. They're new."

"So now you're sure," Riordan said, waiting.

"We need to get this to the Bureau," Ben said, holding out the letter.

"We."

"You could get it to the right desk faster. One of their own."

"Retired. It's not exactly a two-way street with the Bureau. They
have to be careful, doing favors for the congressman. People get touchy
about that."

"Dennis."

He sighed. "Why the Bureau?"

"They're interested in the same people Minot's interested in. Look,
somebody sent this to Danny. Which means they sent it to you, too.
You've got an interest here. Nobody has files like the Bureau. I'll bet
there's one on me."

"Security check," Dennis said automatically, then half smiled at
Ben's reaction. "You asked."

"All right," Ben said. "So, my point. And who'd know better than
Danny? He was a source. You the only one he dealt with? Maybe there
was someone else he got to know. With access. How much do they give
Minot? A spoonful once in a while?"

"They're careful. I said."

"So maybe Danny found a backdoor."

"You don't know that."

"Let's see where the letter comes from. What the lab says. That's the
stuff they're good at, right? Every typewriter has its own signature. Paper
comes from somewhere, has to. What they're famous for."

"You know what they're good at? Sitting in a car all day, watching who goes in and out. I know. I used to do it. Now you want them to run a full investigation just to see who's mailing things in San Francisco?"

"If these names are in their files, they'll want to, don't you think?"

"Why?"

"Because one of them killed a source."

"Former source."

"They still owe him."

Riordan said nothing for a moment, then handed him the letter. "Make a copy. Sometimes things go into the Bureau, they don't come back."

Ben sat down and started to write.

"And if they come up dry with these?"

"There's always a file somewhere," Ben said.

In Frankfurt there had been rooms of them, millions of index cards, the whole crime at your fingertips.

"This doesn't come from Minot," Riordan said. "He's careful, too. No official ties."

"Just warm feelings. Can you get it to them today? Sunday, I know, but the Bureau never sleeps, right?"

"Why the rush?"

"Whoever mailed this didn't know Danny was dead. But somebody else has the key now. How long does he wait for it to show up?"

"Assuming he knows it's coming."

"Then why take the key?"

"Want to be sure? Put a dummy letter in. See if it stays there."

"And if it doesn't?"

"Move out."

He had just finished the names when he heard the lock turn. Without even thinking he covered the paper with another and folded the original in its envelope, his eyes fixed on the shadow behind the translucent glass. Minot opened the door and stopped, staring at them for a second, then took off his hat.

"On your way to church?" he said.

Ben saw Riordan freeze, a burglar caught, too slow-witted to make a move.

"Congressman," Ben said. "You're up early."

"What are you doing here?" he said bluntly.

"Making a report. Dennis was good enough to come down. My only day off."

"A report."

"I spent the weekend with the group—Ostermann, Kaltenbach. You asked, so I wanted to get it down while it was still fresh in my mind. Tomorrow I'm at the studio all day."

"While what's still fresh? Kaltenbach? The Russian consul come, too?" he said dryly.

"It was just the Krauts," Riordan said, as if they'd already been over this.

"We went to the observatory. See the stars." Something easily confirmed.

"And? What happened? That couldn't wait?"

Ben glanced up, aware of Minot's eyes, expectant, waiting to be fed.

"Nothing much," Ben said, flailing inside, looking for something. "But I thought what would interest you is that he's got a new Czech passport."

"What?" Minot put his hat on a table and walked over, galvanized.

"He had one before," Ben said easily. "You probably know. Passport of convenience. But the new government's agreed to reissue, so I thought you'd—"

"Do you know what this means?" Minot said. "He can travel."

"Not yet. He's still trying to peddle an old script at RKO."

"Don't be an ass. You can't leave without papers and believe me, he wasn't getting any from us. We had him. Now he can go whenever he likes."

"With what? Congressman, he's living on handouts."

"He has friends to help now."

Ben held out his hands in a *whoa* gesture. "Nobody was talking about going anywhere."

"Then why does he need a passport?" Minot said, almost snapping, then catching himself. "Look, you're new at this. I appreciate—but we can't afford to take chances. Dennis, we need to get a subpoena. I don't care what passport he's got, he's not going anywhere if he's under subpoena. How long will it take?"

"Ken, it's Sunday."

"I didn't want to move yet," Minot said to himself. "You want to *orchestrate* this. But we can do a closed session. First. No noise, but we keep him here for later. How long?"

"Tomorrow, probably Tuesday."

"Congressman," Ben said, alarmed now. "I think we're overreacting. I was with him. It's the last thing on his mind."

"Not on theirs. You don't know how these people think. The East Germans want him. Why do you think the Czechs got so generous all of the sudden? You think they're sitting there worrying about Kaltenbach? Nobody cares about Kaltenbach."

"Then why do you?"

Minot looked up at him sharply.

"I mean—" Ben said, placating.

"He's my witness," Minot said calmly. "That's why. He's useful."

"But he's not a Communist. He's not anything."

"Read the file," Minot said, nodding to the cabinet. "Socialist Party there. Documented. Speeches, the whole thing. Probably what the books are about."

"That's years ago. Anyway, Socialist, that's not the same thing."

Minot looked at him. "You know that. Thousands don't. They'll just see what he's not."

"What's that?"

"American. You establish a pattern," he said, a willed patience. "Quote the speeches—how far left do you want to go? Gets a visit from the Russian consulate—we *have* this, witnesses if we need them, actual contact with the Russians. Same man works for Warner Brothers."

"A lifesaver contract. They gave them to Jews to get them out."

"I wonder if Jack will mention that," he said evenly, so that Ben looked up at him, chilled now, someone who realizes, his hand still in the cage, what's inside. "Of course, he'll also have *Mission to Moscow* to explain. A lot of activity over at Warners over the years. And here are your old employees drinking tea with the Russians. Thousands won't understand that, either. But they see the pattern."

"But what evidence—?"

"This isn't a murder case," Minot said. "It's not about evidence. It's about what people are. You think he's harmless? Just an old man? I'm sorry, I disagree. I've read the speeches. You put Lenin's name on them and then tell me the difference. And once the pattern is there, you've got a very useful witness. Ask him if he saw—well, who? Let's say you. Did you ever attend meetings with Mr. Collier? And he says no, but now your name's out there, isn't it, whether he says no or not. All we have to do is put it there. Now why would we ask if there wasn't something we knew? Ask a few others, people from the studio."

"You want to use him to squeeze Warner," Ben said quietly, but his voice so neutral that Minot took his dismay for appreciation.

"We need the studio heads," he said simply. "We don't want a fight with the industry. We want to help them clean house. Their own good. I've met Jack—you were there, I remember. I think he's the kind of man who's going to be friendly to the committee. A good businessman looks after his interests. And he thinks he's a patriot. Made *Yankee Doodle Dandy*. That's the story he wants to tell, how he made that, not how the studio took in left-wing Jews. Not that it's about Jews. I know how some people feel, but you don't want to go down that road. I'm looking at the real threat. If you see the pattern. I think Jack'll see it too. So Kaltenbach, he's useful. We'd like to keep him close to home. Come to think of it, if he's got the passport, does that make him a Czech citizen?"

"Technically? I don't know. A passport of convenience," Ben said lamely.

"Good question to ask, though. Foreign national. And a Hollywood address all through the war. Some people, there's no way to help this, are going to think swimming pools. You'd think someone like that would be grateful, not have little parties with the Russians. Well." He went over to his desk and opened a locked drawer. "Some of us do have to get to church. Dennis, you get on that first thing tomorrow, right? You boys almost done here? You want to put that in the file?" He nodded to the papers in front of Ben.

Ben took the copy and handed it to Dennis, who moved to the cabinet before Minot could ask for it.

"You have the date he received it, the passport?" Minot asked Ben.

"Exact? No. But just. Last few days."

"See if you can find out. It helps, having things exact. Makes people think everything you've got is. Ready?"

They all went out together, Ben scooping up the original letter for his pocket when Minot turned to the door.

"Good work," Minot said to him in the hall. "You keep your ears open. It's just like the Commies, isn't it? Pick on the weak one. Kaltenbach—anything'd look good to him. Jackals." He signaled to his car. "Keep an eye on him. Until we get the subpoena served. Take him to dinner. I'll bet he could use a meal."

When the car pulled away, Ben gave the envelope to Riordan. "Where'd you file the copy?"

"Kaltenbach."

Ben watched Minot's car leaving the driveway. "How much of it do you think he believes?"

"All of it."

"How much do you?"

Riordan looked at him, then started down the stairs. "You know, you retire early, you only get half pension."

"Then why did you?"

"I took a bullet. My leg. You probably didn't notice, but I favor my right leg now. My own fault. I should have been paying attention."

Grazing idly, another straggler. Pick on the weak one.

"Let me know what the Bureau says."

It was only after they'd both gone and he was alone in the parking lot that it hit him, a lurch in his stomach that felt like nausea. Is this how Danny had felt after one of his deliveries? He saw Kaltenbach sweating at the hearing table in his shabby suit, asking someone at his side to translate, his eyes frightened, his nightmare finally coming true, what he had managed to escape. No, Germany would have been worse—he would have been killed, or left to rot in a camp. Here they would just hollow him out, use him to snatch someone else. But what was the alternative? Ben had been in Berlin. He had no illusions about Russians, the first wave of rapists and thugs now replaced by a grim occupation, the next thousand-year *Reich*. Nobody could want that, not by choice. And yet there would be pockets of privilege. A prized pawn trapped on the board, but not thrown away. He thought of Kaltenbach at the cemetery, spontaneous tears on his cheeks, mourning the man who had saved him, got him out. But the war, the heroic stories were over. What would Danny do now?

Kaltenbach lived a few blocks off Fairfax, walking distance from Canter's, where his landlady used to work before she'd brought her sick mother over from Boyle Heights to nurse full time. Kaltenbach had the room now, with a ground floor window that looked out on a magnolia tree and a patch of lawn that needed cutting. Ben drove by, struck again by the Sunday stillness of Los Angeles, as quiet as one of those ancient cities where everyone had vanished, leaving their pottery. He had come to see Heinrich, driving fast, but now that he was here, what could he say? Call your lawyer?

The blinds were drawn, perhaps for a nap after the early drive down the mountain. Or maybe he'd been restless, gone over to Fairfax for a whitefish salad and coffee with other Heinrichs. Then there would be the rest of the day to get through. Ben stopped the car, then suddenly didn't have the heart to go in. How could he explain? I know this because I've been informing on you? And then Minot would know. Who else could have warned him? Is this what it had been like for Danny, a balancing act, hiding from both sides? Anyway, in a day or so it wouldn't matter. He'd be stuck. Ben looked again at the quiet house. They couldn't serve the subpoena if he wasn't there. The only thing to do now was buy time. Liesl could take him home—an insistent invitation, no need to explain anything, until they figured out what to do.

He drove back to the Cherokee, stopping for lights without noticing, and parked behind. Nothing in the mailbox behind the little holes. But why would there be? Sunday. And maybe he'd already taken the last piece that would ever come. The new Joel looked at him, indifferent, and nodded when he got in the elevator.

He opened the door with his key, eyes already fixed on the phone table. He heard it first, a soft *whoosh*, then the back of his head exploded with a lightning pain, jagged, so fast there was no time to know what was happening. A pulsing afterimage, like staring into a flashbulb, darkening, then another pain, a crack as his knees hit the floor and he realized he was falling. He put his hands out to break the fall but couldn't find them, off somewhere to his side as his face met the floor, a louder thump, then nothing at all.

Everything was still dark when he felt the animal pawing at him, brushing his clothes aside to get at his chest. Not paws, hands, pulling at his jacket, digging into the pockets, still too dark to see, now at his collar, dragging him. Back to some den. He felt his head scrape on the ground, then a welling, slick, and he knew the blood would excite the animal but couldn't stop it, everything beyond his control.

A change in the air, like a window being opened, a banging as a door hit the wall and even in the dark he knew it was the French window, the black now just a dimness, being pulled again, out toward the air, the balcony, and he tried to open his eyes, panicking, because he knew, not a dream, that he had become Danny. Dragged out to the balcony, heaved over like a laundry sack. His head was throbbing, a toothache pain. They were in the open air now, the animal wearing a hat, not an animal, still dragging him, another yank at his jacket, panting, almost at the rail. And then they were there, the man grunting as he heaved, turning Ben over, grabbing under his arms, about to lift. And Ben already knew what the next second would be, pitched over the Juliet balcony, no scream, jumpers don't scream, and then the crash of garbage cans, Danny, him, a loop.

His eyes still wouldn't open, just slits taking in gray outlines, the man bending forward to secure his grip. In the movies, Ben would leap up now in a violent struggle, but instead he'd become an animal, prey being dragged to the feeding place. He still couldn't find his hands. No time left. Then the man's grip slipped, Ben's head falling again, and as the man reached to grab him, a better angle, Ben turned his head, a move of pure instinct, the effort dizzying, and opened his mouth, teeth connecting with flesh, biting hard on the man's ankle. The howl must have been more surprise than pain, something dead come back to life, but it startled Ben's eyes open, the world fuzzy but there, and as the man jerked his foot away, Ben's hands came up, back now, too, and he held the leg and bit again, the man staggering as he tried to pull it away, no longer pitched forward toward Ben's shoulders, his hands springing back, grabbing onto the French window, then using the other foot to kick, crunching Ben's chest, lunging for him again. There was a shout from somewhere, enough to make the man hesitate for a second before he hammered his fist into Ben's back, a squashing slam that forced Ben's face tighter against his leg, making the man twist free, away from the window now, the fulcrum of his weight flung backward so that Ben felt the pull of the leg moving and let it go, feeling it hit his face then flying free, following the body, turning as the man reached for the rail, then kept going, into the loud scream that filled the alley, the noise Danny hadn't made, and then was swallowed up by the crash, lids clanging, cans rolling away from the impact of the body. Ben grabbed the balcony edge and pulled himself up, just enough to look over, to see the police photos again, the pool of blood spreading from the man's head, but in color this time, dark red, the body splayed out at odd angles, the chalk mark outline where Ben was supposed to have been. He stared at it for a second, nobody he recognized, then heard a window open, a gasp, more windows, the faint sound of a radio, the desk clerk rushing out and looking up at Ben holding on to his balcony, the loop Ben already knew. Soon the ambulance, the crime scene photographers, maybe even Riordan losing himself in the crowd. He lowered his head from the railing, putting his hands in front of him to get up, but couldn't move, falling instead down an elevator shaft until it was dark again.

THE BANDAGE woke him, an unfamiliar weight on his head. The room was all white, which made him smile, a white telephone set, then he remembered the alley. Liesl was standing looking out the window, her back to him, and the loop started running again, Danny's hospital room, this time Ben in the bed. But not dying, everything in focus, the fuzziness gone.

"Is this Presbyterian?" he said, surprised at the croak in his voice.

She whirled around and stared at him, then shook her head, her eyes filling with relief, caught in the same loop.

"Where?"

"Community. On Vine."

"How long have I been out?"

"Most of the day. It's almost four."

"You've been here?" He touched the bandage at the back of his head, then the adhesive tape across the bridge of his nose. A dull throb in his chest. "What else?"

"It's enough. Head trauma—" She looked away.

"It's not the same. Not five stories."

"You still might have died," she said, still not facing him, then turned and came over, brushing her hand against his forehead.

"How about—whoever it was. Is he dead?"

She nodded.

"Any idea who?"

"Some *Schläger*. Kelly knows."

"Kelly?"

"He's here. Outside. He won't go until he sees you. First."

"Okay."

"You don't have to. You've been *out*. You should see the doctor first."

"No, I want to know." He grabbed her wrist. "I'm fine. It's the kind of thing you know about yourself, if something's wrong."

Kelly came in tentatively, the usual jauntiness left outside. "Can you talk?"

"You doing a story? 'I didn't know what hit me.' Pretty lame, except I didn't. Make something up, I don't care. The police out there with you?"

Kelly shook his head. "They want a statement, when you're ready. Dot the i's. They already took the witness's."

"Who?"

"Guy next door saw him punch you, try to throw you off. Day clerk thought he was in the building. Guy comes in, goes to the mailboxes, so the clerk figures he lives there. Of course, if he'd known it was Ray—"

"Who's Ray?"

"The guy. Hired hand. If you need something done. People do, so he and the cops go way back. That's why, when they saw it was him, you didn't have to draw a map. He used to run with the *pachucos,* his mother's a Mex. Then I guess he decided to put it to work, go freelance. He's already been in once for armed robbery."

"That's what they think this is?"

"I have to tell you, don't take this wrong, when I got the call the first thing I thought—I mean, same place."

"Monkey see. Maybe a better story."

"Don't be like that. It's what anybody would—"

"If I'd been the one who went over? I know. That's what he wanted you to think."

"Who? What are you saying?"

"Whoever paid—what was it, Ray?" He looked at Kelly. "Want something better than robbery? First of all, there's nothing to steal," he said, feeling Ray's hands in his pocket again, not something for Kelly. "The door wasn't forced. I had to open it with a key. But he was already in."

"Door's not a problem for guys like that."

"Especially if they have a key."

Kelly looked at him, waiting.

"You know, I never saw his face. He hit me from behind. All he had to do was walk away. If he wanted to kill me, a few more head taps would have done it. So why go through all the trouble? Lugging me out there. Maybe so you'd say, 'the first thing I thought.' Anybody would. They'd think I'd been planning to do it."

"But how would he know?"

"Well, Kelly, how would he?"

"You think he did your brother?"

"Maybe, maybe not. Find out who paid him. But that's how Danny was killed. I know it. For a few minutes there, I was him. Don't worry," he said, touching the head bandage, "I'm not going spooky on you. I just saw how it had to be. Find out who paid him. Work it from that side. Is he the kind who brags? Maybe there's a girl. He get the money yet?"

"You're so sure about this."

"Fine, do it as a robbery. Maybe you get a column. The double jump would have been better, but I screwed that up for you. But a murder? Two? That the police never saw? Exclusive? That's a ticket up." He looked directly at him. "No more moonlighting."

Kelly said nothing for a minute.

"Why don't the police see it?" he said, biting.

"Because they're traffic cops. And they like robbery. Come on, Kelly, nobody was supposed to see it. Ask around. Who paid him?"

Kelly picked up his hat to go. "And the *pachucos* will tell me. Swell."

"It's a bigger story."

Kelly looked at him, a small, ironic smile. "Any studio connection?"

After he'd gone, Liesl moved to the chair next to the bed. "Did you really think that? That you were Daniel?"

"I just saw how it made sense."

"Imagine if you could do that. Know what somebody was thinking. He could tell you—well."

"But I know what he'd do. Maybe it took a knock on the head, but it's clear now."

He began throwing back the covers.

"What are you doing?"

"I have to get out of here."

"Don't be—"

"Listen to me. Heinrich's in trouble. There isn't much time."

"Trouble?"

"I'll explain later. Where did they put my clothes? Help me, Liesl. I'm all right. See?" he said, getting out of bed and standing. "Not even dizzy."

But then he was, weaving slightly, putting his hand on the bed to steady himself.

"Get back into bed," she said, taking his elbow.

"It's my fault, understand? My fault. I have to help." He took a breath, exhaled. "There. I just got winded for a second." He looked down at the adhesive tape on his lower chest. "The rib makes it hard to breathe, that's all. Here, help me with this shirt."

"You can't just walk out. The doctor has to release you."

"What would Danny have done? Would he have waited?"

She looked at him. "That was different."

He walked over to the closet, Liesl trailing him.

"We can't go back to the Cherokee, the cops'll still be there, so we'll have to use your car. My wallet's here. I can use my military ID, they're not going to say no to that. He'll need his passport, though."

"Passport? What are you talking about?"

He took her arm. "I have to get him out. I can do it. But I need you to help me."

"Get him out," she said, looking at his head.

"I'm all right. I'm not crazy."

"No, excited," she said quietly, looking at him.

"Drop me at the house. Then you go to Heinrich's alone, in case anybody's watching," he said, pulling on his pants.

"Why would anyone be watching?" she said nervously.

"Don't pack. His landlady sees a suitcase, she'll start—but anything he really wants. Take a grocery bag, so it looks like stuff for dinner. And the passport, don't forget. I'll explain everything to him when you get back. If he doesn't want to, fine, we give him dinner and drive him home. But he will."

"With a grocery bag," she said. "Like a knapsack. And then what? We cross the mountain?"

"No," he said, buttoning his shirt, too busy to hear her tone. "I get him to Mexico."

"Mexico."

"It's just a drive." Why the movie people came in the first place, dodging Edison's patents, sun, and a convenient border. According to Sol anyway. "Where's my hat? I'm going to need a hat to cover this," he said, fingering the bandage. "Your father's in touch with the Germans there. Some of them will know Heinrich. He'll need help. How much cash do you keep at home?"

"Some. It's something you learn, in case."

"Okay, shoes." He stood up.

"Stop. A minute. Listen to me. You're in no condition to drive. You'll both be killed and then what?"

"I have to."

"Oh, have to. So pigheaded. Just like—" She stopped, looking away. "It's serious? His trouble?"

He nodded.

"All right, I'll drive. Don't," she said, holding up a hand. "Anyway, it's my car."

"You're sure?" he said, pleased, as if he were extending a hand.

She shrugged, a pretend indifference. "You can't go alone. It's breaking the law?"

"Not yet. In a few days it would, but he'll be gone."

"Over the border," she said. "I thought it was finished, all that business."

KALTENBACH GRASPED the situation right away. Ben had expected indecision, an arguing back and forth, but the urgency had jolted him into an oddly calm self-assurance, all his usual dithering put away like bits of stage business.

"A political trial," he said. "Now here."

"No, it's a hearing. Closed at first. It's not the Nazis," Ben said. "It would be a mistake to think that. To decide that way. It's not camps or—"

"But a political trial all the same," Kaltenbach said evenly. "I know what it means."

"There's no danger to you. You're not being charged with anything. Not even being a Communist."

"Just politically unreliable. So no work at the studios."

"You're not working there now," Ostermann said. They were drinking coffee near the end of the pool terrace, the city below, lights coming on in the dusk.

"No, not for a long time," Kaltenbach said. "Now longer."

"I want you to understand," Ben said. "If you leave, you won't be able to come back. They'd make sure of that."

"It's not like before," Ostermann said. "What choice did we have? Now there's a choice. You can't take this lightly."

"That's why you came over? To talk me out of it?"

"No. I talked to Anna in Mexico City. Seghers, you remember. It's not easy to make a call there. An hour to get through. But I thought she would know somebody. Or somebody who—so, here's an address in Tijuana. Who can help with arrangements. I said you'd be there tomorrow. If you go."

"No, tonight," Kaltenbach said firmly.

"Then I came to say good-bye," Ostermann said. "If you're sure."

Kaltenbach turned away, too emotional to face him. "Look at it," he said, nodding to the city. "A mirage. Maybe it's the palm trees that suggest it. But sometimes I think there's nothing really there. Blink—just sand again. Was I here? You and Dieter, all milk and honey, blue skies. But I wonder, even for you."

"Almost ready?" Liesl said, coming out of the house. She had changed into cream-colored slacks and a blouse, resort wear. "Was it big enough?" She pointed to one of Danny's old suitcases, now filled with Heinrich's few changes of clothes.

Kaltenbach turned back to Ostermann. "I know it's different there now." He held his gaze for a second, a silent conversation, then stuck out his hand. "So good-bye, my friend."

But Ostermann, tearing up, took him in his arms, a fierce hug, and Ben saw in his posture that he had done it before, one more leave-taking. When he finally pulled away, he took some money out of his pocket. "Here."

"No," Kaltenbach said, covering his hand.

"You'll need it."

Kaltenbach shook his head. "But Frau Schneider, my landlady. There's rent owing."

"Are you sure?"

"Keep my good name," he said, smiling sadly. "I'll pay you back." A ritual phrase.

Ostermann took one of the bills from his hand. "Here. For cake at the Romanische."

Kaltenbach took the money. "*Mohnkuchen*. Like nowhere else." He touched Ostermann on the shoulder, starting to turn away, then stopped and looked at him again. "If you read that I've said something—something, you know, that doesn't sound—you'll know it's not me, yes? You'll remember that?"

"Of course."

"Even if my name is attached. I may have to— But you know the books. They can't change those. The rest, don't listen. Just the books."

"We should go," Liesl said. "They look all right," she said to Ben, now in Danny's borrowed clothes. "How do you feel?"

"Ready. This all?" He lifted her bag.

"I have to be back. I'm in the scene."

"They can shoot around you for one day." He turned to Ostermann. "Have Iris call in sick for her. Doctor's orders."

"They won't like that."

"We can't just drop him at the border. One day."

They started across the terrace, then froze as the phone rang.

"Don't answer," Ben said. "That'll be the hospital, wondering if I ended up here in my nightgown. What did you say at the nurses' station?" he said to Liesl.

"That you were sleeping. I'd be back tomorrow."

"Good. So I'm the only one missing. Walking around somewhere near Vine."

"You'll be in trouble for this?" Kaltenbach said.

"Not unless they catch us."

They followed Ostermann's car down the hill and stayed behind until he veered off with a small wave. Kaltenbach waved back, his eyes fixed on the featureless boulevard, a last look before it shimmered away. By the time they turned on Sepulveda, heading down the coast, he seemed to have lost interest, letting his head rest on the backseat, eyes closed, like someone on a long railroad trip.

"Don't go too fast," Ben said. "We don't want to get stopped."

"Why are you so nervous? Nobody has any idea. Why are we supposed to be going, if anyone asks?"

"The races. Everybody goes down for the races. Fishing in Ensenada. I don't know, why does anyone go?"

"Your brother used to say, don't think about anything," Kaltenbach said. "Pretend it's the most natural thing in the world. If you worry at all, they sense it. Like dogs."

"And did you worry?"

"I was terrified. You know what I think got us through? Alma. The way she's in her own world. At the border she seemed surprised to see the guards, you know, anything in her way. They didn't even question us. Of course your brother made a gift to them, but even so. They usually asked questions, to make a show. But not Alma. *Sí, señora.* Up goes the crossing bar. And all I could think was, don't sweat, don't let them smell it on you. And you know, if it had gone the other way—well, it was another time. I owe my life to him. Now you."

"No. This isn't the same."

"It feels the same. All that climbing, I was afraid for my heart. Now look, a chauffeur. But the same." He was quiet for a minute, watching the night landscape pass, dark houses and miles of streetlights stretching down to Long Beach. "I never said good-bye to Alma. I wonder if she'll notice that I'm gone."

"Everybody will," Ben said. "You'll be in the papers."

"So. You have to leave to make an impression," he said, playing with it.

They drove past Huntington Beach, the lights getting fewer, Liesl sneaking glances at him.

"What's wrong?" he said.

"Nothing," she said, a little startled, unaware that he'd seen.

"I'm all right, really."

"It's not that. The jacket. I bought it. I was remembering when I bought it."

He fell asleep without realizing it, his head against the window, dreaming of the stars spilling across the sky on Mt. Wilson. Then he was at the Cherokee, watching blood spread in the alley, someone else's blood, not his. Had Danny fought back? He woke when she stopped for gas, the station overly bright in the black landscape.

"Where are we?"

"Nowhere. Another twenty miles to La Jolla. Maybe we should stop there. It's a long drive."

"No," Kaltenbach said from the back, "it's important not to stop." Another lesson from the Pyrenees. "Even to rest. People notice you. You see that car? It's been behind us. Now it stops, too."

"It's the first station for miles," Liesl said.

"Go to the toilet," Ben said. "See if they follow. I've got your back."

The attendant came over to start the pump.

"You encourage him," Liesl said.

"He's careful. Want a Coke?"

He went over to the ice cooler and pulled out a bottle and opened it, glancing at the second car as he drank. Two men on a Sunday night.

Going where? Kaltenbach came out of the station, head low, his face shadowed by his hat.

"They're still there?"

"Getting gas. I think it's all right."

They paid and left, Ben driving now, one eye on the rearview mirror.

"How would anybody know?" Liesl said to him, using English, Heinrich just a child in the backseat, swiveling his head from time to time. "You think they were watching his house?"

"He's not the only one in the car. You heard Kelly. The guy was a hired hand. And I'm still here."

She took this in, thinking for a minute. "And yet you do this. Out here. Where it's easy for them."

He said nothing.

"They were going to use Heinrich anyway. You didn't make them."

"I helped."

"So it's all on your shoulders. All the problems of the world." She looked out the window, quiet. "You and Daniel."

"What do I do? Just sit there?" He looked at her. "It's not much, considering."

"They're turning off," Kaltenbach said, looking out the back.

After La Jolla there were more lights, the hilly outskirts of San Diego. Liesl was fiddling with the radio, Kaltenbach keeping watch for cars.

"In the movies they always hear about themselves on the radio," Liesl said. "But listen, just music. So we're safe." She turned the dial, picking up a Spanish-language station. "We must be close. What will they think of us? Different passports."

"They don't care much going out. It's getting back in. It'll be easier, just the two of us."

"With a bandage on your head." She was quiet for a minute. "Why did he want to kill you? You never told me that part. Why?"

"He was paid."

"The one who paid him."

"Maybe I'm getting close."

"Close," she said, not following.

"Who killed Danny."

"Why do you think that? There's something you're not telling me."

He shook his head, dodging. "But I must be."

"Then he'll try again," she said flatly. "You have to go to the police."

"With what? Tell them Danny was a snitch for Minot? I have to stay close to Minot. That's the connection."

She looked down. "He wasn't that. I still don't believe it."

"Maybe he thought he had a reason," Ben said, letting it go.

"We're coming to the border," Kaltenbach said, his voice nervous and melodramatic, as if he had seen guard dogs and soldiers with guns. In fact it was only a string of lighted booths under an arched sign.

"Go to sleep," Ben said to him. "I don't want to use a Czech passport if we don't have to. He'd remember. He's probably never seen one."

"I don't have to show it?"

"We can try. Close your eyes."

He pulled up to the booth, holding his ID out the open window. A uniform like a state trooper, with a broad-brimmed hat.

"Driving late," the guard said, checking the ID.

"Want to be early for the races."

"Not tomorrow you won't. No races. You didn't know?"

Ben could feel Liesl tense beside him. "I guess we'll have to find something else to do," he said, the suggestion of a leer in his voice.

The officer glanced at Liesl. "I guess."

She began to hand over her passport, but he ignored it.

"Who's that?"

"My old man. He likes the ponies. And the tequila." He nodded to the back. "Got a head start."

"He'll feel it, that stuff. Careful tonight. You know where you're going?"

"We've been before."

"Then I don't have to tell you. Watch the car. They'll steal the tires while you're still in it."

He stepped back, waving them on, and they drove through the no-man's stretch to the Mexican booth, another bored officer who just looked at them and said "*Bienvenidos*" and then they were over, suddenly in Tijuana.

"It's done?" Kaltenbach said, almost deflated, cheated out of an expected drama.

"You're free," Ben said, stumbling on the word, an unintended irony. "No subpoenas."

The city was noisy even at this hour, bright with strings of bare incandescent bulbs. San Diego had been asleep, but here there were still crowds, peddlers and shoe-shine kids and Americans in Hawaiian shirts, the smell of frying food, makeshift buildings as dingy as carnival flats. Men with mustaches idled on corners waiting for something to happen, like extras, their eyes following the car. Kaltenbach kept staring out the window, expecting it to get better, but the blocks streamed into each other, the same glare and sinister languor, and for a second Ben wanted to turn around, take him back, make some deal with Minot. But now he was here, even more displaced.

They went to the biggest hotel they saw, with a guarded parking lot, and Ben paid for the rooms in dollars. The desk clerk, a Mexican Joel, barely lifted his eyes as he handed out the keys. There was a restaurant two doors down and they sat in a booth, exhausted, and drank beer, picking at the chiles rellenos the waiter had brought, all that was left before closing.

"How long do you think I will have to stay here?" Kaltenbach said.

"We'll see Broch tomorrow. I think there's an airport. Maybe we can get you on a plane for Mexico City."

"A plane?" Kaltenbach said timidly.

"You don't like to fly? Oh, such a baby," Liesl said fondly. "It's like a bus."

"In the air."

"A man who crosses borders. An escape artist."

Kaltenbach smiled weakly. "Not so difficult. Find a Kohler." He looked at Ben. "'My old man.'"

Ben tipped his glass in a toast.

"The other time it was sherry. Your brother found a place, after we got through, and we all drank sherry. It's what they have there, Spain." He glanced around the room. "It's the same language, but this—"

There was a shout from the street, a bar argument that had moved outside.

"Border towns are like this. It'll be different in Mexico City," Ben said, wondering if it were true.

"Better food," Kaltenbach said, looking at it. "Imagine living in such a place. Stealing tires."

Ben stared at the scarred table top, remembering a wrecked Horch abandoned in Jägerstrasse, tires gone, gold on the black market. Children selling K-rations, as slippery as the kids outside. Where he was sending Kaltenbach. But where Kaltenbach wanted to go.

"It's an odd feeling," he was saying. "No one knows I'm here."

"None of us," Liesl said. "You could disappear here." She met Ben's eyes. "If someone were looking for you. You could—just go. Anywhere. Be safe."

"Unless you wanted him to find you," Ben said, looking back at her.

"You could stop."

"Not now. He won't stop. I'd always be looking over my shoulder. You can't live that way." He touched her hand. "And there's Danny. Do you want me to walk away from that?"

She raised her head, her eyes wider, as if she were startled to find him there.

"What are you saying?" Kaltenbach said, not following their English.

"Nothing," she said quickly, sitting up. "Just how it's like before. When we got out."

"This place?"

"Yes, everything. How worried I was. What if they turn us back? And then at the border, how easy and you thought, it's a trick."

"Yes, that's right," Kaltenbach said.

"Then a drink to celebrate. Like this. Everything," she said, facing Ben again.

"And how calm he was, your brother. Well, and you. 'My old man.'" He grinned. "But not this," he said, gesturing to the beer. "Do you think they have schnapps?"

"They may call it that, but it won't—"

"You can't celebrate with beer. Not something like this."

They were another hour, sipping a harsh, burning brandy with a Mexican label, Kaltenbach getting sentimental but not yet maudlin, Liesl smiling to herself as he talked.

"And you'll come to see me. How far is Berlin? Imagine the neighbors. A movie star. In old Kaltenbach's flat. Everyone looking, just behind the curtains. You remember the courtyards, how everyone knew your business? Nothing said and they know everything. So you'll come. Look at you. Since a child. You don't forget these things. Your mother, so protective. Everything for you, for Hans. Everybody but herself. And then she couldn't protect you anymore."

Liesl reached across the table. "Heinrich."

"Yes, I know, I know. Don't speak. Like Hans. But then, you know, we begin to forget. They go away from us." He turned to Ben. "Can I say something to you? Your brother was very brave. I know. This thing, maybe it's hard for us, but we can't pretend it didn't happen. We don't talk about it, it goes away, but then they go away, too. Look at Hans, he never talks about Daniel now. It reminds him. Once it's there, in your head—"

"What does he mean?" Ben asked Liesl.

"My mother was anxious. She had pills for that. So one night too many. Maybe an accident. We don't know, Heinrich," she said to him. "Not for sure."

"Ach." He waved his hand. "So it's not for sure. And that's why Hans won't talk about it. But it's in his head."

The kind of idea that can lodge there, Ben thought, so you come back to it, over and over. Use it. Something people don't want to be sure about, a car off the road, a fall, something they'd rather not see, not even laid out in a pattern. A convenient way to make people look away.

"He talks about it to me," Liesl said quietly.

"Forgive me, it's the schnapps. I don't mean anything by saying this."

"I know."

"But your brother," Kaltenbach said, switching tack. "That was someone. Right past the guards, not a drop of sweat. Always an answer. 'Who's this?' The signature, you know, hard to read. 'Pétain.' On a laissez-passer. Imagine, Pétain. But they believe him." He cocked his head, looking at Ben. "I used to think, so different, but now I see it. Not the looks, something else. Don't you see it, Liesl? Doesn't he remind you?"

She looked at Ben for a second, then finished her glass. "It's late," she said, standing up.

At the hotel there was a message in Ben's box.

"Someone's here," Liesl said, apprehensive.

But it was only a flyer from a bar down the street, offering the first drink free.

"Stop worrying," Ben said, handing it to her.

"Think how easy it would be to do here. Who would know? Somebody in the alley. Another one."

They were in the hall now, Kaltenbach opening his door.

"So good-night. Thank you again." He hugged Ben, clamping him on the back, then kissed Liesl. "You'll knock?"

"Get some sleep," Liesl said softly. "Lock the door. You, too," she said to Ben as they moved down the corridor. "It's not safe."

"It is tonight. We're off the map. For one night, anyway."

"And then what?" She stopped at the door. "He's so old," she said, nodding to Kaltenbach's room. "All of a sudden."

"You just haven't been looking."

"No, no one has." She touched the bandage on his nose. "How is your rib?"

He shrugged.

"The brandy will make you sleep. You must be tired. It's not easy, all this."

He kissed her forehead. "Easier than getting over the mountain."

She looked at him, eyes darting across his face, suddenly tearing up.

"What's wrong?"

"I can't do it twice."

"What, the border?"

"You. Him, now you. What if it happens again?" She ran her hand over her eyes. "It's the brandy. Go to sleep."

"It's going to be all right."

"How do you know?" she said, her head still down. "Was it all right for him?" She started shaking, fighting back more tears.

Ben put his hand to her cheek. "Stop."

"It's too many parts. I can't do so many."

"Which one do you want?"

She sniffed, a stifled laugh. "War bride. That's what I want. Turn here, feel this. Be that. Not these. Heinrich's memory. Your—your what?" She raised her head. "I can't do it twice."

"I'm not him."

"No," she said, her head sinking again, her voice breaking. "No one is."

She began to shake harder, pitching forward with sobs, trying to stop by gulping air, so that for a second he thought she might be sick. And then she was letting go, her shoulders suddenly slack and drooped, as if her body were sliding away from her. He put his hands on her arms, holding her.

"Now I do this," she said. "After all this time. All this time. My god, what a place."

He followed her glance down the hall, the dim sconces and fraying carpet.

"Ssh," he said, letting her forehead fall on his chest, a child who'd just tripped, cut her knee.

"Do you know what he said? When I asked him to stop the work? Do you want me to walk away? The same words. You say it and he's saying it." Blurted out in a rush, unscripted. "All day he's there. Still there."

She started shaking again, and he put his arms around her, holding her, but then the words came back and this time he listened, went still, the smell of her suddenly different, someone he had never held before. He tried to think of her somewhere else, their own time, but his mind went blank because he saw that she had never been there, already taken, somebody else's. He drew in a breath, stunned by how fast it had happened. Maybe this is how you died, without warning, without the chance to hold on. One minute it was there and then it wasn't.

She moved her head back, as if she had felt the shift, too, some fluttering away, and looked at him, biting her lower lip. For a minute neither of them moved, letting the air settle.

"It's not your fault," she started, but that seemed wrong and she stepped back, her hand over her mouth. "It's late. I'm not making sense."

Rewinding, pretending it hadn't happened. But too late. "No one is." Spoken out loud, there, everything different.

"Where's your key," he said, a disembodied voice.

"I can do it. I'm sorry." She was wiping her face. "It's just—I don't know. Some foolishness." But still looking at him, seeing something go out of his face, irretrievable. "Too much brandy." She put her hand up to his neck, just a touch, uncertain, then turned with her key.

"Lock your door," he said.

In his own room, still dizzy with it, he stood smoking and looking out the window, the room dark except for the weak pool of light by the reading lamp. There were a few people below, moving in and out of shadows, a car radio playing. Why didn't it all look different? Everything had changed in a beat and no one in the street had the faintest idea.

BROCH HAD already organized the plane.

"Anna will meet you in Mexico City, so someone you know. There's a group there, they can help you with the arrangements. Did you have any trouble at the border?"

"No. They didn't even look."

"Yes, it's like that. If you want to stay, of course, you need a permit. You might consider Mexico for a while. It's not a bad place."

Broch was short, with thinning hair and a soft German accent, Bavarian or even Austrian.

"You mean here?" Kaltenbach said.

"Well, Mexico City. But of course there are business opportunities here."

He wore a rumpled tropical suit and Mexican sandals, and Ben imagined him in cafés arranging shipments, border-town business, one eye to the door.

"No, I want to go home," Kaltenbach said.

Broch looked surprised at the word, but didn't say anything, then took Ben aside. "Are they looking for him? The authorities?"

"No, no, it's all right. Nothing illegal. No risk to you."

"I only ask—" He looked back at Kaltenbach, now huddled with Liesl. "Everyone here is waiting for a quota number. To get in. But he leaves."

"Can you get him to the airport? We should go."

There were more hugs, Kaltenbach looking wistful. Liesl had stayed near him all morning, solicitous, but also shy of Ben, watching him with side glances, unsure of things.

"So I'll see you in the *Kino*," he said to her. "Ten feet high. Make a sign, eh? Like this." He touched his eyebrow. "Then I know you don't forget."

"I won't forget," she said, brushing his lapel.

"And you, my friend," he said to Ben. "I can never repay you."

"Just don't tell anyone how you got here. Our secret."

"Who would ask?"

"They're going to interview you. You know that. The prodigal son."

Kaltenbach looked away. "It means wasteful, you know. Maybe it's true. Wasted years. It's not serious here. It's too much sun, I think." He looked up at the hot Mexican sky, already a bright reflecting tin. "We need clouds sometimes. But what choice was there?"

In the car Liesl was restless, checking the passport in her bag, then turning back to the dusty streets lined with open stalls. When they stopped at a corner a woman in a peasant skirt rushed over to sell them a ceramic Madonna.

"I hate it here," she said.

"We're almost out."

"I saw you give him money," she said.

"He'll need it. You think this is bad." He nodded to the street. "I wish I thought we were doing him a favor. Here we go." The crossing booths were now just down the street. "Got your passport?"

"Just once, not to be nervous. I think they're going to send me back. Every time."

"Don't worry about the Mexicans."

"No, them." She looked toward the American gates. "My own," she said, ironic. "And with this head. So much to drink last night." Putting it behind them, one glass too many, the evening hazy and vague. "How do I look?"

He turned. "You look fine."

But different, as if he had changed glasses, the exact same features subtly altered, a shift in definition. She seemed unaware of it, her skin just as it always was, her hair falling loosely on her shoulders, the way she had looked yesterday. But something had been said and now he saw it through a different lens, everything the same but different.

The Mexican guard barely glanced at their papers, but the American flipped through her passport. "Buy any smokes? Liquor?"

"No."

"You been away how long?"

"Just overnight."

"Purpose of your trip."

"Tourism," Ben said, deliberately not looking at Liesl, letting the guard do it. An unmarried couple.

He took Ben's ID card. "Just a minute," he said, turning in to the booth.

"What's wrong?" Liesl said under her breath.

"Nothing."

The guard was on the phone, then he was back. "Okay, pull up over there." He pointed to a building on the right.

"What's the trouble?"

"Just pull up over there," he said, beginning to walk beside the car, still holding their papers.

Two men in suits hurried out. Ben put the car in gear and headed slowly to the building.

"Oh my god," Liesl said, her voice panicky.

"It's probably just a spot check," Ben said, a willed calm.

"Check for what?"

"Get out of the car," one of the men said. "Hands on the car," he said when Ben stepped out. The other began to frisk him.

"What's going on?" Ben said. "Is there some trouble?"

"That depends."

"On what?"

"What you have to tell us."

"You want the cuffs?" the other man said, but the first shook his head.

"Tell you about what?"

The man flipped open a wallet to show an FBI badge.

"Let's start with espionage."

AMBUSH

THEY SEPARATED THEM, taking Liesl down the hall, her eyes startled and jumpy, like a deer's, and leading Ben into what seemed to be a lounge for the border guards, a big coffee urn in the corner. He sat at a table across from yet another agent answering questions, not complaining or hesitating, because he saw that was expected, the air hostile, and hoping the questions would tell him what had happened. All he knew was that the letter he'd given Riordan had set off an alarm in the Bureau, still ringing. After a while the questions began to repeat themselves, as if asking them again would produce different answers. But the agent was no longer bristling, settling in for the long haul. He offered Ben a coffee.

"Is this where you tell me I have the right to call a lawyer?"

"You don't have any rights."

"How about a cigarette then? That allowed?"

The agent put an ashtray on the table.

"Now can I ask you a question?"

"No."

"You seem to forget. I called you. You wouldn't be here at all if I hadn't given you the letter. Last time I heard, we were on the same side."

"So what's the question?"

"Who are they? The names."

The agent said nothing.

"Not even a day and you're here jumping on me. I didn't know the Bureau could act that fast. So they must mean something to you. They pop up in the files, or did you just know?"

He shook his head. "I can't— You don't have clearance."

"Dennis didn't—"

"Dennis doesn't have clearance, either. Not even before. Not now."

"Just you. Even though I've already seen them."

"So why ask? Who do you think they are?" the agent said, turning it around.

"Communists."

"Hardly," the agent said, unexpectedly amused. "Let's hope not, anyway."

"Then how is this espionage?"

The agent looked at him over the rim of his coffee cup. "You're in the Army. Know what an order of battle is?"

"Organization. Commanders in the field."

"This is a kind of order of battle, okay? It's important, that's all I'm going to say. We need to know where it came from."

"So do I."

The agent raised his eyebrows.

"I think somebody on it killed my brother. Who, by the way, in case nobody told you, used to work for you."

"I know that," he said tersely.

"Which makes it all the worse, is that it? You think he was a spy, your own guy?"

The agent put down the cup, not responding.

"Neither do I. So you want to know two things: where it came from and where it was going. It didn't end with Danny. What was he going to do with it? Anyway, he's dead. And it still came. So who was it for? The only person you know it *wasn't* for is me or I wouldn't have given it to you in the first place. You following? Where it comes from I don't know—that's for you to figure out. But whoever it was on this end maybe I can help you with."

The agent stared at him. "Help us how?" he said finally.

"Well, let's talk about that. But first, can I assume that I'm not under arrest and we can start this over? Or do you want to keep grilling me?"

"For two cents I'd—"

"Except you're flying blind here. I've been listening. You came all this way. Let's talk."

"Talk," the agent said, his voice low, dragged out of him.

"First, Liesl. You're not going to charge her, either—she knows less than I do—and you're probably scaring her to death."

"She was his wife."

"Was," Ben said. Is.

"And Mexico?"

"We were giving a friend a lift. Nothing illegal."

"Dennis says—"

"Dennis isn't even allowed to know who we're talking about. And if he's already told you about Kaltenbach, you know about Mexico, so we're wasting time."

"You don't make friends easy."

"Well, we started off on the wrong foot—you throwing me against a car and accusing me of things. It put me off. Can we get Liesl now?" he said, then, seeing the agent hesitate, "I'm the only shot you've got."

"How do you figure that?"

"Whoever wants the letter thinks I have it. He tried to kill me for it. I think he'll try again."

The agent looked at him for a minute, then pushed back his chair with a scrape and walked over to the door. "I'm Agent Henderson," he said, turning halfway.

Liesl was brought in a few minutes later, her face still pale, drained. "You all right?"

She nodded, mute.

"I thought you'd better be here for this. It's going to concern you."

"Because of Heinrich?" she said, still puzzled.

"No. Danny. They think he was passing secrets."

"What?"

"Well, receiving anyway." He turned to Henderson. "Is that right?"

"Close enough."

"Secrets?" Liesl said, confused, almost sputtering. "Like a spy? Daniel? No, it's a mistake. What secrets?"

"Classified information was sent to him. By name. His address. We don't know for how long. Once would be enough."

"To the house?"

"The Cherokee," Ben said. "His other name. The place was used as a mail drop."

"I don't believe it. How would he know—secrets."

"He didn't have to know them. He just had to pass them on." Ben looked at Henderson. "Assuming he did."

"What do you mean by that?"

"They were sent to him but we don't know that he picked them up, do we?"

"We can assume."

"But we can't prove it. The guy who went over the balcony—my burglar. Ray. Police find a mail key on him?"

Henderson said nothing.

"You must have asked. Given your interest. Or didn't anybody think of it?"

"We asked."

"And? Great partnership," he said when Henderson didn't answer. "Look, I can find out anyway. But I thought there was some urgency here." He stared at Henderson. "It's important."

Henderson nodded, then said, "Now tell me why."

"Because he didn't take mine. So he already had one. Danny's. Which he either took from him, or which Danny never had. It's possible somebody else picked up the mail." He looked at Liesl. "It's also possible Danny did. Either way."

"And either way he's part of it," Henderson said. "He had to know."

"About the mail, yes. Not necessarily what was in it."

"Small difference."

"Not to us," Ben said, including Liesl. "Anyway, Ray had a key. Which means whoever hired him gave it to him. Which also means he doesn't have it anymore. And that's where we come in," he said to Henderson.

"Back up," Henderson said.

"Guy goes to the Cherokee, checks the mail but nothing's there because I'd already picked it up. So he checks the apartment, still nothing, and after he knocks me out, he goes through my pockets and still nothing. Then he goes over. And now the police have the key. But not the letter, or all kinds of bells would be going off. So whoever hired him is stuck. No key, no letter. But he knows it was sent, so where is it?"

"You have it," Henderson said quietly.

"Right. And the important thing is that he doesn't know we're having this little talk. He doesn't know I gave it to you. Unless somebody leaks. We don't know where he has friends."

"Nobody's going to leak."

"Make sure, okay? Or he won't move. He won't take the bait."

"The bait being you," Henderson said.

Ben nodded.

"What are you talking about?" Liesl said. "Bait?"

"If the letter's already here, I must have it. If it's still on its way, then I'd get it. No other keys. Not to mention he won't want to risk checking the boxes at the Cherokee. After what happened. Police might be taking an interest. So if he wants it, he has to get it from me. With any luck, before I start asking anybody about it. So he doesn't want to see me with anybody." He looked at Henderson. "No watchdogs. But Liesl's a different story. That's why I wanted you here, so you'll know. I want you to put someone on the house," he said to Henderson. "Not sitting out front in a hat, either. A gardener, maybe, something like that. But who's there all the time. And somebody right behind, when she goes out. So she's always covered."

"You're taking the case over now?"

"You were going to put some guys on me, weren't you? Just switch them to her. He'll watch me. He has to think it's all right, to make his move."

"Try to kill you, you mean," Liesl said.

"Which he might do," Henderson said. "And then we're nowhere and you're dead."

"That's the chance you'll have to take."

"You're the one taking the chances," Liesl said. "You don't have to do this."

"He'll come anyway. He's already tried once. Besides we have some names to protect," Ben said, leading him.

"Protect."

"You moved in hours. If you had files on these guys, criminal files, you'd be rounding them up. So they're in the other files."

"Which other files."

"Security clearance is my guess. Of course, I'm not cleared to know."

"Does it make any difference?"

"I'm putting myself in a gun sight for you."

Henderson looked at him. "I'll see what I can do. I'd need approval."

"Protect yourself," Liesl said. "Don't act like this. You should have someone."

"You wouldn't even know he was there," Henderson said. "We can do that."

"He'd know. And then he'd know you were after him. He'd duck. We have to do it this way. I've got a guy looking into who hired Ray. It's a back way in, but maybe we'll get lucky. Otherwise—"

"What guy?"

"A reporter. Knows a lot of rats. Sorry I can't say who—you're not cleared."

"Very funny."

"How about the Bureau issuing me a gun?"

"A gun?" Liesl said, alarmed.

One of the other agents knocked and opened the door. "Phone," he said to Henderson.

"In a minute."

"It's long distance. Berkeley."

Henderson frowned, annoyed. "I have to take this." He hurried out of the room, closing the door behind him, leaving them alone, the air suddenly thick with quiet.

"This is what you think, he was a traitor? It's *fantastische.*"

"I don't know."

"How can you say that? I know."

"Because you're still in love with him."

She jerked up her head, meeting his eyes for a minute, then looked away. "You take everything too seriously. I didn't mean—"

"I didn't see it. Maybe I wasn't looking."

"What difference does it make?"

"His widow, that's one thing. His wife—"

She smiled grimly to herself, still staring at her lap. "Not seemly." She was still for a minute, then got up, pacing to the other side of the table. "So now you want to get yourself killed to prove this? First an informer, now, what? From bad to worse. That's what you want?"

"To get killed? No. I want to talk to him."

"Talk to him."

"I want to know what happened. What Danny did. Not guess. Know."

"Why?"

He looked at her. "So I can let him go."

She stopped, folding her arms across her chest, swaying slightly, holding herself in. "And me," she said.

Before he could answer, Henderson was back, the same brisk hurrying.

"Any luck?" Ben said.

"With what?"

"The San Francisco postmark. Wasn't that the call? Berkeley?"

Henderson shook his head. "Something else. We have other cases, believe it or not. Now, we were—"

"You were going to get me a gun."

"We're not a store. You'd have to be deputized."

"Fine. It's a family tradition, working for the Bureau. Maybe this time it'll be for something worthwhile, not just chasing Communists."

Henderson turned to him. "You're a little mixed up on this," he said.

"How?"

"I told you. Those names are like an order of battle. The only people interested in that now *are* the Communists. That's who your brother was working for."

RIORDAN SHORTSTOPPED him in the hall. "You don't want to go in there. Not even near. Not the way he is today. He'd do it with his bare hands."

Riordan was carrying an envelope, in a rush, his eyes darting toward the parking lot.

"What's the problem?"

"Are you kidding? Warning Kaltenbach? C'mon, before he sees you."

"Then how about you going in there, quiet, and getting my copy of the list and I'll be gone."

"Forget it. Get it from the Bureau. Ever see him crossed?" He paused. "Why'd you do it, anyway? I mean, who was he to you?"

"Nobody. Just a friend of the family."

They both turned as the door opened, Minot coming out so fast he almost bumped into them.

"You've got a hell of a nerve," he said to Ben. "What are you doing here? Dennis, I thought you had something to do." He slammed the door behind him. "Let's go. Or do you want me to have Frank throw you out?" He began hustling everybody down the hall.

"Congressman—"

"I don't want to hear it. Just get out. You come here again, there'll be orders to call the cops. You hear that, Frank?" he said to the guard at the door. "Take a good look at this one. You want to remember, if he shows up."

"Yes, sir."

They were outside now, Minot watching his car pull up.

"He was an old man," Ben said to him. "There wasn't much to squeeze."

"That's not for you to decide, is it?" he said, his voice fast, a whiplash. "Or maybe you think it is." He looked at Ben. "It isn't. He was my witness and he's gone. Dennis." He nodded toward another car pulling into the lot. "Let's get the subpoenas served before Paul Revere here has any more ideas."

"What subpoenas?"

"You think I'm going to let this happen again? Once is a lesson. Twice is stupid. I learned my lesson. Thanks to you." He stopped, his face breaking into a jagged smile. "That's right, isn't it? They'll all owe it to you. Maybe we should let them know. Make you a popular guy." He switched tone. "I didn't want it like this. I wanted more time, do it right. Now I don't have a choice, I have to use a net. But there's something to be said for surprise." He smiled to himself again. "Catch the lawyers off guard."

"Mine too? You going to put a lamp in my face?"

"I don't want to see it again. Ever. I trusted you." He shrugged. "Another lesson in life."

"You're a lot upset over very little."

"That depends. Maybe you're right, maybe I don't need him at all. But I sure as hell don't need you. So I'm throwing you back." Another smile. "We'll let the others take care of you." He opened the car door and got in. "Dennis? Make sure he gets out of here."

"What others?" Ben said after Minot had left.

"What?"

"Taking care of me. He meant something by it."

"He gets mad, that's all. He likes to get even. In other ways."

"Such as?"

"Targeting Continental. They get to go first. Kind of a payback."

"To me? That's crazy."

"You shouldn't have crossed him."

"When is this?"

"As soon as the subpoenas—" He stopped. "Get out of here, okay? You don't have to warn anybody. They'll know soon enough. Maybe nobody'll connect the dots."

"To me. The dots in his head."

The other car had pulled up.

"Hey, Kelly," Ben said. "Still picking up Polly's laundry?"

Kelly took the envelope from Riordan, a little embarrassed.

"Anything yet on Ray?"

"I just put out a feeler yesterday."

"And then you got busy," Ben said, looking at the envelope. "Is Polly getting a lead this time or still playing shill?"

"What's it to you?"

"I like to see you get ahead."

Kelly looked at Riordan, a thanks for the envelope. "I'm doing all right."

"I'll walk you to your car," Riordan said.

"I can find it," Ben said. "You're busy."

They watched Kelly drive away.

"So who were they? In the letter," Riordan said.

"I don't know. They wouldn't say."

"They wanted to find you in a hurry."

"You know what I think? They don't know. They were looking to me to tell them."

Riordan made a face, skeptical. "Communists?"

"Haven't you got enough?" Ben said, cocking his head toward the office.

Riordan didn't bother to answer. "Maybe we'll run into each other some time. Lunch at the Market."

Ben headed for his car, then turned, watching Riordan go in. So who were they? Friedman. Someone the San Francisco operator didn't have. A few names lodged somewhere in the back of his mind, the rest in a drawer, unavailable. He looked at the building, the guarded back door. Minot's office would face the side street. He followed it toward the front entrance on Wilshire, trying to guess which windows were Minot's. There, both open now, but locked tonight. High enough to require a jump to catch the sill. And then what? He saw himself dangling in the street, pulling himself up, breaking the window, the sound of smashing glass—impossible, something even the Partners would find absurd. The way into any office was through the door.

He skirted the building, going in through the Wilshire entrance. Also locked at night, presumably part of Frank's rounds. He walked down the long hall to Minot's office, then stood near the door. Behind the translucent glass he could hear voices, Dennis and the secretaries. Did they all go out to lunch together? But then they'd lock it. He looked at the doorknob, the keyhole in the middle. Something Frank could open with a master key, but not Ben.

A man came out of the next office and crossed the hall to the restroom, looking at him. Ben took the knob, pretending to enter, until he heard the men's room door close, then noticed Frank turning the corner down the hall. He jerked his hand away and went into the next office. Statewide Insurance. An outer room with three secretaries.

"Yes? Are you here to see Mr. Herbert?"

"No, I—I think I've made a mistake. Congressman Minot?"

"Next door, on your right."

"Thanks," he said, hesitating, listening for Frank, then saw that she was waiting and that he had to move. He opened the door, and looked down, hiding his face. But Frank had passed. He hurried back to Wilshire, the files still behind him.

At the studio, people already knew Minot was going to make a move. The power of Hollywood gossip, Ben thought, impressed again, no warning flares needed.

"Bunny's been with lawyers all day," Hal said.

"But nothing's happened."

"It's going to. Polly's got a column tomorrow. She says it's about time."

"For what?"

"Housecleaning. Makes you think of a duster. Joan Leslie doing a little tidying up."

Ben glanced at him, surprised at his tone. "But you're all right. I mean—"

Hal nodded, smiling a little. "But you had to ask, didn't you? Take a walk around the lot. You can feel it, people just waiting to see."

Bunny came in without knocking.

"Oh good, both of you. How's your head?" he said to Ben and then, at his expression, "You made the papers. Well, the burglar did. Some building."

"Still a little sore."

"Can you work? We need to get this wrapped up."

"Sure. Why?"

"You think you've got a headache? Wait till the messengers get here with their little papers. Tomorrow? The next day? The suspense is killing us. Except it's not going to. We stay on schedule." He turned to Hal. "Two things. The overrun was *not* authorized. It's an Army film, let Fort Roach do the processing." He stopped, taking in Ben, too. "We bring it in on budget or we bail. I mean it. Second, I need to see you. In the office." This to Hal, his voice lower.

"Me?"

"I want you to talk to the lawyers."

Hal took a step back, his whole body a question mark.

"What's going on?" Ben asked for him.

"You know Schaeffer, over at Fox?"

"We made a picture together," Hal said, suddenly hoarse.

"Well, they're going to want to know everything he ever said to you. The lawyers need to prep you."

"Slow down a minute," Ben said. "What's going on?"

"A run-through," Bunny said. "Rehearsal for taking on the majors. Minot wants to show them how disruptive this can be, what it can do to your business. Encourage them to be friendly. Just like we're going to be," he said, looking now at Hal. "All friendly witnesses. We understand the *gravity* of the situation. And he goes away and we close the door and we're still here. Then it's Jack's turn and Zanuck's and—and they won't even have to be told. They watched him do it to us. Now, okay? My office. They're waiting."

Hal left without saying a word.

"Who else is going to be called?" Ben said.

"We're not sure. We're trying to anticipate."

"Talk to him. I thought you were pals."

"And what would I offer him? You? I gather you annoyed him. Even wounded." He pointed to Ben's head.

"I don't want to make trouble for the studio. Do you need me to take a walk?"

"You're not making trouble, *he's* making trouble. We're easy, the first bite. Small enough to chew and spit out. He thinks. You notice he's not taking on Warners. Or Metro. Yet. Just somebody he can push around." He looked up at Ben. "He wants to tear this industry apart. To make himself a star. So we help him. And then we help him move on."

"You're going to cooperate."

Bunny glanced at his watch. "Now look at the time." He raised his head, Ben's eyes still on him. "I'm going to keep things going. Call Liesl, by the way, and get her in here. Sick day. We send somebody over there, and she's off on some joyride with you. Don't bother." He held up his hand. "It wouldn't even be good. The *point* is that we have to move up the picture. Tick, tock. We may have a hole in the schedule. We can't go into Christmas without an A."

"Why would you? Have a hole?"

"In case a picture's in trouble," Bunny said, turning away. "In case we had to shelve it."

"If someone were testifying."

Bunny looked at him, then put both hands to his temples. "Didn't I tell you? It's already starting. Why don't you *help* and just save the questions?"

"Want an aspirin? You'll feel better."

"Wouldn't that be nice?" Bunny said, heading for the door.

"Bunny? Before you go?"

"I can't hear you."

"Studio have a locksmith?"

Bunny stopped, surprised.

"I'm having trouble with my door."

"That's all? Lucky you. Rogers. Carpenter shop. Two hundred and forty-one." No detail too small.

Rogers, like everyone else, wanted to be in the movies.

"What kind of lock?"

"Like this," Ben said, touching the doorknob, similar to Minot's. "The scene calls for the guy to pick the lock. Trouble is nobody knows how it's actually done. So I figured you—"

"You don't need a pro for that. Anybody could pick that. Get a Yale. Maybe a dead bolt. You can stretch the scene."

"But this is what we have."

"You only find these in buildings like this. Standard spring, the guards are the security. Hotels, sometimes. They're cheaper. The door chain's your real lock. This is a heist? They'd have to pick something a lot stronger."

"No, just an office. So maybe he's not a pro. How easy is it?"

Rogers took a slender rod from his tool belt and, holding the door ajar, inserted the rod, flicking it up in one quick motion that released the lock.

"That's it? Show me."

"This groove here. Put her in there, all the way to the right, then up. You're going to do this in close-up? You're better off with a Yale."

Ben tried it twice before it worked.

"Can I borrow this?"

"Sure. Smooth slice up. You could jiggle, have it slip or something, but that's not going to fool anybody. You should change the lock."

BEN WAITED on the Wilshire side until just before closing.

"The problem isn't getting in," he said to Liesl. "It's getting out. After six, everybody goes out the back. That hour, they're heading for the lot. So I'd have to get past Frank."

"Unless he's not there. You've explained it."

"I just need a few minutes. Keep him with you. Your boss?"

"Mr. Herbert. Who's going to kill me if I don't do those papers tonight. Why are you doing this?"

"Because the Bureau's never going to help. What names? The only thing they're willing to do is let me get killed. Okay, let's go. Park on the side street."

"And wait for the window shade. Then do my scene with Frank. Funny, now I'll be you."

He looked at her, puzzled.

"In the series. The one who helps. The good one."

He went in through the Wilshire door, moving quickly down the hall, late for an appointment. There were only a few people around, stragglers or assistants doing last-minute jobs, cleaning ladies collecting waste baskets. Lights still on in Minot's office, probably a secretary with a letter to finish. Riordan, he knew, had already left. He went into the men's room, took the last stall, and sat down to wait. The building was alive with sounds when you stopped to listen: a typewriter click, footsteps, somebody laughing, then nothing for a while, just the creak of the building settling, the scrape of a chair. When someone came in, everything sounded loud, the splash of pee, the running water, a throat clearing. Ben imagined him—the insurance agent?—adjusting his tie. Then the thud of the door closing.

It got darker earlier now, even in California, and Ben watched the window over the sinks get dimmer. He got up and switched off the overhead light, then peeked out. No lights at Statewide, but somebody was still in Minot's office. What if she stayed late? They'd come to clean the restroom soon, mopping everywhere. But then Minot's door swung open. One of the secretaries with fresh lipstick, locking it behind her, then checking it by twisting the knob. Ben ducked back behind his door, listening to her high heels going down the hall. Give it a few minutes, in case she forgot anything. The hall needed to be clear. There was nothing suspicious about being in the men's room, not yet. Once it got dark, though, no story would work.

He waited for what seemed like hours but was probably ten minutes, then opened the door again. No one, the only sound the clang of a pail near the Wilshire end, the cleaning ladies starting. He palmed the rod and crossed over to Minot's door. Act as if you're using a key. He inserted the rod, jagged right and up, but nothing happened. Again. Why did he assume they were all alike? It must be a different mechanism. He tried left, a variation, his hand tense, then stopped, taking a breath, feeling a bead of sweat on his upper lip. But it had been so easy at the studio. Don't overwork it. Think of Rogers's hand, the deft flick right, then upward. He tried it again, almost making a sound of relief when he heard the click.

Inside, there was barely enough light to see, the shades half-drawn. Liesl would be outside, watching. Minot's personal office was in the next room, but all the files were out here, where the staff worked. For a second he was tempted, now that he was in, to go through Minot's desk, but that would be actual theft, not just collecting something of his own. He crossed over to the file cases. What if Riordan had already taken it out? Something he didn't want Minot to find? But it was still there, in Heinrich's now useless file. Ben folded it quickly and put it in his jacket pocket. Now get out before the cleaning staff started working its way down the hall. He returned the file and went over to the window, pulling the shade, then raising it back into position, and waited by the door. It would take at least a few minutes for Liesl to talk to Frank, helpless and panicky.

Ben jumped, his skin tingling, when the phone rang. Was someone supposed to be here? For one terrible second he expected it to be picked up in the inner office, but it kept ringing, so shrill that everyone must hear, and then finally stopped. He breathed out, his ears still filled with sound, listening now to the hall. Why so worried? Everything was fine, what he'd expected. There were even footsteps now, a woman's voice, Liesl on time. He put his ear near the edge of the door to hear better. Liesl was thanking Frank, slightly scatterbrained, someone likely to have forgotten her work. They were now at Statewide, Liesl thanking him again as he used his passkey. Take him inside. Two, three minutes and Ben would be out. He opened the door a crack. They were going in, Liesl still talking, keeping him busy. Now. He opened the door.

He saw them before he heard them, two shadows followed by the sound of footsteps, clunky, not furtive. He pulled back in, banging his shoulder, and listened. Closer. Then Frank was back in the hallway, alert.

"Congressman," he said.

"Thought you were catching forty winks somewhere," Minot said, genial.

"No, just helping next door. Little lady forgot something."

Could Liesl hear or would she blunder out into the hall?

Ben slid his hand toward the knob, turning the lock quietly, hoping the sound would disappear under Frank's voice. If it were open, Minot would wonder. He looked toward the window, frantic. Too late to fiddle with the sash lock. Under a desk? Did Liesl think he was already gone? But what choice would she have, once she'd got her papers? A new voice now, Minot's guest. The shadows were larger against the glass. Another look around the office. Nobody hid under desks, something out of Mack Sennett. Minot was taking out his key. Ben tiptoed away from the door. Next to the filing cabinets there was a supply closet, not a real closet with a door you could close, just shelves covered by an accordion screen. He wedged himself behind, his back flush against the shelves, trying not to move anything.

"This won't take a minute," Minot said, opening the door. He flicked on the overhead light.

Ben glanced to his left—did he make a shadow?

"But I did promise. And you know people—think nobody's busy but them."

"I can imagine," Bunny said.

Ben went still, his mind racing, almost jumping again when the phone rang.

"That'll be him," Minot said, picking up and talking, the words bunching together, slipping past Ben, just business.

A meeting with Bunny arranged by whom? Minot just another union, another negotiation? Bunny was walking around the room, politely distancing himself from Minot's call. Maybe looking out toward the hall, where Liesl would be any minute. But she'd see the lights, realize people were here. Ben imagined her in the hall, being swept down toward the back door by her own story—she had the papers, why stay? Her voice now, to Frank. Don't say any more. If he could hear it, Bunny could.

"You're a peach," she said. "You saved my life."

Distinct to him, or was he the only one listening, Bunny preoccupied? Then the sound of her heels.

"Everything okay, Congressman?" Frank said, his head in the door.

Minot nodded and waved him off. Now he'd follow, let her out, and she'd go to her car, expecting to find Ben, alarmed when she didn't. Don't come back.

"Sorry about that," Minot was saying. "Now where— Ginny was supposed to leave— Here it is." Ben heard the ruffle of paper. "We can talk more in the car."

"I think I know what you need. You understand, our records aren't anything like this." Ben imagined him waving to the cabinets.

"No, these are the best anybody has, thanks to Jack Tenney."

"It's understood that Mr. L won't be called," Bunny said.

"I see no reason for that at this juncture," Minot said, oddly formal.

"He's not Mayer. No real press value for you. And the studio heads might see it as an attack, close ranks."

"We wouldn't want that."

"Besides, I'm not sure he really understands what this is about." He dropped his voice. "He's out of it. That's understood."

"He hired Schaeffer," Minot said.

"So did Zanuck. Anyway," he said, switching tack, "who talks to writers? People on the set, not the front office. We can help you there. What kind of charges are you going to bring?"

"Charges? This isn't a criminal trial. I'm not looking to send anybody to jail. Takes time and then you make martyrs out of them. Of course, if he perjures himself—but I doubt that, don't you? Especially with all the corroborating testimony. Schaeffer's a Commie and he knows we know. I don't want to put him away, I just want everybody to know he's *there*. Anyway, the public isn't going to care about Schaeffer. They'll want—" He stopped, evidently aware that he was saying more than he needed.

"Actors," Bunny finished. "Stars."

"Well, let's just say people they know. Not necessarily Reds. Maybe just people who are as concerned as we are. Friends."

"I understand," Bunny said, interrupting him. "Faces for the news-reels."

"Well, just so we do understand each other," Minot said, annoyed. "How mutual interests work. The studios. The committee. We want to be on the same side here. As I say, I'm not looking to put people in jail. I'm expecting the studios to do their own police work. You wouldn't want one working for you, would you?"

There was a pause. "Not even a suspected one," Bunny said quietly, taking this in.

"That's right. And once people know the studios feel this way, that it's about their *jobs*, I think we'll have a whole different situation. You fire one, everybody sits up. They'll know it's not going to be tolerated. Not in American movies. You don't want to employ people who are against everything you stand for. You get together on this, hell, you could put the committee out of business."

"Their jobs," Bunny said. "Then why not give us names. We can take care of it before you have to call them. Saves expense."

"Maybe in time. But right now—I don't have to tell you about the value of publicity to get things rolling. That's mother's milk to you people."

"Preview of coming attractions."

"That's right. We understand each other?"

For a minute Ben heard only the clock ticking.

"Mr. L is out of it," Bunny said. "And the union contract?"

"That's not in my gift. But I can promise that Mr. Stein will be otherwise occupied. That should help things along. Funny how they're always Jews, isn't it? Well, I have to get going. Do me a favor, will you, and reach behind? Get me an envelope for this? There should be a box of manilas in there."

Ben fixed his eyes on the edge of the screen. What an animal must feel, he thought, finally outrun, trapped, a rush of blood to the head, then an eerie stillness, everything stopped, waiting. A hand, then a body blocking the light, Bunny turning. Ben reared back, flattening himself against the shelves, as if he could disappear, out of Bunny's startled gaze. He expected Bunny to jump but instead he put his hand to the shelf, maybe to steady himself, still staring. A second passed, then another, neither of them making a sound, so that of all the things racing through Ben's mind, what stuck was Bunny's control, a will stronger than shock. And then it was too late for him to say anything, the moment over, both thinking, not breathing, trapped by each other.

"The door slides," Minot said. "They're back there somewhere."

Maybe coming to help. Ben made his eyes go to the shelf beside him, a direction, then repeated it, like a flashing light.

"I see it," Bunny said, reaching to the box on the shelf, his hand grazing Ben's shoulder, complicit now by his silence, suddenly Ben's protector. They looked at each other, a whole exchange without words, beyond the obvious question.

"I'll have Andy drop you home," Minot was saying, his voice sounding closer.

"No, the studio," Bunny said, still looking at Ben. "I have a meeting. Somebody I need to see." His voice now pitched directly at Ben, unmistakable. He took the envelope, then pulled the accordion screen closed, hiding Ben. "Here you go," he said, handing it to Minot, and it was only then Ben heard the first waver, Bunny's nerves finally engaged, not wanting Minot to know.

"This late? Well, I know how that is. Come on, I'll get you back. I feel good about this. I think we got something done tonight."

Ben heard them cross the room and then the light went out and the door slammed. He breathed out, the blood coming back, and realized he was sweating. He nudged the screen back, trying to do it silently. Give them a few minutes. He looked around the dark office. He'd have to use the window after all.

He leaned against the wall, waiting, thinking about the conversation. Their jobs. He was going to get the studios to do it for him. And they would. Buying time, feeding him one piece at a time, staying 100 percent American. Even Bunny, who understood, would have to give him somebody, a face to start with. He thought suddenly of Bunny's face as it had been, guileless, a Freddie Bartholomew tear running down his cheek. An orphan. If you were fired at one studio, you'd never work at another. It would be understood, the way Minot wanted it.

Some headlights went by outside the window. Minot's or just another car? Not yet. He looked at the files. Any one of them. And then he knew who it would be, the pragmatic choice. The file was right here, easy for him to take. Would it make any difference? You could reconstruct a file. If you remembered the sources, knew the cross references, had the time. And Minot now was in a rush. Danny had tried to help her once, never reported a thing. She must have meant something to him. Ben glanced at the file drawer again. Right here. Be Danny one more time.

He went over to the files and flicked through the tabs. Miliken, Millard, Miller. He took it out, bulky, and put it in his jacket, feeling his blood rush again. He glanced around, a thief's involuntary gesture, then closed the drawer and went over to the window, trying to estimate the drop. Not far, the first floor, but you'd have to dangle a second before you dropped or risk your ankles, just the second a car might be passing. But everything seemed quiet. Wilshire was always busy, but the side street mostly took the outflow of the parking lot. He waited another minute, listening, then opened the window and swung out. When he was over, still hanging from the lintel, he tried to reach up with one hand to bring the window back down, but it jammed and putting his weight on one hand made it begin to slip, so he brought the other back and let himself down, dropping slowly until he was a few feet from the ground. Now. He hit the ground just as a pair of headlights swung around from Wilshire. He was wincing from the dull shock of the jump, but forced himself up before the light could reach him. A crouch would be suspicious. Your body told the story. Somebody walking, heading for the lot. The car passed.

Liesl was still down the street.

"I didn't know what to do. It was Bunny, wasn't it? What was he doing?"

"Fixing things. He thinks. Drop me at the studio. I told him I'd be there."

"He saw you? What did he say?"

"Nothing. He was more upset that I saw him. Kind of thing you like to do by yourself."

"What?"

"Make deals."

She was quiet for a minute, moving them into traffic. "What's going to happen?"

"I don't know."

She fixed on the windshield, shivering a little. "It's like before. Today, at the studio, I felt it. The way it was before the war. The quiet. Nobody talks. Everybody knows and nobody talks. So it's like that again."

There were a few lights on in the Admin building, but Bunny's office was dark so Ben headed over to the screening room. He touched the letter in his jacket, aware suddenly of the shadows and the deserted alleys between the sound stages, a perfect place to wait. No shots, another crack on the head, fatal this time, Carl oblivious at the gate while someone went through Ben's pockets.

Bunny was alone in the screening room, running a picture.

"Just a minute," he said, motioning Ben to sit. "Watch this." Not rushes, an old feature, Claudette Colbert in a gold lamé evening dress, clearly gold even in black and white. "Watch her wiggle in the seat." A society party, people listening to a classical singer. "She got in with a pawn ticket and now they're onto her. Barrymore knows. Look at the way they size each other up."

But Ben was watching Bunny, his face soft with pleasure, living in the picture even as he talked.

"Now Hedda makes the announcement. See the one with her back to us? That's Polly."

"Polly?"

"Mm. Her greatest performance. Hedda gave her her start, with the column. Watch Barrymore's eyebrows. Nobody could ham like that. The way they play off each other. Her eyes. It's perfect, isn't it?"

Claudette was getting up, summoned by a butler, and Bunny picked up the phone.

"Stop it there, Jerry. Thanks." His eyes were still on the screen as the lights came up. "One week at the Paramount and it's gone. But it was perfect. That look, like a grace note. That's what we're supposed to be doing here, putting in grace notes. Making things better."

"What's the picture?"

"*Midnight*. Before the war." He got up. "There's a sequence I wanted to see, a bit with taxis. But I don't think we can use it." He turned to Ben. "What were you doing there?"

"If you don't know, you'll never have to answer that," Ben said, feeling the weight in his pocket.

Bunny looked at him, then moved away, running his hand over the back of his seat. "I suppose you heard everything, behind your little arras."

"Faint mumblings."

"I should have had a sword. Run you through. But I find I never do have one, when I need it." He stopped. "Don't interfere in this."

Ben nodded, noncommittal.

"I mean it. Just put it out of your mind. We'll both do that. What *were* you doing, though?"

"Catching up on my filing. They make interesting reading."

"Not anymore. Stay out of it."

"Don't give him anybody."

"You think I'm enjoying this?" He walked down the aisle, away from Ben. "It's business, that's all."

"No. It's going to get worse."

"Not for us," Bunny said quickly. "Look, I'm walking a tightrope here." He lifted his arms from his sides a little, a balancing mime. "Don't shake it. Don't huff. Don't puff." He looked at Ben. "Don't anything. Or you're off the lot. Mr. L or no."

The back door to the Cherokee was kept locked now, so he went through the front, past the new night clerk, attentive, maybe a Bureau man, planted too late. Upstairs he flicked on the light before going in and flung the door open, in case another Ray was waiting. He opened the French windows to let in some air, then went back to the door and wedged a desk chair under the knob. Would he really try here again? Dropping somehow onto the balcony?

Ben sat on the bed and pulled out the sheet of names. Wallace. Gilbert. No more recognizable than before. Not here, not in San Francisco. Friedman. He stopped. A name he had heard. Literally heard. A voice saying it. But whose? He tried putting it in people's mouths to see how it would sound—Liesl, Bunny, anyone he knew, but nothing came. Still, he'd heard it somewhere. On the lot? Lasner's party? Let it go. If you tried to force it, nothing came. You had to let it pop into your head.

He looked at the door again, barricaded, what his life was going to be like now. What if he never came? But he'd want the list. Unless he'd decided to write it off as a bad risk, move on. Still, he'd tried once, a man dead. A day, two. Or he'd have to use more bait.

MINOT PRESENTED the hearings as a preliminary fact-finding inquiry, something local, but he was staging them like a full Washington investigation. The press had its own section in the hearing room, behind the newsreel cameras, but half were still outside covering the witnesses arriving, a premiere without the broad smiles. The public seats filled almost immediately, with a few front rows reserved for the witnesses, studio VIPs, and anyone with a friend on Minot's staff. Ostermann, surprisingly, was in the press section, near Polly, who kept leaping up and down to talk to people, then scribble notes, a blur of eager restlessness. The committee sat at a long table, not a raised judge's bench, but the arrangement, looking across at the witnesses and their lawyers, still had a courtroom effect.

What Ben noticed most was the noise. The galleries buzzed with talk. In the side rooms, telephones rang almost constantly and aides ran back and forth with messages. When Minot came out to take his place at the table the hum rose even higher, the room busy, anticipating. Ben thought of a Coliseum scene in the old silents, everyone in jerky motion, waiting for the lions.

The first bang of the gavel was startling, followed by a murmur, a second bang, quiet. Minot, his face flushed with confidence, gave the opening speech—a great industry undermined from within, the values and moral fabric of the culture itself at risk, the unwitting comfort extended to traitors in our midst—and then, just a few seconds before the audience could get restive, called Dick Marshall.

"I thought he was going to start with Stein," Bunny whispered, half to himself.

A logical choice, the strike still daily news, and Stein's sympathies so well known he would have been an easy first shot, but for once Bunny's instincts were off, not the point Minot wanted to score. As Marshall approached the table, there was an audible rustling of interest. A movie star, someone, Ben suddenly remembered, who'd once actually played a gladiator.

It was clear from the first moment, Minot's head nodding with respect, that Marshall had come as a friendly witness, there to add a glow and demonstrate that he was as American as everyone assumed him to be. There were soft questions and patriotic answers, more nods from the committee, Dick's very presence, his concern, somehow affirming their own. Bunny watched carefully, head on his pyramid fingers. Marshall was Continental's most valuable name, a marquee favor to Minot. But why call him? Ben looked at his tanned, smooth face. An arm dangling from a chaise. Minot, he saw, was ignoring the Continental row. There were complicit glances at the rest of the audience, direct appeals to the cameras, but he never met Bunny's eyes, acknowledged the gift. Marshall was his.

"Now you yourself didn't serve in the military?" Minot said.

"No, I was 4-F. Perforated eardrum."

Bunny sat up but didn't say anything, maybe a question not in the script.

"But of course you served your country in other ways."

"I did what I could, yes. During the bond drive, we raised—"

"Well, I meant more just by doing what you do. Your pictures. I can tell you, when I was in the Pacific, there were times the boys thought you were winning the war single-handed."

Everyone laughed and Marshall tilted his head modestly.

"I had a little help. About four million guys, in fact. They're the ones who won it."

"Christ," Ben said under his breath.

"Don't snipe," Bunny said.

"But I think we can all agree," Minot said, "morale's important, too. As someone who did see active service, I can tell you those pictures meant a lot to us. Now I wonder if I can ask you about one of them. In 1943, you were in *Convoy to Murmansk*. You remember that?"

"Sure. I was in the Navy in that one."

"Escorting a convoy of freighters, wasn't it?"

Dick nodded. "Dodging U-boats."

"Dodging U-boats. Now of course they were all over the Atlantic. And the book the movie was based on—were you aware of this?—was English, about convoys heading for England. *Convoy* it was called."

"That was the original title of the picture, too. The first script, I mean."

"Oh, the original. And were you going to England in the script?"

"Yes."

"Then all the sudden, Murmansk. Now why is that, do you think?"

"I don't know. That would have been up to the writer. The director. I just say the lines."

"The director, the writer—same fella on this picture, is that right? On *Convoy to— Murmansk*," Minot said, emphasizing the last word.

"Right. Milton Schaeffer."

"You ever ask him why he changed it?"

"Just in a kidding way. Made things harder to pronounce, the places."

"In a kidding way. And what did he say?"

"Well, at the time we were trying to show how all the Allies were in it together. He said this was a way of bringing Russia in."

"Including a new Russian character." He looked down at his notes. "Andrei Malinkov. Soviet Naval attaché. Dick Marshall couldn't get through the Baltic himself, is that it?"

Dick smiled. "The idea was, we were working together. He knew the mine fields."

"Americans and Russians side by side. Just like they were any folks. Let me read you something." He picked up a paper. "'We're not just carrying food. Equipment. We're carrying hope. They're taking a terrible beating. We have to help. How can we eat if they're going hungry?' Recognize that?"

"I said it. In the picture."

"It's in the book, too. Of course then you're saying it about London. Now it's—what? Leningrad? You think it's the same thing? London, Leningrad? Is that what Mr. Schaeffer said?"

Dick gave a side glance to his lawyer, who nodded, a cue.

"He said the suffering there was even worse, in Russia, but nobody was doing pictures about it. This would help draw attention. That we needed to help the Russians."

"Help the Russians," Minot repeated. "Well, that we certainly did. The ships in *Convoy*—excuse me, *Convoy to Murmansk*—were carrying Lend-Lease. Millions and millions to help those people Mr. Schaeffer said were suffering so much. Know how much of it they've paid back? Not one cent. Not one kopek." He looked up. "Did you ever suspect at the time that Mr. Schaeffer might be a Communist?"

"No, sir," Marshall said, appalled.

"No, you don't find that word in the script, not once. Just those friendly Russians. But they must have been, mustn't they? Why not call them Communists?"

"I don't know."

"Maybe you'd have found that harder to say. Maybe everybody would have found it harder to watch. Better not to tell people what the picture is really about. That's how they work. How would you feel now about *Convoy*? Knowing what you know today?"

Another glance to his lawyer, Bunny still, staring ahead.

"I guess I'd ask to be taken off the picture. If, like you say, it wasn't good for America. All my pictures, I've always thought they were a hundred percent American."

"Mr. Marshall, no one here is questioning your loyalty. We're just concerned that some people might use it for their own ends. Maybe you need to be a little more careful in the future. Not just say the words. Think a little bit about what's behind them." A school principal to a truant.

"Yes, sir."

Dick lowered his head slightly. Ben thought of him climbing into the fighter cockpit, eager to take on Japan, and saw that the nod had been the real point of the testimony, a kind of salute to the new commander at the long table.

"Anyone else on the committee have a question? If not, I think we can take a short break. You'll be available to us later, if we need you?" he said to Dick.

"Congressman, I'm here to help. I believe in fighting for America— and not just in the pictures."

Ben glanced across at the press section. Everyone was scribbling but Ostermann, his eyes fixed on Minot.

"That was fine," Bunny said to Marshall. His lawyers were gathering up papers from the witness table.

"Nice to say that about my pictures. Seeing them over there."

"What he *said* was that he was in the Pacific and you weren't. That's all anybody heard."

"Still."

"Never mind, you were fine. The fight line was good. They're all going to use it."

"I meant it."

"That's what makes it so convincing," Bunny said, not missing a beat. "I didn't know where he was going with the 4-F, but it was fine."

"Where he was going?"

"Well, we don't want anybody poking lights in your ears, do we? Anyway, it's done." He put a hand on Dick's shoulder. "Polly," he said, spotting her.

"Dick, that was wonderful. Wonderful. Read the column tomorrow," she said, patting him. "You're going to be very pleased." She turned to Bunny. "I have a bone to pick with you."

"Oh, Polly, a very small bone, I hope."

"You promised me an interview with Liesl."

"And you'll get it."

"When, after the picture opens? I thought she'd be here today. Why isn't she?" she said, her voice pointed now. "You'd think she'd want to be here with Dick."

"Polly, she's *shooting*. Some of us have to work. Of course she wanted to be here. She also wants to get the picture out."

"You mean you do."

"Because I've seen it. You won't believe how good she is. Bergman." He held his hand up, being sworn in. "Have I ever lied?"

Polly laughed. "You? No. You don't have it in you."

"A heart to heart, I promise. The kind you like. Just let her finish."

Polly waved this off. "See where I'm sitting? Right next to the Other Mann. Maybe I'll get him to ask. Somebody with influence."

"Call my office in the morning. I'll have Wendy set it up. Anyway, I thought you were doing Dick."

"A companion piece. You should want this," she said, tapping Bunny's arm. "It makes her more American. Especially after today. I could tell Ken was pleased. It's a great thing he's doing."

Bunny watched her trail after Dick, then turned to one of his assistants. "Where's Rosemary? I thought she was supposed to be here."

"Rosemary?" Ben said.

"She hasn't been served yet," the assistant said.

"That's funny," Bunny said, frowning, a detail out of place. "Go call and see what's up."

"Why Rosemary?" Ben said, walking out with Bunny.

"He can't lean on Schaeffer all week. Where's that going to get him? Murmansk?"

"Where's Rosemary going to get him?"

Bunny looked at him. "Stay out of this."

In the hall, people huddled in groups, smoking. Dick Marshall posed for a few more pictures. Ben made a circle, looking for Ostermann, and instead saw Henderson, leaning back against a fire extinguisher.

"What are you doing here?"

"Sure," Henderson said, reaching into his pocket. "Right here."

Then, in a lower voice, "Take out a cigarette. I thought you didn't want us to talk."

"I thought you weren't going to follow me," Ben said, leaning forward for the light.

"I'm just watching."

"What?"

"Things. See who's watching you. It's a good place for it. Who'd know? I figure he'd like to keep tabs. I would, I was him."

"And?"

"It's early. Now you got your light."

"Clearance come through yet on those names?"

"I'm working on it. You're welcome," he said louder, nodding.

Ben stood for a minute, stymied. "Don't ruin this," he said.

Henderson smiled. "What? Your unexpected demise? I'm looking forward to it. As long as I see who does it."

He moved off, leaving Ben to watch the crowd. Could he really be here? Someone on his way to the men's room. The photographer who wasn't. Anybody.

When the hearings reconvened, Ben had Dick next to him, Bunny on his other side.

"Why start with you?" Bunny said to Dick, still preoccupied with the order of things.

"I'm just glad to get it over with."

"But there's no build. Here they come."

This time Minot did look at them, an unexpected anger. At first Ben thought it was directed at him, the Kaltenbach grudge, but when Carol Hayes was called, a Fox contract player, Minot's eyes were fixed on Bunny, gauging his reaction. Bunny, clearly surprised, shrugged back.

"He's doing this wrong," he said. "Why her?"

"Picture in the papers?"

"Below the fold," Bunny said, dismissive.

Ben watched the newsreel cameras track her as she moved to the table, motors whirring. "Who is she?"

"Priscilla Lane. Diana Lynn," Bunny said, casting.

"I mean here."

"Probably a Schaeffer picture at Fox. But he just did that. There's no build. Carol Hayes."

"The cameras like her."

Bunny frowned. "Something's wrong." He leaned across again to one of the publicity staff and whispered, sending him out of the room.

"And you talked to Mr. Schaeffer about the script?" Minot was saying.

"I didn't want to," she said. "You know, you don't like to make trouble. But I just didn't feel comfortable with some of the lines."

"On the seventh take," Bunny said under his breath.

"And why was that?"

"They didn't seem— I don't think it's like that in this country. I mean, my dad was a businessman and he just wouldn't have done that, what happens in the picture."

Ben thought at first that Minot was heading somewhere with this, but after a while saw that he was just treading water. Everything Hayes said, her fear of being used to promote an underlying message, had been said. After she stepped down, another break, Bunny caught Minot as he passed.

"I don't understand what you're doing," he said quietly, a private conversation as people passed around them.

"No? Not exactly what we agreed, is it? I don't like sloppy seconds, either. You people," Minot said, an undisguised contempt. "Look at that."

Off to the side, Carol was smiling, her face lit up by flashbulbs.

"Then why did you—"

"You want to protect your property? That it? And I get this. So the surprise is on me. Live and learn. Who'd you use? Him?" He jerked his finger at Ben. "Handy Andy. No, he wouldn't have the balls. One of your studio goons probably. But I'll tell you something. The next surprise is on you. I can't call her without the file—that'll take a while to put together again. But there's always another way. A little whisper and there's no end to the shit they can stir up." He turned his head toward the reporters. "You shouldn't have done it."

"I don't know what you're talking about."

Minot dropped his voice. "Who do you think you're playing with? You fix parking tickets. You don't fix me. Not me."

"I still don't—"

"No? Then maybe she did it herself. Such light fingers," he said, wriggling his. "It doesn't matter. You're both fucked."

"Ken—"

"Can I get a word in edgewise?" A voice behind them.

"Polly," Minot said, rearranging his face, stepping back. "You there all this time?"

"Now don't run away. I've been trying to get you all morning. They're running the column out front."

"As the news?"

"In addition. Two stories. And a picture."

"That's a mighty good start," Minot said, smiling.

"Mm. I'm doing the color. Bunny, you don't mind, do you? I'll bring him back in a minute. Who else are you calling? Schaeffer?"

"You bet." He looked at Bunny. "And that's just the first day."

"What was that about?" Bunny said when they left. "Light fingers?"

"I don't know," Ben said, a little shaken, back in the supply closet, waiting to be caught. But she wouldn't be called. Something for Danny.

"I've never seen him like that."

"That's who he is."

Bunny's face, ashen just a minute ago, hardened. "He's not going to do a thing about the consent decree."

"Then make it harder for him. Don't give him people."

Bunny looked up. "Well, now I haven't, it seems. This isn't your doing, is it? Is that what you were— But why would you?" he said, talking to himself. "You know what he'll do now." He turned toward the door, watching Minot leave. "He'll feed her to Polly. Before we go into release."

Henderson seemed to have disappeared, now just another hat in the crowd, but Ostermann was there, standing alone by a window, looking out.

"It's usually gone by this time," he said, nodding to the fog. "Not today. No sun. Dark times, eh?"

"You haven't been taking any notes. Are you really going to write about this?"

"If he calls Germans, then it's something for *Aufbau*. Brecht, at least, I would think, wouldn't you? He'd make an interesting witness."

"It's a farce."

Ostermann nodded. "It always begins that way. Nothing to trouble about. Then each day a little more. Well, that's not so serious, either. And then one day—"

"You're writing your piece," he said, one eye still looking for Henderson.

A short man with wire-rimmed glasses, surrounded by lawyers, was crossing the hall, drawing photographers away from Carol Hayes. Schaeffer, he guessed.

Ostermann smiled. "Just thinking out loud." He looked at the crowd. "They don't see it. It's new to them. But it's the same. A farce. So say nothing and then it's too late. Like us."

In the hearing room, Bunny was still talking to the lawyers at the witness table so Ben was forced to take the open seat next to Dick. Their shoulders touched as he sat down, a slight brush, then a quick drawing away, and suddenly Ben was aware of him as a body, the height of his shoulders, his bulk filling the suit, hands placed on his knees, waiting. His tanned face oblivious to any change in the air around him, Ben invisible.

What had it been like? Had Dick stood by the pool's edge, watching her legs open and close? Or had that scene been just for him? The sounds, the way she clenched him. Ben turned, facing the long table. Something that only happened to you, what everybody felt, each time. Was it over? Someone else she hadn't loved. Still Danny's wife.

The sound of the newsreel cameras made him look up. Minot was calling Milton Schaeffer. The tone in his voice, with its hint of blood sport, almost gloating, had made everyone sit up. Carol Hayes, even Dick, had just been there to set the stage—Schaeffer was actually a Communist. But as the cameras followed him, Ben's attention shifted to them, the familiar whirring sound suddenly distracting, like someone whispering in his ear. Newsreel cameras.

Minot shuffled through papers, a promise of evidence to come, as Schaeffer approached the long table and was sworn in. He seemed slighter than he had in the hall, wiry and pale. Minot kept putting his papers in place, letting a hush fall over the room before he pounced.

"Mr. Schaeffer, are you now or have you ever been a member of the Communist Party?"

No one had expected a direct jab at the opening, and it might have worked, caused the excitement Minot had clearly been hoping for, if Schaeffer had been defiant or uncooperative or even evasive. Instead, he answered Minot's questions with a resigned fatalism that seemed to diminish their importance. Yes, he had been a member of the Party. No, he had resigned in August 1939, after the signing of the Non-Aggression Pact. No, he had not attended meetings since. He knew the names of the national Party officers (known to everyone) but not any of those in the local chapter.

"Don't know or don't want us to know?" Minot said.

"Names weren't used."

"No names. But they had faces? You'd recognize them if you saw them?"

"I suppose. It's been six or seven years."

"You didn't stay friends?"

"It was a discussion group. Not—well, just a discussion group."

"What did you discuss?"

"Political theory."

He still believed in the plight of the underprivileged, but no longer felt the CP was an effective tool to help them. His testimony was listless and damp, like the fog outside, waiting to be burned off. Minot had clearly been expecting something else and finally he saw that Schaeffer's answers, easily given, made him seem no more threatening than the bank clerk he resembled. The cameramen looked disappointed, not interested in the quieter drama, Schaeffer politely ending his career.

"He's losing them," Bunny said.

"Are you seriously suggesting to this committee that for five years—five years—you were part of an organization that owed its loyalty to a foreign power and this was a youthful indiscretion?"

"I have never been loyal to any country except the United States. I am an American. At no time during my association with the Party was there any question of disloyalty. When the Party adopted a position that I felt was not in our interests, I resigned."

"And up until then they acted in our interests?"

"What I thought should be our interests, yes."

"Should be. A rude awakening, then, when you found out what the Party's interests really were. A smart fellow like you ought to have known, don't you think? Or are you trying to say—it's some defense—that you didn't know what you were doing?"

"I thought I did. I thought I knew when I got married, too. Things change."

People laughed, grateful for a light second. Minot used his gavel.

"Mr. Schaeffer, do you think these proceedings are a laughing matter?"

Schaeffer looked around. "Not yet."

Just a gentle poke to the side, a tap, but this got a laugh, too.

"I can assure you, you won't be laughing when we're finished. This committee doesn't think subversion is a joke. This country—"

The rest was lost, background noise as Ben stopped listening again. The laughter, small as it was, was taken by Minot as an affront and Ben saw that Bunny was right, he was losing the audience, confusing them, his confidence turning petulant. Even his staging was off. He had kept the other witnesses in the room, but that meant they were now only a few feet away from Schaeffer, avoiding eye contact, their testimony suddenly personal, everyone smaller.

One of the publicity assistants, hurrying in, squatted down next to Bunny, leaning over to whisper in his ear.

"What?" Bunny said out loud.

Minot looked up, then smiled to himself.

Bunny left, huddled with the assistant, half the room watching.

"What did he say?" Ben asked Dick.

Dick shrugged. "Something about Lasner."

A summons from the studio, Bunny on call even here. But when he came back ten minutes later his face was grim, disturbed. Something more than a studio crisis. Ben looked at him, waiting.

"They've called Mr. L," Bunny said.

Ben took a minute, thinking this through. "He can get it delayed," he said.

Bunny shook his head. "They'll tell the papers he asked. Which means he has something to hide."

"Does he?"

"Don't be ridiculous. The only Reds he ever knew were fighting cowboys. Bastard," Bunny said, looking toward Minot. "To drag him into this."

Minot, noticing, smiled again.

Bunny left for another call, then two more, a small frenzy of activity, back and forth.

"I have to get to the studio," he said. "The lawyers want to coach him. Hal, too."

"Hal?" Ben said.

"He worked on *Convoy*. Bloody picture, we didn't even make money on it."

"We didn't?" Dick said. "I thought—"

"In second release, yes."

"The trades liked it. They said I—"

"Dick. Nobody could have done it better," Bunny said, impatient, his tone weary, like rolling his eyes. "I have to get back."

Before he could leave, however, Minot had called a break and they were trapped by the crowd in the hall.

"Bunny," Schaeffer said, extending his hand. "Don't worry. Nobody's taking pictures."

Bunny shook it. "I'm sorry, Milton. You know what it's like."

He looked around the hall. "I know what this is like anyway. How's Sol?"

"They're calling him, Milton."

"Sol? What for?"

"What for."

"Because I worked for him?"

"No, he's doing a picture with Stalin. What for."

"This wasn't my idea, Bunny."

"I have to run, Milton."

"Bunny. They're not going to pick up my option. Not after this. I can work quiet. No credit."

"I can't, Milton," Bunny said, meeting his eyes. "I can't." He glanced over Schaeffer's shoulders. "Look sharp. Here comes Judge Hardy."

Schaeffer moved away without bothering to turn, as if Minot were a scent he'd picked up in the air.

"You said you wouldn't call Mr. L," Bunny said, his mouth clenched.

"We both said things."

"Call it off."

"The subpoena's been issued."

"Dismiss it."

"You think the studios run this town, don't you? Nobody elected the studios."

"He's not a good enemy to make."

"Neither am I. Don't get yourself in a swivet. You tell Lasner to behave. He cooperates, everybody's fine. He gets to be a patriot and I get to send a message."

"To whom?"

"You think it's still twenty years ago, picture people can do anything they want. What did Comrade Schaeffer say? Things change."

"Don't do this. I mean it."

"You mean it." He made a face. "I appreciate the advice."

"Want some more? Professional? You're flopping in there."

Minot blinked, then looked at him steadily. "Things'll pick up tomorrow."

Ben decided to leave before Minot had finished with Schaeffer. The testimony had grown repetitive, used up. Once Schaeffer had admitted to being a Communist, Minot was left with the less exciting story of what he'd actually done, discussion groups and petitions and rallies no one remembered. Still, a Red in the industry—how many more?

He found Hal in the cutting room, finishing the last of the camp footage.

"I thought you were with the lawyers," Ben said.

"I was. Now I'm supposed to be thinking of anybody who could have been—you know. So I thought I'd get this done. In case things get busy. I hear Dick did a little flag waving."

"It's that kind of occasion. What did the lawyers tell you?"

"Be polite. Don't volunteer. Make him work for it. Whatever that's going to be."

Ben leaned toward the Moviola. "Didn't we already cut this?"

"I was just trying something."

"What?"

"Seeing how it would work without the Artkino footage," he said, self-conscious, trying to be casual.

"How does it?" Ben said quietly.

"You don't want anybody saying—" He looked away. "It's just in case. You have to pick your fights. You want this made."

He ran into Lasner in the Admin men's room, a surprise since his office had its own bathroom.

"Lawyers. It's the only place I can get some peace," Lasner said to him in the mirror, his face sagged, slightly withdrawn, the way it had looked during the street fight on Gower, trying to make sense of things. "So you were there? What's he going to want?"

"Keep himself in the papers for a while."

"No. From me."

Ben joined him at the sink. "To go along. Treat him like a big shot."

"That's what Bunny says. It'll blow over. What'll blow over? I don't know, a man comes, eats in your house, you make a party for him, and then this. So maybe Bunny doesn't know what he's talking about, either."

"It worked with Dick. It was all right."

"Did I know I was hiring Commies? Jesus Christ, Milt Schaeffer. If that's what the Russians got, we don't have a thing to worry about."

"He's not trying to make you look bad."

"I thought you knew something about pictures." He raised his hands, framing. "You argue with him, you're a Commie—sticking up for them, same thing. You don't argue, yes sir, you're an idiot for using Milt in the first place. Either way, he's a smart guy and you're a putz."

Ben said nothing.

"So that's what everybody thinks? Bunny. You. Keep your head down. Be a putz."

"He can make trouble for the studio."

Lasner nodded, conceding the point. "When did that happen? I've been thinking about that. When did we let that happen, he wins either way?"

Ben looked at him, suddenly back with Ostermann. "A little bit at a time."

THE NEXT day a steady drizzle came with the morning fog, blurring visibility, everything beyond the next block only half-seen through a gray scrim. Bad weather anywhere else was just part of life. Here it became disturbing, a form of disillusion. Wet palm fronds drooped, pastel stucco walls streaked grime. Without the lighting effects of sunshine, the city was shabby, the realtors' promises turned into streets of disappointment. Traffic barely moved. The hearings would start late.

Ben turned on the radio to cover the dull squish of the windshield wipers and found Minot on the news, an interview from the federal building, predicting more revelations.

"Where's the front line in this war? Not some ditch, some atoll in the Pacific. It's in everything we see and hear, the values our children are being taught. The Commies don't fight where we can see them. They'd rather sneak something in with the popcorn."

Go to Berlin, Ben thought, there's a front line there—machine guns and checkpoints, right out in the open. Talk to some of the DPs, the ones from the east, watch how they scuttle away from the Soviet soldiers, an animal fear. But Minot never brought up the genuine horrors, the show trials and mass executions. Communism was for him a purely domestic threat. The Russians, the visible menace, weren't on trial— Milt Schaeffer was, who'd left the Party in '39. Assuming anyone really left. Danny apparently hadn't, working for them, according to Henderson, right up to the end. But doing what? Playing both sides against each other, or only deceiving one? Or had the loyalties become so tangled that he no longer knew? Ben grimaced, seeing Danny at the witness table, facing the committee, finally answering for whatever he'd done. Except that he had already answered.

Minot started with Hal Jasper. At first Ben thought, Bunny's lesson taken, that Minot was building his case, then realized there was a pettier motive—he wanted to make Lasner wait. He had been the big draw earlier in the hall, Fay on his arm, both smiling for reporters. Now, wedged in the Continental row with Bunny and the lawyers, he was just another witness, with Minot calling the shots.

"Mr. Jasper, it's our understanding that Mr. Schaeffer requested you for *Convoy to Murmansk*. Were you aware of this?"

"No."

"In writing. There's a memo to that effect."

Ben glanced over at Bunny. Something that could only have come from him, in more cooperative times.

"Can you think of any reason why he would do that?"

"No," Hal said again, not giving him anything.

"You'd never worked together before?"

"No."

"Had you done any action pictures? Before *Convoy*?"

"One or two."

"What were their names, do you remember?"

Hal looked puzzled, wondering where this was going. "*Apache Trail.* One or two others."

"These were Westerns?"

"Yes."

"Not war movies. And yet Mr. Schaeffer requested you. Someone who had no experience with this kind of picture. Why do you think that was?"

"The process is the same. You're still cutting action scenes."

"I see. Posses, convoys, it makes no never mind."

Hal said nothing, waiting.

"It couldn't have been for your political sympathies, could it?"

"No."

Minot smiled pleasantly. "Just your Western expertise. I'd like to show you a photograph. Put it up here on a screen so we can all see it." Behind him, a slide was projected, Hal fighting in Gower Street. "Now that fellow there, center right, I think we can all agree that's you?"

Ben saw Lasner shift in his seat, restless.

"Like to tell us where this is?"

"Outside Continental."

"And what were you doing there?"

"Trying to get to work."

"That's quite a commute you have there from the looks of it," Minot said, getting a laugh. "Now isn't it a fact, Mr. Jasper, that the police were called in to break up a union riot? Isn't it a fact, unless there's something wrong with my eyes, the photograph shows you in that same riot? Fighting with a policeman, in fact. And isn't it a fact you were later treated for injuries at Continental with Howard Stein—practically brought in together is my understanding? That's the Howard Stein whose affiliation with the Communist Party has been under investigation for years. That

Howard Stein. And that's his union outside in the picture and you in it, throwing punches with the rest of them. Now," he said, pausing for effect, "I don't doubt that Milton Schaeffer, a self-confessed Communist, confessed right in this room, in fact, admired your skills with Western movies. But isn't it just possible—I can't help feeling there's a chance of this—that he also liked to have people around who agreed with him politically? Requested people like that. Especially when he was about to make a few *changes* to the picture. Changes to make us feel a little better about the Russians. I'd just have to say this was possible. Now I'm not asking you to tell us which union you support or how you voted—that's your business. I'm just saying things like this," he said, pointing back to the screen, "might give somebody the impression you lean—" He broke off, covering the mike with his hand as an aide whispered in his ear. "Excuse me," he said after the aide left. "Now let's talk about *Convoy*. Yesterday we heard how all those Bundles for Britain ended up going to the Soviets instead. Was that already settled when you came on the picture or did Mr. Schaeffer discuss it with you?"

"No."

"No, he didn't discuss it with you?"

"That's right."

"Well, now, that's interesting, because we have testimony, and we'll get it sworn in later, that Mr. Schaeffer actually reshot scenes—a pretty expensive proposition I'm told—after consulting with you. Do you recall that?"

"We didn't have enough reaction shots. He took a few more, that's all."

"Reaction shots of who?"

"Brian Hill."

"That's the fellow playing the Russian. Make his part bigger, that the idea?"

"In that scene, yes."

"Quite a bit bigger, in fact. That's where he talks about the Russian people, isn't it. How they're hungry because the Nazis took over their farms. Now some of us were under the impression that all started a little earlier, when the Soviets did it, forced them into collectives, but we're not here to give history lessons and neither was *Convoy to Murmansk,* I guess. Just make the Russians look like all-around good guys. That was more the point, wouldn't you say?"

Hal said nothing.

"Wouldn't you say?" Minot repeated.

"I'm not sure I understand the question."

"Well, not so much a question. More a general impression."

"Of the picture? I thought Schaeffer did a good job, considering."

"Considering what?"

"He had to shoot it in a tank. Technically, it's a headache, Navy pictures."

"I meant your overall impression of the story line. What the movie was saying."

Hal shrugged. "It was a U-boat picture. A war picture."

"Did Mr. Schaeffer ask you to feature the Russians, when you edited scenes?"

"No."

"But you did in this scene."

"You cut to whoever has the dramatic moment. Who the audience would want to see."

"And in this case, they'd want to see Lieutenant Malinkov, our friend from Murmansk?"

"What the hell is this about?" Lasner said, his voice low, but loud enough to be heard in the row. Fay put a hand on his arm, shushing him.

"Were you aware at the time of Mr. Schaeffer's political affiliations?"

"No."

"I've been told that the editor is the unsung hero on a picture, the one who makes the real decisions. What we see up there, that's pretty much what you want us to see. How you want us to feel about it. You agree with that?"

"You can only work with what they shoot."

"A modest man. But Mr. Schaeffer put a lot of trust in you. From what

I hear, he gave you pretty much a free hand. Easier when somebody knows what you're after. Heart in the right place, so to speak. I'd like to return for a minute, if I may, to Mr. Stein. Your comrade, if I can use the word, in that little dustup on Gower Street. Was that the first time you'd met him?"

"No."

"Oh, you knew him, then."

"I've met him, I wouldn't say I knew him."

"Where'd you meet?"

"I don't remember exactly. Somebody's house. Socially."

"Come now, Mr. Jasper, it was a little closer to home than that, wasn't it? Would you like to identify the name Elaine Seitzman for the committee?"

"She's my sister."

"Seitzman's her married name?"

"Yes."

"A housewife. And a secretary. Isn't that right?"

"Yes."

"A paralegal secretary. Howard *Stein's* secretary for a while, isn't that so?"

"Her firm did some work for him once. That's a lot of years ago."

"Got arrested with him, in fact. A public disturbance. Or maybe she was just on her way to work, too," he said, smiling to the audience. "It seems to be an unlucky family that way. She introduce you to Howard Stein?"

"She may have. I don't remember. I only met him to shake hands."

"Even though she was working for him."

"Her firm worked for him."

"All right, I'm not here to contradict you. Her firm. She stay with them?"

"No, she left after she got married."

"But she kept working. This time for the government. Care to tell us in what capacity?"

"As a paralegal."

"I meant which branch of the government. Turns out it was the NLRB," Minot said, picking up a note. "That's the National Labor Relations Board, for anyone here doesn't know. Is that where they're recruiting now? Howard Stein's office?"

Ben noticed Ostermann raising his head at this, interested.

"This was eight years ago," Hal said.

"All right, we'll bring things closer to the present day, if you prefer. You know the public record's a useful thing. Memory can play tricks on us, but when you've got something down in black and white—I'm thinking now about a paid ad in the *Los Angeles Times*. Open letter to President Roosevelt with your name on it. Ring a bell? Organization called the Motion Picture European Relief Fund. Decent size, I guess. Whole bunch of names on the letter. Would you like to tell the committee what the fund was for?"

"To help refugees get out of Europe."

"Get them here, in other words."

"Here, Cuba, Mexico, whoever would take them."

"These were Jewish refugees?"

"Not all."

"Not all. What were you asking the president to do?"

"Change INS regulations. To allow more refugees in."

"And did he do this?"

"No. There was congressional opposition," Hal said, looking directly at Minot.

"Maybe they were a little uneasy, seeing who was making the request."

"Those people died," Hal said simply.

Even Minot paused. "Well, now I doubt that was Congress's intention."

"They still died."

Minot nodded. "I think everybody here knows that, Mr. Jasper. We fought a war to stop it. All of us. But right now I'd like to look at that letter you were sending the president. Remember who was on the steering committee?"

"No."

"You don't. Well, like I said, have something in black and white and it comes in handy. Let me refresh your memory." He picked up a piece of paper. "Quite a list, but I'd like to draw your attention to the S's. Milton Schaeffer. Howard Stein." He looked up. "Maybe this is where you met him. To shake hands."

"What, Hal's a Red?" Lasner said to Bunny. "Jesus Christ, this is the guy you said was going to help us?"

"Was."

Minot was reading more of the names. "Gus Pollock. Passed away, sadly, but I'm sure you know Mr. Pollock wrote more than letters. In fact, he got a cowriter credit on *Convoy*." He paused for effect. "It's a small world, isn't it? Mr. Schaeffer. Mr. Stein. Mr. Pollock. And of course yourself. All in the same letter. We could go on with this," he said, raising the paper, "but I think you get the point. A small world. But you and Mr. Schaeffer never discussed any changes. A small world. But you didn't know Mr. Stein from Adam in that street brawl." He shook his head. "It's quite a memory lapse we're talking about here." He glanced at the aide. "Why don't we recess now for a few minutes." He looked at his watch. "Say, fifteen. Give it some thought, Mr. Jasper. Maybe something will come back to you."

There was a rush for the phone booths in the hall, the sound of matches being struck.

"We can go in here," Bunny said, indicating a large room that had been set aside for witnesses and lawyers.

"I'm not going to sit around here all day," Lasner said.

"Take it easy," Fay said. "It's one day."

"If he gets around to it. We're looking at lunch next. Then what? Forget it. I'll be at the studio. Tell him to call me when he's ready."

"You can't," Bunny said.

"What, I'm under arrest?"

"You could be, if you leave."

"Sit," Fay said. "I know you like this. Sit down before you break something."

"They have coffee," Bunny said.

"I'm awake," Lasner said. "So we just wait till he's good and ready? To ask me what? Is Milt Schaeffer a Commie? He already said so. So what's the news? And what the hell's this about Hal's sister? Who's she supposed to be?"

"Rosa Luxemburg."

"Who?"

"Nobody. He wants to play sheriff, that's all."

Lasner looked at him. "Sheriffs are the good guys. This isn't right. A cutter, for chrissake. We're supposed to protect our people."

"He's got four lawyers, Sol. Ours. All he has to do is be polite. Yes, sir. No, sir. Thank you. And it's over."

"That's our legal strategy."

"Sol."

"All right, all right."

Ben watched him go over to Hal, Lasner consoling and blustery, Hal's shoulders sagging.

"Keep an eye on him, will you?" Bunny said to Fay. "He's not happy."

"Because he has to roll over and play dead? He's not good at that."

"Just don't let him pick a fight. What do we win?"

"I have so much influence."

"Minot wants to embarrass the studio. If Sol doesn't—"

But now he was distracted by one of the publicists with a small stack of phone messages, Continental not yet running by itself.

"He listens to you," Fay said to Ben.

"Sometimes."

She patted his upper arm, a kind of reply, then went to join Lasner.

Bunny was looking at the top message. "Now Breimer in casting. He's going right through the studio. Everybody who worked on *Convoy.*"

"You gave him Schaeffer," Ben said quietly.

"Schaeffer's at Fox," Bunny said, an automatic reply, then looked up. "I didn't 'give' him Schaeffer. They already had him as a Party member. Your wonderful brother probably. If you want to be technical about it."

"You gave him the paperwork to set it up. And now he's using it against the studio."

"He wouldn't be if someone hadn't—" He broke off. "Isn't it a little late in the day to be splitting hairs like this? Or is it all supposed to be my fault? Funny how things go missing. Maybe next time they should check the closet."

Ben said nothing.

"I still don't understand what she is to you."

"Who?"

"Who."

"Does it matter? She doesn't deserve this."

"Who does? Hal? My god, reaction shots." He stopped, as if his train of thought had run out. "All right, I thought Schaeffer would buy us a little peace in our time and now it's biting us in the ass. And now I'm the one putting out fires." He held up the messages.

"I'm just saying, don't give him any more."

"I don't *have* any more. Do you actually think there are Communists at Continental? Or did you find someone else on your brother's list?"

"His list?" Ben said, looking up.

"Whatever he was feeding Minot. If there are, let's not keep our cards too close to the vest. I've had enough surprises. Oh god, Liesl's father," he said, spotting Ostermann over Ben's shoulder. "Down here with the field hands. He thinks I'm ruining her. Her Von Sternberg or something. Imagine. Run interference—I've got to call Breimer before he throws a fit." He paused. "Look, blame who you like. There's plenty enough to go around," he said, looking pointedly at Ben. "But right now we're circling the wagons. I could use some help. Go keep an eye on Mr. L, will you? He trusts you. I can't think why."

Ostermann had been talking to Polly, his improbable new friend.

"She writes down everything," he said to Ben, amused. "Everything he says. Her Cicero."

"But you're not. Still nothing for *Aufbau*?"

"No. Who's on trial? For once, not the Germans. The Comintern? No. The New Deal, I think. A political exercise."

"It'll burn itself out," Ben said, glancing toward the cameras in the hearing room.

"Not yet. The start only."

Across the room, Hal was now standing with his lawyers, listening as he sipped coffee, his face pale, making his five o'clock shadow even darker. Schaeffer, who had requested him, sat farther back in the room, smoking, looking at the rain.

"So how do we stop it?"

Ostermann shook his head. "I don't know. In books, a brave man does it. Fights back. But I've never seen that happen."

They went back to their same seats, only Bunny missing, still on the phone. Schaeffer was on the other side of the aisle, quietly wiping his glasses, people talking around him. When he glanced over, presumably unfocused, not really seeing anything, Ben felt it had been to look at him, some reminder of Danny. Who'd fed Minot's files. Could he really ever have imagined Schaeffer as someone dangerous, one of the old comrades who needed watching? Ben sat up. But he hadn't known him then. Schaeffer had left the Party in '39, before Danny had arrived. Which meant Danny had got the information from someone else. His reports always checked out, Riordan had said. If he said to look, there was something to be found. Because he'd been there, too, Ben had assumed, like the meeting with MacDonald. But not this time. So who had told him? The Party didn't keep files to rummage through, like Minot. You had to know, be part of its secret world.

"Mr. Jasper, I believe you testified that *Convoy to Murmansk* was the first time you'd met Mr. Schaeffer."

"No."

"No?"

"No, I said it was the first time we'd worked together." He nodded apologetically. "I'm trying to be precise."

"We appreciate that, Mr. Jasper," Minot said, but irritated, unable to spring some minor trap. "So you knew each other."

"A little."

"Could you quantify 'a little' for us, Mr. Jasper?"

"A few times."

"More than once? Five times, ten times? To be precise," Minot said, playing to the room.

Hal raised his head, not answering for a second, as if he were taking aim. "More than once. Less than five. Somewhere in between."

"This was at his home?"

"Once."

"And the others?"

"Around."

"Around. Well, we'll get to those later. Right now I'd like to go back to the meeting at his house."

"It wasn't a meeting. A party."

Minot moved some papers in front of him. "Maybe we're not talking about the same occasion. I'm referring to the evening of March 7, 1941. You were one of the guests, I believe."

"That sounds right. I can't be exact on the date."

"The evening I'm referring to had people giving speeches for the European Relief Fund. Do the parties you attend usually include speeches?"

"It was a fund-raiser. And a party."

"I see." Minot picked up a magazine. "Are you aware that *Red Channels* lists the Relief Fund as one of their suspected Communist front organizations?"

"No."

Ben saw Lasner take out a pad and begin to write, a memo he must have forgotten, trapped at the hearing.

"And how had you come to be invited to this party?"

"I was a contributor."

"So you gave some money to this organization, and Mr. Schaeffer invited you to his home. This was in the nature of a thank-you?"

"Partly, I guess."

"And the other part was to raise more money? Did they actually collect cash?"

Hal looked at him steadily. "Checks, mostly."

"Not just spare change, then. Who else was at Mr. Schaeffer's party?"

Hal glanced quickly at the lawyers, some code they'd been waiting for. "I don't remember. Other people from the Relief Fund, I guess. The ones in the letter you have."

"But you don't remember which ones precisely?" Minot said, biting the last word. "Was your wife there?"

"Yes."

"Your sister?"

"No. It was an industry event. People in pictures."

"So you remember their occupations, but not who they were."

Lasner squirmed in his seat, jotting something down again, his breathing audibly impatient.

Minot pulled out a copy of the letter. "Let's see. Mr. Schaeffer, of course. How about Howard Stein? Was he there?"

Another quick look to the lawyers. "I don't remember."

"Gus Pollock?"

"I think so, I'm not sure."

"Not sure. Ben Friedman. Was he there writing checks?"

Friedman. Ben's mind went to Danny's list. Friedman. But not Ben, he'd remember his own name. Another Friedman. A voice saying it. He looked away from the table, trying to remember, hearing it instead. One of the newsreel cameramen was changing film, the other camera still whirring.

"Ben Friedman?" Minot said again.

No, Alfred. Alfred Friedman. He jerked his head toward the cameras, hearing the name, then stared, not moving, afraid even a blink would make it go away. Newsreel, a voice in a newsreel. Alfred Friedman. The camera panning across a group of men. Suits and uniforms.

Minot was talking again but his voice had become a background sound, like noises in the woods, Ben's mind racing. What did it mean? A man in the group. Follow the logic. His thoughts ran everywhere at once, water rushing downward, separating, branching off until it was stopped, blocked, then backing onto itself. If he knew Friedman, he knew the others, who they must be. Follow the logic, like gravity, one step flowing down to another. Then a split, a whole branch that led nowhere, stopped at Paseo Miramar. Unless Genia had been an accident after all, something that didn't need to fit. The cameras kept whirring but his mind was moving even faster, in a panic now, because while things snapped into place a dread was spreading through him, where all the logic led, Danny doing something that could not be forgiven. He felt himself growing warmer, as if the body could literally burn with shame. His brother. Someone Ben hadn't really known at all.

"What?" one of Bunny's assistants whispered, but Ben shook his head "nothing" and faced forward again. He tried to listen to Minot, something again about Schaeffer's party, but kept hearing Friedman's name in the newsreel.

Assuming it was the same Friedman. He needed to be sure, something more than instinct. One foot, then the other. But he kept moving in leaps. If he was right, then the list wouldn't be enough bait. They'd run to ground, not take any risks now. He'd need to offer something more, a direct threat, exposure. He glanced toward the press section, Polly's hand moving on a pad as she watched Hal testify. Ostermann looked up, his features suddenly Liesl's, the fine stretch to the chin, and Ben met his eyes for a second, then quickly went back to Polly. Did he owe Danny anything now? Was there ever a good reason for betrayal? Anyway, how could you betray the dead? This one would be for the still-living.

Assuming it was the same Friedman. He got up, crouching, the way people left the theater halfway through. "Phone," he said to the assistant, the all-purpose excuse, this time true. In the hall, he felt his pockets for change, heading for the phone booths.

"Long distance," he said, getting the coins ready.

The call took a while to put through but only a few minutes once the connection was made. Afterward he sat in the booth, his hand still on the receiver. The first piece, but not everything, the water still running in too many directions. Even now, when he thought he knew what

Danny had done, his mind kept drifting back to the Cherokee, to police details, instead of what he really wanted to know, why.

He looked up. Across the hall, Bunny was standing in the witness room, no longer on the phone, not doing anything, in fact, just leaning against the wall and staring. His chest moved in small heaves. Ben got up and went over, directly in his sight line, but Bunny seemed unable to see anything until Ben was in front of him. Then a quick blink, startled, his throat moving in spasms, as if someone were choking him, cutting off his air. He swallowed, constricted.

"You all right?"

He didn't answer, just swallowed again, his eyes talking now, screaming somewhere, mute.

"What's wrong?"

Bunny looked down at the phone, then back at Ben. "He's gone," he said, a whisper, all the sound he could manage. "Jack's gone." Then nothing, another swallow, trying to breathe, now that it was said.

"When?" Something to fill space.

"Last night. This morning," Bunny said, vague, but less ragged.

Ben looked at him, not sure whether to touch his arm, a gesture that might seem too intimate. Instead he nodded. "Go. They don't need you in there."

But Bunny still didn't move, mesmerized by his own news, all the echoes of it.

"They just called?" Ben said, trying to keep his attention.

"They had to wait," Bunny said, mostly to himself, his eyes getting moist for the first time. "Until they got the next of kin. They have to do that, tell them first. They didn't want to wake her."

"Who?"

"His mother. In Oregon. They had to tell her first. He's been there all morning."

"Go," Ben said again. "Really. There's nothing you can do here anyway."

"She wants the body shipped back. She can do that. Ship it up there. He hated it up there." He looked at Ben, catching himself. "I have to see him. Before they do that."

Ben nodded. "Go."

"I can't," Bunny said, looking down at his hands, an invalid displaying his paralysis. "I don't think I can drive."

Ben looked toward the hearing room, then gripped Bunny's elbow. "Come on."

In the car, Bunny said nothing, staring blankly at the half-visible streets, as if the rain were in his head, not something outside the window. Ben had to hunch over the wheel, peering out, watching for lights and corners.

"Is there anyone else? Besides the mother?" he said, trying to draw him out, but Bunny didn't even turn his head.

"Me," he said. "They're going to ship him up there."

After that, Ben let him drift, his eyes fixed out the side window. They took Washington all the way out, through Culver City, past the white colonnades of MGM, maybe next on Minot's list. More stars than there are in heaven. The rain stopped in Venice, leaving just patches of fog on the coast highway. At the Sunset turnoff Ben thought of Paseo Miramar, the sharp curves as slippery now as they had been when Genia had driven up. Why? An invitation to Feuchtwanger's? But he didn't know her. A convenient excuse for the other car, though, if anyone noticed. But no one had.

As they got nearer the hospital road he could feel Bunny stirring beside him, sitting up straighter, gathering himself. He even glanced into the side rearview mirror, a last-minute dressing-room gesture. Closer than blood. How close was blood anyway? More than obligation, scraps of shared memories? Were he and Danny even the same blood type? O-negative, the universal donor. Another thing he hadn't known, that didn't matter. But Otto's blood had, binding Danny in a kind of loyalty oath, while Ben had been somewhere else. Or was that just another excuse, another out for Danny? What possible out could there be, to have done what he did?

"At least it wasn't in action," Bunny said suddenly. "They just send you the dog tags. At least he's here."

They went straight to MacDonald's room, not bothering with the front desk, but it had been emptied out, the stripped bed not yet re-made, the personal things in the bedside cabinet already taken away. Ben thought of his mother's hospital room, another body whisked away before anybody could say good-bye, the white loneliness of it. Danny wouldn't know until a cable reached him, an ocean away, and by that time Ben had arranged the burial, all the family gone now except for the thin stream of flimsy V-mail sheets, the last blood tie. But how close was blood?

"Where is he?" Bunny said to the nurse who'd hurried after them.

"He's—downstairs. They're preparing the body. He's going to be—"

"I know. I want to see him."

"We're not supposed to—"

"I want to see him," Bunny said, not any louder, but in control. Ben remembered that first day at Continental, people making way as Bunny walked by.

He waited in the room, smoking on Jack's balcony while Bunny went downstairs. No mention of how it had happened. But people never liked to talk about that. How easy it had been to make Danny an accident, convenient for everybody. He touched the rail, thinking of the Cherokee. Why kill him if he were passing on the list? Unless he wasn't, another Danny fast one, but not fast enough. Or unless they were just covering traces, wiping every pawn off the board, Danny not important enough to be worth the risk of what he knew. Better if it died with him, everyone safe.

He turned, hearing Bunny come back. "You okay?"

"Yes, fine," Bunny said, his own voice again, embarrassed to be asked. "Thank you for coming." A polite, receiving-line phrase, as if the panic choking and the drive out had never happened.

"It's not easy. I've done it."

"What?"

"Been with somebody. After."

430

Bunny walked closer to the bed. "I had a scene once. In a picture. My grandfather, I think. Everybody upset, in floods. But it's not like that, is it? They're not really there. Just a body."

"I'm sorry, Bunny."

Bunny glanced up at this, then let it in, nodding. He touched the bed frame. "There wasn't anybody here. When it happened. He was alone." He stared at the bed for another minute. "Did I tell you? His playing—he had the lightest touch."

"Mr. Jenkins? Sorry to intrude." A woman in a suit, not a nurse. "Some papers to sign."

She looked over at Ben, hesitant, someone she hadn't expected, not next of kin, either, and for a second, less than a blink, Ben felt what it must be like to be Bunny, every quick disapproving eye movement, try-ing to explain him.

"Papers," Bunny said.

"Yes, for the shipment. The additional charge. The expense isn't covered in the monthly rate."

"I pay to ship him?"

"I'm sorry. I understood you were the responsible party. My records say all expenses."

Bunny looked at her, a final twist in. "Yes, that's right. All expenses. Yes."

He looked down at the bed again. For a minute everyone just stood there, not moving, and yet it seemed to Ben that he and the woman were disappearing, wisps of fog, the room itself receding, so that Bunny was completely alone.

"I'll be with you in a minute," Bunny finally said, an executive dis-missal, then turned to Ben. "You'd better get back. Mr. L will want watching."

"I can wait."

"No, we have some things to do here," he said. "Did his mother give any instructions?"

"She said, whatever you decide."

"Did she. The navy blue, then, I think. The worsted. *Not* the uniform. Where did you put his ties?" He turned to Ben. "We'll be a while."

"But how will you get back?"

"I'll have the studio send a car," he said, in charge again. "It doesn't really matter now. If anyone knows." He stopped, glancing at Ben. "Still. It's nobody's business."

Ben met his eyes. "Nobody's," he said.

He started back down to the coast highway but had to pull over at the second curve, unable to see through a new bank of thick fog. He felt back in the hospital room, everything white, gauze and empty sheets, Bunny standing in a void. But this white was moist air, beginning to drift, the other had been still, an absence. The dead are gone. And yet we hold on—a loyalty, a debt, to make up for something. Didn't he owe Danny that much, to let it die with him, a crime that could only bring shame now. Paid for. But who had decided that? What do we owe the dead? Dress the body, the blue worsted, keep the memory intact. What did he owe Henderson, willing to use him as bait? There were all kinds of debts, even, finally, one to yourself. Do the expedient thing. Or the crime would go on, maybe taking him with it. Danny's name was a price, but the dead never blamed you.

He sat for a few more minutes, trying to think. The list wasn't supposed to stop at Danny's mailbox. But nobody had moved yet, playing safe. He had to make them come for it. Something public, a spotlight they'd have to put out. Another car was coming up the hill, grinding slowly around the curves, the sound muffled, a little like the newsreel cameras. For a second he was back in the hearing room and then he was looking across to the press section, Ostermann watching quietly and Polly scribbling beside him.

He found Lasner with the lawyers finishing lunch at Ristorante Rex, the kind of place where they usually brought clients to celebrate deals, all black enamel and art deco ocean-liner trim. Today the mood was anxious, Lasner fidgeting, impatient.

"Where's Bunny?" he said when Ben took a seat.

"Something came up."

"Serious?"

Ben shook his head, knowing Lasner meant a studio problem. "He'll be here later," he said vaguely.

"So will we, by the looks of it," Lasner said, glancing at his watch. "The goyim like a long lunch."

"You should eat something yourself," Fay said.

"Talking to Hal like that. He's a Commie, his sister's a Commie. Hal. He couldn't wipe Hal's shoes."

"Nobody cares about Hal," one of the lawyers said, an attempt to smooth things over.

"I care about him," Lasner said.

"I didn't mean that. I just meant he won't be that way with you. He'll want to play it friendly."

"While he's stabbing me in the back."

"Where?" Fay said, running her hand over it, a calming smile.

"You hit the studio, you hit me. I built the studio."

"He's not hitting the studio, Sol," the lawyer said patiently. "I told you. He's making some noise. In a day or two, he'll take it somewhere else."

"Already we're getting calls from the exhibitors. What's going on? Why all these people from Continental? You know we depend—we don't have our own theaters."

"Well, neither will anybody else, the way things are going," the lawyer said.

"They get nervous, we're the first people they say no to. They're going to fuck Mayer?"

"Some language. That'll sound wonderful in there," Fay said.

"He sends Eddie Mannix," Sol said, ignoring her. "All the sudden they're booking musicals again." He paused. "You know how long I know Hal? His father was cutting for Sennett. Sennett, for chrissake, before that nose wipe was even thought of."

"Well, they're thinking of him now," the lawyer said. "And listening, so let's all just take it easy. You know what to do."

"Yeah, I know," Lasner said, still with a hint of defiance, but Ben could hear the nervous tremor under the bravado, as wary as anyone brought before a judge. "I never knew Milt Schaeffer was a Red. I'm as surprised as anybody. I would never have hired him. Continental doesn't hire Reds. We're certainly going to be more careful from now on. Thanks to you, Congressman. You want to see me hit my marks, too?"

They took studio cars the few blocks back.

"What's with Bunny?" Lasner asked Ben.

"A little fire to put out. You know."

"Everything's a crisis with him. Sometimes you have to step back. See the whole thing."

"That's what you should do, step back," Fay said. "You're getting all excited."

"You see Hal's face?" he said quietly. "Why would you do that to him? Guy like that. You know him," he said to Ben. "He try to sign you up for the Party? Labor agitator yet. Where? Fort Roach? You see the way he looked?"

The car pulled up to the curb.

"There's Polly," Ben said. "I'll meet you inside."

"That bitch," Lasner said.

"Wonderful," Fay said. "Be sure to say that when you're on."

Polly was surprised, then skeptical.

"What kind of drink?"

"To talk. I have something for you."

"What, something you tried to peddle to Ken? You're not exactly flavor of the week there."

"He didn't level with me. He's not leveling with you, either."

She looked up at this, caught, suspicion part of the air she breathed. "What do you mean?"

"Six thirty?"

She hesitated for a minute, then started to turn. "Don't waste my time. I'm not Ken. I've been doing this a lot of years. You have something for the column, call my assistant. It doesn't check out, don't call twice. I don't just print things, they have to check out. Then we'll see."

"Not for the column. The news page."

"Really. Just for me. And to what do I owe the favor?"

"I want something from you."

"I'll bet."

"It'll be worth it. One drink. You'll want to hear it."

"What did you mean about Ken?"

"That's what we're going to talk about."

"He's a friend of mine."

"Polly."

She looked at him. "What's this all about?"

"Six thirty. You pick the place. You don't want the story, at least you get the drink. I could give it to Kelly but I figure you could make a bigger noise. A hundred twenty-three papers."

"A hundred twenty-seven."

"On the other hand, he could use a break. He's lucky he's still got a job there, working for you on the sly. Not very nice of you."

She narrowed her eyes, enjoying this. "Well, I'm not. Very nice."

"That's why I thought of you."

Lasner was already seated at the witness table when Ben got to the hearing room. This time the lawyers sat behind, not flanking him, a subtle shift to suggest that he wasn't on trial, as Schaeffer had been, just there for a friendly exchange. Minot started with a formal appreciation for Lasner's giving up his valuable time to help the committee, implying that he'd offered to come, no subpoenas necessary. The approach was courteous, Minot's way of signaling to the other studio heads what to expect, his conciliatory tone something their people would notice and report back. Nobody was out to get anybody—they were, after all, on the same side.

"Now, Mr. Lasner, you are the president of Continental Pictures. How long have you held that title?"

"Since nineteen fifteen. I started the company."

"And before that it was Mesa Pictures?"

"That was one. There were a few others. We combined them to make Continental."

"I see. So a mighty oak from several acorns, not just one." He smiled, either at the line itself or Lasner's obvious confusion over it.

"You could say that."

"And how long have you lived in this country?"

"How long? All my life."

"Well, not quite all your life."

"Since I was a kid."

"And before that? Where were you born?"

"Poland."

Minot looked at a paper. "Yes, except then it wasn't Poland, was it, where you were. It was part of Russia. From what I hear in Washington, it's going that way again. Hard to keep them out." This as an aside to the committee, but pitched to the audience. "So you were born in Russia."

Lasner sat up straighter, his eyes now fixed on Minot. "We thought of it as Poland."

"But not officially. And after you left Russia you came here and became a U.S. citizen?"

"Yes, sir."

"And worked your way to the position you have now. A great American story."

"It's a great country," Lasner said.

"And may I ask your religion?"

Lasner glared back at one of the lawyers, a can-he-ask-this? expression. "I don't practice a religion," he said.

"But you believe in God, I hope. Your parents, then. What religion were they?"

Lasner looked at him steadily for a minute, an assessment. "Hebrew."

"Hebrew."

"That's right. Why do you ask?"

Minot leaned forward, as if he hadn't heard. "What?"

"Why do you ask? Is this strictly a curiosity question or are you saying—"

"I'm not saying anything, Mr. Lasner, just trying to establish your background for the committee.

"I thought we were here to discuss Communists."

One of the lawyers touched his back, the way you pat a horse to slow down.

"Indeed we are. Now if you don't mind, let me ask the questions."

"I don't mind. That's what you're here for. But maybe I can save us both some time. You're a busy man. So am I. I didn't know Milt Schaeffer was a Communist when we hired him for *Convoy*. As a matter of fact, from what we heard here yesterday, he *wasn't*, so I'm not sure what this is about."

"He had been, Mr. Lasner. I'm sure you remember that testimony, too."

"You mean it's like having diabetes—once you get it, it never goes away?"

There was some laughter at this and Minot tried to ride with it.

"Mr. Lasner is known for being a colorful figure in the industry," he said to the audience, then looked back to the witness table. "But I know he agrees these are serious matters. You say you didn't know Mr. Schaeffer had been a member of the Communist Party. But you did hire him to direct a Russian-themed picture, is that correct?"

"It wasn't about Russia when we hired him. That came later."

"Why did you hire him, then?"

"He was available and he works fast. We had a deadline. You hire somebody like Wyler, we'd still be on the convoy."

This brought enough laughter to make Minot bang his gavel.

"Mr. Lasner," he said, wearily.

"All right. Why? He knows his way around a set. I liked his work. And I like him." He turned his head slightly toward the row where Schaeffer was still sitting. Behind Lasner, the lawyers huddled.

"There were no political considerations, then?"

"What political considerations? It was a picture."

"Now, Mr. Lasner," Minot said, switching tack, "you may not think about politics, but Continental's a big place. I don't imagine you do everything yourself. Who exactly decided to hire Mr. Schaeffer? The line producer, wouldn't it be?"

"A thing like that, it stops with me. It doesn't matter who the line producer was. You think I wouldn't know? You're just trying to get me to say—"

"Mr. Lasner, I'm not trying to get you to do anything but answer the question."

"No, you're saying I didn't know what was going on in my own studio. A bunch of Commies come in and pull a fast one, that's where you're going with this. Well, nobody pulled anything. Nobody was a Communist. Not that I knew of. Milt, I don't know, he says 'no' under oath, I believe him. You make a big deal he requests Hal. Everybody requests Hal. He's the best cutter in the business, something you'd know if—" He stopped, hearing himself, but only for a second, rushing now. "And Gus Pollock, you try to bring him in, make it seem—"

"Mr. Lasner."

"Wait a minute." He took up one of his papers with notes. "Passed away, you said. I hope it was just a mistake, your staff didn't tell you how. Gus came home in a *box*. A Silver Star. You think he was working against this country? But you don't mention that. And what's all this business with Hal's sister? We're after the steno pool now?"

Minot banged his gavel again. "Mr. Lasner, you're out of order."

"I'm out of order?"

One of the lawyers rushed up to Lasner's table, signaling at the same time to Minot, whose head had swiveled upward, as if he were literally scenting a change in the air. One of the cameras had moved closer, its motor drowned by the buzzing in the public section. Minot nodded to the lawyer.

"The witness's counsel is requesting a recess."

"We don't need a recess," Lasner said, his voice louder. "Let's get this over with."

Minot banged again. "We'll recess for ten minutes." He turned to the rest of the committee, who looked disoriented by the unexpected outburst, and shuffled some papers for the camera.

Sol's table was now surrounded by lawyers, blocking him from sight. "Are you crazy?" one lawyer said.

"He's an anti-Semite," Lasner said, still boiling. "You think I don't know when I see it? I know it like air."

"So what?"

"So what?" He stared at the lawyer.

"You never met an anti-Semite before? Had to deal with one?"

"All my life. I never *elected* one."

"You didn't elect this one, either. Now listen to me—"

Sol held up his hand. "I'm listening to you. Are you listening to him? You don't want to put a stop to this?"

"That's not up to us."

"Who is it up to, then?"

"Fay, talk to him."

Fay put a hand on his shoulder. "You all right?"

"I'm great."

She made a half smile. "I know. You're enjoying yourself."

"Gus Pollock, for chrissake. Comes home in a *box*."

"Fay," the lawyer said again.

"What can I tell you? He's a grown man. Am I his mother? If you ask me, they're with him," she said, pointing to the public section.

"There's a way to do this," the lawyer said.

"What way?" Lasner said. "Wait for somebody else?" He looked at Ben. "You're the one who showed me. What happened. We're making a goddam *picture*, what happens everybody waits. Who did he bring down here? The country club? No, a Jew business. I know," he said, catching Ben's expression, "it's not the same. But how different? You tell me. What? Wait for somebody else?"

Ben looked at him, then glanced quickly over to the press section, everyone standing and talking but Ostermann, who sat still, his eyes on the witness table, seeing something new.

"Not if you can do it," Ben said finally.

"Ha."

"Why do you say that?" the lawyer said.

"You don't have to ask me," Ben said to Lasner. "You're going to do it anyway." He paused. "He can hurt the studio."

"More?" Lasner said. He turned to Fay. "How many times I worried about that before? It doesn't change."

"Neither do you. You think it's still Gower Gulch."

"Where do you think he gets all this from," Lasner said, sweeping his hand to take in the room. "Pictures. He doesn't even *know* where he gets it, but it's pictures." He looked at Ben. "I know pictures."

"Then fight him with that," Ben said.

When they resumed Minot was sitting up straight, the papers in front of him stacked, everything back in control.

"Mr. Lasner, have you had enough time with counsel?"

"Yes, sir. Thank you."

Minot looked up at this, but played along. "Good. Now if we can continue."

"Certainly. But first I'd like to apologize if I expressed myself—"

"No apologies necessary, Mr. Lasner."

"It's just that I appreciate the importance of these hearings and I didn't want you to waste your time on—"

"We're not wasting time, Mr. Lasner."

"On *Convoy*. I mean, for all the people saw it, it wouldn't have done the Russians much good anyway."

"It was my understanding the movie was a success."

"Well, that depends on whose accountants you talk to."

There was an amused murmur, everyone in the press section now following closely.

Minot referred to a paper. "Mine said fifty thousand net."

"With second release," Lasner said smoothly. "Yeah, we made our costs back, I'm not saying that, but wartime that's not hard to do. Everything gets an audience."

"The military audience, you mean," Minot said, not even aware he was following Lasner.

"Overseas? They get it free. Part of the war effort. The industry paid for the prints, those pictures you used to see," he said, Minot suddenly a GI again, young. "The boys, we didn't make a dime on them. Wouldn't. Your gross was in the home market."

"And not enough of them wanted to convoy to Murmansk," Minot said, trying to be light, but sounding forced.

"Not until second release."

"And yet you're full of praise for Mr. Schaeffer—everybody who made it, in fact."

"It was a good picture."

"You say that even though—"

"There were timing problems," Lasner said, going somewhere else. "They put out a Bogart early so all the sudden we're up against that in the first run. Plus *Cover Girl* was still—you know, you're going to do tremendous business with a Hayworth."

Ben noticed that the names made the audience more attentive, as if the stars themselves had entered the room.

"Mr. Lasner," Minot interrupted, sensing this, "the fact remains that millions of people saw *Convoy to Murmansk*. We're not interested in the studio's account books. We're interested in what the movie had to say, how it was changed to say it. Now I can appreciate you want to make money, I guess most of us do, but we're here to see how these people work, how they get their message out when the rest of us are just going about our business—you up there counting your money—" He broke off, seeing Lasner's face grow tighter. "Now I also appreciate that as head of the studio, you want to take responsibility for everything that happens there, but one man can't do it all. These are people who know how to play on sympathies. It's not just what happens in the front office, who decides this or that, it's what happens on the ground—I guess we'd say on the sound stage. And what happens off."

"What happens off."

"Social life's an important part of the business, wouldn't you say? Sometimes you want to know about a person, you can tell by who he knows."

"You mean like you coming to my house?"

Minot said nothing, blindsided, barely noticing the ripple of interest in the press section, a new detour.

"I know what you mean," Lasner said. "People listen to us a while ago—" He raised his hand slightly, deflecting an argument. "My temper, I know. But they wouldn't think you'd been to my house. Had dinner. But maybe we have more in common than they think. This country, how we feel about it. Of course, I don't know what it says about you and Milt Schaeffer. I mean, both of you being there, at the same party."

"Mr. Lasner, we're not here to discuss my social—"

"Just Milt's, huh? I thought maybe the two of you had talked. You were the guest of honor. The point was to meet you. But there were a lot of people. Sometimes it's like that, you don't get to talk. At least this time it wasn't a fund-raiser, unless you were raising funds I didn't know about," Lasner said playfully, the scene his now, as if the tables themselves had changed places.

"Mr. Lasner," Minot said stiffly, "can we get back to—"

"I was just making a point. You said you can tell a lot, who people know, but, see, we can't really tell anything about you by the fact that you and Milt were both there."

"Your point being?"

"So Hal and Milt were at the Fund party. Does it mean anything, they were both there?"

"Those were very different occasions," Minot said, defensive now.

"I'll bet. I've been to Milt's parties. You're lucky, you get cream cheese on a Ritz cracker."

Everyone laughed, even Schaeffer, a little color now in his cheeks. Minot waited it out.

"Mr. Lasner."

"I'm just saying, we don't even know if they talked. You just said they were there, is all."

Minot stared at him, trying to close down the volley with silence.

"Because if you don't know anything more than that, there's no reason to bring it up, is there? It's just like you and Milt at the house."

Minot covered his microphone and said something to the other committee members, a quarterback running through plays.

"Mr. Lasner, I'm not going to debate this with you. The event we were discussing is part of a much larger web of association."

"What, like that letter in the paper?"

"Among other things."

"I was wondering about that. I wanted to ask you—"

"Mr. Lasner, we're asking the questions here."

"I'm sitting here all morning, I don't even get one?" he said, facing away from Minot to the rest of the committee, one of whom leaned over and whispered to Minot.

"Ask me what, Mr. Lasner?"

"That letter in the paper, for the European Relief Fund. You say Milt signed it. And Hal. Gus Pollock."

"That's correct."

"And you think that means something."

"*Red Channels* has listed the Fund as a suspected Communist front organization."

"What's *Red Channels*?"

"It's a publication that— Mr. Lasner, this is all beside the point."

"Not to me. Who are they to accuse me—"

"Nobody's accusing you of anything."

"No? You're pretty quick telling us Hal signed that letter. So they're all in it together, Hal and Milt and— But you don't say who else signed it. Take a look. Jack Warner, I remember. Selznick for sure. Even Mayer, I think, but I can't swear to that. I know they asked. How? Because I signed it, too. And gave them money. Is that why you got me down here? With a subpoena. Under oath. Because I gave money to save some Jews before they were killed? Are you calling me a Communist, too?" All the cameras had now swiveled toward him, the entire room pitched forward, waiting. "Who's *Red Channels*? Bring them here, so we can take a look. Let them call me that to my face." His voice kept rising, then dropped. "Or is that what you're doing? Calling me a Communist?"

"Mr. Lasner, this isn't getting us anywhere."

"No? Where are we going? I thought you got me down here to tell me there were Commies in the industry. Making trouble. And all you've got is Milt giving parties? Who's paying for all this, by the way?" He threw his arm out, expansive. "You got a budget on this thing or do the taxpayers just keep forking it over till you dig something up? All right, I'm under oath?" He raised his hand. "I am not a Communist. I don't even *know* any Communists. Milt wants to think it's a paradise over there in Minsk, let him, I don't care. I make pictures, that's all."

"That tell the American people what to think," Minot leaped in, visibly angry now, finally drawn out of public politeness. "Nobody here has accused you of anything except possibly a political naïveté so profound—"

"Naïveté, what's that?"

Minot stopped, flummoxed. "Innocence," he said. "A political innocence, or indifference, that allows people, clever people, to exploit—"

"Now you're calling me stupid?"

"To exploit an industry without your being aware of it."

"I don't know what you're talking about. But I guess that makes two of us because you don't know what you're talking about, either. Are we finished here?" He scraped back his seat, getting ready to go, startling the lawyers behind him. "Because I am."

"Mr. Lasner, with all due respect, you are testifying before a committee of the United States government. This kind of—grandstanding will not be tolerated. This is not a theater."

"No, a circus. A congressman. I expected better from you."

Minot flushed, as if he'd been slapped. "You are out of order, Mr. Lasner," he said, furious, his face twisting. "This is not Continental Pictures where you can strut around, make people jump just because you say so. This committee doesn't work for you."

Lasner looked at him, then stood up, a move so abrupt that the committee started with alarm. Two lawyers jumped up to hold him, but Lasner brushed them away, swatting flies, all the calculated restraint gone now, jabbing his finger into the air at Minot.

"That's just where you're wrong. You do work for me. I learned that in civics. That's a class you take when you first get here. From *Poland*. Maybe you ought to take it. You work for *us*. We pay you. We elect you. Once, anyway. And as far as I'm concerned, you're off the lot."

"Sit down," Minot said, rising himself, both glaring at each other.

"Or what? You going to put me in jail? Is that what happens when somebody stands up to you?" He turned to the room. "We should all watch this. What happens when you stand up to these people. Maybe you'll be next. Any of us. Anybody in pictures." He looked back at Minot, a beat while the room waited. Even Polly had stopped writing, looking around the room, disturbed. "What happens? Or do you think everyone will be too scared to stand up?"

Minot banged the gavel again, even though the room was quiet, mesmerized.

"You are still under oath."

"You want to know about *Convoy to Murmansk*?" Lasner said, almost shouting, so worked up now that the committee seemed to draw back, out of the way. "I'll tell you. Want to know who changed it? What Commie? Me. I asked them to change it. Want to know why? I got a phone call. From the president. We need your help. We've got an ally doesn't think we're pulling our weight. We'd like to show them we know what they're going through. A picture would be a big help. Is there anything we can do? Asking me. I had tears in my eyes. He's calling me. It was the proudest day of my life." He looked around, emotional, shaking a little. "The proudest day. And this? What's the opposite? I feel—shame here. Not of this country. I'll never feel ashamed of this country. I'm ashamed of you in it," he said directly to Minot. "I'm ashamed anyone listens to you. I'm going to work. You want to arrest me, do it here, because you won't get on the lot. That's me at the gate stopping you." He pointed to his chest and it was then that Ben noticed the film of sweat on his forehead, a white fleck of spit-tle in the corner of his mouth. Lasner leaned on the table with both hands, under the heat of the camera lights, almost vibrating with emo-tion, the same sweat and tremor Ben remembered from the train. "You want to make fun of me, go ahead. You think I 'strut' around? I do. I'm proud of Continental. And I'm not letting you have it. You think I don't know what you want?" He turned to the audience. "What he wants from all of us? He wants to take over. Tell us what to make. Who to hire. Who to fire. Well, I run the studio. Me. You don't tell me who works there. Milt," he said, turning to him, "you looking for a job? If he doesn't lock you up, give me a call." He turned back to Minot. "I run Continental, not you. Go tell Warner what to do. If he has any sense, he'll throw you out, too. You're finished here. If I can see it, with my—what's it? naïveté?—they can all see it. I thought this was about politics. About the good of the country. And what is it? Just another *pisher* wants my job. Not my studio. Not my—"

His hand went to his chest so fast that the room saw only the body slump forward, but Ben had been watching for it, waiting, so as he leaped out of his seat, pushing past the lawyers, he saw the hand clench, grabbing suit cloth, as if it could stop the pain by squeezing, then the head hitting the edge of the table as he fell over. There was a frozen mo-ment of shock, then screams, gasps, everyone standing, beginning to surge toward him, but Ben was already there, turning Lasner over on his back, reaching into his pocket.

"Oh my god," one of the lawyers said.

"Where are his pills?" Ben said, searching, not even aware he'd said it aloud.

"Here." Fay, dropping to her knees next to him, clawing at her purse, behind them a roar of noise.

"Give him air! Call an ambulance," Ben yelled to the circle around them, grabbing the pills and shoving two into Lasner's mouth. "Water."

A glass appeared out of the air and Ben forced water between Las-ner's lips, waiting to hear him choke, afraid the white, sweaty face was beyond responding. But there was a kind of hiccup, a faint sign of life, not yet gone. Ben undid the tie, tearing the collar open, as if the problem were air, not his heart. Lasner had cut his head in the fall, so now there was blood, too, seeping in a small stream, inching toward Fay's nylons. She was clutching Lasner's hand, watching Ben as he undid the collar, then massaged Lasner's chest, the rhythm a makeshift substitute for the heart, a pretense that you could keep life going from the outside. He bent down to Lasner's mouth, listening for air.

"Give him room."

Behind them the crowd tried to back up without really moving, pressing against each other. Polly had wedged her way to the front.

"Oh," she said, distressed, her hand at her mouth. "Is he dead?"

"Give him air," Ben said.

Lasner's eyelids fluttered open for a second, taking in Ben and Fay, the circle of faces, then closed again.

"Did you get them down?" Ben said to him. "Try one more." He pushed the pill between Lasner's lips. "Swallow. Try."

Lasner opened his mouth a little, obedient, and Ben watched his throat move, his face tightening with the strain.

The committee had now reached them, Minot pushing his way through. He stood for a second looking down, appalled and confused, then stepped back when he felt the flashbulbs go off, catching him looming over Lasner, an unintended boxing ring pose.

Ben took out a handkerchief and wiped Lasner's forehead, then held it against the cut to stanch the bleeding. "They need a minute to kick in," he said to Fay, then grabbed a folded paper and started fanning Lasner's face, forcing air toward him.

"Breathe," she said to Lasner. "Sol, can you hear me? The ambulance is coming." She tightened her hand on his.

Now that Lasner had responded, the crowd grew louder with talk. "All of the sudden, like *that*," someone said, snapping his fingers. Ben opened another button on Lasner's shirt.

Fay glanced up at one of the studio people. "Did anybody call Rosen? Dr. Rosen. Bunny knows the number." She turned to Ben. "You knew about the pills. What, on the train?"

He nodded. "It's worse this time. We have to get him to the hospital." He felt Lasner's wrist. "It's weak."

"I'm not dead," Lasner said, then winced.

The ambulance was there in a few minutes. As the crew lifted Lasner onto a stretcher, more flashbulbs went off. Fay grabbed Ben's hand, drawing him along with her. Lasner opened his eyes, aware of the movement.

"They're here," Fay said. "Just hold on."

Lasner struggled to say something, but managed only an indistinct sound.

"Don't try to talk," Fay said. "You've said enough."

Lasner glanced at her and started to smile.

In the ambulance, Fay and Ben in the back with him, Lasner began breathing more regularly, his color better.

"That's twice you're there," he said to Ben, his voice scratchy but intelligible.

"Shh. Don't excite yourself," Fay said.

"You see his face?" Lasner said.

"Quite a finish," Ben said.

"I told you. He didn't know how to play it. He's done."

"Don't talk crazy," Fay said.

"He should fucking go out and shoot himself. Like Claude Rains."

Ben laughed. Fay shot him a look, but Lasner, pleased, smiled and closed his eyes again.

"What did you give him?" the doctor said as they brought the gurney into the emergency room.

Ben handed him the pills. "Two, three."

The doctor nodded then said something to a nurse, ordering an IV, and after that nothing made sense, medicine its own foreign language. Ben and Fay were shunted aside into a waiting room, the air stale with smoke. Ben opened a window. Fay sat down, covering her eyes with her hand.

"Thank you," she said, and then neither of them spoke, trying to slow things down, all the urgency of the last half hour finally wheeled away somewhere else.

Ben glanced around the room: a pastel seascape on the wall and a stack of *Reader's Digest*s on a coffee table. No wonder people paced.

"How bad was it on the train?" Fay said finally.

Ben shrugged. "Not great. But he got through it."

"How many times can you do that?" She started to cry quietly and Ben looked away, giving her room. "What am I supposed to do? A house that size?"

After they moved Lasner to a room, Ben and Fay were allowed to sit with him, a vigil, until Dr. Rosen arrived and put them in the hall while he conferred with the hospital doctors.

"Is he going to be all right?" Fay said, when he came back out to them.

"That depends what you mean by all right."

"He's going to live?"

"Not like now." He looked at her. "No studio."

"He won't."

"He'll have to. This time it went off," he said, pointing to Lasner's chest. "It goes again, he's gone. I'm sorry, Fay. I don't mean to—"

She waved this away. "And that would buy him what?"

"I don't know."

"Odds?"

"I can't answer that."

"He'll ask. A few months sitting around? Is that all he's going to get anyway?"

"A month is a lot, if it's your last. A year—? What's numbers? Don't go soft on me, Fay," he said, seeing her face begin to tremble. "You're the only one can talk to him."

She flicked the corner of her eye, drying it. "Wonderful."

Bunny arrived when they were sitting with Lasner, awake now but not talking much, preoccupied.

"Now he gets here," Lasner said, but patted his hand, affectionate.

"Sol, I—" He didn't finish, turning instead to Fay, putting a hand on her shoulder.

"I'm going to be out a few days," Lasner said.

Bunny nodded, playing along, but his eyes were examining Lasner, appraising without the pyramid fingers, and Ben watched him grow paler, shaken, and knew that Lasner was dying, the doctor's assessment just something to comfort Fay.

"He didn't call Rosemary like we thought," Lasner said, talking business.

"He might."

"Let's release the picture anyway. Fuck him."

"Let's talk about it when—"

"We're talking about it now."

"No, you're not," Fay said, playing nurse. "Doctor's orders. Look at you. It's not enough for one day?"

"What do the doctors say?" Bunny said, but Fay didn't answer, instead rolling her eyes toward the door.

"What do they always say?" Lasner said. "Listen to them, everybody should go live in Laguna."

"Watch I don't take you there," Fay said. "You look tired. Close your eyes for a while."

"Don't leave," he said, a child's voice.

She put her hand on his forehead. "Never," she said softly.

Ben stared at Lasner, hearing his words again, an echo effect. But not the way Danny had said them, meaning something else.

"I'll come out with you," Fay said, dismissing them, and for a second Ben saw a twitch in Bunny's face, annoyed at their being lumped together.

Lasner managed a half wave from the bed. "Don't be scarce," he said.

In the hall, Bunny huddled for a minute with Fay, presumably getting a medical report, then joined Ben at the elevators. "I turn my back for two hours," he said.

"There was nothing anybody could do. Even you. He knew what he was doing."

"Mm. Putting himself in here. And Minot's back tomorrow."

"I don't think so."

"With a grudge. A little tantrum from Mr. L and you think he's all taken care of."

"He will be."

Bunny looked up sharply. "What do you mean?"

"Read the papers tomorrow."

POLLY HAD suggested the Formosa, and when Ben got there she was already settled in a red leather booth, nursing a Gibson.

"I went ahead," she said after he ordered. "Talk about a day for it. Gives you a turn, seeing that. I've known Sol a lot of years." She looked up, narrowing her eyes. Her hat, the mesh veil thrown back for drinking, was tilted slightly. "You were at the hospital. How is he?"

Ben shrugged, noncommittal.

"They said stable. Stable could be dead. I should probably be there, in case. But they just stick you in the waiting room. Anyway," she said, switching, "I have this meeting. Where you're going to give me a story and I'm going to do you a favor. Surprise me. Tell me you're not trying to get into somebody's pants." She finished off the drink and raised her finger for another. "So what do you want?"

"Want to hear the story first?"

"No. First tell me what it's going to cost."

"Minot fed you some material on Rosemary. I want you to kill it. For good."

"Christ," Polly said, picking up her fresh drink. "Her pants. That's not even a surprise."

"It would be to her."

"So why— Anyway, how do you know he fed me anything?"

"Because he did. Jump page stuff, I've seen the file. You can do better."

"With you." She looked at him. "Now why is that? You don't even like me, do you?"

"I think you're a cunt."

She stopped sipping her drink, then laughed into it, almost spitting. "Well, that puts it right out there, doesn't it?"

"It got your attention."

"No, I think you mean it. So why are we here?"

"To do a little business."

"You're lucky I don't throw this drink in your face." She stared at him for a second. "All right. What have you got?"

"You kill the Rosemary story."

"You going to tell me or just sit there and play with yourself?"

"My brother worked for Minot. A supplier. Trouble is, his supplies were tainted. He was also a Communist. A real one, Party member. Still active. The Communists have been setting Minot up. A lot of the stuff he's using he got from them. Some of the stuff he gave you, too, probably, but you don't have to mention that. Minot had a Commie working for him and didn't know it. To undermine the hearings, make him use bad information. Which could blow up in his face. Will. Unless somebody blows the whistle first."

Polly said nothing, just sat looking at him, then raised the glass to her mouth, her head shaking a little. "Somebody like who?"

"Brenda Starr," Ben said, opening his hand to her.

Another silence.

"And how do I back this up?"

"You have an exclusive interview with his brother. On the record. I can tell you how Minot's files were set up, how they marked the information from him. He ever give you any files direct? I'll show you how he sourced them. I can fill you in about Danny's Party membership. Since Germany. How he gave Minot stuff only another Communist could know. Not ex—still. You want to back up further than that, you can source Riordan. Off the record, but he'll back me up about the files."

"You can prove this? Documents?"

"If I have to. But I won't. Look where it's coming from. His brother. I *know*. Straight from him. Anybody comes after you, they're really coming after me. I'll give you an escape hatch. But who's going to deny it, the Commies? When I'm the source? Nobody else has this. Interested?"

She looked into her drink, thinking. "You didn't like your brother much, huh?"

Ben looked away. "Not much. Not now, anyway. That I know what he was. If he hadn't died, he'd still be doing it. Setting Minot up."

"How do I know you're not setting me up?"

"For what? Look, if you don't want it, I can go somewhere else."

"But you're so fond of me."

"You know you're the first person I met out here? Union Station."

"And I have some dirt on your girlfriend."

Ben shook his head. "Not only that. You hate Communists, everybody knows that, so who better? And it's your town. Maybe you deserve each other. But here's a chance to show what the Commies are trying to do to it. Minot uses this net with all these holes in it and who gets away? Who wins?"

"Look at you. The all-American canary."

"No, Minot's the all-American. Too bad he's also a fool."

"This would— Ken's a friend of mine."

"Don't make me laugh."

She looked over at him, bristling.

"Don't make me laugh," Ben said, slower this time, a lead-in. "I was in that hearing room today. Know what I smelled? Blood. You smelled it, too, didn't you? He's finished there, he made a fool of himself, even before it comes out how the Commies were using him. Lasner's going to die, and everybody's going to blame Minot. The whole town. Including you. The big funeral piece. One of the giants of old Hollywood. You can even throw in that fucking barn where DeMille started. The old days with Rex. You won't even have to say Minot bullied him to death, everybody already thinks it. They'll thank you for showing him up before he could go after anybody else. You have a lot of friends in the industry, it's where you live. He's just passing through, see what he can get out of it. And he's already on the floor bleeding."

He waited another minute while she digested this, her eyes wide, calculating.

"You want to do the interview we should go to your office, not sit in a bar. Tape it, if you want. On the record. I've got some paperwork, too. So you won't be nervous about using any of it. Do you want it? Part one?"

"Part one."

"There's more, but we don't want to throw everything out there right away. It's all page one, milk it. In fact, that's part of the deal, you saying there's more. Even more sensational. What Danny was doing beside feeding Minot. Exclusive from me. I'll help you write it."

"But you're not going to tell me what it is."

"I will."

"How do I know?"

"Because I'm promising you. Or another story, just as big."

"What?"

"A murder."

"Yeah? Whose?"

"Mine."

She blinked, then took up her glass. "Ha ha."

"Don't worry. I'm good for it. One or the other."

"You'd better be. You hang me out to dry and I'll kill you myself."

"So we lose the Rosemary story?"

"There's just one little problem with that. I gave it to Kelly. Not all of it, but enough to get him some space."

"Then pull it back."

"That doesn't leave him with much."

They met each other's eyes, holding their glasses as if they were looking over cards.

"Dick Marshall and Liesl. Inside the romance. Pictures at her place, by the pool. Exclusive."

She nodded slowly, still looking at him. "I remember that train. You're a quick study."

"It's an easy place to read."

"Yeah, I guess," she said, finishing the drink. "Union Station. And now here we are at the Formosa. They all go that way, don't they? All the stories here."

"Not all of them," Ben said.

POLLY WORKED for the afternoon paper so Ben spent the morning waiting, trying to keep busy. When he started stacking papers and arranging them in piles he realized that all this methodical make-work was simply a pretense, putting things in order while his stomach jumped, restless with nerves. He checked the gun in the drawer. Somewhere, miles away, paper had streamed through inked drums and been baled, thrown onto trucks. They'd have to come now. How long before they wondered what else Ben would say?

Bunny was already at the gate when Ben went down to check on the afternoon delivery. He glanced up briefly from the paper, then went back reading, handing Ben another copy from the pile.

"The phone's been ringing," he said, an explanation.

Lasner had made the front page with the picture of Minot looming over him, but so had Polly, the left lead. MINOT DUPED BY RED INFORMER. STAFFER WORKED FOR COMMIES SAYS BROTHER. Two columns with a jump to page eight, the entire story Polly had filed, including the more to come.

Bunny read through to the end, then folded the page under his arm. "My, what a big tongue it has," he said.

"Minot had it coming."

Bunny looked at him. "Every time I think we understand each other—we don't." He turned, Ben following. "There'll just be another one. Maybe worse. It's not going to stop."

"It will for a while."

"At least you kept Liesl out of it. Family feeling?"

"It's about Danny, not her."

"She was married to him." He paused. "If anybody remembers. I gather you promised Polly some pictures. She's already been asking. I didn't realize you were running Publicity now."

"I had to offer her—"

Bunny waved his hand. "Save it. I'm going to move up the release date. Before anybody remembers. So a spread will come in handy. By the pool, wasn't it?"

"The picture's ready?"

"Just the prints. I can pull a booking at the Egyptian."

"Not Rosemary's."

Bunny looked over. "No, not Rosemary's. We haven't booked that yet."

"You can. There's not going to be any trouble."

"Is that what this is all about? The girlfriend? Not both of you. Double dunking? You don't find that a little tawdry?"

"I just said—"

"Like one of those loops where they leave their socks on."

Ben just looked, waiting.

"As a matter of fact, we haven't booked it because we're doing some retakes. I think we can fix it."

"No other reason."

"No other reason. Now that you've chased all the storm clouds away. What else are you going to do for us? Just so I'm ready."

"Mr. Jenkins?" A secretary came up to them. "The union's here. About the musicians."

"Right there," Bunny said.

"Musicians? I thought Continental didn't do musicals."

"We didn't have Julie before. She's good. And we signed her cheap. It's worth a shot." Already head of the studio.

"Sam'll be happy."

"Well, there's that, too," Bunny said, dismissive, moving away. He opened the paper again, then shook his head. "No more stunts? Please."

"He lied to you."

Bunny handed Ben the paper. "Everybody lies to me. Mr. L will be pleased anyway. Like a one-two punch team, aren't you?" He looked up at him. "Fay said you saved his life."

"She's exaggerating. I was just there."

"He'll be grateful," Bunny said, his voice flat.

Henderson turned up an hour later.

"Everywhere I look, what do I see?" he said, tossing the paper on Ben's desk. "You all over the page."

The paper had landed with the bottom half faceup. A picture Ben hadn't noticed before, pushed below the fold by the Minot story: Kaltenbach at a press conference in Berlin, surrounded by men in bulky suits.

"I didn't know you guys read the papers," Ben said.

"You've got a mouth for brains, anybody ever tell you? Let's take a walk."

"You can give me the lecture right here. Don't worry, there isn't any more. The Bureau isn't going to come into it. If that's what—"

"Give me a preview. Tomorrow's edition."

"This is it."

"That's not what it says."

"We don't need any more. Once they see this, they'll come running. Look how fast you got here."

Henderson stared at him. Ben picked up the paper, scanning the Kaltenbach piece.

"So he made it."

"You didn't see it? He denounced Ostermann. A real German would come back, build a new Germany. Ostermann's a 'cosmopolitan.' Not even a German anymore."

"They made him say it."

"They'll make him say a lot of things. Drove himself to Mexico. Funny, isn't it, since he couldn't drive."

"Couldn't he? Who told you that? Danny?"

Henderson motioned his head toward the door. "Show me the lot."

Ben took him past the sound stages to the New York street, empty today, the brownstone fronts as silent as a ghost town.

"You're trying to get yourself killed," Henderson said.

"That was the idea, wasn't it?"

"The idea was to find your brother's mailman. Make him come after the list. Not after you."

"When did you get all protective? They've already tried once. We both knew how this was going to work."

"Not by going to the papers."

"What are you worried about? That I'm going to embarrass the Bureau? Give away state secrets?"

"What state secrets."

"That's right. There is no list."

"It's classified," Henderson said evenly. "It has to stay that way."

"It will. You think I'd tell Polly? I'm that crazy?"

Henderson turned. "I'm not the one setting myself up as target practice."

"Look, they know I have the letter. But nobody moves. Still safe. Even with you hanging around. But I go public, they've got to stop me. Come out where we can see them." He opened his hand. "Then you go to work."

"There's talk of bringing you in," Henderson said slowly. "Preventative custody."

"To prevent what?"

"You talking out of turn."

"That's why you're here?"

"I just said it's been discussed. People are nervous. Kind of thing, nobody ends up looking good."

"You forget, I came to you," Ben said.

"Well, let's just say you got to us anyway."

"Give it one more day. They'll bite now. We're on the same side here, aren't we?"

Henderson had stopped, looking at the street set. "There's nothing behind that, right? You look at those windows, you think there's a room there. It's something, how they do that."

Ben waited.

"You know, it's a funny thing, people in the field, I've seen it happen. They work so many sides, it gets confusing. They don't know which side they're on anymore. I think something like that happened to your brother."

Ben shook his head. "You didn't know him. We're alike."

Henderson raised an eyebrow.

"He knew. It just wasn't the right side. That was the hard part, figuring that out."

Henderson took this in, thinking, then started back. "I'm going to put a tail on you."

"Somebody could pick us off right now, if he wanted. What good would that do?"

"Might make him work a little harder for it. Find a better spot."

Ben glanced up at the set. "Unless he's already found it."

After Henderson left, Ben drifted back toward the Western set. Some workers were trimming branches off the giant cottonwood, the whine of their buzz saw drowning out the carpenters in the partial saloon, all the noises a comfort now, safety in other people. Beyond the cottonwood there was a stand of live oaks, where posses tied up horses for the night, and then the raised wooden sidewalk in front of the general store and the sheriff's office, lined with hitching rails. Had the real towns been any more substantial? Thrown together in a few weeks, the same dusty clapboard fronts and fading paint. He was standing now in the street where gunfighters faced off, hands hovering near their holsters. He looked down to the corner, half-expecting someone to appear. But it was too soon. There'd be some better plan. From the top of the building, someone with a rifle could take him with a single bullet. One shot, then glide away in the confusion as the carpenters raced out to the street. But it wouldn't happen that way, either. A hired *pachuco* at the Cherokee wasn't enough anymore. How much did Ben know, what had he already told Polly, how far had the stain spread? What Henderson didn't seem to understand, one reason Ben had set it up this way—first they'd have to talk to him.

He was still at his desk, waiting for the phone to ring, as the production units closed down for the day. He could hear people outside heading for their cars, the line of idling motors at the gate, the lot thinning out. He tried to imagine the call, wondered where the meeting would be set. Why not Paseo Miramar, a sentimental choice. But too public at this hour. When the door opened, no knock, he jerked his head up, every part of him alert.

"I was wondering how long it would take you," he said.

Liesl hesitated, still holding the doorknob. "I didn't think I was going to come at all." She walked in and put the newspaper on his desk, a presentation gesture, Exhibit A.

"You got all dressed up."

She glanced down at the bare-shouldered evening gown. "Publicity," she said, offhand, distracted.

"For *War Bride*? In that? More like Dick Marshall's bride. How's that going? Or isn't it?"

She stared at him, thrown, not expecting this.

"I told you. It didn't mean anything," she said finally.

"Well, neither did I."

She looked surprised again, slightly lost. "Is that what you think?"

He met her eyes, not moving. "Go on, say it."

"What?"

"What you were going to say. When you didn't think you'd come."

"Bastard. I was going to say what a bastard you are," she said, emotionless, repeating lines. "To do this to him."

"He's dead."

"And this is the memory you want for him? An informer? So everyone knows," she said, pointing to the paper, her voice stronger. "And now you're the good one. It means so much? To be better than him?"

"It's true. He was an informer."

"That's not everything he was."

"No. Worse."

She stopped, dropping her hand to her side. "What do you mean, worse?"

"Treason? What every Russian wants to know. What did Henderson call it? Our new order of battle."

460

"The list," she said, ignoring his tone. "You found out who they are?"

He nodded. "It took a few calls. Of course some of them don't have phones. They're nowhere. New Mexico, I guess. Like in the newsreel. That's when it clicked. I remembered Friedman. The Livermore lab. Berkeley. Bingo. In Danny's newsreel. At home. Maybe you watched it together."

"What are you talking about? What treason? You're going to put this in the paper? Make it worse?"

"That depends on how you read it. The Communists will think he's quite a guy. You do. Except for his love life. But maybe that was just a get-even screw. He didn't take her there, you know. The Cherokee love nest. That was your idea. That's not what it was for. Party business."

"Party business."

"You remember the Party."

"Remember what?" she said, confused.

"You were in it, too."

She said nothing.

"You came here to talk, didn't you? Let's talk. Don't worry, I'm not running to Minot with it. And Bunny will keep you miles away. Not even a hint of red. No idea what Danny was up to. Somebody else he duped," he said, looking at the paper. "But not over there. You'd have been a lot closer. Somebody he could trust. Doing what he was doing. You'd have to be one of them. I should have got that right away. Anyone from the outside would have been too risky. A death warrant. You'd have to be. Is that how you met?"

She looked down, shaking her head. "It was for him. A card even," she said, her mouth suddenly crooked, almost in a smile. "He couldn't. Too incriminating. They weren't so worried for me." She looked up at him. "I threw it away. A little ceremony. A new place, new start. For both of us. I thought it was anyway. He lied about that, too."

"And not you? 'Everybody was a little like that.' Isn't that what you said? The first night we went to bed, come to think of it. The first lie. One of them."

"You think there were so many. It was—in the past. Why bring it up again?"

"And I bought it. And went around in circles for a while. I didn't see a lot of things."

She stared at him.

"Something gets in your eye, a little speck, and you miss things. I kept seeing you at Genia's table, it kept coming back to you, and I'd look somewhere else. And then there we were drinking brandy—brandy—and I saw the glass and started seeing other things. The Paseo. Just visiting Uncle Lion if anyone had asked. The balcony. I remembered that in a clip. Girl your size. You just need leverage. The hospital. He said, don't leave me, but I did. I saw you there, too."

"Stop it," she said, her voice edgy, upset.

"Even then I thought I was just—seeing things. What could I prove? If I wanted to. It wasn't going to bring him back anyway. But not after the list. Not after I saw that. You should never have let me leave the house. I suppose you didn't think I'd move to the Cherokee. Right to the mail drop. That must have been—" He stopped. "You should have kept me close." He looked at her. "It would have been easy to do."

She met his eyes for a moment, then looked away, picking at the newspaper, something to do. "So now it's this. I'm a—what? A murderer? That's what you think?" She held her arms out. "Do you want to look? Maybe there's a gun in my dress."

"No, you just came to find out how much I told Polly. How far it's gone. And I'd tell you, wouldn't I?" He nodded. "The dress helps."

"Stop."

"Give me a name."

"A name?"

"I don't think you hired the kid at the Cherokee. A *pachuco*? That had to be someone else. Give me the next guy, who had the key. I can tell Henderson I got to him through Kelly, keep you out of it. They have him, they can roll up the rest. You retire. Unless they turn on you, but I'm betting they won't. But you retire. For good."

"Why would you do this? If I'm—"

"It's enough damage," he said, indicating the paper. "Right now Danny's a Communist who made a fool out of Minot. Some places that even makes him a hero. But this is something else. I'm not going to do it to him. Make him carry that mark around. So let it stop here. Let the Bureau have the others. And there's your career to consider."

She raised her head, about to speak, but he cut her off.

"No one else knew I had it. And didn't know what it meant. You saw that with Henderson at the border. Why didn't anyone come after me? Even Henderson was surprised. One try at the Cherokee and then— nothing. But by that time you knew it could stop there—Henderson didn't know where to go with it. You were safe. No one else knew, Liesl."

Her eyes opened wider at this, unsettled. "No one else," she repeated, a little breathless, catching up with it.

"Give me a name."

"How can you believe this?"

"What? Because of us? Let's not do that again. I thought—" He broke off. "Tell me something, though." He waited for her to turn to him. "Was any of it real? A few lines?"

She shaded her eyes with her hand. "A few."

He said nothing for a second, letting it settle. "Give me a name. Then let's talk about why."

The phone rang and her hand jerked away from her face, a startled reflex. They both went still, looking down, the second ring louder.

"Yes?" he said, grabbing the receiver, just to stop the noise.

The night operator, sounding bored. "A message from Miss Eastman. She wants to see you on Sound Stage Four."

For a second he didn't respond, as if he were still waiting to hear, the sound out of synch.

"Miss Eastman," he said, jarred, looking across at Liesl.

"That's right. Sound Stage Four."

Now he heard it, still looking at Liesl, his stomach beginning to slide. The floor itself seemed to move. He placed the fingers of one hand on the desk to steady himself.

"She just called?"

"The AD. Is there some problem? I called as soon as—"

"No. Thank you."

He put the receiver back. Liesl was watching his face, confused, then alarmed.

"What?" she said.

But he could only look at her, the room still sliding, everything wrong.

He picked up the receiver again. "Get me Carl at the gate, will you?" He waited for the connection, Liesl still staring at him. "Carl? Ben Collier. I want you to close the gate. Nobody goes off the lot, not until I call back. Got that? Anybody asks, say it's orders." He put the phone down, now feeling eerily calm. "You're asking for me on Sound Stage Four."

"I'm asking—?" She stopped as he reached into the drawer and took out the gun, checking it.

"Stay here," he said.

He went out the back of the building, then swung behind the writers' wing. It didn't have to be Sound Stage 4 itself, just anywhere on the way. He took a parallel route, away from the exposed main road, his eyes scanning side to side. A few grips were unloading flats from a truck down by the Western set, but otherwise the lot was quiet. The sun was almost gone, the dreary plaster walls now a light apricot. On the other side of the street, the prop building's hangar doors were still wide open, spilling out bright light. Acres of tables and settees and mirrors, stacked chairs, all of it easy to hide behind if you'd planned it that way. He felt the gun in his hand. What could he say if anyone saw? Slinking behind buildings with a gun. But these weren't real streets, people carried harmless guns between sets all the time.

The door to Sound Stage 4 was closed but not locked, the red light off. He opened it and stepped into a darkness so complete that he felt swallowed up in it, like a stray crack of light. He fumbled behind for a switch. The utility lights flashed on, not as bright as overhead stage lights, but enough to see the set, the wood-frame backing and ramps for wheeling the cameras. Ben blinked, disoriented for a second. It was the nightclub in Rosemary's picture, the bar just where it had been but the dance floor repositioned, down a short flight of stairs, the tables dressed now in white cloth with center lamps, swankier. He stepped carefully toward the bar, using the long mirror to check the space behind him.

"Liesl?" he said, playing along. He moved his arm in a slow circle, the gun pointed, ready. "Liesl?" he said again, his voice the only sound in the big space. He stood for a second, just listening. Quiet enough to hear a watch, someone breathe, but there was nothing, then suddenly a creak, a foot on wood, and he turned to it, not expecting the explosion, the noise of the shot, his hand burning, a searing pain as his gun fell and he clutched his hand, already smearing with blood. He ducked, an instinct, to reach out for the gun on the floor, then reared back when another shot went into the wood next to it.

"The next one goes in your head," a voice said, coming out of the shadow at the end of the bar. He waved his gun, motioning Ben back as he stepped forward, finally reaching Ben's gun and kicking it aside.

"Dieter," Ben said, still in pain, clutching his hand.

"Did you think we were going to play with guns? Like cowboys? Who is faster? Don't be a child."

"Dieter," Ben said again, trying to focus, watching his hand run with blood.

"What a trouble you are, this family. This time it's not so easy to arrange. Bullets. There'll be questions." He paused. "If they find you."

Dumped somewhere, off the lot. Another accident? The thought darted in and out of his mind, not yet ready for it, still hazy with surprise.

"I don't understand." But even as he said it, he did, all the scenes coming back to him now with a different face. A brandy glass. Don't leave me. Dieter also at the hospital, more than just family. Ben tried to remember the sequence—racing for the doctor, Liesl where? The nurses' station? Just a minute or two, all that would be needed. Concerned. In Danny's room. Don't leave me alone.

"What?" Dieter said.

Everything snapping into place. His hand throbbing, just the first shot. Keep him talking.

"Who told you about Genia?"

Dieter moved his head, physically taken aback. "At such a moment that's what you want to know?" he said.

"Liesl told you."

"Liesl," Dieter said, dismissive. "You told me."

"Not Liesl," Ben said, as if he hadn't heard.

"You. On the beach. After Salka's lunch. A great favor to me, to know that. I had to act. If she talked to you, she would talk to others. I was always secret. Only someone from those days would know and here she was, talking to—well, Otto's son, maybe she thought it was all right. But no discipline. Even Otto's son. Something happened to her in the war, I think."

"So you killed her."

"I had to," he said easily. "Once you told me. So I thank you for that. You know, I have an idea that she knew. What had to be done. When I called her, she came, no questions. The old discipline."

"Because she was a threat, just knowing you," Ben said, still stitching things together.

"Do you have any idea what we are doing here? How important it is? They're making weapons so powerful—well, that's for another time."

"I want to know."

"Why? You'll be dead. What can it matter to you? Or do you think someone's coming to save you? Texas Rangers, maybe. The marshal," he said, drawing the word out, sarcastic. He shook his head. "No one is coming."

Ben glanced around. His gun had been kicked toward the door, too far away. Something else. A nightclub table to duck behind. A bottle to smash. Any kind of weapon. But what was real? If he smashed the bottle would he have jagged glass or breakaway Plasticine? The stage telephone, the fire alarm, everything useful, was behind him, impossible to reach. Keep talking.

"You're not going to kill me yet."

"No?"

"Not before you know how much I know."

"It doesn't matter what you know. You'll be dead."

"Or how much I told Polly."

Dieter looked at him.

"You don't want to kill her if you don't have to. You don't want that kind of attention."

Dieter sighed, a mock concession. "So what did you tell her?"

"First you tell me."

"What?"

"Why you killed Danny. I want to know."

Dieter shrugged. "I said, it's a difficult family. Always their own ideas." He nodded to Ben. "Not in the beginning. Otto's son. Anything we needed. But this place, it changed him. The life here. Liesl."

"Liesl?"

"You know a wife changes things. In France, I thought, well, it's good, he can get her out, he'll make her serious. But it was the other way. *Kino,* this stupid *Quatsch* he makes. She was ambitious for him. No politics here, it's another country. Well, what did she know about it? So he has to hide it from her, the work he does for me."

"Hide it?"

"Of course. What would she think? Her father."

"Slow down," Ben said. "Her father."

"That was the beginning. They wanted someone close to Hans." He smiled. "Him they worried about. The Conscience of Germany. What did he think? Who did he see? So Riordan talks to Daniel, they know each other from those movies, he thinks Daniel's a good American. Well, he was a good American. But also a son-in-law. Close, you understand. So he comes to me. What should I do? And of course I see at once what a thing this is. At first, even, suspicious—what if it's a trap? But no, an opportunity. To work with the FBI. To have a man there.

Not high up, but still. Just how they make the files. The organization. Even this is valuable. They want to watch the German community? Good. Show them where to look. Imagine, Hans Ostermann's son-in-law. Their man inside."

"Their spy."

"Well, what was there to spy on? Even Brecht. Daniel tells them about the girlfriend, and of course that's all they can see after that. They even follow him to New York. Where does he sleep at night? How long does he stay? *Quatsch*."

"But not you."

"Me? I don't have girlfriends. I don't go to New York. I salute the flag. I'm happy to be alive. I think here it's paradise. My colleagues. My numbers. It's all I need, my numbers. Nothing else in my head. It's more interesting, Brecht's secretary."

"And some of those colleagues are at Northridge."

"Yes, some. And I know what some of them do. So that's one piece. And of course they investigate us. Are we loyal? Can we be trusted? Look at my FBI file, a German, yes, but now American. It's all in the file."

"And Danny knew what you were doing?"

"There was a loyalty there, from Otto. He knew the FBI was watching the émigrés—his family, his friends—why not protect them?"

"But not the other? The work at the labs? The weapons?"

"It's so important to you, this distinction? He worked for us. He was one of us."

"But he didn't know."

"You have to understand how this *worked*," Dieter said patiently, wrapped up in his story now.

Ben looked to the door again. The fire alarm. But he'd be dead before he pulled the lever. Get Dieter to take him off the lot, wherever he was going to stage a disappearance. There were still people outside. He wouldn't want to be seen dragging a body to a car.

"No one knew," he continued. "Just his piece. Daniel wasn't at

Livermore. Or Cal Tech. Not out in New Mexico with the Project. He was here, making these foolish reports. Making them look where there was nothing to see."

"Away from you."

"I was a messenger, that's all. But nothing could come to me. I had my security clearance, but you couldn't risk the mail. They still look. It had to go somewhere else."

"What did he think it was? All the mail."

"Party matters. A convenience, for me. I was always secret, you see. He understood that. Otherwise I wouldn't have been able to work."

"But why help Minot?"

"Another opportunity, to make them look somewhere else. He had credibility. Do you know how valuable that is? The Bureau could vouch for him. Anything he said—"

"But Minot was after Communists."

"But which ones? Hollywood," he said, his voice brushing it off. "Circuses. Of no importance. But think what it means. Minot asks the Bureau to help him. Investigate. Verify. They're not supposed to do it, but of course they do. Time and men, all for this distraction. They catch one, they want more. You see? They were right. More time, more men. So give them another. But always the same kind. Of no importance to us."

"Party members?" Howard Stein. Milton Schaeffer. Written off. Distractions.

"The Party here is never going to amount to anything. It's not a political force in this country. A cover, sometimes, but now that's difficult. So, another use. A small sacrifice. Old members. People who left in 'forty. Some actives. These people are of no consequence. So Daniel cooperates. It's useful to us."

"And what about the people he gives them?"

"What about them?" He looked at Ben. "Another sentimentalist. So you're alike that way. 'Why are we doing this to—?' Well, whoever. To ask such a thing. No discipline. Not like before. Something changed for him here."

"That's why you killed him? You asked him to throw them somebody and he refused?"

Dieter smiled, the idea itself unlikely. "No, he started reading the mail."

"And realized—"

"Not immediately. But then, yes. What we were doing. What *he* was doing, too, don't forget."

Ben saw him in the screening room, running the newsreel over and over, each time worse, smothering.

"So he decided to stop," Ben said. The crucial point, the one redemption.

Dieter nodded. "And *told* me. Imagine the foolishness. I should stop, too. Not just stop. Give the Bureau names in exchange—for what? Clean hands? There are no clean hands. Foolish. But dangerous—all our work. What else could I do?"

"How, exactly?"

"How? What is the point of this? You know how."

"Was he unconscious? When he went over?"

"It matters to you, to know this? Yes, on the head," he said, hitting his own. "I thought the fall would kill him. A very strong head."

"So you went to the hospital. To make sure." Don't leave me. A pillow. A minute.

"A long wait," Dieter said, annoyed, as if the inconvenience of it still rankled. "Are you finished now?"

"How did you get out? The Cherokee. You locked the door—you had your own key, you must have—so everybody would think he'd been alone. And then what?"

"I left," Dieter said simply, the question not worth raising. "Everyone was in the alley. So I went out the front. I had a story, if anyone asked. I was family, and I'd been worried about him and now, my god, too late— But nobody asked. So."

"One more. How did you know I had the list? Did you miss a pickup?"

Dieter shook his head. "It was not so regular. It was late, in fact. But you had to telephone. First at the faculty lounge, then even on the mountain. What's so important, I thought, to call from the mountain?

And you're living there, you said—Liesl never mentioned that. A worry. So I listened."

"And then had someone waiting."

"Another strong head, it turns out. But here we are. So. Did you tell Polly?" He tilted his head. "Or are you just trying to buy time. Waiting for the *marshal*."

"No marshal. Just us. But you don't want to kill me here."

"No?"

"Carl has orders not to open the gate. My orders. So it would be a lot easier to have me drive you off the lot." Picked up by Henderson's tail. "You don't want anyone finding bodies lying around."

"More *Kino*," Dieter said, almost sneering. "And then the fight and you save yourself. Not with that fist anyway." He nodded to Ben's hand.

"You won't get through the gate."

"Change the orders. Call." He jerked his head toward the phone behind Ben.

"What if—?"

"There are no what-ifs. Say one thing wrong and I'll put a bullet in your head. Mine, too, if I have to. So it ends here. No need to explain anything."

Ben looked at him, thrown. "Why?"

"Make the call."

"You'd kill yourself? You can't really believe in it anymore. Not after everything."

"I did believe in it. So that's something. You don't—betray that."

"Just your own people. And kill them. What did that feel like, killing Danny? All those years."

"It will be easier to kill you. You wouldn't keep out of this. Daniel—" He stopped. "I don't know why he changed. 'I won't do that to my country.' Foolishness. What country? We don't have a country."

"Not Russia?"

"Russia," he said, a hint of scorn. "No, no country. The future. The rest is—politics. They want to scare themselves to death here. Look under your bed, what do you see? A Communist? No! So give the fools a few Communists. But not the weapons. You don't give weapons to children. You can't put guns in their hands."

"Just yours." He looked at Dieter, suddenly weary, something seeping out of him with the blood. "Do you listen to yourself anymore? The future." He shook his head. "It was a mistake. You wasted your life on a mistake. Like my father."

Dieter stared back, surprised, as if he'd been struck.

"And Danny."

Dieter said nothing for a moment, then motioned the gun toward the phone. "Make the call. Slow steps. Not too fast."

Ben turned, feeling Dieter following behind. A fire alarm lever he could pull, but that would be a suicide move, the bullet in his back before the lever was down. Overhead light switch, but not the master switch, a fuse box farther away. The phone itself, some kind of coded message out? But Dieter had already thought of that, reaching around to pick up the receiver himself, the gun close to Ben. He asked the switchboard for the front gate, then handed the phone to Ben.

"Carl? Mr. Kohler," he said, a name all the émigrés still thought he used. "You can open the gate again." But would Carl hear the name change or simply recognize the voice and move on? "Sorry for the inconvenience," Ben said, but Dieter was waving him to finish and hang up, and Carl didn't reply.

"Over there," Dieter said, indicating the stage door, the smaller one people used, not the huge sliding wall for the sets, activated by a button switch.

"You can't hide a body in here," Ben said.

Dieter pointed to one of the large black storage cases stacked by the wall. "Move the light out of the way." A flood lamp, heavy.

Lights. He looked back to the nightclub set, the floods already set up, spotlights hanging in rows from the high rigging, a boom set up for a mike, the camera at the top of the ramp, pointed down toward the dance floor. Lights, camera, action. A phrase he'd never actually heard on set. All right, people, let's go. Okay, Jimmy? Action. But never the full phrase. Why was he even thinking about this? A case big enough for a body. Do something. He's going to kill you. Lights. Already connected, ready to go tomorrow. Action.

He flicked the switch on the lamp, swerving to face Dieter, a blinding light in his eyes, like a flashbulb that kept going, so that he raised his arm against it. An automatic response, a second, enough to let Ben duck and roll away to his right, into the set, hidden by one of the tablecloths.

"Don't be stupid," Dieter yelled, but the flash had disoriented him. He headed toward the door, the logical place for Ben to have gone. Ben moved farther into the set, a kind of desperate table hopping, until he was under the platform for the band, then out behind, moving slowly counterclockwise. Lath and plaster. Dieter moved over to the flood lamp, still bright, and tilted it down, beginning to search the tables, a lighthouse sweep to the bar.

"Come out," he yelled, focused now on the bar, an easy hiding place.

Ben tried to remember where his gun had gone, slithering across the floor. Toward the door. Exactly in Dieter's field of light. He had now reached the camera platform. Across the dance floor, the long shine of the mirror behind the bar. Dieter was still moving the light, shafts reflecting off the mirror, his back to Ben but still between Ben and the door.

Ben heard the sound of his own breathing, a ragged panting, and tried to close his mouth, holding it shut. A vacuum quiet. You could actually hear a footfall, the faint mechanical turning of the lamp. His whole body tensed with a feral alertness. Not like the war, people yelling over all the noise, shell explosions and the whistle of flying shrapnel. War was about luck. This was something else, a hunt, crouching with ears up, waiting to hear a twig snap.

He looked behind: the shadowy clutter of the sound stage, cables and dolly tracks, equipment that never appeared on screen. The sound console. A diversion. He breathed out a little and slipped over to the panel, trying to remember how it was operated. No time. He shoved a whole row of switches, hoping for anything, and got the squawk of feedback, then ran in the other direction. Dieter swung the light around, walking carefully now toward the sound, pausing at the foot of the ramp to peer into the dark behind of the stage, using the lamp as a kind of flashlight. Another sweep. Ben lifted himself up onto the platform, the upper tier of the nightclub, and crawled on his stomach toward the camera, his sounds still masked by the screech coming out of the console. Dieter took another step, wary, as if the sound were a trap, looking at each side of it, not hearing the clicks on the platform as Ben carefully unlocked the brakes on the camera wheels, the whole heavy weight now free. Action.

Ben rose slightly on one knee and pushed the camera to the edge of the ramp, the rubber wheels gliding smoothly, responsive, the way they would during a shoot, steady. It was only after they had tipped down the ramp, pulled by gravity, that they wobbled with speed, racing, finally loud enough to make Dieter turn and jerk away from a direct hit, so that only his leg was caught, the crash bringing him down, but not crushing him, knocking over the lamp, which crashed, too, sputtering out.

Ben rolled off the platform, running hunched over across the club floor, exposed now. He heard a grunt, Dieter trying to pick himself up, then a shot, louder than the sound console. He dropped flat, heard the smash of bar bottles as the bullet struck. Real glass, not breakaway. He lunged again for the door. The gun was here somewhere, but no time to look. Instead he reached up for the hangar door switch and pushed the button, then jumped away from it before Dieter could fire again, and moved along the wall, toward the console and heaps of equipment. Another grunt as Dieter got up, lurching toward the door, the obvious place, sliding open now, a loud clunking on its tracks. Where Ben would try to rush out.

But Ben burrowed deeper into the equipment pile, every sound hidden by the door motor, the console still squawking. He moved farther back. There had to be other exits, not yet lit up as this one was, the nightclub lights now spilling out in shafts onto the back lot. He raised his head to see Dieter standing in place, turning side to side, then reaching down to his leg, evidently hurt by the falling camera. The console would draw outside attention now, the soundproof stage open to the night.

Still aiming his gun at the door, Dieter started moving back to the panel to cut it off. There would be a fumbling with switches, just a few seconds, but a distraction. Ben kept moving back, picking his way over cables, afraid of knocking into something, an unexpected sound. Dieter was close enough now to hear, even with the door still winching open. It was dimmer here, almost dark, and then blank, a temporary wall thrown up to divide the stage. He followed it, feeling for a door. There must be another set behind, another outside door. His hand touched a knob.

He turned it carefully, hoping no light would shoot in to give him away, but the other stage was dark, the floor empty of clutter. Nothing was being shot here. He closed the door behind him and moved back to the outer wall. Suddenly the hangar door motor stopped, presumably all the way open now. The console feedback was lower, too, intermittent. In a second Dieter would find the panel switch, every sound Ben made audible again. Perfect for stalking.

He took another step and bumped into something waist-high, putting his hands out to steady himself, prevent anything from crashing over. A table? Some prop. He moved his hands over it. Big, a construction. Then, like Braille, plaster rising out of the smooth surface in jagged clumps, mountains. Japan. Continental's contribution to the war effort. He tried to remember the layout, how near it had been to a door. An entire country lying on trestles, waiting to be photographed, what the bombers would see. The console stopped.

Ben looked up. The quiet had become physical again, something you could feel. He heard Dieter moving, then saw the ceiling get lighter. More lights in the nightclub, Dieter now obviously at the central switches near the stack of camera cases. Ben looked at Japan. Nothing else on this part of the stage, not even a spool of cable. A few footsteps, Dieter exploring. Don't panic. He ducked down and slipped between the trestles, a hiding place. But all Dieter would have to do was shine a light underneath, catch Ben's eyes. He felt above him. The whole frame was supported by slats lying across the trestles, nailed in place to prevent wobbling. The diorama itself was like an attic crawl space—if you managed to climb into it, you could lie on the slats, off the floor. Japan over your head.

The spaces were irregular. Ben tried to wedge up into one, but couldn't get through. He tried to remember the shape, where the load-bearing sections would be. Think of it as a box spring, the springs clustered, not even. He moved toward the center, where the plaster would rise highest, allowing more wiggle room. A mountain range. If it worked anywhere, it would work here. He put his head through, then grabbed two of the slats to pull the rest of him up. His shirt caught, then freed itself with a tug. His feet were off the floor, another push with his elbows, then inching forward over the empty space onto another slat, trying to distribute his weight, slat, space, slat, space.

His head bumped into wood. Of course there'd be cross struts. His feet were still dangling, but he managed to draw them up a little, so that only his toes dropped over the slat. There was nowhere else to go, his body suspended now, his hands clutching hard to the slat on either side. The injured hand was still throbbing, and he tried to relax its grip. Maybe a bone had been smashed, shooting out darts of pain. But it wouldn't be much longer. Dieter would check the sound stage, then inevitably be drawn back to the door and out, the logical escape. Just try to stop breathing. Become, literally, part of the woodwork.

The floor beneath him got lighter. Dieter must have found more switches. These would be the utility lights above the catwalks, making the stage visible while the gaffers arranged the set lights on the rigging. The light would come straight down through the open ceiling, flat, not strong enough to make shadows. Ben clenched his hand on the slat again. Keep still. Footsteps on the other side of the dividing wall, a shout, as if Dieter were testing the echo effect. Over his head, lights were shining down on the simulated hills. It occurred to Ben, a surreal idea, that his body was under Hiroshima.

"Can you hear me?"

The voice seemed nearer. Ben held his breath. The slats might creak if he moved. In the silence, there was a sound so small it might be inside his head, light as a bubble popping, no, a drip, an invisible tap, a single bead of water. He looked down. Not invisible. A red dot on the floor, now another. Frantic, he looked at his hand, blood seeping, a line moving down off the side, then falling. He relaxed his grip, turning his hand. The line changed course but kept flowing down, another drip. There was nowhere to move the hand without shifting his weight. Impossible. But you'd have to be on top of it to hear. And now it fell on the previous drip, muffled, not like a fresh drop on the floor. He stared at the hand, willing it to stop.

"It's very foolish." Dieter's voice again, moving with him through the door, flicking on more lights.

Ben looked down. A tiny puddle, not a river. But still dripping, a little more quickly. Dieter had stopped, probably trying to figure out the map. Another minute, fascinated, like any set visitor.

"You know I have to do this," he shouted finally. "It's nothing to do with me." His voice lower, reasonable. What everyone thought, dropping bombs, firing into streets. Years of it, something that couldn't be helped. "You don't use the door," he said, loud again, not sure where Ben was. "Hide and seek. Shall I tell you my plan? It's good—no bullets to explain." He waited, as if expecting an answer back. Ben stared at the blood. "These places. They should clean up. Did you see the paint cans? Thinners. A hazard. One match. Well, a few, to make it all go at once. The door locked. It's a good idea, don't you think? A pity. A whole building for this. And such a way to die. To burn. What they say will happen in hell, it's so terrible. Much easier, a bullet. Quicker. You decide. One or the other. Are you listening?"

Another silence, Ben watching the droplets on the floor.

"I know what you're thinking. The fool leaves, I make an alarm. Ben. Not such a fool. It's easy to disable. I'm a good mechanic, did you know that? No alarm. The door locked. Yes, they see the light maybe. But paint makes so much smoke. You know most people die from smoke in a fire. Before they burn. So by the time— Are you listening?"

But it was Dieter who suddenly paused, hearing a noise, indistinct, behind him. Ben could see his feet move back to the partition door. "Hello?" No answer. Dieter waited another minute to be sure, then moved back toward the map. "So is it fire?" he said to the rafters.

Ben went still, watching the blood run along the floor, a thin line, but moving.

"We don't have time. With the barn door open," he said, a forced joviality. "Before the horses get out." Another pause. "So."

Ben saw his feet turn back to the nightclub and the equipment piles, stepping carefully, still listening. The blood seemed to be following him, almost at the edge of the trestles now. Leave. Even a fire would give him a chance. Dieter couldn't disable the sprinklers. Unless the heat didn't reach them in time, high up, designed to save the building, not someone trapped in it.

Dieter turned, taking a last look around the stage, and stopped. He began walking back slowly, coming directly toward Ben, shoes getting closer, not stopping until they were at the trestles. Close to the blood, but not yet touching it. Ben waited. Then he saw a finger reach down, swiping at the blood and moving up again. Was he tasting it or was the look enough? All he'd have to do now was shoot through the plaster, leaving Ben's body to hang, unseen for days, until someone followed the smell.

Instead his face suddenly appeared, crouched down. "So. Come out now."

Ben looked at him, gulping air. "Why?"

"As you wish," Dieter said, raising the gun.

Every second a bargain, maybe a chance. Ben began to wriggle back, dropping his feet, moving down to the floor and out from under the map. The line of blood streaked as he pulled himself up, now facing Dieter.

"The preservation instinct," Dieter said. "It's wonderful, yes?"

"Why didn't you?"

"Then burn down the studio? Such a colorful ending." He shook his head. "It's a question of attention. Something quiet." He motioned him toward the dividing wall, back to the nightclub. "A fire. Everyone wants to know. Questions."

"They're going to ask anyway. There are always questions."

"Not always," he said, nudging him with the gun into the nightclub. He swerved suddenly. "Who's there?" He tilted his head, listening.

"You're hearing things," Ben said. "Conscience?"

A diversion. He reached down to nurse his hand, hurting again, then looked up and stopped. The wall phone, its receiver dangling. Someone here. He moved to his left so that Dieter would face away from it.

"Stay."

A sound of movement, rustling, then a faint cling, something touching metal. Keep him talking.

"Hadn't you better close the door? The whole studio will hear the shot."

"Quiet," Dieter said, listening.

"Security would come running."

Dieter looked at him. "You're right. There's not much time."

More footsteps somewhere, a whisper, then a hum of one of the studio carts passing outside. Night sounds. Air moving through the cottonwoods. Carpenters. No posse coming. Dieter held the gun out before him.

"They'll hear it."

"Yes, I heard it, too. Where do you think it came from? Shall I help them look? But not there." He nodded to one of the camera cases.

A thump, unmistakable this time, inside the sound stage. Dieter swung toward the bar. "Come out!"

"I'm here," Liesl said, coming up behind him.

He whirled around and froze, taking in the gun in her hand, the improbable gown, the whole moment inexplicable. "Liesl."

"Stop. I can shoot."

"Get out of here. You don't know—"

"Yes. It was you. I know now. So you'd have to kill me, too."

"Don't talk crazy. Put down the gun. Where did you—?"

"By the door," she said simply. "Someone dropped it." She looked at Ben.

He started to move toward her, but Dieter stopped him with the gun. "No. We finish this."

"What do you want?" Liesl said. "Everyone shoots?"

"You won't."

"Yes, I can do it. It's loaded, I checked. I took the safety off. They taught me. For *War Bride*. I shoot a soldier who's trying to rape me. It's my secret. So I know how. Move away from him," she said to Ben.

He took a hesitant step, but Dieter grabbed his upper arm, holding him, gun still raised.

"No," Liesl said. "It's enough, Dieter. It's the end now. Not him, too." She stepped forward to maneuver him away from Ben. "Not him, too."

"You don't know what you're doing."

"Yes. Now I do." Her voice trembled a little, not as steely. "My god, do you know what I said to him? To Daniel. When he asked me? What to do? I said, 'Go ask Dieter. He'll know what to do.' The sensible thing. I sent him to you."

"And now what? You want to shoot me for that? A man who was unfaithful to you?"

She shook her head. "That? Little lies. But for you, big lies. To everyone. He didn't betray me with her—with you." She nodded at Ben. "Let him go."

"I can't do that," Dieter said calmly. "What do you think this is? It's real now, not acting."

But for a second Ben felt, the gun still pointed at him, that they had merged. She was still moving, glancing up quickly as if she were hitting marks, positioning them for a take, under her key.

"Go. You don't want to see this." Dieter raised the gun higher, to Ben's head.

"I'll shoot," she said, her voice not as steady, still moving.

"No. Shall I tell you what will happen? I have to shoot him. It's not so nice, to see that. It's better to leave now. You won't shoot me."

"My father was right. You never listen."

"Now," he said, then clicked back the hammer on his gun.

"Go!" she yelled to Ben, but all he heard was the explosion in his ear as his body jerked. For a second he wasn't sure whether he had ducked or whether this is what it felt like to be shot, pushed away by the blast. But it was Dieter who was staggering, the gun no longer at Ben's head, his hand clutching his chest. "Get away!" Liesl yelled. Ben dived to the floor, rolling to the side.

Dieter stood holding himself, his eyes disbelieving, and turned the gun toward Ben again, determined to finish. Ben saw the hand come up, the red patch on the chest, a sheen of sweat, still not dead. They stared at each other, the only people there. Then suddenly, with a *whoosh* of air, Dieter was crumpling, one of the overhead lights smashing down on him, a terrible thud as the heavy weight hit his body, pinning it to the floor. Ben heard footsteps running on the catwalk, Liesl's name being shouted, but his eyes were fixed on Dieter, gun hand sprawling on the floor, the heavy block of metal sliding halfway off his chest, his head already open, leaking blood. He bent over and took the gun from Dieter's hand, not yet trusting death, then looked up at Liesl. She was still holding the gun, her hand shaking now, eyes blinking. Behind her, someone was climbing down the catwalk ladder.

"Is he—?"

Ben said nothing, his head still pounding, everything around him slow.

She looked up to the empty spot in the rigging. "I tried to move him faster," she said vaguely, to no one in particular.

"Darling, you got there," Bunny said, visible now, a soft reassurance. "Are you all right?"

She handed him the gun. "So now I've done this."

Bunny took the gun, looking at it, suddenly queasy. He put one hand to his mouth, collecting himself, seeing Dieter's head in the pool of blood, then the gun again, his eyes darting. He breathed out. "Whose?" he said to Ben. "Yours?"

Ben nodded. "From the Bureau."

Bunny began wiping it with a handkerchief. "So it'll want explaining. You must have left it lying around. On your desk. So he—" He turned to Liesl. "Go and change. Before anyone comes. You were doing lines in your trailer, waiting for him. You know how people wander. When they visit." He held her arms. "All right? I'm sorry you had to—"

She was staring at Dieter's body. "We were fond of each other," she said quietly. "All my life."

Bunny glanced at her, alarmed at the trance quality of her voice, then held her arms tighter, almost a shake. "Well, that's what makes it worse, isn't it? These accidents—"

"Accidents?" Ben said.

"Darling, now," Bunny said to her. "Before the Keystones. I'll be there in a few minutes. Just stay calm. It's over." He looked at Ben. "Giving orders to the gate. Nobody gives the gate orders. Was that supposed to be a *signal*? Never mind. Off you go," he said to Liesl. "It'll hit you now, so be careful." He looked at her gown. "Something simple. A blouse and a skirt. All right?" He was moving to Dieter, placing Liesl's gun in his hand.

She came over to Ben, touching his bloody hand, then moving hers up to his forehead, brushing it. "So," she said, a whole conversation.

"Please," Bunny said.

"Come with him. I can't do this alone," she said to Ben, then left, slipping out onto the dark lot.

"Get rid of that," Bunny said, nodding to Dieter's gun, still in Ben's hand. He looked down at Dieter's body. "Are you finished now?"

Ben didn't answer, staring, seeing the police photo again. The same twisted body, same dark blood around the head, soon even a crowd around it. Finished. What had he expected to feel? This void? I found him. I know. But now there was not even that to keep Danny with him, no hold.

Bunny twisted something on the metal frame, his hand still wrapped in a handkerchief. "I had a hell of a time with these bolts."

"Accident," Ben said.

"Just what we're always afraid of," Bunny said coolly, arranging Dieter's body. "You should see the insurance premiums." He looked up, gauging the fall's trajectory. "People don't know. They think the equipment— Of course, visitors."

"He's shot. He has a bullet in him."

"Freakish, wasn't it? The crash, setting that off. People who carry guns should keep the safety on."

"You think they'll believe that?"

"Why not?" Bunny said. "It's what happened." He looked at Ben. "Isn't it?"

"You're covering up a—"

"Now you listen to me. Liesl's not going to be explaining anything. Is that understood? I mean really understood this time? She was never here. You came looking. People get lost on the lot at night. When they don't know where they're going." He paused. "You might thank me. The gun was pointing at you. And here we are—"

"I have to tell the Bureau. About Dieter. It can lead them to the next."

"I don't care what you tell them as long as nothing leads here. It's an accident in tomorrow's papers. They'll have to live with that. Make them," he said, looking at Ben, then away. "She's valuable to the studio. Anything else here needs taking care of?"

"Some blood under the Japan map. A camera got loose down the ramp."

"I saw. Naturally one of the new ones."

"Did she come to find you? Liesl? She was worried?"

"We found each other. Carl called. To check on the orders." He gave

Ben another look. "Your hand," he said noticing it. "You better get over to the infirmary. Patch it up. Think how you got it, will you? That makes sense? Maybe you cut it trying to get the light off him. In your haste."

"It's got a bullet in it. How do we explain that? The doctor—"

"It's the studio infirmary," Bunny said, then held his look. "I'll fix it."

SUNSET

THEY HAD SET up bleachers for fans down one side of the long temple entrance to the Egyptian and put the cameras and reporters behind a rope down the other, the red carpet between. The line of studio cars seemed to stretch all the way back to Highland, the spillover crowd craning necks to look into back windows, hoping for glimpses. There were searchlights and live radio feeds and an a party scheduled at the Grove, signs that the premiere itself marked a shift at Continental, the old modest openings something now out of the Gower Gulch era.

Ben looked at the giant posters behind the floodlit palms—Liesl with her head tilted up, her eyes fixed on the GI who was taking her home. The real Liesl was in a soft off-white gown and a fox cape, and her appearance had drawn *oohs* from the kids on the sidewalk. He watched her on the red carpet, surrounded by studio people, first greeting the audience, waving, then turning to tell the reporters how thrilling it all was. And wasn't it? The air was bright with flashing lights, something new, the rhythm built up, car after car, gown after gown, heady just to be part of it. Her escorts were in uniform to represent all the forces—everyone's dream war bride. Dick would follow later, another squealing entrance and another interview.

"The soldiers were a nice touch," Bunny said as they watched from the side. "You can feel it, can't you? It's going to happen. Look at them."

He nodded to the reporters, surging around her but keeping a distance, some invisible royal line, not pushing microphones in her face. Even Polly, speaking to her now on the radio, seemed respectful, paying court. Ben thought of Rosemary at Lasner's party, surrounded, everyone smiling. Her moment.

"What's it costing you?" Ben said.

"Don't keep books. How much is air time worth? Mr. L never understood that, either. These people haven't even seen the picture and look at them," he said, still fixed on the reception. "It just comes to her. They all have it, that instinct."

"Did you?"

Bunny didn't answer.

"You don't know her. She could walk away from it tomorrow."

"No one ever does," Bunny said, turning. "No one." He took out a cigarette. "You've been scarce. I've been meaning to talk to you. Come have a smoke." He drew them away from the temple courtyard into the lobby, waving away some ushers who darted over. "I wanted you to hear it from me. We're not picking up Rosemary's option."

"Why?"

"The picture's doing nothing."

"You dumped it."

"Now you're an expert on distribution, too. We didn't dump it. It's last year."

"So put her in something this year."

Bunny took a drag on his cigarette. "Look, I don't know what she is to you. But you're a big boy now. That's the way it is."

"You know what this is all about. You're going to let him tell you who to hire? He's finished."

"He's embarrassed. He's calling off the hearings. For now. He may even be in a little trouble next election. But he's still in office. He'll re-group. When this starts up again, Continental's going to be absolutely clean. No associations, not even relatives."

"Or close friends. If they're alive."

Bunny said nothing at first, squinting through the smoke, reluctant to cross a line. "That's right. If they're alive."

They looked at each other for a minute with the weary familiarity of an old couple, stuck together by everything that had happened, too tired to untangle it.

"Hal tells me the picture's finished."

"Some dubbing."

"You'll be thinking, what next? They were wondering at Fort Roach."

"They called you all by themselves."

Bunny stuck the cigarette into the sand of the standing ashtray. "They're winding down. The exhibitors don't want any more informa-tion films. The training films—"

Ben shrugged. "My separation papers'll come through any day."

But Bunny was going somewhere else. "They've agreed to a limited distribution. The Nuremberg picture didn't do what they hoped. This would be the last anyway."

"How limited," Ben said, alert, listening to code.

"Limited. Strictly speaking, we don't have to distribute at all. There's no agreement."

"Sol agreed."

"Well, Mr. L—"

"Is still head of the studio."

Bunny looked up. "Keep your socks on."

"You can't do this," Ben said, his throat suddenly tight. "Dump it. Not this one."

He saw the pan shot of the guards' faces, the slow walk into the camp, evidence.

"I'm not dumping it. And you're leading with your chin. Anybody ever tell you not to do that here?"

Lasner on the train, clutching himself, never weak.

"Show them what you really want?" Bunny finished.

"I really want this," Ben said, his voice steady. "It's important."

To whom? The dead, the survivors? It occurred to Ben that he had become a believer in images, their power to change things, even though of course they didn't. Show the faces. Maybe that's all it was, a record too late, but at least it was there. The dead are never avenged. All we can do is leave markers.

"I said limited. Major cities. After Christmas. Don't worry, you'll get your credit."

"It's not about that."

Bunny raised a disbelieving eyebrow.

"Sol wants this picture."

"So you keep saying. And I wouldn't want to disappoint him. He knows what the exhibitors are like, but if we can sell it as—"

"What do you want?"

"Want?" Bunny said, raising both eyebrows now. "I'm not a pawn-shop. It's a picture, not a watch. I said I'd do what I could." He paused. "What I'd *like*, though, is a little favor from you."

Ben waited.

"I hear you've been spending a lot of time at Cedars. Little chats."

"He likes to tell stories," Ben said carefully, wondering where this was going. "The old days. My father."

"Funny how that happens. He never used to dwell on the past." He looked up at Ben. "I know Mr. L pretty well. He gets—enthusiastic. He's likely to think things can happen that can't happen. That people can do things—and they can't, really. They don't know enough. They'd be in over their heads."

"They could learn."

"Not on this job."

"You're ahead of yourself. Sol hasn't offered me anything."

"Then it's a good time to move along, before it comes up. Fort Roach. Wherever. You don't want to disappoint Mr. L, either."

"How would I do that?"

"By having to say no. The job's filled."

Ben gave a quick half smile. "You really want this," he said, an echo.

Bunny looked up at him. "I already have it. Now take yourself out of it."

"That's not up to me. Or you. Sol's still head of the studio."

Bunny shook his head. "Not anymore. But that's something we'll keep to ourselves, shall we? Feelings being what they are. Acting Head is fine with me. Mr. L can live with that. As long as he does. Let's make it easier on everybody."

"And what's the favor? Go away? Why?"

"For Fay."

"Fay?" Ben said, surprised.

"There's a lot you don't know about running a studio. The first thing—I'll bet it's never even occurred to you—is who owns it."

"Sol owns it," Ben said, suddenly not sure.

"Not all of it. Not enough. You know that Rex still has his original eight percent. He's very excited about the television deal. Sam owns a piece, too, did you know? And I'm happy to say he feels very confident about the direction we're taking. So does New York. Very panicky they get when there's a health problem. They like a certain stability. That leaves Sol. Or, rather, Fay. I have enough voting stock to do it without her—I'm *already* running the studio, which seems to escape you. But it would be much nicer with. One happy family, not taking sides, squabbling over something that isn't going to happen anyway." Another direct look at Ben. "Some deathbed whim. Fay's been lovely to me. I'd like it to be her idea, too. Sol's idea. Not something that was forced on them in a proxy fight. And it wouldn't be, if you weren't here."

"You really want this," Ben said quietly.

"It's not a lot to ask, considering, do you think? Think of all the favors I'll have to do for Polly now, because of you."

"Don't do me—"

"Well, it's not just you, is it? Polly's a girl who hates being stood up. Vindictive, really. She still thinks you're holding out on her. But we don't want her going after you, opening things *up*. Looking into accidents. I've got seventeen writers and I'd still rather just let things lie as they are. Think of all the people involved. Luckily, Polly likes access to studio heads. She's not one to hold a grudge when there's so much else she might be doing. And of course, if you're not here, to put her in a temper—out of sight, out of mind."

"She won't be out of Minot's mind."

"Oh, they'll make up. Well, at least go back to their corners. They need each other, when all's said and done, always a point. A little go-between work and before you know it, it's lunch at Chasen's and off we go. It's you they won't forgive. There's nothing you can do for them."

"Only for you."

"For Fay, really. No point in having any unpleasantness. Especially when it's done."

"You're sure. Maybe you underestimate me."

"No. I did. Not anymore. Why do you think we're having this chat at all? This time, we need to understand each other. Lou," he said, voice raised, eyes over Ben's shoulders. "Good to see you. You know Lou Katz, from Abe Lastfogel's office?"

"Nice to meet you. Jesus, this is some night."

"Wait'll you see it."

"I hear, I hear. Listen, we should talk sometime about Julie. Who does a musical for two hundred dollars a week? I mean, it's wonderful what you're doing, a production like that at Continental? But she's wonderful, too."

Bunny nodded. "So let's keep her happy. Monday, okay? We keep the steps, but we can do something on the front end. Just don't plead poverty. Not the Morris office."

"What, it's for her. She's still in some crappy efficiency on La Brea."

"Not after this."

"Zanuck never saw it."

"Well, Sam Pilcer. He's got an eye. You know Ben Collier? He's producing a documentary for us. The end of the war. Footage you won't believe." He looked at Ben. "We think it's an important picture. *San Pietro,* in that class. Awards, even."

"Jesus, at Continental. How's Sol? I hear so-so. That was something, though, wasn't it? What he pulled with that fuck Minot?"

"Like something out of the movies," Bunny said flatly.

The others were moving in now, filling the lobby. Liesl was posing with the servicemen, two on each side. Her father, looking slightly lost, had arrived with Salka. She was beaming, reminded perhaps of the old opening nights at the Ufa Palast, but no one in the bleachers paid any attention. Only Polly recognized them, nodding to Ostermann, her neighbor at the hearing, now someone she mentioned in her columns. The Conscience of Germany. There was talk of a Nobel, she'd heard. Behind her, Kelly was holding her mike, doing a remote check. When he looked up he caught Ben's eye for a minute, an odd questioning, the sound stage accident mixed up with the Cherokee somehow, a scent nobody was following, Ben an inexplicable connection. But Kelly had moved on to another beat, no longer doing Cagney, and Dick Marshall was getting out of his car, the story he'd come for.

Ben went in, sitting in one of the back Continental rows, watching the rest of the audience kissing and waving across aisles, a party. Bunny hurried down front with Rex and Sam and some men from the front office, talking as he went, Lasner on the carpet at Grand Central. Little Brian Jenkins, quick as a bunny. Then Liesl came in between the Army and the Navy and the lights started to dim.

It was the kind of company audience that applauded the credits, little salutes to their friends. Imre Tabor, ten years out of Budapest, had directed, and Epstein had done the music and Simco the photography, all Europeans, but whatever edge they may once have brought had been smoothed out, maybe forgotten. It was a studio picture, bright, every eyebrow in place. Ben wondered for a second what might have happened to Kaltenbach if he'd stayed, got lucky with *Exit Visa*, shepherding Danny's story through rewrites. A vehicle for Dick. Stranger things had happened.

On the screen a process shot of ruins dissolved to a studio interior, the family waiting for the Allied liberation. Then Liesl's first appearance, riding a bicycle, hair blowing. Applause. Her face in close-up, young, fearless, the one Danny must have known. In a second a re-treating German soldier would grab the bicycle, force her into the door-way, struggle with her until she got his gun, shot him. The scene that would come in handy in real life, holding the gun steady in the night-club set, standing over Dieter on the floor. Ben standing there, too. Are you finished now? Bunny had said. Danny finally avenged. But how could you ever be finished with murder? An endless accounting. There was always more. Reasons. And once you did know, what did you do? Not all deaths are alike.

Liesl was heaving, distraught, racing to safety. Now the advancing GI who would discover her, deliver her, and then come to call. The war as Continental saw it. Not the rest of it, not what Ben had seen. He glanced down toward Bunny. There were a hundred ways he could in-terfere, keep the faces off the screen. Would it matter? What was it worth to them, already gone? Had it mattered to Danny, Dieter finally lying in a pool of his own blood? But it had to, somehow. To us. What if we never saw the faces, stayed in the dark?

He felt the hand on his shoulder just as the screen Liesl shot the gun, making him jump. An apologetic publicist, drawing him quietly out to the lobby, a waiting phone.

"He's asking for you," Fay said. "I know you're in the middle—"

"Is he—?"

"I don't know. He keeps coming back. An ox."

"But you called."

"I have a feeling, that's all," she said, her voice small, afraid.

"I'll be right there."

The same hospital smell as he walked in, sharp disinfectant cutting through air thick with blood and waste, the same as Danny's hospital, all of them. The linoleum in the corridor, just mopped, glared in the overhead light.

Fay was sitting in the room with Paulette Goddard, waiting to-gether, maybe as they'd once waited in casting offices to show their beautiful legs. Now they both looked drawn, sober, their usual sparkle muted. The way his mother might have waited for Otto, if she had been there, if any of them had. They squeezed his hand, a silent hello.

Sol was lying half propped up, eyes closed, his skin gray, thin hair pasted down with sweat. A plastic tube hissed oxygen in his nose, and a bottle hung next to him, dripping fluid through an IV. His face looked slack, old, the corners of his mouth white with dried saliva.

"How's her picture?" he said, opening his eyes a little.

"The audience likes it."

Sol grunted. "They're on the payroll."

"How are you?" Ben said, coming over to the bed, resting his hand.

"I'm signing up with Arthur Murray."

"I'll teach you for free," Fay said.

Sol smiled. "Let me talk to Ben for a minute. Why don't you and Paulette get something to eat? Like birds. A celery stick, they call it a meal."

Paulette came over and tapped his nose. "You want me to get fat?" she said fondly.

"Fat." He smiled at her. "Another pound wouldn't hurt."

"We'll be outside," Fay said to Ben. She nodded silently to a buzzer on the nightstand. "If you need me—"

"Go eat," Sol said. He waited until they left. "They're good girls. You know they go way back?"

Ben nodded. "How are you feeling?" His hand still on the sheet, seeing Otto's bed again. But there hadn't been one, no hospital room, a bullet somewhere, no one waiting outside.

"I feel like shit," Lasner said. "Don't bother with the pills next time." He closed his eyes, drifting a little. "You know on the train? The way you were? It reminded me. My first trip out here. Looking at everything. I didn't know what to expect. A desert. For asthma. Now—" He opened his eyes fully, lifting his head. "I want to talk to you."

"Minot called off the hearings," Ben said, heading him away.

"Yeah?" he said, pleased, then sank back against the pillows. "And then who? All these years. We made something great here. From nothing." He looked out, as if there might be marquee lights, not just dull hospital windows. "It's all going to fall apart now, isn't it?"

"No, it's going to change."

"At my age, same thing. That union business," he said, another thought. "On Gower Street, for chrissake. To see something like that on Gower. Clubs." He was quiet for a minute, thinking. "We had the audience. Now, I don't know. You know what I think it was? The war. Everything made money. You didn't have to think about the audience, maybe they want something else. Whatever you gave them. You think they don't change. But how do you go through something like that and not change? How's your picture?"

"Done. We'll put it out after Christmas."

A weak smile. "First Crosby and the nuns. Then the dead Jews." He looked at Ben. "So we did that. I want to talk to you," he said again. "I have to make some decisions."

"You just have to rest."

Lasner waved his hand. "I still get tired. I'm tired all the time now. You notice they don't send me home? I couldn't have nurses there? So what do they know I don't know?" He paused. "Nothing," he said, answering himself. "So maybe the only way I'm getting out of here is in a box."

"Don't talk that way."

"You don't have kids, you have to think about things. Who's going to take over? Keep things going. You remember on the train? Even then I had an idea. Somebody moves like that. Keeps his mouth shut. You don't always say what's up here." He pointed to his head. "That's like me. And Otto's kid. Christ. In the blood."

"Sol—"

"They even give you a—what's it? MOS? Even the government, for chrissake. You know what I'm saying to you? What I'm thinking?"

"I can't, Sol," Ben said simply.

Lasner waved his hand again. "Fay helps. You'd be surprised what she knows. And maybe I'm not out of here so fast, either, who knows? You pick things up. Me and Fay want it, New York goes along. Believe me, that's how it works."

Ben looked away, embarrassed, and reached for the water glass on the table. The way it used to work.

"Here," he said. "Drink a little."

Lasner took a sip. "There's no surprise here," he said. "Don't tell me that. I see you watching everything, figuring it out. You know what I'm saying."

Ben looked at him, feeling suddenly winded, caught. Be my son. Something no one had ever asked him before. Otto and Danny, one life passing to the other. He felt as if he were actually being touched, a stroking along his skin. Chosen. For something already decided, no longer in Sol's hands. And for a second he wondered if it were possible, Bunny's hold fragile enough to loosen. Would New York really say no to Fay, would Sam? A dying man's wishes? A fight he might be able to win, if he really wanted to. But even as he imagined it happening, shuffling people in his head, he knew that things had already been arranged in a new order, any attempt to upset them as futile as Lasner's grandstanding in the hearing room. Sol had already lost the studio. The point now was to salvage the rest.

"We've always been straight with each other, haven't we?" he said.

"Somebody says that, they're going to start pulling something," Sol said.

Ben shook his head. "You want to do the right thing for the studio? Call Bunny. He'll be good at it."

"He's a pansy."

"No," Ben said, not flinching. "He's you. He got everything from you. He can do it."

"And you can't?"

"Not like him. It's all he cares about, pictures. Like you. He's got the instinct."

"For pictures, maybe. But look with Minot. Just roll over. So who's going to fight the next one, him? There's always somebody coming after the studio. You want somebody's going to fight. You would. I saw you do it for Hal."

Ben shook his head again. "I don't even know who the bad guys are anymore."

Lasner made a face, impatient. "It's just this business with your brother. Whatever the hell he was up to. It's not like that. You don't know what's right, something like that happens with family."

"That's just it. I think everybody's like him now. Maybe that was the war, too. I think we're all in-between. Somewhere gray. Pictures were never good at in-between."

"What, gray? I'm offering you the studio," Lasner said, his voice rising, a gift so priceless any hesitation seemed crazy.

"Offer it to Bunny, Sol. He can fight. He's tougher than I am."

"You're tough enough to say no. To this. You don't want this? What do you want?"

He looked around the hospital room. What did he want? He thought of watching Liesl in the pool, of wearing Danny's clothes, a life that didn't belong to him.

"I don't know yet," he said. "Not this."

"Just like that," Lasner said, opening his fingers. "The whole goddam world."

Meaning it, Ben realized, the rest just something vague, east of Gower.

"I want the picture to come out. I want that."

"There's some problem with that?" Lasner said, suddenly alert.

"No, no. Bunny wants to give it a big release." He paused. "Talk to him. He'd appreciate it, I think, coming from you. Personal."

"Like you did."

"You know what it means to me? That you asked?" He looked down. "I'll probably regret it."

Lasner leaned his head back into the pillow. "That's what he said, too. Otto. When he took a powder. For Germany, yet. Christ, what a family. If he had stayed here, think where he'd be today."

At Cedars, Ben thought, the odd transference happening again, listening to the oxygen. Thinking about his credits. Wondering.

Sol closed his eyes.

"I'd better go."

"Stay a little," Lasner said, reaching his hand out to anchor Ben's. Don't leave me.

Ben felt the hand, still warm but light, as if it were disappearing.

"Think about it," Lasner said. "You don't want to decide too quick. Something like this."

"Okay," Ben said. Both of them saving face.

He glanced out the window, feeling claustrophobic. Another hospital room. His mother had held on to him, too. Danny. Now Sol— Otto—whoever he was. One more loss. How many people could you lose before there was no one left?

He stayed like that for a while, watching Sol's face, almost expecting the shallow breathing to stop, both of them at an end. You could hear the footsteps outside, rubber-soled, nurses answering calls. Just like the ones outside Danny's room, Dieter waiting in the hall. Picturing it over and over in his head, making the final cut. Not all deaths are alike. Then even the footsteps stopped, the hospital asleep. How long should he stay? Fay would want to be here. He slid his hand out from under, a silent good-bye. Sol opened his eyes again.

"What do you want?" he said, still puzzled, a real question.

Ben stood there for a second, then patted Sol's hand. "I want you to get some rest," he said, because it was better not to say anything else.

WAR BRIDE would be over now so he headed straight to the Grove. The afterparty was even more lavish than the premiere, fake palm trees this time but an orchestra and passing trays of champagne glasses. Liesl was being photographed yet again, hundreds of pictures tonight alone. Primitive peoples thought one could rob the soul.

"I wonder what her mother would have said," Ostermann said, making conversation, but stiff. "All this. Your own child. You're well? I haven't seen you since Dieter's funeral."

An endless afternoon in Pasadena, all the émigrés, long tributes from faculty members, flowers from Continental. Henderson deep in the back, just to see who came.

"She's a success," Ben said, nodding toward the photographers.

"Maybe it takes her mind off things. It's a difficult time for her. She was his favorite. Always spoiling her."

Ben thought of her looking down, the gun still in her hand. Another thing that had never happened. The camera bolt loose in the rigging, nobody's fault.

"I wish I'd known him better," Ben said, a polite phrase, now surreal.

"I've been wondering—you don't mind? When you asked me about the hospital. Daniel. Why did you want to know?"

Ben shrugged. "Loose ends. I was remembering that day, and then I couldn't. Like a crossword you can't finish. It bothered me, that's all."

"Ah," Ostermann said, looking at him blankly, a translation he didn't quite get.

"Don't mention it to Liesl. I think it still upsets her, thinking about it."

"Yes, but you know one has to be sensible. It was a mercy. So much brain damage. All the doctors said. He would have been—what? Who knows? But not himself."

"Still. Her husband."

"And your brother," Ostermann said slowly, wanting to say something, then deciding to hold back instead. "Ah, Liesl."

"Salka's looking for you," she said, kissing him on the cheek.

Ben could smell her perfume, something new. Her hair was shiny, lit up, and he thought of Paulette on the train, the same glow. Movie stars. She turned to face him, suddenly awkward.

"How have you been?"

"Congratulations," he said, taking in the party.

"You moved from that place," she said, ignoring this.

"I'm bunking in with Hal. Until the picture's out. Then I'm going back," he said, a decision just made, but clear, as if someone had turned on a light. "Work for the newsreel."

"Back? To Germany?"

"Wherever they send me," he said, suddenly filling up with it, the whole world east of Gower, where it wouldn't matter what Polly thought, whether Minot held a grudge, if you knew things you shouldn't know. Where everyone else lived.

"You're leaving here?" Liesl said.

"The picture's finished. There's no reason to stay."

"Maybe it's better," Ostermann said, then, self-conscious, began to back away. "Well, I'll find Salka."

"What did he mean?" Ben said, watching him go.

"He doesn't understand. The newspaper, what you said about Daniel. How you could do it. I can't explain. You know it's one of those things we can't talk about."

"Danny was spying on him."

"But to tell a newspaper—it's confusing to him."

"People always made excuses for Danny."

"Maybe we all need that. Someone to make excuses." She bit her lower lip. "Why are you leaving?"

"Too many people to avoid. It's easier to get out of the way."

She said nothing for a minute, taking this in. "You can't even look at me anymore. I always thought, a secret, it makes people closer, but it's the opposite. That's all we're going to see now, when we look at each other. What happened."

"Let's not talk about it. It didn't happen, remember?"

"That's why you never come to the house anymore?"

"I didn't think you'd want to see me. After everything. The things I said in the office." He looked over to her. "I made a mistake. I'm sorry. But that doesn't count for much, does it?"

"It doesn't matter."

"Yes, it does. To think that. You must have—" He stopped, meeting her eyes. "I'm sorry."

"No, don't be sorry. Not about anything."

He was still for a second then looked away, uncomfortable. "I have to go."

"Not like this. Come with me a minute." She began pulling him away from the club floor.

"The party's for you."

"For them. No one will notice. Come."

They went down the side hall to the parking lot entrance. Outside, the same scent of orange trees, the row of palms outlined beyond the cars.

"We've been here before," he said, the memory of it tangible.

"Yes. And then up with Dieter. And all the time he—" She broke off and reached up, putting her hand behind his neck.

"What are you doing?" he said, feeling her breath.

"We can't leave it like this. I know you. Why you said those things. You know what I remember? You said, 'Was any of it real?' So bitter. You already knew the answer. But it's wrong. It was real. I never lied to you."

"You just pretended I was someone else. Maybe I did, too."

She looked down. "Always the same. Always putting him there. He wasn't."

"You're in love with him."

"What a boy you are," she said, moving her hand across the back of his head, smoothing his hair. "You think it's like *War Bride*. Love forever. But how can it be like that? Nothing is like that. You know, when we first left home, left Germany, I thought it's all finished for me, everything. But then Vienna. France. All right, it's somewhere new. Not the same, but I can live here. I think it's like that. Not the same. Another place. But you can live there for a while. And you don't forget it, it's something special to you, somewhere you lived."

He looked at her, silent, his skin alive with her again. "As long as it lasts."

She smiled weakly, her hand moving to the side of his face. "It's not enough for you? A place you can live? There was no one else there. Nobody was like you, the way it felt. It was different. When I was next to you, the way we used to lie there, it wasn't somebody else. How could it be? It was you."

"And now it isn't."

"No," she said softly. "Not anymore." She leaned into him, putting her head down.

"Liesl—"

"Just stay for a minute like this, like before."

He felt her against him, as natural as his own skin, and for a second he was weightless, not holding on to anything, falling. All he would have to do was lift her head. Another second passed, suspended, then he leaned down, kissed her hair, and stepped back.

"It can't be like before. Not now."

She looked away, then nodded. "I know. I just don't want to forget. The way it is now, that's not how it always was. Maybe I want you to remember, too. Someday—I don't know, we'll be in a room somewhere." Setting a scene, her voice caught up in it. "Years from now, an accident. And you see me. I want you to think, I used to live there once. It was nice."

He stood for a minute, unable to move, in the scene with her. "I'll remember," he said finally.

She opened her mouth to speak and then stopped, out of lines. Instead she nodded, then kissed him lightly on the cheek, a good-bye. "Let's not say any more, then," she said.

"No," he said, watching her turn and move to the door.

Secrets didn't bring you closer. He thought of all the things he'd never say now, things only he would know. How he went over that day in the hospital in his mind, working out its choreography, who was where, until finally he thought he knew, and then asked Ostermann to make sure, that Dieter had always been with him, never alone. That only she had been in the room. That all deaths were not alike, that some secrets had to be kept. That she was the only place he'd ever lived.

He heard the band music through the door. No one would miss him. He drove to the Egyptian to catch the late showing. The picture had already started, so he slipped into a back row. A scene he'd already been in, Liesl looking up at him, luminous, catching all the light. "I don't care," she said, eyes darting, her face soft with love. She leaned forward to kiss the GI and the audience seemed to lean forward with her. No sound, not even a gum wrapper. "I don't care." Everyone in the scene now, wanting her. Thinking she was wonderful.

AUTHOR'S NOTE

STARDUST IS A work of fiction, not history, and readers familiar with the period will see that liberties, a few chronological, have been taken with events that inspired some of its scenes. Labor unrest in Hollywood actually began before the war was over, in early 1945, but reached its most violent stage in the fall, as in the street brawl here. An information film about the Nuremberg trials, *That Justice Be Done*, was released in October 1945, but no feature film about the death camps themselves was ever made or, so far as I know, contemplated. (A rough documentary compilation of captured newsreels about the camps, *We Accuse*, was released in May 1945.) Minot's hearings are meant to be a premature trial run, a preview, of HUAC's assault on Hollywood in 1947, but even in 1945 Representative Rankin had announced the committee's intention to investigate Hollywood, "one of the most dangerous plots ever instigated for the overthrow of this government," and California state senator Tenney's fourteen thousand files had been compiled during the war and were certainly in place then. Jack Warner did indeed become a friendly witness but for reasons of his own, not those suggested here. No studio head, in fact, ever stood up to the committee. After a meeting in November 1947 at the Waldorf-Astoria Hotel, some fifty studio executives issued the anti-Communist Waldorf Statement, effectively starting a blacklist that would last for a decade. Sol Lasner's principled stand here is imagined, something that might have happened in the movies.

STARDUST

Joseph Kanon

A Readers Club Guide

INTRODUCTION

IN POST-WWII HOLLYWOOD, Ben Collier has returned from the front lines to find that his brother Danny has died from a fall off a hotel balcony. But the information surrounding Danny's accident is blurred, and Ben makes his way to Los Angeles, wondering why Danny, a successful filmmaker, would leave behind a life of promise and respect. Or was it not his choice after all?

In Joseph Kanon's most intricate novel to date, *Stardust* follows Ben on an informative and mysterious trek through the glamorous world of 1940s Hollywood. As he attempts to piece together the specifics of his brother's death, Ben is hurled into a maze of secret deals, political maneuvering, and the beginning murmurs of the Hollywood Communist witch hunts.

With a lush depiction of the era, Kanon weaves a tale of intrigue, suspense, and romance that looks behind the film lens and into the hearts of émigrés and American moviemakers of the time. Lights, camera, action . . .

QUESTIONS AND TOPICS FOR DISCUSSION

1. Did you expect the final outcome? Did the identity of Danny's murderer come as a shock?

2. Discuss Liesl and her numerous lovers over the course of the narrative. (Consider Danny, Ben, and Dick Marshall.) Did she ever love Ben, or was he just an extension of Danny? As Ben asks, "Was any of it real?"

3. Discuss the courtroom debate between Minot and Lasner. Who do you think won in the end? Did Lasner successfully thwart Minot's attack on Hollywood, or did he merely delay the inevitable?

4. Ben is supplied information (and misinformation) by a variety of questionable sources. Did you trust his various informants? (Consider Kelly, Riordan, Polly, Minot, and Bunny Jenkins.)

5. Bunny is one of the more complex characters within the narrative, a child star turned Hollywood Studio second-in-command and "fixer." Discuss his evolution and multiplicity. How did you interpret his relationship with Jack (the mangled veteran)? Or his compliance with Minot's proposed witch hunt? And, of course, consider his role in saving Ben's life. Did you ever have a firm grasp on his character or intentions?

6. Did you trust Ben's deductive skills? He was led down the wrong path on numerous occasions. Were Liesl and Riordan right in persuading him to let Danny go? Was he any better off once Danny's past allegiances were uncovered?

7. Murder plays a large role throughout the story, as two killings spur Danny to uncover the secrets behind the studio and the Red Scare.

Were you certain why Danny had to die? What about Genia, the Holocaust survivor?

8. Where do you think Ben goes after watching *War Bride*?

9. Who was your favorite starlet in *Stardust*'s versions of Hollywood? Rosemary? Paulette Goddard? The new and improved Liesl Eastman? Are any of them safe from Minot and Polly Marks?

10. Who makes a better case for Ben's future in Hollywood, Bunny or Lasner?

TIPS TO ENHANCE YOUR BOOK CLUB

1. Read another thriller/mystery novel, such as John le Carré's *A Most Wanted Man* or a title from Robert Ferrigno's Assassin series, and discuss the way the writers build up and establish intrigue, and the methods they use to reveal the truth.

2. There is an immense amount of misinformation, secret connections, and crossed lines throughout the narrative. See if you can draw a map that clearly indicates how everyone is associated, who supplied whom with information, and how Dieter's machinations work underneath it all.

3. The novel is a representation of a very specific era of Hollywood. Watch some of the movies from that era to get a better idea of what Tinseltown was producing during the 1940s. Watch *You'll Never Get Rich* (Rita Hayworth, 1941) or *Casablanca* (Ingrid Bergman, 1942).

4. Continuing with the previous question, do you find any Communist or Socialist undertones in these films? Could you make a case for or against an imaginary Red inquisition?

5. Whom would you cast in the *Stardust* movie?

A CONVERSATION WITH JOSEPH KANON

You obviously did a great amount of period-specific research for the book. What was the information-gathering process like for such an undertaking?

All my books begin with a place. I have to know where my characters live, how the streets look to them. The best way to get a feel for a city is to walk it—for *The Good German* I spent days walking all over Berlin, trying to imagine the ruined city of 1945 beneath the modern one, a kind of literary archaeology. Los Angeles resists that kind of walking— you have to drive it—but the period details required a similar reimagining. Many of the settings in *Stardust* still exist: the émigrés' houses (Feuchtwanger's, Salka Viertel's, etc.), the studios, Mt. Wilson, the Farmers Market, Union Station. But they exist in a very different city. In 1945 there were no freeways—streetcars ran down Hollywood Boulevard. There were still orange groves in the Valley. And it felt more remote. The fastest train from Chicago took 40 hours (and a full weekend from New York). Beverly Hills a generation before had been bean fields.

You can learn a great deal from old photographs and histories, but by far the most useful source of period details are memoirs. Luckily, Hollywood has provided an almost endless stream of anecdotes, memoirs, and biographies. While they're often self-serving or misleading about their subjects, they're usually accurate about the way people lived. This kind of research can be so enjoyable that the problem is having to stop.

The more serious area was the political climate—the union infighting, the red-baiting, and the beginning of witch hunts. The trick here is getting not only the background right, but getting the tone right. It's impossible to quote directly from the actual transcripts of the hearings. The exchanges are so ludicrous and shameful that they seem implausible now. So in an odd way you have to elevate them, give them an intellectual seriousness they never had, and still somehow capture their almost surreal circus atmosphere.

Ben seems to possess an inexplicable detective's intuition. What makes him such a good sleuth?

I don't know that he's a particularly good detective—he's just following his nose and wherever logic seems to lead him. I've never written a book with a professional detective because I don't have any idea how they actually work, what tricks they know. I just have Ben do what anyone would do. If you suspect something's wrong, how do you go about finding the truth? Of course, playing detective is simply a convention of the genre—if there's a murder, somebody has to investigate or you don't have a story. But I found it useful to have Ben get things wrong too. *Stardust* is about *seeing*, about the dust that gets in the way of our seeing things clearly, sometimes because we'd rather not see. And, of course, it's complicated here by being set in a community whose business is illusion.

What are your favorite movies from *Stardust*-era Hollywood?

The year 1939 is generally considered Hollywood's *annus mirabilis*, the peak year of the studio era, but the golden period continued right through the '40s, when *Stardust* is set. Favorites? Too many to list, but I never tire of watching Preston Sturges's *The Lady Eve* and *The Palm Beach Story*, to me the wittiest comedies ever filmed. *Notorious* is perfect entertainment, *Double Indemnity* still the best—and best written—film noir. Is there anyone who doesn't love *Casablanca*? *Meet Me in St. Louis* is a beautifully made sentimental piece. *Citizen Kane* is inevitably on the top of every list.

It's important to remember, though, that even during the golden years, first-rate movies like these were rare. We know the movies that endured, not necessarily the ones audiences liked then, and few things change faster than pop culture. The Crosby-Hope *Road* pictures, big hits at the time, are barely watchable now. *The Bells of St. Mary's* was far and away the most successful movie of 1945. To us the big stars of the '40s were Humphrey Bogart, Ingrid Bergman, Rita Hayworth, Cary Grant, and indeed they were big stars, but the box office champs were Bing Crosby and Betty Grable, and her musicals aren't even redeemed by camp now—they're just inane.

Considering the subject matter of *Stardust*, it must have been useful to see *The Good German* translated to film. How do you feel about literature adapted for Hollywood?

I wasn't involved in the making of *The Good German*, so the one really didn't affect the other. I did, however, visit the set and that was useful because the director, Steven Soderbergh, wanted to make the movie the way it would have been done in 1945—shooting on sound stages and studio back lots, even using the same camera lenses that would have been available then. So in a sense I got to spend time on a set that actually might have been in *Stardust*. This even extended to the breaks between setups. Because *The Good German* was a period movie, all the actors were in 1945 dress—upswept hair, bright lipstick, uniforms. To see the extras milling around the lot was to see exactly how it would have looked in 1945. The movie was shot on the old Columbia lot on Gower, just across the street from Continental in *Stardust*, so even the buildings had the right period feel.

The book-to-movie transition has always been difficult for writers—they are notorious complainers about film adaptations—because what they really want to see is an illustrated version of the novel that's already in their heads. But film isn't a visual translation, it's a medium unto itself, made by other people. The best a writer can hope for is that talented people are taken by something in his material that prompts them to do good work of their own.

I don't think there are any hard and fast rules about adaptations. It's often just the luck of the draw. *Lolita* didn't seem a natural for the screen, but Kubrick made an interesting movie from it anyway. The 1940 adaptation of *Pride and Prejudice* (script by Aldous Huxley) is still a delight, if not what Jane Austen intended. But does it really matter?

The original books remain just as they were, still available, as rich and complex as ever. Why can't we enjoy both?

The problem is that movies are so central to our popular culture that we tend to think of adaptations as replacements. They're not. And the better the book, the less likely it is to be replaced. I suppose you could see *Gone with the Wind* without ever reading Margaret Mitchell and not miss much, but even though Greta Garbo is in *Anna Karenina* and Gwyneth Paltrow made a fine *Emma*, imagine how much you'd miss by not reading the books. Of course, this process also works the other way—a movie can drive readers back to the book, which is always a good thing.

There has always been a large interest in following a child star's coming-of-age. How do you view Bunny's rise to the upper echelons of studio business? Or is it a fall from the limelight?

Bunny is one of the most complicated characters in the book and to me, in some ways, the most interesting. He represents the generation that will succeed the pioneering moguls and as such will steer the studio system through radical change (and eventual collapse), but he's very much a product of that system—he grew up in it—so his feelings are contradictory. There is a built-in poignancy, a sense of loss, to the lives of child stars. Very few of them ever carry their careers into adulthood (Elizabeth Taylor being a notable exception). But there's a built-in toughness too—they learn at an early age how arbitrary and unfair life can be.

Bunny has both these qualities. He prides himself on being pragmatic and shrewd, but he is still hopelessly romantic about movies. He knows that Hollywood will change—he is alert to the rise of television, he is willing to compromise people and principles for the sake of the studio—but he is not yet one of the corporate suits who would take over what was left of the studios in the '60s and '70s. He cares about making movies, not just making money. He can be manipulative, even Machiavellian, a cold-blooded plotter, and yet when he stands outside a closed set he's looking at his own version of paradise lost, when he worked with people "closer than family." Now he's the boss. He's clear-eyed about this—what's past is past—but a part of him will always feel outside too.

This novel has a very cinematic feel. Did you think about a big screen version while writing it? Whom would you cast in the *Stardust* movie?

To me writing is like making a movie in your head, the only one you can control, that's really yours. What appears on the screen is inevitably someone else's. So I don't consciously think of movies as I write, what would work on the screen. But possibly what makes the books feel cinematic is that I tend to shape the narrative in scenes and rely heavily on dialogue. I like scenes where more than one thing is happening at once—in this case, say the dinner party at Sol Lasner's house, when four or five plot elements are overlapping. The challenge for the writer, aside from the dialogue itself, which keeps the scene going, is knowing when and how to shift emphasis, moving the reader through it, in much the same way as a director has to know where to place the camera.

As for casting, this is everybody's favorite parlor game. At bookstore readings I'm constantly asked whom I think should play a character or even whom I had in mind when I was writing. The truth is that the characters have to be so real to you that they only can be themselves, not look like anyone else. That having been said, there's no denying the extraordinary power of film. I may not have thought of Jake and Lena as George Clooney and Cate Blanchett when I was writing *The Good German*, but that's how they look to me now. As a matter of fact, I think they'd look right in *Stardust* too.

With all the duplicity and background connections in the book, did you have a hard time keeping track during the writing process? Was there a particular way in which you organized the book?

No, I never work from outlines or plans. Aside from having a general idea of what will happen—and certainly the whodunit—I tend to make things up as I go along. I like that surprise of seeing where the story will take you, the detours. In *Stardust,* though, I did reach a point where things became so complicated that I started keeping track of the scenes—what in the movies would be called continuity. This mostly had to do with chronology, when somebody would have known something, etc. And there were broader problems of chronology in the backstory—when did Danny and Ben last see each other, how old would Ben have been when his mother died, etc.

Strictly speaking, none of these really affect the ongoing action, but I find that readers tend to trust the larger story more if you get the small details right. The congressional hearings in *Stardust* take place earlier than the actual ones did, but the schedule for the Super Chief is accurate, right to the minute. And since I assumed, or hoped, that *Stardust* might appeal to film buffs, all the industry details are true: Paulette Goddard was about to do a picture with Milland, *Saratoga Trunk* was released as described, the palms in the Cocoanut Grove really were from the set of *The Sheik,* or so sources said. This sort of thing may seem insignificant, but I think details give the story weight. And of course they're fun to research.

What was the most challenging aspect of writing such an intricate narrative?
Trying to keep it to a manageable length. The material is so rich that I wanted to do more, particularly about Hollywood itself, but the book kept getting longer and you don't want to try the reader's patience. The front story—the crime and Ben's solving it—inevitably takes up space at the expense of the backstory, which to me was a portrait of Hollywood just before it began to fall apart.

The seeds of that fall are there but some aren't covered as extensively as I originally intended. The all-important Justice Department consent decree (separating the studios and their theaters), which would hit the studios with a financial body blow, is referred to here—it's the reason Minot's been invited to Lasner's party—but not in great detail. The internal politics of the labor unions were too complicated (and, frankly, dated) to develop, so I had to be content with some conversation and a strike action. Television appears only in one scene, but at least that's consistent with how little attention the studios themselves gave it in 1945.

Other factors in the decline—the sense of the audience changing, the complacency that set in with the wartime boom years—were more subtle and could be explored through the characters. Only the anti-Communist hearings became a centerpiece in the story, not only because they're inherently dramatic, but because they open a window on Hollywood's vulnerabilities: its reliance on fickle public opinion, the special sensitivity of an industry run largely by assimilated Jews, revered for its patriotism during the war and now accused of being traitorous and un-American. The poison that these hearings introduced into the American body politic would go on for years and affect virtually every aspect of American life, but the poison began in Hollywood, where the headlines were. And the stardust.

Ben is the son of a German film director and his brother had close ties to German émigrés. What made you introduce so many Germans into a Hollywood story?
Actually, the Germans came first. I was originally drawn to Los Angeles as a setting because of the extraordinary group of German refugees who ended up there—a phenomenon still very little known, even in Los Angeles itself. Hollywood had always been a magnet for talent from the German film industry, especially in the '20s and early '30s, when the move was motivated by career opportunities or family ties, as well as politics. F.W. Murnau, Ernst Lubitsch, Fritz Lang, William Wyler, Billy Wilder, Peter Lorre, Marlene Dietrich—a long list, all early arrivals.

The Germans who came later were somewhat different, an increasingly desperate group of exiles, part of the European intellectual diaspora that was Hitler's inadvertent gift to America. In a sense, this was for me a continuation of *The Good German*. That had been a book about a city utterly devastated by war, both physically and morally. But what about the people who had been lucky enough to get out?

I was particularly interested in the group that went to L.A.–whether for the climate, the cheaper cost of living, or hopes of finding work in Hollywood–because of the great cultural dislocation L.A. represented in their lives. This was a city, after all, that even most Americans at the time considered exotic, a sunny Eden. Imagine its impact then on the émigrés, often representatives of high culture, who had literally just escaped with their lives, sometimes a few steps ahead of the Gestapo, and now find themselves in a world of palm trees and swimming pools and milkshakes and a popular culture largely indifferent to them. This seemed to me a story rich in dramatic possibilities, especially since, as technically enemy aliens, they were subject to FBI surveillance (and hounded for any leftist sympathies), the very kind of political intimidation they'd left Germany to escape.

The émigrés are still very much a part of *Stardust*, but book ideas often grow in ways you don't quite expect and as the story went along I began to see that the Germans were only a part of the larger story, that what they really offered me was a way to look at Hollywood from a different angle.

In *Stardust* you combine history and storytelling to weave your tale. What plotlines or characters from the book are historically based, and which are your own inventions?
The major plot lines–the murder, the motivation for it, the love story– are all invented. Only the background is historically based. But of course the background is an important part of this book and it needs to be as accurate as possible to make the fiction plausible. None of the principal characters are intentional composites or stand-ins for anyone real, except possibly Kaltenbach, who was inspired by Heinrich Mann. Some real people do appear–Paulette Goddard, Jack Warner– but they are only real in the sense that this is how I imagine them to have been. You listen to their voices in memoirs and anecdotes (and of course film) and hope they sound that way here, but in any case these are minor characters in the larger story.

I have mixed feelings about using real people in fiction, in part because readers can bring their own sense of the character to the page and find yours inconsistent. In fact, this is the first time I have done so since *Los Alamos*—how could Oppenheimer have been anyone else? But celebrity is so important a part of the culture of Hollywood that some stargazing seemed inevitable, and I found that using real people could make a point about the ephemeral nature of celebrity itself.

I avoided enduring icons like Bogart. The movie people who appear here were certainly famous at the time, but perhaps not so well known today. At Lasner's party Paulette, Ann Sheridan, and Alexis Smith all make an appearance (and dress up the party) but so does the fictional Rosemary, whose shining moment this is, and my hope was to make them interchangeable to the reader, Rosemary being just as real as the boldface names—and now all of them faded. Real people also appear from the émigré community—Brecht, Feuchtwanger, Alma Mahler—but again this is primarily to lend more plausibility to the fictional ones (Ostermann and Liesl). What isn't made up is the mixed blessing of their exile, saved but now rootless in a town of strangers.